The Price of Silver

Solis Invicti: Book II

JOSIE JAFFREY

CONTENT WARNINGS & SERIES RECAPS

There is a full list of content warnings at the back of this book, and also available at Josie's website at the link on the left below.

Recaps of the Silverse books are available on Josie's website at the link on the right below.

By Josie Jaffrey

Stories from the Silverse: the World of the Silver

The Seekers Series
Killian's Dead (short story prequel, free to Josie's
subscribers)
May Day
Judgement Day
Winta's Day
Valentine's Day
Dark Days
End of Days

The QuickSilver Trilogy
Kill Me Quick
A Quick Study
Quick and the Dead
QuickSilver Omnibus Edition

The Solis Invicti Series
A Bargain in Silver
The Price of Silver
Bound in Silver
The Silver Bullet

The Sovereign Trilogy
The Gilded King
The Silver Queen
The Blood Prince

Silverse Serialised Stories
Dead Box
Dead Road

Silverse Short Stories
Encounters: Silverse Short Stories

Other Fiction

The Deluge Series
The Wolf and the Water

Short Stories
Broken Wings (collection)
Ring The Bell

For Zoë, the world's best ex-wife

PROLOGUE

My head and ears thumped with the ringing noise of the blast, and the lights behind my eyelids were strobing and blinding. As my vision started to clear, I could see the stars blinking peacefully in the sky above me and it took a moment for me to realise what had happened, to remember where I was.

We must have been very close to the surface, because an access hatch above us had been blown up and apart, exposing us to the open air beyond. From what I could see of the rest of the tunnel, it looked as if it had collapsed in on itself entirely, filled with rubble from its own ceiling, from the street above us.

The torchlight in what remained of the room was dim and it seemed to be getting darker by the moment. I remembered that the rebels had brought down the perimeter wall circling the safe zone.

Soon the Weepers would come.

I tried to reach my hand out to my right, but my shoulder was pinned at an awkward angle and I couldn't shift whatever was holding it in place. I could make out a figure to my left, half-buried beneath lumps of masonry and twisted pieces of metal and concrete. It was Oliver, lying on his side with a dark circle of liquid spreading from beneath his shoulder.

He wasn't moving.

I'd been a fool not to go back for more help when I could, but there hadn't been time, and they would have stopped me from coming here if they'd known.

In retrospect, that probably would have been a good thing.

I was going to die here tonight, a fragile human, trapped and powerless.

My name's Emmy, I'm twenty eight and I'm still alive. For the moment, at least.

CHAPTER I

Thursday

Leaning towards the mirror in the en suite of the Palace's guest room, I put one of the pins to the top of my right eyebrow and braced myself.

This was going to hurt like a bitch, but it was unavoidable.

I gritted my teeth and pressed it into my skin, drawing it across my forehead and into my hairline. It only needed to be a shallow cut, so it bled only a little and wasn't as agonising as it might have been. Still, the pin was unhelpfully blunt and the graze stung in a way that made me stamp my foot in an attempt to shake off the pain.

It was only the first.

Tears welled in my eyes as I drew a second line with the pin from the right corner of my mouth to the outside of my right eye, the sensitive skin paling before it swelled and flooded with colour. A single teardrop spilled over and the salt burnt the surface of the cut as it ran down my cheek. I wetted some cotton wool under the tap and wiped it across each of the grazes, removing the excess blood, then looked at my face appraisingly.

They would do. They were in more or less the same positions as the original injuries and they looked like they were just pink from where the cuts would have reopened under the hot water of the shower I had just taken.

Less than twelve hours ago I'd had a badly skinned knee, scarring scratches across my face, a load of stitches in the palm of my right hand and three separate bite marks on my neck. This morning, they were all gone, a small pile of stitches left sitting in the palm of my hand, apparently magically expelled from the skin intact during the healing process.

Now I needed to recreate those injuries, or risk revealing to the world that Drew had bonded to me: the Secundus of the Silver in love with a human girl.

I looked at my bare chest in the bathroom mirror. The silver handprint that was the mark of his healing touch shimmered under the surface of the skin under my collarbone, an eerie echo of the mark found on the corpse of Cara Alton, whose death was the catalyst for the Revelation.

It was the brand of a connection I wasn't sure I was willing to accept, a connection that would bring his death at the same moment as mine. It was the downside of the Silver bond: you live together and die together.

Drew had used the power of the bond to erase my wounds as if the last week had never happened, but I was raw with the memories. I felt weak, like I'd been drinking too much coffee after too many sleepless nights. My head was cocooned in a lethargic fog at the same time as a restless panic raced my heartbeat, pounding irregularly in my chest.

I wondered if I would ever feel normal again.

Drew had saved my life last night, pulling me back from the brink and into the world, but I wasn't sure it was a world I wanted to live in anymore.

It had only been a week since the Revelation, a week since this vampiric race had first made its existence known to us: the Silver, named for the silver colouring that filled the blood vessels patterning the whites of their eyes.

With them came the Weepers, zombie-like creatures who

carry an infection in their blood that could wipe out humanity. If that's their aim then they seem to be doing a pretty good job of it so far.

The Silver have made a bargain with the remaining human population of England: we work for them and make regular blood donations in return for their protection from the Weepers. They have told us that America is lost to the infection, that submission is our only option, but we don't know about the rest of the world.

Maybe we're the last humans left.

Then again, maybe that's just what they want us to think.

I rinsed the pin under the tap and took a deep breath, staring steadily into the mirror as I prepared for the next round.

Now for the bite marks.

The bites of the Silver weren't the clinical punctures that I had been led to expect from decades of vampire films. Instead, they were two neat arcs of incision, the top deeper than the bottom, that seemed to bracket the skin. It was much like I imagined a human bite would appear.

I hadn't seen the marks that had been left on my neck from the attack last night, the third bite, before they were healed, but I guessed that since the attack wasn't common knowledge I wouldn't need to replicate it. Instead, I just scratched shallow marks into my neck on each side in the places where Sol had bitten me.

I wasn't going to be able to erase the traces of my night with him so easily after all.

He was the Primus, the ruler of the Silver: Solomon, and I'd slept with him. On the terrace of his club, where I work. And I let him get a little… bitey. Well, okay, I asked him to bite me, but in my defence it had been a long night and I'd nearly been killed.

Sol had saved my life and I was grateful. It may not be the best reason in the world to have reckless sex with a vampire, but I swear it made perfect sense at the time.

Before Sol, I'd thought I was a rebel. I'd wanted to escape.

But the way he spoke… he made the bargain the Silver offered seem undeniably better than the alternative. I wasn't sure where I stood now, but I suppose I'd resigned myself to the futility of fighting human subservience. The truth was that I hadn't really been required to submit in the same way as the rest of the humans, so maybe it didn't seem that bad to me.

Sol had given me a free pass.

I cleaned the wounds on my neck and cleaned up the sink. It's pretty difficult to make accurate cuts on your own neck when you can't get the angle right to see what you're doing and when your eyes are watering from the pain, but I decided they were good enough to allay suspicion at least. They'd have to be, because they were the best I could do.

There was no sign of my skimpy work uniform in the bedroom and I wondered whether it had been trashed in the attack last night. My stomach lurched at the memory and I sat down heavily on the edge of the bed, hanging my head between my knees until the lights stopped flashing in front of my eyes. My forehead prickled with sweat as I breathed deeply through my mouth, desperately trying to calm myself down.

Last night, a Silver called Benedict had tried to kill me, and so kill Drew, and apparently there's nothing Drew or Sol can do about it. If they were to imply it's a big deal that a Silver nearly killed a mere human, then not only would they risk drawing attention to the bond, but it would be political suicide. That would put Ben in charge, and that's not something any of us want.

If the humans were slaves to the Silver now, it was nothing compared with what would come with Ben's rise to power. I didn't know what he was planning, but I knew it would be a hell of a lot worse than Sol's bargain.

This time, whenever he made his move, at least I'd see him coming. I wouldn't go with him willingly like a gullible sheep to the slaughter.

Unfortunately, Ben was far from the only Silver who thought Sol was too kind to humans. A sizeable percentage, I wasn't sure how many, thought that we weren't even people, that imprisonment would be better than allowing us any freedom at all. The Silver world was at war with itself, and I was stuck in the middle. If any of the others found out about Drew's bond to me, things would just get worse.

One homicidal Silver was enough for me.

I set my jaw and pulled myself together. This was not the right moment to fall apart.

I wasn't sure what time it was, perhaps early afternoon, but it was overcast outside and it felt cold for the middle of the summer. The wind was howling down the street outside, rattling the sash windows in their frames. I guessed there was a storm on the way.

I shimmied into some skinny jeans and a high-necked T-shirt I found in the bedroom's wardrobe. Finally, I grabbed a couple of bandages and wound one around my right hand. I was relieved to find my trusty flat-soled boots by the door to the suite. They, at least, had been salvaged after last night's attack. Slipping my feet into them, I prepared to leave.

As I turned to go, I saw there was something lying on the pillow of the bed. It was a circle of black lace with a lily design picked out in silver: the choker Sol had given me to mark me as his, thereby exempting me from blood donations and protecting from the attempts of any other Silver to drink my blood.

There was a small slip of paper pinned to it.

It read: *Wear it this time — S.*

CHAPTER II

I made my way back over from the Palace quickly without seeing any of the Silver I knew. In fact, the whole place seemed to be running on a skeleton crew.

The club and the dorm were both completely empty.

Where was everyone?

The only person in the dorm was Nix, a tortoiseshell kitten I'd been nursing back to health with the help of Alice, the girl who bunked in the bed next to mine. So yes, technically Nix was a cat rather than a person, but she was a friend to me. She was curled up on my bed, the closest one to the window at the end of the room. I sat down next to her and tickled her behind the ears as she blinked up at me sleepily.

"Where's everyone gone?" I asked her, the back of my neck starting to prickle with anxiety.

Was it weird that I was talking to the cat? Either way, I found it reassuring to hear her purr in reply.

My head jerked up as a gentle thunking noise came from outside the open window. Giving Nix a final stroke, I perched myself on the wide windowsill and leaned out tentatively to investigate the source of the sound. It was coming from the end of the road, from the barricade to my left. A couple of Silver were laying what looked to be massive blocks of stone in a line across the road, about twenty feet in front of the sizeable pile of rubble that marked the end of the Weeper-free safe zone.

They were building a wall, the stones settling into the line of the foundations they had dug across the road. It would mark the boundaries of Sol's city: our new, diminished London. The blocks stacked on top of each other swiftly as I watched, the Silver almost unseen as they moved at speed to lay the stones in place. They could zip around at an unbelievable pace when they wished, but it took more energy than normal movement and increased the amount of blood they needed to sustain it.

The wall grew before my eyes, more Silver joining in as it quickly topped ten feet, fifteen feet, then twenty feet high. They were sealing us in, corralling their humans away from the Weeper threat beyond the barricade.

But what good was a wall when the Weepers could surge up it, breaking against it like a wave and throwing themselves on top of each other to reach its crest? We'd seen it on the broadcasts the Silver had shown us: video feeds from America showing rising peaks of Weeper bodies creeping up against skyscrapers to reach their occupants.

The Silver must be intending to patrol the walls, I thought. Or the barricades, which is what they'd been doing for the past week. As soon as the Weepers caught sight of a Silver they backed away, repelled in some indefinable way by their strength, or by their smell, or by something else entirely. I wasn't sure. If they saw a human, it was a different story: they descended en masse, piling on top of each other and digging down to the meat.

Wall or no wall, our only hope of survival lay in staying close to the Silver.

Maybe the walls were intended to keep the humans in rather than to keep the Weepers out.

Despite the dangers beyond the wall, I was uneasy about it. We were trapped, hemmed in and isolated. Although I hadn't voluntarily moved much beyond the club and the

Palace in the past week, the imposing spectre of the wall loomed in front of me with terrible finality. It was a stark testament to something of which I had been vaguely aware for a week: this tiny slice of London was now my entire world.

Propping my feet on the ledge, I watched the builders for another quarter of an hour or so with a growing sense of claustrophobia itching under my skin. I leaned back against the window frame as the blocks thudded into place, drumming the rhythm of my anxious heart.

The new line of the Silver domain would have one welcome effect: it was removing the street where Danny had died from the safe zone. The day after the Revelation I'd managed to find three of my friends from the club. They had hidden from the Silver and the Weepers, and together we planned a resistance.

It failed.

Ben killed all three of them, but Danny was the only one whose death I had witnessed. His neck had snapped effortlessly in Ben's hand, who had smiled when he saw me watching. At the time I'd thought Ben's smile was one of recognition, but now in my memory it was twisted into a mocking grin. He'd already killed Jeff and Sarah back at the club. He'd known I was the only one still standing and he had planned to make that as painful as possible for me. To make me think that Drew, the Silver who'd saved me from the Weepers and for whom I'd been having some seriously confused feelings, was responsible for Jeff and Sarah's deaths.

Ben was a bastard. He needed to die, if only for the sake of my sanity.

I just had to work out how to make that happen.

I was pondering this when a noise rose from the other end of the street behind me, opposite the wall that was growing swiftly before my eyes. The street was filled with people pouring towards the club and the Palace Hotel across the road, voices loud and excited. There must have been a gathering in Paternoster Square, maybe another broadcast.

I'd find out soon enough.

As people started thundering into the club beneath me, I caught sight of the stragglers walking towards the Palace.

I spotted Tommy and Cam, a couple of the Solis Invicti with whom I had become friends over the past week, but they didn't hold my attention.

Drew was with them. He was dressed in his usual khakis and leather jacket, the wind lifting his shoulder-length, dark hair away from his face. There was a seven o'clock shadow on his chin and I imagined I could hear the rumbling timbre of his baritone voice from where I was perched.

He looked upwards, turning his gaze towards my window. I caught my breath and hated myself for doing it, because no doubt he'd have heard it. A lazy grin spread across his face and my fear was confirmed.

Dammit.

There was something about the way his eyes twinkled with his smile that hit me right in the chest. On the first night I met him, he'd made me feel safe and protected. Now I wasn't sure how I felt, but I had missed the feeling of security Drew's presence had given me, the certain knowledge that I was home.

Had that feeling even been real? We'd hardly spent much time together and we couldn't be around each other now without risking exposure of the Silver bond. I'd never even kissed him and I couldn't now. If we did somehow manage to find a private moment alone, a kiss from Drew would leave a scent mark behind it. That scent mark would tell every Silver I came across that I was Drew's property which, besides the obvious unwelcome sexist implications, would give the game away as far as the Silver bond was concerned.

The failed rebel in me was irritated in principle at the concept of the bond, the concept that love could be subject to such predetermination. I chafed under the removal of choice. More than that, I resented the fact that Drew's bond to me was a burden to him.

For any Silver to bond to a human is a weakness, because we're so easy to kill. But for the Secundus to bond to a human is a security risk, that the Primus's military leader could be eliminated so simply by my death. So I had to hide the shining palm print and pretend there was nothing between us, just as Drew had to pretend that the diffusion of silver threading from the whites of his eyes into their irises was a result of his bond with someone else, a legitimate mate, a Silver.

I sighed and shook my head at Drew through the window.

He just smiled contentedly back at me. I'd said I needed time to grieve for my friends, to sort my head out, and he'd told me this was enough for him: for us to be friends and nothing more. But would it be enough for me? Now, more than ever, I longed for protection, for something to hold onto as my world lay in ruins around me. I'd never felt so powerless, so weak as I did today. Ben had stolen my strength away from me when he showed me how casually he could end my life.

Until recently I'd been living in a world of rules and law, where people were generally good and crimes had consequences. I hadn't appreciated how different the Silver were, despite having reminded myself of this at every opportunity. Silver society was ruled by the powerful for as long as they could stay that way. The weak were simply victims. The parasitic nature of the vampires kept the humans safe, but that protection was by no means absolute, as I had discovered.

Even if I had felt nothing for Drew, the protection of a strong Silver was a welcome prospect in the circumstances. But that protection would be dangerous for both of us if it risked revealing the Silver bond.

Whatever I told myself, it was going to be difficult to prevent Drew's allure from becoming an irresistible attraction. If I had learned anything from Sol in the past week, it was that making something forbidden would only make it more desirable.

I made to move away from the window as I heard my dorm mates walking up the stairs towards me, but as I did so I saw Sol join Drew and the others on the street beneath me.

His eyes flicked up to where I stood at the window and then back down to Drew, his face clouding with disapproval as he directed Drew towards the Palace.

Even a smile could be dangerous when the stakes were this high. I was all too aware of why I had to avoid contact with Drew, or any action that might indicate there was anything between us. Apparently I just wasn't very good at it so far.

"I'm sorry," I said quietly, knowing Sol would hear me.

He waited in the street below until Drew had walked into the Palace with Tommy and Cam, then looked up at me with his blue eyes. He stood with his hands in the pockets of his dark suit, the breeze from the direction of the new wall ruffling the golden curls on the top of his head.

He was beautiful, but intimidating. He radiated power. It flowed around him in the quiet confidence of his bearing, in the self-possession of his strength. As he stood below me he looked cold to the touch and as solid as if he were carved from stone. I knew he was neither of those things.

I'd used my brief fling with him to take me away from myself and I'd found something I hadn't been looking for. He had set me on fire, but I couldn't decide whether he'd illuminate me or burn me away.

I had been told by a couple of the Solis Invicti not to expect anything from him. They feared and respected him, feelings borne from a shared history of which I had no knowledge. Worse still, they seemed to pity me for the attention he had shown me, and I didn't think that boded well. I wondered what they had seen that made them avoid my gaze when they talked about him.

Now there seemed to be a distance in his gaze when he looked at me, a hardness I hadn't seen since we'd first met. The cool blue shone like ice, brittle and chilling. It broke something inside me, snapping a thread in my chest.

I steeled myself and tried to tamp down my anxiety, knowing that he'd be picking up on it. I rubbed my hand across my chest where my T-shirt covered the Silver mark and wondered if I'd ever feel safe again.

The urgent clatter of stiletto heels behind me alerted me to Alice's imminent arrival and I turned, my heart racing with alarm.

Nix took fright at the noise and jumped past me out of the window and onto the ledge that ran around the outside of the building. I felt an urge to follow her.

From there, she leapt down onto the fire escape below and bolted off into the city. I hoped she wouldn't go far. I wasn't sure whether or not the Weepers would go after cats, but I didn't want her to risk it.

I forced a quick smile to Sol before hopping off the windowsill and turning back into the dorm room.

"My god, Emmy," Alice squealed as she tapped down the aisle between the beds, "where were you?"

It looked like she'd dressed up to go to the broadcast, which was fairly normal behaviour for Alice. She worshipped the Silver and did everything she could to catch their attention. I suspected it was why she hung around with me. I had friends she wanted to share.

I didn't mind. It was nice to have a friend who was human, and they didn't come any more human than Alice. I found her light-hearted presence strangely reassuring after the trauma of last night.

Today she was wearing jeans and a halter-neck top that showed plenty of skin, twinned with her usual stiletto knee-high boots. Her blonde curls were swept off her neck into a pile on the top of her head, the tracery of her dark veins visible under her porcelain skin. She was vamp bait, but she must have been freezing.

I rubbed self-consciously at my chest again, reassuring myself that the brand was hidden from view.

"I had a bit of an accident, so I went to see the medic over at the Palace."

"Oh," she replied, clearly unsure how to react.

"I'm okay," I said, to save her the embarrassment of having forgotten to ask, though I'm not sure Alice was bothered by such things.

"Good. Well, you'll never guess what happened!" she continued without pausing for breath.

The rest of the occupants of the dorm were filing in now and heading over to their bunks. I wondered idly whether people had been given time off for the broadcast. We hadn't had one for days.

"What happened?" I asked obediently.

"There was a broadcast."

"Yes," I replied patiently. "I'd guessed that much."

"Okay, well, you'll never guess what the Primus announced in the broadcast."

She paused for effect and I circled my hand at her to hurry her up.

"They're making more Silver!" she said, clearly delighted. "We could be Silver, Emmy! Isn't that awesome?"

Drew had told me this morning that Sol was bringing in some 'changes'. I hadn't realised he meant it so literally.

I looked around at the other faces in the dorm. Some were talking excitedly in corners, mostly the young but sometimes older people too. I wondered if they were hoping that turning Silver would prolong their lives or cure them of disease. There seemed to be a lot of that in this dorm.

Other people sat quietly or muttered to each other, dropping their heads in sadness or gesticulating angrily. There were as many negative reactions as there were positive, but Alice couldn't see how this could be anything but an opportunity.

"Not really."

"You don't want to be Silver?" Alice asked me, her pretty brow wrinkling in confusion.

"No," I replied quietly. "I don't want to be Silver, Alice."

I really didn't. I'd made that decision already. I didn't want to lose who I was to a craving for human blood. I didn't want to become like Ben and his friends: detached, haughty and murderous. More than anything, I didn't want to live forever in a world where all the people I loved were dead.

"They're making four a year," said a young man on my

right as he sat down on a bed, "as a reward for our compliance."

He spat the last word like a curse. This was one human who wouldn't be lining up for a Silver makeover. A group of lads on the bed behind him murmured their agreement, approving of his tone.

I'd seen him around the dorm in the past week, but never in the club itself. I supposed he must work over at the Palace. He looked to be about thirty and stood six feet tall, with light brown hair that fell in unaffected waves to the nape of his neck at the back and to his earlobes at the front. His eyes were the most unusual thing about his appearance: an incongruous shade of grey that seemed at odds with his Mediterranean colouring. It was an attractive combination; his long, dark lashes setting off the brightness of his irises.

They drilled into me, challenging me to respond.

"You let the monsters play with you, Emilia," he continued.

I bristled at receiving such an insulting judgement from someone I'd never spoken to before. Who the hell did this guy think he was? I took an instant dislike to him, resenting his pretentious tone and his over familiarity.

Did everyone know that I was the girl who'd let the Primus drink her blood? I was never going to be allowed to forget it at this rate. I craved a bit of anonymity, but I suspected hanging out with Alice didn't help. She loved to brag about how close her friend Emmy was to the Silver. Then, remembering the bite marks I had recreated on my neck, I realised how unfair that was. I'd hardly hidden my association with them. It wasn't Alice's fault that everyone knew I'd let one of them bite me.

I wondered if the presence of the apparent supporters behind the bright-eyed man was egging him on. I wasn't in the mood to be intimidated by them, not after everything I'd been through over the past few days. Compared with Ben, these humans were about as imposing as puppies.

"What did you say to me?" I asked aggressively.

"I wonder if you know their plans, the inner workings of this veil of lies," he said.

I raised my eyebrows at his florid turns of phrase and stifled a snort of laughter. It seemed to me that he was mimicking the way Sol spoke. Badly. It was incongruous given that he appeared to be so anti-Silver.

I knew there were things I'd been told that weren't common knowledge, like the fact that the Silver had yet to find a safe way of killing and disposing of the Weepers that wouldn't increase the risk of infection to the humans. That wasn't something I was going to share with this would-be agitator. I felt far more loyalty to Sol than I did to a human I barely knew, and frankly I could see why the Silver had kept that particular piece of information from the human population. It would only engender fear.

Then there was the Silver bond and its effect. I could only imagine that keeping it quiet was as much in my interests as it was in the interests of the Silver.

"I'm sure the Silver have secrets," I replied, as if talking to a small child, "but that doesn't automatically mean they're deceiving us."

The bright-eyed man scoffed as if he thought me stupidly credulous. I felt my cheeks flush with anger.

I knew Drew had kept more from me. I'd never found out about the history of the Silver, how they were made, or what had caused the Weeper plague. Sol had always seemed happy to answer my questions openly, but maybe I hadn't asked enough of them, or the right ones.

I was intrigued despite myself.

"What do you think they're hiding?" I asked.

"Ah," he replied with a cryptic smile, "the million dollar question."

He knew nothing, a puerile bigmouth who fancied himself insightful. I kicked myself for rising to the bait.

"Conspiracy theorist, are you?" I asked in a mocking tone.

"Realist."

He put his hands behind him on the bed and leaned

backwards, looking up at me with a smug expression that made me want to slap it off him. I was about to lose my patience.

Fortunately, Alice's tolerance for distractions was even more limited than mine.

"Come on, Emmy," she interrupted. "They're looping the broadcast in the new café in the Square. I'm just desperate to go there! You can see it for yourself."

We had a café now? What else had I missed this morning?

"Hang on," I said as she grabbed my hand. "I need to find Laila to check whether or not I'm working tonight."

"You're not," she replied impatiently. "No one is."

I looked at her, confused.

"You'll see," she said. "Come on."

With one last glance at the irritating man, I let her lead me out of the door.

CHAPTER III

I followed Alice down the stairs and out of the club, her heels clacking as we crossed the floor of the main bar to the street. I surreptitiously checked that the road was clear as we entered the open air, my anxiety ramping up now that we were outside.

The wind was still whipping between the buildings and it felt like rain might be on the way.

"Do you know that guy?" I asked as we hit the pavement, trying to distract myself from the thudding of my heartbeat.

"That's Oliver," she replied. "He was with us at the safe house before we came here."

The majority of the humans here had been housed in a single building for a couple of nights last week while the Silver cleared the Weepers out and set up the barricade. I hadn't been with them, but Alice had. I'd been back here at the club, vainly trying to reclaim the life we'd had before the Revelation with my ineffective Resistance.

"He seems like a bit of a dick," I said.

"He's had a bad week."

Hadn't we all.

We walked along the middle of the road towards Paternoster Square. I wrapped my arms closer around myself and wished I'd brought a jacket.

"So there's a café now?" I asked.

"Yeah, isn't it awesome?" Alice squeaked. "It turns out that the Silver love coffee as much as we do, so they got one up and running. So now they've got the club, the restaurant at the Palace and a coffee shop in the Square." She tapped each of them out on her fingers as she spoke.

"And how many of those establishments cater to humans as well as vamps?"

She gave me a disparaging look.

"You really shouldn't call them that, Emmy. They don't like being referred to as vampires. They're the Silver."

I smiled at her indulgently. How ironic that Alice, who to my knowledge had barely spoken to the Silver outside the club, was lecturing me on how to address them properly. Apparently she was now an authority on all that was Silver.

"We can go to the café," she continued, "it's totally allowed. You'll see when you watch the broadcast. Oh, and you haven't even heard the best bit!"

"But what about the Palace and the club?" I persisted.

"Well, I don't think we're really allowed to go to there recreationally unless we're guests of the Silver," she replied dismissively, "but listen, everything in the café's free!"

So the Silver were still retaining the Palace and the club as human-free zones, with the exception of the workers of course. I could see the logic of keeping the Palace as vampires only, it was their headquarters after all, but the greater the inequality between the races the greater the feeling of deprivation and enslavement. Plus, it just irritated me that I couldn't go where I wanted. We were so restricted in the way that we could move around the safe zone: free to go to each others' dorms and to walk in the streets, but unable to explore all of the buildings around us, to find out what they looked like on the inside. It was frustrating.

I couldn't be the only one feeling this way. In fact, Oliver had demonstrated that I wasn't, and I thought it was counterproductive to reinforce the line between Silver and human. This wasn't the cooperative future many (arguably the more gullible) had imagined and I was worried that there might be repercussions from the disillusioned.

Oliver was playing on my mind. I wondered how many people he'd been spouting off to, how many people agreed with him. Going by the expressions in the dorm earlier on, the Silver might have something to worry about.

I accepted that there was an intrinsic bias towards the Silver in the bargain they'd offered. After all, we were their workers and they needed our blood. But they were clearly trying to integrate us and build loyalty, as was evident from this new carrot: the opportunity to turn Silver.

But I thought it was an offer that was more likely to prove divisive than cohesive.

It seemed like the wrong move when they could have a much happier workforce (and blood supply) if we were simply allowed access to somewhere like the club, somewhere we could unwind. I'd spent a night off at the club with Cam last week, and there hadn't been any trouble. Well, not much. On the other hand, maybe it was wise to keep us away from free alcohol in the circumstances. For some of us, the adjustment had been rougher than for others, and it was far from over.

Thunder rumbled above us as we turned into the Square. The sky roiled with black clouds and as I looked up to it I felt the first heavy raindrop splash heavily on my cheek.

Yup. Definitely should have worn a coat.

"Oh no!" Alice squealed.

We ran across the Square to the glass double doors of the café as the downpour started, huge drops of water tumbling from the sky to detonate on the pavement below. A hot, steamy smell of cooling tarmac surrounded us, and the warm light shining through the windows was like a beacon through the storm. By the time we pushed our way inside the first set of double doors we were soaked from head to foot, clothes and hair plastered to our skin, and we weren't the only ones.

Another set of double doors separated us from the café, which was completely packed. Despite the ominous weather, masses of humans had turned out to experience the new coffee shop for themselves. I supposed it was the first luxury many of them would have experienced since the Revelation, possibly even the first time most of them had been allowed to go somewhere other than their dorm, their workplace or the Square. That made me feel a little guilty about the decadent circumstances in which I had awoken this afternoon.

"They've expanded it upwards into the building," Alice said to me in hushed tones. "Four floors, big ones too. Can you believe it?"

"And we're allowed on all of them?" I asked, immediately suspicious.

"Well, no. Not the top floor."

"Right."

What did it matter anyway? I doubted access to an extra floor in a café would placate Oliver and his friends. A few days living in Sol and Drew's world seemed to have blinded me to the essential truth of the Silver bargain: we want to be safe from the Weepers, so we work for the Silver and we give them our blood. There just wasn't any way to soften that or get used to it if you were living down in it. I'd been exempted from giving blood by Sol, kept from having to work too hard by Sol, kept safe by Sol and his Invicti. I'd been seeing our new world through blinkers.

The only threat I saw from the Silver was Ben, because it was the Silver who had protected me from him. I'd walked more in their shoes than I had in those of the humans around me. I was more sensitive to their concerns than to those of my own race.

I was out of touch.

A counter ran across the back wall of the café, where coffee machines whirred and steamed to serve a long line of humans backed up to the inner door. I pushed through it slowly, nudging it open to avoid slamming it into the crowd inside. They'd kept the original branding of the shop from before the Revelation, a salve to those swimming in an unfamiliar sea. Personally, I found it a little disconcerting, a reminder of everything that had been lost and was unlikely to be reclaimed. I wondered what had happened to the baristas who once manned the milk frothers and cash registers here. They were probably gone too.

I shook off the rain as best I could and looked around the room. There weren't any free tables. In fact, a lot of people were standing around tables whose chairs were already occupied, crammed into every available space. Also, there were no TV screens.

I looked at Alice.

"We have to go up to the second floor," she yelled over the noise of conversation around us. "There's a screen up there."

She pointed to a stairwell in the far corner of the room. I nodded to her before weaving my way across the room towards it. Alice's stiletto heels slid on the wet, polished wood floor and she grabbed onto my arm to stop herself from falling. Even if she had toppled, I suspected that the crush would have kept her upright. I had to push physically through the bodies, winding my hips sideways to slip between the standing people, who all appeared to be human. The atmosphere was steamy, loud and hot, the smell of wet clothing and coffee pervading the air.

When we finally reached the stairs, we struggled up them through a stream of people going up and down. I was exhausted by the time we reached the first floor, which was just as packed as the ground floor below us. Alice pointed across the room and, with a sigh of resignation, I fought my way to another stairwell on the other side. There was no service counter on this floor, just a load of tables and chairs. It was huge, maybe the same size as the first-floor bar at the club, but there wasn't a free seat in the house.

I didn't hold out much hope of finding space on the second floor, but I was surprised. There was no one going up or down the staircase and, when we reached the top, I saw why. Alice gasped and clasped her hands together in glee.

Immediately in front of us, perhaps six feet away, was a service counter with coffee, cakes and cold drinks. A wall ran behind it across the width of the room. To the right of the counter a set of glass doors led into a huge, dark room beyond.

"It's a cinema!" Alice said excitedly. "I knew they were showing the broadcast, but I had no idea it was on this scale!"

To the right of the doors was a second counter selling popcorn, sweets and every other kind of confection you could wish for. They had an excellent set up, but no customers. I supposed that everyone must have already seen the broadcast so enthusiasm to watch it again would be limited.

"Don't people realise there's another coffee counter up here?" I wondered aloud. They were queuing like crazy on the ground floor, but it looked like Alice and I were the only ones up here.

"We've only just opened," said an attractive redhead behind the coffee counter. "Literally just now."

She smiled at me and I smiled back. She was human, but the man behind the other counter wasn't. The redhead saw my eyes flick sideways and nodded at me.

"Don't worry, ladies," he cut in. "I'll be out of your hair in a moment. I'm just finishing the wiring for the fridges."

As he spoke, a light flickered on in one of the counters and I saw what it contained for the first time: ice cream. Not ideal in this weather, but when the summer heat cranked up again...

"How did you manage ice cream?" I asked the Silver, incredulous.

He tapped the side of his nose and, with a cheeky grin at me, slipped out from behind the counter and down the stairs behind me.

"That's Patrick," the redhead said to us when he had gone, with a hint of a sigh. "He manages this place. He'll have gone downstairs to get the rest of the counter staff and proclaim this floor officially open, so let me get your orders before the hordes arrive."

"Er, wow," I said, surveying the choices in front of us. "I don't know. What do you want, Alice?"

"Everything's free, right?" she asked, her eyes widening

hungrily.

"Yup," the redhead confirmed. "For the moment, at least, so I'd make the most of it if I were you."

"I'll have a large white chocolate mocha with vanilla cream, cinnamon and chocolate sprinkles, please," she said quickly.

I laughed happily at her enthusiasm. It sounded like it was an old favourite of hers. She smiled shyly back at me.

"I'm a bit of a sugar freak."

"No kidding," I replied.

"Aren't we all?" said the redhead, grabbing a jug and getting started with the milk foamer. "And you?" she asked me.

"Just a white tea, please." I paused for a moment. "And a bit of that cake," I continued, pointing through the glass counter at an iced carrot cake, one of my favourite things.

"And can I have a bit of that Victoria sponge?" Alice asked.

"Sure, let me box them up for you then you can take them through to the screen."

"I haven't had cake for weeks," Alice said to me. "If I'd known the world was going to end, I wouldn't have bothered dieting."

"Ah, I see. The sugar cravings make a bit more sense now."

"Well, it's not like there hasn't been loads of sugar around, pre-packed and all that, but fresh baking? That's something different."

I nodded, agreeing wholeheartedly.

"We've got a proper pastry chef supplying us here," the redhead said as she handed the boxes of cake to us over the counter. "They're really getting the food sorted out now. I think it's as much for them as it is for us."

"Then it's a good thing they like cake," Alice replied.

The redhead turned to finish off our drinks as we heard the first footsteps on the stairs.

"Lucky we got here when we did," I said as she passed us our drinks.

When we reached the double doors to the screen, the line for the coffee counter was already trailing down the stairs.

"Alice," I asked, pulling open the door, "what have you been doing for food for the past week? In the dorm, I mean."

I'd eaten at the restaurant, in the rooms at the Palace (courtesy of Sol and Drew) and from the tins I still had stashed in my backpack, under my bed. I'd eaten cereal from the kitchen at the dorm, but that was all I'd seen there.

"To start with, there were packaged foods brought into the safe house from the shops outside," she replied with a shrug as she followed me into the dark cinema. "I heard that they've cleared out all the shops now, though. I guess they didn't want to risk people raiding them."

The seats were slightly tiered in three columns separated by stairs. The room probably held about five hundred when it was full. It must have been an old lecture hall. For the moment, the screen was blank.

"After that," she continued, taking the right-hand set of steps, "when we moved to the dorm, there were some tins and stuff. There's more variety now. We help ourselves whenever we like, and the cupboards are always stocked. There are loads of cereal bars and chocolate bars and stuff that lasts a couple of weeks, like rye bread and cheese. Haven't you seen the fridge?"

"Not for a good few days."

"Well, there's more there now. Veg and stuff. We could probably cook, but I don't think the oven works. Do you want to go here?" she asked, indicating a row towards the back of the seating and on the right.

"Sure, wherever."

We put our cardboard cups into the cupholders in the arms of the padded chairs and sat back with the cake boxes on our laps, staring at the blank screen. We were the only ones in the room and it didn't look like anyone was going to join us. I wasn't particularly surprised by this; the broadcast had taken place in the Square just outside, so most of the people in the café had probably been there to hear it in person.

I looked around the room at the rows of seats surrounding us. It was a little surreal. It felt so strange to be sitting in a cinema, oddly incongruous in the circumstances of our modified and diminished existence. For me, going to the cinema had always been a rare treat. Now it was one of the few normal things we had, even though most of the humans in this hybrid settlement apparently couldn't even manage to get a hot meal.

I felt like priorities were skewed, that the measures implemented by the Silver weren't really taking account of actual need. But then I suppose they had everything they needed. They could afford to focus on the luxuries, the non-essential marks of civilisation, because they had all the fundamentals in place: rich housing at the Palace, good food, the club. Blood on tap. They didn't have to worry so much about the Weepers. Not like we did. They were no threat to the Silver, only to their blood supply.

Then again, maybe they were deliberately trying to lull us into comfort by retaining some semblance of normality in our lives.

If things had been less awkward between us then I could have spoken to Sol about it.

The screen flickered into life in front of us.

Speak of the devil.

On the screen, Sol approached a microphone set on the stage out in the Square. The camera zoomed in to focus on his face. He looked straight into the lens, his ice blue eyes burning into me.

"I want to offer you an opportunity," he said enticingly, his clear voice chiming across the microphone. My stomach flipped a little at the sound and my heart raced. He looked good on the big screen.

Shit. I wasn't expecting to have this reaction.

"I offer each of you a chance to become like us, to become Silver."

There was an audible gasp from the original audience of the recording. Sol looked on placidly, giving his congregation time to absorb this information. The noise of the crowd grew, excited laughter mingling with shouts and, in the very background, mumbles and murmurs of uncertainty and disapproval.

After a couple of minutes he raised his arms and silence fell, instantly.

"Although any human may apply, a maximum of four each year will earn the right to attempt to turn Silver. That maximum applies not just here in London, but across the entire country, so it is possible that no humans from this zone will succeed this year. The selection and transformation processes will not be simple, nor are they guaranteed."

I imagined that was something of an understatement. I knew the process was difficult. Sol had told me before that the circumstances had to be right for people to turn Silver. Apparently, he was still keeping the details of those circumstances under wraps.

"Each of you who wishes to participate must have a Silver sponsor to present you at the Casting a week on Wednesday. Each Silver may present only one applicant, and a selection process starting next week will determine which four humans will prevail."

An uneasy sense of inevitability settled over me. I could already anticipate Alice's question.

That's why she'd been so eager to get me over here to see the broadcast. She was going to ask me to find her a sponsor.

I forced myself to keep staring at the screen, to resist the urge to look her way. I could almost feel her eyes on me.

"Attendance details will be given to all sponsors in advance. Candidates must be nominated by their sponsors by this Wednesday, a week before the Casting. All queries can be directed to the Palace."

He stepped away from the microphone and turned to the back of the stage as the camera panned back. A lot of the Silver on the stage looked unhappy. Unsurprisingly, Ben was chief amongst them. I could have guessed that he wouldn't be thrilled at the prospect of humans turning Silver. Less blood for the rest of them.

Another Silver hove into view on the screen and I saw with surprise that it was the guy we'd just seen outside fixing the ice-cream fridge. He smiled widely at the camera. He had curly black hair cut short on his head and brown eyes that were warm and made him look approachable, even gentle..

"Hi all, my name's Patrick and I wanted to announce that this afternoon I'll be opening the café behind you for business." He indicated the back of the Square behind the camera, and most of the heads in the audience turned to look. "Come by and see us. We've got hot drinks and snacks, and it's all free!"

Excited chatter rose from the audience. Patrick waved from the stage as the screen faded to black. The lights in the cinema steadily brightened until it was fully lit.

"Well, that was short and to the point. I guess we were the only people interested in seeing it," I said, turning in my seat to scope out the rest of the room. Still empty.

"I haven't even started my tea and cake," I said, too cheerfully and too quickly, not pausing to let Alice get a word in. I was prolonging the inevitable, but I didn't know how I was going to respond when she asked me. Firstly, I didn't think she should be so eager to turn Silver, particularly without understanding the risks involved. And secondly, I didn't know whom I could trust enough to recommend as her sponsor.

No, I thought, cutting myself short. That was a lie. I just didn't want to share the ones I trusted. Not Sol or Drew. Not Cam either. Not the ones I cared about. Not with Alice. She was so…

"It's okay," she said, crestfallen.

"Alice…"

"I just thought I'd ask. I thought you might help me."

Dear god. She looked so small, so young, so disappointed in her goth Barbie outfit. Young as she was, she certainly knew how to pile on the guilt.

"It's not a golden ticket. Didn't you hear Sol? It's not

guaranteed. And who knows what he means by that? Maybe you'll die. Have you thought about that?"

"I don't care. It's a chance, and that's good enough for me. I just need help finding a sponsor."

"Alice, this isn't what you want."

"Don't tell me what I want," she replied, anger igniting in her eyes. "I'm not a child, you know. I know there are risks, and I know it's not going to be perfect, and I know it's not what you'd choose, but it's all I have." She looked down into her hot drink, blinking back angry tears.

"They see you," she said, her voice rising as she gesticulated towards the screen. "They accept you. I've seen you drinking with them, eating with them. You talk to them outside the club, hang around with them. It's normal for you. And you're not fazed by anything. You know who you are. But I'm not you. I can't have that. That's not who I am, not like this." She gestured down at her body, encompassing her entire self.

I was confused.

"What are you on about? You're gorgeous. They drool over you constantly at the club, like they can't get enough of you."

"But none of them know me. They see me, but they don't see me. I don't matter."

I knew how she felt. In the world of the Silver, it was difficult to feel like anything other than a second-class citizen. Apparently everyone was finding different ways of dealing with that inequality: just as Oliver was working out ways to beat them, Alice was set to join them.

"They don't all accept me, you know," I said quietly. "They hate us, some of them. They'd kill us all in a heartbeat if they had some other way of getting blood. Do you really want to be like that?"

"But they're not all like that. You know that, Emmy, better than any of us."

I had to concede her point. I knew they weren't all monsters. Some of them cared, even loved. Some of them could be trusted. Sometimes.

"I just want to belong," she said desperately. "Can't you understand that? I can find a place there, with them, as one of them. I just know it."

Her words brought back the memory of my first meeting with Sol. He'd told me I could find a place, that I could belong in this new world if I chose to. As far as Alice was concerned, apparently I already did. It was a terrifying thought.

"I'll think about it," I said.

Her face exploded into an expression of pure joy.

"Oh, Emmy…!"

"That's not a yes," I replied firmly. "I said I'll think about it, and I mean it."

The lights dimmed around us in preparation for round two of the broadcast.

"I'll catch you later," I said abruptly, gathering up my tea and cake.

I left Alice transfixed by the screen. I had to get out of there.

Awkwardness be damned; I had to speak to Sol.

CHAPTER IV

The storm had passed by the time I finally manoeuvred my way back to the ground floor. I wove through the crowds with my hands held high above my head to preserve my precious cargo: my tea and cake. There was plenty of jostling on my way to the door, but I ran the gauntlet with my burdens intact.

I'd only been in the building for about half an hour, so on the plus side my tea was still hot in its insulated cup. On the minus side, I was still soaking wet from the rain. At least my boots had kept my feet dry. There was nothing I hated more than having cold toes.

As I pushed through the doors and into the Square, the sun burst through the black rain clouds above me and shone off the puddles that had collected on the paving. If I'd been a little less nervous about being on my own, I might have stopped to sit and enjoy my afternoon snack in peace. As it was, I was concerned that any moment alone was a moment when Ben could catch me undetected. He could kill me in a second and no one would ever be able to prove it had been him. Then again, maybe the Silver wouldn't care even if they could.

I grew more anxious as I strode across the Square, back

the way I had come from the club. I'd been an idiot to leave the café on my own. In fact, it hadn't been a great idea to leave the dorm with Alice in the first place, but I was aggravated by Oliver and I got caught up in her excitement.

Stupid.

My heart pounded in my chest. I was getting myself worked up and that wasn't helpful. Taking a few, deep lungfuls of air, I tried to control my breathing. It was starting to work, but, just as I reached the edge of the Square, a breeze whipped towards me and deposited a figure on the pavement next to me. A Silver, moving at speed. Ben, come to kill me finally.

Panic overcame me. The box of cake fell from my hand. I breathed in sharply, my heart racing in horror as I anticipated my imminent death.

"Emmy?"

I stared at the figure in confusion for a few seconds as my brain processed the images it was receiving from my eyes.

It wasn't Ben. It was Tommy. And he had caught the box before it even hit the ground.

Relief coursed through me and I exhaled heavily, unaware until now that I had been holding my breath. Then I thumped him on the arm. Hard.

"You scared me senseless, you idiot," I gasped.

"I'm an idiot? What the hell are you doing out here on your own? Are you trying to commit suicide by Silver?"

"Yeah, I know," I waved him away wearily. "I didn't think."

"Well, I wish you would. It's not just your life on the line here, you know. If anything were to happen to Drew because of your carelessness…"

I held up my hand in contrition. He had a right to be angry.

"I'm sorry. I'll be more careful. I'm an idiot. Okay?"

He paused and the anger in his expression dissipated, replaced by his usual pragmatic stoicism.

"Will you accept a guard?" he asked as I retrieved the cake

from him.

"Really? How are you going to explain that one away? On what possible basis would a human merit the protection of a Silver?"

He fell silent, thinking hard. Even indicating that a single human life meant enough to be worth protecting at all would raise eyebrows amongst some Silver; they had plenty more. But using a Silver to protect a human? That was on a whole other level.

"The Primus favours you," he hazarded.

"I'm not sure that's going to fly anymore. And besides, you know he can't be seen to care about a human. It would make him seem weak."

Sol had told me as much himself. This morning, in fact, though it felt like it was a year ago.

"Is that why you're not wearing the choker?"

Dammit! I kept forgetting to put it on.

"Shit," I said, kicking myself for my absentmindedness and checking my pockets. "I must have dropped it in the Palace."

Tommy pursed his lips and looked at me with disapproval.

"I know," I said. "I'm being careless, but it's not intentional. I'm on my way to the Palace now. I'll get it while I'm there."

"I'll walk you."

I didn't feel like I was really in a position to argue as Tommy fell into step beside me.

I sipped at my tea as we walked, and thought wistfully about when I might get a moment to enjoy the carrot cake. Not for a while, I guessed.

"I'm sorry about last night," he said quietly.

"What about it?"

"I should have realised about Ben. When he came into the cellar, I should never have let him take you." He gestured angrily as he spoke, his eyes fixed on the pavement in front of him. "We, me and Cam, we just… I'm so sorry."

I smiled at him and said nothing until he looked up at me.

"It's okay, Tommy. He had us all fooled."

"No," he replied, shaking his head. "He didn't. We've known him for years. Decades. Some of us for centuries. We know what he's like, how he feels about humans, deep down. We should never have trusted him with you. We panicked. We made a mistake."

Juggling my tea and cake, I reached out and took his hand for a moment as he walked beside me.

"It's okay. I forgive you. You didn't know."

"I should've known."

"But you didn't. Stop beating yourself up about it, you martyr."

He smiled a little at that.

We turned out of the Square and into the street towards the Palace.

"We just never guessed that he knew about the bond, that he knew what you were to the Secundus."

Ah, yes. The Silver bond.

"You knew, didn't you? When we first met?"

He nodded back at me.

We'd met in the Square when Drew had taken me to watch one of the first broadcasts. Tommy had seen silver glinting on my arm, a mark left behind from Drew's healing of a small cut. I remembered Tommy's reaction as he realised what it meant: horror, anger and then pity. Pity for Drew that he, the Secundus, had silvered for a human. Such a weakness for one so strong.

"You kept his secret," I said flatly.

I knew with absolute confidence that it was a statement rather than a question. Tommy would never betray Drew. Of that much I was certain.

"Yes."

"But you pity him."

"You don't love him," he replied.

I was a little taken aback by the statement.

"What?" I asked, not sure I'd heard correctly.

"You don't love him," he repeated.

"I barely know him. And how would you know?"

He paused for a moment.

"His eyes," he said.

I remembered something Ben had told me last night as I lay dying on a rooftop outside the safe zone, drained of blood, my pulse slowing to the point of no return as he watched. He told me the story of Cara Alton, the American girl whose abduction by her Silver lover had apparently incited the Revelation. He mentioned something about the colour of her Silver's eyes changing when Cara returned his love for her.

Tommy looked off down the road beyond the Palace and towards the wall, twenty feet high, that now blocked the rest of the city from view.

"There's an old song the Silver sing at our version of weddings," he said. "It's really pretty. I can't sing for shit so I won't assail your eardrums by trying, but the chorus goes: 'Etched in skin and shining eyes, "Now to have and ever hold" swears the mark that never lies. Bound in silver, sealed in gold.'"

He paused as I digested this.

"It's a bit poetical," he added after a moment, "but you get the idea."

"Gold?" I asked.

"Gold," he replied quietly.

We walked a little further in silence until we were about two hundred yards from the Palace. The tea was warming me up on the inside, even if my wet clothes were freezing the rest of me.

"So," I said, eager to change the subject, "how do you feel about this 'opportunity'?"

"The Casting?" he asked.

I nodded at him and he shrugged back.

"I don't feel much about it either way. Some of the Silver are livid, but I don't have a problem with it." He cast a canny glance my way. "It would be a really good thing for Drew if you put yourself forward. Hell, I'll sponsor you if he won't."

"I don't want to be Silver."

"Why not?" he asked, genuinely confused. "You don't

want to live forever?"

"Not particularly."

"Well, would you rather live forever or not see the end of next week? Because with Ben after you, the latter is a real possibility."

"You fill me with confidence at your bodyguarding skills."

"No," he said, stopping and turning towards me, "seriously. Why would this not be something you'd want? You'd both be safe. You'd be stronger, faster, practically immortal…"

I interrupted.

"I'd have to drink blood to live, I'd lose my humanity and, oh yes, possibly die in the process of turning Silver."

He fell silent and walked on towards the hotel. I took his silence as confirmation of my suspicions.

"It's true then," I said softly as I finished my tea and threw the empty cup into a nearby bin. I wondered who was responsible for emptying it now.

He looked back at me briefly as I ran a few steps to catch up with him.

"People can die in the attempt to turn?"

Tommy said nothing.

"Well, can they?"

"I'm not talking about this anymore, Emmy. You've clearly already made up your mind."

"Can you blame me when there are so many unanswered questions surrounding the process? I'm not just going to walk in mindlessly. But…"

I stopped talking, wondering whether or not I should continue.

"Well?" Tommy asked, all trace of good humour gone.

I decided to take the plunge.

"I have a friend who asked me to find her a sponsor."

There, I'd said it. If Alice wanted to be Silver so badly then she could deal with the consequences herself. I couldn't make her decisions for her. Nonetheless, I knew I'd be agonising over enabling her application if Tommy came through for her.

He smiled grimly at the massive perimeter wall in the distance as we approached the steps of the Palace.

"I'll sponsor your friend if, and only if, you agree to participate yourself."

"Tommy…"

"No, that's the only offer you'll get. And don't get any ideas about trying Cam or Viv, either; I'll speak to them as soon as I've escorted you back to your dorm. You'll get nowhere with them."

Damn. Viv was my back-up plan.

"And Sol and Drew?" I asked.

"I wouldn't go offering them up to your friends as sponsors until you know what their role would be in the selection process."

That sounded suitably ominous.

"Well how am I supposed to know if you won't tell me?" I snarled at him in exasperation.

"Just trust me," he replied with a wide smile.

With that grin he looked about as trustworthy as a used car salesman with a gambling habit, but I knew I should follow his advice.

I sighed. Sol and Drew were off the cards. It looked like I was going to have to bring bad news back to the dorm for Alice, but maybe it was for the best in the long run.

As we walked up the steps to the Palace together I passed the cake box to Tommy so I could braid my damp hair before we got inside, securing it with a small strip of ragged bandage I ripped from the edge of the one wrapped around my right hand.

"Good thinking to recreate your injuries," he said as he passed the box back to me. There was so much respect in his tone that I felt a little insulted, like a puppy who'd performed a particularly impressive trick. Like standing still.

"No, really, they're pretty good," he added, noting my wry expression.

"Good enough?" I asked with concern.

He smiled as he opened the door to the Palace for me.

"They'll do fine."

We stepped into the double height atrium and walked across the marble floor towards the grand staircase at the back of the room. There weren't that many people about, just the receptionists behind the desk (human), the guards stationed around the room (Silver) and a giggling group of five girls walking down the staircase towards us (too far away to tell).

"It's quiet," I said to Tommy.

He shrugged.

"It's not dinnertime yet. Wait an hour or so and the place will be packed with people heading for the restaurant," he said, indicating the door to our left as we walked past it.

I'd been in the restaurant before and wasn't that keen to repeat the experience. There was a small menu of nice, wholesome food. After all, the Silver liked to eat and drink as much as us humans. There was also bottled blood available for their particular needs. Then there was the table service, for vamps who preferred to drink straight from the vein, much to the apparent enjoyment of their servers. I shuddered a little at the memory.

As we drew level with the reception desk, I saw that the girls approaching us were all human, with the exception of a single Silver who was apparently escorting them. They were all beautiful, wearing wonderful dresses, well-groomed and much younger than me. I immediately felt scruffy, like I was ruining the ambience by sharing their space.

I glanced down at myself and exhaled heavily. Tommy laughed softly beside me.

"I can get you a dress, if you like," he teased.

"Okay," I replied with a smirk, "but only if you get one for yourself at the same time so we can both dress up and go clubbing together."

"And dance round our handbags?"

"You've clearly done this before."

"What can I say?" he grinned. "I know how to accessorise."

I smiled incredulously. Tommy had a sense of humour.

Who knew?

I idly surveyed the accessories of the approaching group and gasped in recognition when I clocked the first one's necklace.

"She's wearing my choker," I said in confusion.

"No," Tommy started to reply.

"Wait a minute," I said, looking at the whole group. "There are three of them wearing it…"

I stopped walking and turned to Tommy in incomprehension. The girls walked past us, giving me odd looks as they went. Almost glaring. Maybe they'd heard me speak, because the three who were wearing the chokers were fingering them possessively as they clacked by in their stilettos.

"What's going on?" I asked.

"Oh, Emilia," said a voice behind me. Tommy's eyes narrowed, focussing above my head, and I whirled round to face the speaker. "Surely you didn't think you were the Primus's only pet?"

"Benedict," I gritted out between my teeth, like what I really meant to say was 'Bastard'.

He was a hulking figure, so heavily-muscled it was difficult to believe it was natural, but Cam had reliably informed me (when extremely drunk) that it was. Despite his bulk, he was oddly graceful, like he had perfect control of every part of his body. It hadn't bothered me before the attack last night, but now I found it creepy.

"How delightful to see you looking so well," he replied with exaggerated enthusiasm, dark caprice sparkling in his eyes.

I backed away, still pathetically clutching my box of cake, until Tommy's hands settled on my shoulders.

"No need for that," Ben continued in a frivolous tone. "You're quite safe here with your bodyguard. For now, at least," he grinned, but there was no joy in his eyes. It was like he was wearing a theatre mask, where everything lied except the eyes.

"So, what brings you to the Silver Palace today?" he asked.

"I'm here to see Sol," I said, as confidently as I could, clenching my hands around the box to stop them from shaking.

"You mean the Primus?" he emphasised the title, spitting the word. I wasn't sure whether he had a problem with my failure to address Sol correctly or whether he was showing his distaste for the fact that Sol held the position. Maybe both.

"Yes, the Primus," I replied, affecting a weary tone in an attempt to hide my fear. I stuttered the last word a little, which rather spoiled the effect.

"Quite out of the question, I'm afraid. He has matters of state to attend to and he is not to be interrupted by the likes of you. Besides which, as you have seen," he added, indicating the direction in which the glamorous girls had gone, "he has plenty of other donors from whom he has already taken his fill. You are… surplus to requirements."

I knew Ben was trying to rile me, but my heart squeezed in my chest. I knew how Sol fed. Well, I knew how he had fed on me.

He was fierce and strong. He was fire. And for one night, he'd been mine. Or, at least, I thought he had been. Maybe I'd never been his only 'donor'. He'd always refused to drink blood in public, saying it was something private. I hadn't thought much of it at the time, but maybe he always drank from the vein. And maybe it was only ever girls…

Ben laughed at me, a rich, rolling laugh that echoed off the marble of the atrium.

Either way, I'd pushed Sol away. I could hardly blame him for moving on. In any case, it wasn't as though we'd discussed the concept of fidelity. Maybe he just wasn't the faithful type.

Tommy slipped an arm around my shoulders and turned me towards the exit. I wondered if he felt as impotent as I did, unable to challenge openly the Silver who was only two people away from the Primacy.

"You're not leaving so soon, surely?" Ben cried in mock concern, walking alongside me. "We haven't even discussed the Casting. I imagine you'll be putting yourself forward?"

I shook my head, my eyes fixed on the doors to the street.

"Shame," he said. "I was so eager to sponsor you. In fact, I assumed that you had come here precisely to ask me to do so. All that time alone together, it would have been incredibly… satisfying."

I glanced over at him. He was looking off into the middle distance as the corners of his mouth rose slowly into a grin that bared his teeth. I wondered what he was imagining, what he pictured in his mind that made him smile so sickeningly.

He snapped out of his reverie and caught my eye, but I couldn't hold his gaze. I looked away.

"It's probably for the best," he said abruptly as we reached the door. He held it open for us. "If I had my way, your sort wouldn't be permitted to dilute our bloodlines and diminish our resources. And, my dear Emilia," he suddenly leaned close to me to whisper softly in my ear, "I will have my way, sooner or later."

I flinched and Tommy jerked me sideways, away from Ben's toothy grin. His laughter followed us out into the street, chasing us down the steps as I walked as calmly as I could to the door of the club.

CHAPTER V

"We're watching him, tracking him all the time. He'll never reach you without one of us being right beside you in an instant."

The sun was mellowing as it descended over the city, bathing us in its evening glow. I shivered and Tommy wrapped a blanket around my shoulders. We sat on the roof of the club, part of which had been turned into a garden terrace. I'd wanted some air, wanted to see the sky, but I wasn't comfortable on the other terrace of the club, not since I'd nearly died falling from it on Monday night, and everything that had followed.

Like I said, it had been a bad week.

"There's nothing you can do though, is there? He outranks you."

Tommy sighed with frustration.

"If it's just us and Ben then I won't let him hurt you, regardless of rank. If not, then I can at least call Drew."

That wasn't as reassuring as he probably meant it to be.

"So I'm only safe with Drew, but I can't be seen with him? That's really helpful."

The club was closed tonight following the announcement of the Casting, so on our return from the Palace I'd left

Tommy in the downstairs bar with my cake while I went up to the dorm to change into some dry clothes. We had intended to have a drink, but as I'd reached the first floor, nausea had overcome me, so I'd pushed through into the toilets off the first-floor bar and been promptly and violently sick.

I was glad I hadn't eaten the cake. It would have been such a waste.

Then I'd started crying and couldn't stop, curling up in a ball on the floor in one of the toilet cubicles. Seeing Ben so soon after the attack last night… I was completely hysterical.

After half an hour or so, Tommy had come and found me. I'd locked the cubicle door, needing to cry this one out on my own. He'd left me there.

A few minutes later I had heard footsteps and frozen. A stack of warm, clean clothes, a towel, a toothbrush and some toothpaste were pushed under the cubicle door. He'd told me he'd be right outside and left me to finish my crying jag.

When I'd emerged, thoroughly ashamed at my lack of control, Tommy was still waiting.

I sat on the roof terrace with my back to the Palace, on the wide edge of a large rectangular planter filled with jasmine. It was new, as were all the other plants, trees, ornaments and pieces of furniture littered around the roof. They'd even paved it and gravelled it until it was a pleasant roof garden. Tommy stood at the ledge, looking out across the city. There weren't so many fires glinting among the buildings now. When dusk fell, things were mostly dark.

My coveted carrot cake sat untouched in its box at my feet. I still felt too nauseated to eat.

To my right, the perimeter wall stretched between the buildings and away into the distance around the safe zone. There was a distant cry from out in the city, a howl that was returned by hundreds of other voices: the Weepers calling to each other through the night.

"Sometimes I think I can hear them in the cellar, in the sewers, in the walls," I said quietly.

"The Weepers?"

I nodded.

"Crawling and grasping, fingernails scraping at the bricked and cemented tunnels to find a way in. Sometimes in my mind's eye they wear faces I know. Danny. Cassie. Sometimes you." I looked up at him as he turned to face me.

"I'm not like Ben, Emmy."

"I know that," I whispered back.

I also knew that Danny was dead. Properly dead. But Cassie... Cass, as she always preferred to be called, and so many others, I didn't know about. I'd lived with Cass. She was my flatmate, one of my closest friends. As far as I knew, she hadn't made it. I wished I knew for sure, one way or another.

"There's a list now," he said.

I looked at him, confused.

"A list of names, of people who are here. Do you want me to check it for you?"

I hesitated for a moment, then gave him Cass's full name. He pulled a phone out of his pocket and fiddled with it for a moment, excitement rising in my chest.

She might be here after all. I might not be alone.

But after a few seconds he shook his head.

"She's not on the list. I'm sorry."

I made him check for each of the names of my friends from the club, not just in the safe house here in London, but in all the safe houses in the country. Not one of them was listed.

The disappointment was crushing, sending me even further into a state of dejected hopelessness. Minutes passed as I stared out into space, dark silence hanging around me.

"Why are you here, Tommy?" I asked abruptly.

"Here where? Here England? Here London?"

"Here with me. I'm sure there are more important things for you to be doing. Don't get me wrong, you've been great today, but we're not all that close, are we? And won't you be missed?"

He sighed.

"I like you, Emmy. I actually do, though I wasn't expecting to. But mostly, honestly? I'm here for Drew. He needs to know you're safe and, if an opportunity presents itself, he needs to see you."

"So you're here to find that opportunity?"

He nodded.

"He'd be here now, he'd like to be, but the Primus has him entertaining." Tommy tapped his earpiece. It was so discrete that I hadn't noticed it was there until he pointed it out. "The defunct oligarchs are still here."

I looked at him blankly.

"You know, the former leaders of the disbanded safe houses."

"Oh," I replied.

Initially, there had been a lot of different safe houses all over the country, formed from existing Silver hierarchies, which took in humans after the Revelation. Now they had been consolidated into only five: London, Glasgow, Oxford, Norwich and Leeds. That consolidation had left a lot of petty rulers without anything to rule, and they were all here to see Sol, fighting to regain some semblance of power. Amongst them was Charles, an arrogant pervert who had been set on me last night by Ben.

Charles had drained me nearly dry before he was interrupted by Tommy and Cam. Ben had swept in, acting the saviour, but instead of taking me to get medical help he dumped me on a rooftop to die.

I couldn't imagine Drew entertaining the oligarchs, especially if Charles was with them. He wasn't particularly good at politics, probably because he tended to say what he thought without necessarily thinking it through first. In the circumstances, Drew and Charles in the same room was probably a recipe for disaster.

"So you're babysitting?" I asked. It had already been a pretty humbling day and this indignity was the cherry on top.

Tommy gave me an apologetic look. He walked across the

roof and perched beside me on the edge of the flowerbed. We sat in silence for a few minutes, watching the sunlight fade as it glanced off the glass buildings around us.

"I knew him when he was human, you know," he said.

"Who?" I asked, my brow furrowed in confusion. Drew had told me that, unlike Sol, he had been born Silver.

"Benedict."

"Were you human?" I asked.

"Not then, though I was once."

I thought for a moment.

"If Ben used to be human then why is he so hung up about the bloodlines not being defiled by the Casting?"

"He was a prince," he replied. "Germany, I think it was. I was just passing through and, when I saw that another Silver had taken up residence in the royal palace, I didn't stay long."

"He was royalty?"

"Yep. Explains a lot, don't you think? Inbreeding, arrogance, insanity…"

I smiled. He was trying to cheer me up, in his own way, but I really didn't want to talk about Ben.

"What about Drew?" I asked.

"He's common as muck," Tommy laughed for a moment then looked surprised. "He hasn't told you his story?"

"No. I know he was born Silver. I know his parents were Silver, but other than that…"

I shrugged.

"I can't tell you that story, not with Drew in my ear." He tapped his earpiece again. "He promises to tell you himself."

"He can hear everything we're saying?" I asked, horrified. I did a quick mental rewind to check I hadn't said anything I didn't want him to hear.

Nothing sprang to mind.

"He's not always listening."

Tommy paused for a moment.

"He's switching to a different feed and he says not to worry, he just wanted to check you were okay. He's only been tuned in to us for a couple of minutes."

"Is that true?" I asked, startled by the intrusion.

He shrugged. Maybe this was just life with the Solis Invicti. Tommy didn't seem to find it at all out of the ordinary.

"All I can hear now is hobnobbing. He's talking to some woman about how wonderful Wimbledon used to be in its glory days."

I smiled a little.

"I spoke to her last night when I was serving in the VIP bar. She seemed nice."

We watched the sun dip a little further down the sky, me trying to overcome my inner demons and Tommy presumably listening in on Drew's chitchat.

"What about Sol?" I asked tentatively. "Was he a prince too?"

Tommy raised his eyebrows at me then shook his head, looking away into the city. He settled his elbows on his knees, leaning forwards and clasping his hands together in front of him.

"He was a king," he said, "and more than a king to some. Still is."

"Always?" I asked.

"Long enough," he replied.

"So Ben's plans…"

"It'd take a lot to get the Primus out of the way, I can tell you that much. People love him, and not just here. He's a legend. But Ben's arrogant enough to think he can step in and take in a day what Solomon has built over the course of millennia."

"Could he?" I asked.

"I don't know. Maybe he could gain control here, but even if he manages to supplant the Primus, that wouldn't give him an outright win. There are some of us who would follow Solomon to the ends of the earth, wherever he goes."

"You?"

"Yes."

He was quiet, contemplative, but determined.

"Even though you think him incapable of emotion?"

"Ah," he replied, moving his hands to rest on the edge of the planter at his sides, "now you're twisting my words. I've never said he's incapable of emotion. I'm just not sure he's capable of the kind of love that Drew is."

I knew where he was going with this and I didn't want to have this conversation with him, not with Drew possibly listening in. He wanted me to forget Sol and choose Drew, but I couldn't. If Drew and I didn't keep our distance, we risked someone finding out about the Silver bond. It wasn't a chance worth taking when I didn't even know how I felt about him.

I shook my head, dismissing Tommy's unspoken question.

"I can't see him," I said. "You know that. He knows that. It's too risky."

"We can take precautions, make it safe."

"Can you? Can you ever do enough to prevent detection by the Silver? Who hear everything, see everything, smell everything?"

He was quiet for a moment.

"There's always going to be a risk," he conceded, "but isn't it worth hazarding a little on this?"

"So now you want me to put my and Drew's lives on the line? You've changed your tune from this afternoon."

Tommy pursed his lips, exasperated. Then he seemed to reach a decision.

"We've got a plan," he said.

"Oh?"

"A decoy. If Drew spends time around a particular Silver woman, then hopefully people will assume he's silvered for her."

"It's hardly foolproof," I scoffed.

"No," he replied, "but it would reduce the risk of detection, so we think it's worth doing."

"Do you have someone in mind for the role of fake girlfriend?"

"Viv's already volunteered."

I liked Viv a lot. She was a very friendly, kind, but above all beautiful Silver. I wasn't sure I was happy about her cosying up to Drew, even if it was for my sake.

Tommy clocked my reaction and smiled.

"Jealous?"

I sighed heavily. I needed to make up my mind one way or another. I couldn't keep bouncing between two different Silver without actually being involved with either of them. One was bad enough. I felt like a deluded teenager.

"She jumped at the chance to play the role," Tommy added, rubbing it in.

"And Sol's okay with this, is he?" I asked sarcastically. "He's happy for his Invicti to be involved in this deception?"

Tommy's face fell. He'd thought he had me.

"No," he growled with irritation, "of course he isn't. It's not something we're planning on sharing with him. He wants you and Drew as far away from each other as possible. You know that."

We sat in silence for a while as the sun disappeared behind the vista of roofs and towers, the residual red sky lighting the world in a pinkish hue.

"He's always had the girls, you know," he said.

"Who?" I asked.

"The Primus. He's always had the donors. Or a harem. Or groupies. Whatever was appropriate for the time."

I nodded.

"You'll never be the only one, Emmy. It's just not how a leader like him works. He doesn't have the time or the energy for love. But he'd sure as hell be your only one. It's at his convenience and it always will be."

I took this on board. Sol and I had only spent one night together. That was it. He'd seduced me, and then what? I'd run a mile and he'd let me.

No, that wasn't fair. I'd told him I wouldn't let him put me in a cage and call it romance. I didn't want to be kept or controlled. He'd tried to respect that, but he'd also made it clear that he wanted me to be his.

But had he only wanted to add me to his collection?

"How many chokers?" I asked.

"I don't know," Tommy replied awkwardly, rubbing the back of his neck with his palm.

"How many?" I insisted.

He sighed.

"Used to be maybe twenty a week. Altogether..." He shrugged.

I did some quick mental arithmetic.

Twenty a week was more than a thousand a year. For thousands of years. A million for each millennium.

Shit. That was a lot of chokers.

Tommy looked up as he heard a light crunch of gravel on our left.

"I see my Invicti are telling tales again."

CHAPTER VI

"You're upset," Sol said to me as he walked across the roof garden towards us.

Tommy jumped to his feet, clearly mortified. He'd put himself in a difficult position.

As Sol approached, the evening breeze catching at his suit jacket, he looked at Tommy then flicked his eyes towards the edge off the roof. Tommy took the hint and sped away, leaving me alone with Sol.

"It's not his fault," I said, pulling the blanket closer around my shoulders. "I asked."

"Do you regret having done so?"

I looked down at my hands, unsure how to reply.

Sol reached the flowerbed and, leaning towards me, plucked a jasmine flower from the plant at my back. He held it briefly to his nose before spinning it in his fingers, whirling it like a tiny cocktail umbrella.

"I'm not infallible, Emmy, but neither am I the incorrigible philanderer some imagine."

He walked away and I looked up abruptly, concerned that he was leaving me. I didn't want him to go. I told myself it was because I was worried about being alone with Ben on the loose, but in truth that was only part of the reason. His presence warmed me.

I thought of the millions of chokers and tried to crush my emotions down, but that was not an easy proposition when I still felt so close to the precipice of hysteria.

He stopped about fifteen feet away from me next to a circle of metal chairs arranged around a table, and I relaxed a little. Hooking one of the chairs with his fingers, he carried it back across the terrace and set it down a respectable distance away from me.

He was giving me space.

"I was once the man Thomas paints me to be," he said as he settled onto the chair. "In fact, I was renowned for my conquests in every context."

He crossed his ankles and leaned back into his chair, looking out at the sunset colouring the broken city.

"Significant failures either craft us into better people or break us utterly," he continued. "Subtle failures, acceptable failures, are more insidious. We cast them as peccadilloes then worship them into vices until they become our sole motivation, our sin."

I looked up at him, confused, but he kept his gaze fixed on the warm rainbows of colour painted across the width of the dimming sky.

"I once yearned to conquer, to control, to possess, but the nature of the prize was irrelevant. My sin was never lust, Emmy. It was avarice."

I remembered his possessive gestures following our brief liaison earlier in the week. Once I had let him mark me with his kiss, he was unwilling to let any Silver touch me but him. He wanted me to belong to him, but when I pushed back hard enough... he let go entirely, slipping away through my fingers in the face of my resistance.

"And now?" I asked quietly.

The beginnings of a smile skirted the edges of his mouth as the reflected light of the setting sun danced along the silver threading in his eyes.

"A different sin entirely," he replied cryptically.

I ran through the list of deadly sins in my head: lust, avarice, gluttony, sloth, wrath... I couldn't remember the last two.

"I gather that you came to see me today," he said, abruptly changing the subject.

"Yes," I replied, "but your pitbull sent me packing."

"I heard."

I shuddered with the recollection of my encounter with Ben.

"I am sorry about Benedict."

"You're sorry?" I replied, incredulous. "He's going to terrorise me at every opportunity until he gets me alone, and then he's going to kill me. You do know that, don't you?"

"We have him under surveillance."

Apparently that was all the comfort he had to offer me. I snorted in contempt.

"We can control him, Emilia."

"Yeah?" I retorted irritably. "How? He didn't seem particularly under control earlier today."

Sol looked at me sadly.

"There is no neat resolution here. If I send you away, he will find you. If I step down and give him what he wants, my position as Primus, your whole race will suffer under his regime. His support is too strong, politically and physically, for me to exile or attack him. Any such action would expose you, expose Drew and challenge my sovereignty. Again, the humans would suffer as a result. Would you have that burden on your shoulders?"

"You know I wouldn't," I replied, anger and shame warring in me.

"And so we watch him," he said calmly. "We look for ways to undermine him, to draw support away from his side. When we find any vulnerability we shall exploit it, just as he is using Drew's love for you against us both."

The stark acknowledgement hung in the air between us.

Drew loved me.

"You knew?" I asked.

He looked down, watching the jasmine flower as he turned it in his fingers.

"Sol," I said deliberately, "did you know?"

"Not at first," he replied softly, his clear voice lilting as he spoke.

"When?"

"After I marked you."

That left a wide margin.

He had marked me with his kiss the morning after we met, during my admission to the safe house. His kiss had released a drug into my system, dulling the pain as he'd stamped tattoos onto the insides of each of my wrists. One tattoo bore my blood type and the other designated me as a member of Sol's safe house, a stylised 'SI'.

"Did you know before the…" I started, not sure how to finish the sentence. Affair? Encounter? Sexual interlude?

"Before the terrace," he said.

A chill skittered through me as I remembered the feeling of Sol's body pressed up against mine, his tongue on my lips, the scrape of his teeth on my neck as they sank into my flesh. I wrapped the blanket closer.

"You knew," I asked, "but you still did it?"

He nodded back at me, meeting my eye once more.

I was a little surprised that he hadn't taken into account the fact that his Secundus had silvered for me. Silvering wasn't something common, so it wasn't taken lightly. Nor, as I understood it, was the bond between the Primus and the Secundus.

"Why?" I asked.

"I wanted to," he replied simply. I'd asked him a similar question when he first kissed me and had received the same reply.

I wondered whether that desire had entirely passed now. He was always detached, but seemed even more so this evening.

"And Drew? Didn't you even consider him?"

"Didn't you?" he retorted calmly. "All's fair in love and

war, Emmy, and I'm something of an authority on the latter, if not the former."

"You should have told me."

He shook his head.

"There was no deception on my part. It was his place to tell you, and he chose not to. That was his decision to make. Besides, he had a surfeit of my Invicti to entreat you on his behalf. It seems that he still does."

He paused for a moment as he placed the jasmine flower on the side of the planter.

"Perhaps they are correct to compare me to him unfavourably, in the circumstances."

I didn't know how to respond, so I said nothing. I was finding it impossible to compare the two of them. Until recently, I'd demonised Drew. I'd been drawn to him from the first moment I met him, but I'd buried that attraction and tried to deny it existed. Being around Drew had made me feel like I was home, safe, protected. Now I was having trouble dealing with the fact that he apparently loved me, so quickly and for no reason other than that fate determined he should. It was…unsettling, and the fact that it had been so instantaneous somehow undermined its credibility. It had everything to do with what I was, but nothing to do with who I was.

And then there was Sol, so volatile and raw when he was unleashed. He was fire in my veins. A fire I'd chosen to extinguish.

"You should know that the Silver bond is not the eternal trump card amongst the Silver that Andrew imagines it to be," he said, "nor does it make his emotion more valid than your own. His love for you should not change what you feel for him."

There was a moment of silence as his eyes met mine. We were skirting dangerous territory.

"I thought he had killed my friends, Sol. Knowing that was a lie, that's what changes things."

And it really had. I hadn't given Drew a chance. Instead,

I'd denied my desire to be close to him, putting space between us in an effort to ignore it. It was fair to say that it hadn't brought out the best in him. He'd been angry and desperate, and at last I understood why.

But I couldn't say that I wouldn't have ended up on the terrace with Sol regardless. There was power in the Silver bond, but Sol had a power all of his own. Where the bond was comfortable and reassuring, proximity to Sol provoked emotion that was fierce and unrelenting.

"You regret your choices," he said. It was a statement, not a question.

"Regret is the wrong word." I was unsure how to express myself. I fidgeted in my seat, pulling the blanket around me again. I wasn't ready to talk about this, to expose myself by discussing this openly. Not with Sol, and not when he was giving nothing away himself, the distance still evident in his eyes.

"He wishes to see you," he said after an uncomfortable moment, steering the conversation away from the subject of our brief association.

"I know."

"Do you want me to let him?" he asked quietly.

I was quietly outraged at his presumption.

"You think you can stop him? Or, for that matter, that you have the right to?"

He was silent for a moment, as if marshalling his emotions.

"As Primus," he replied deliberately, "I have the power to do almost anything."

He looked at me with such intensity that the hairs on the back of my neck stood on end.

"Although," he continued more softly, "I appreciate that ability and entitlement are not necessarily concurrent. In any case, he intends to see you whether I allow it or not."

"Of course he does, Sol."

"And do you intend to allow it?" he asked in a dull tone.

I nearly said no, but, as Secundus, Drew should know whether or not any opportunity that might present itself was safe. I didn't think he'd take it if the risk was too great. He had a plan and I trusted him to protect me. After all, he loved me, apparently.

I needed to see him. There was a lot for us to discuss, one way or another.

I nodded.

"Even though it will endanger you both?"

I sighed, uncomfortable talking about Drew, but painfully aware that it meant I could avoid, or at least delay, having to discuss directly my feelings for Sol and his for me, if he had any. That would be an awkward conversation that I would rather manage obliquely if possible.

What can I say? I'm an emotional coward.

"What would you do in his position?" I asked.

"It's difficult to say, for I'm not in his position," came the cryptic response.

He looked at the flower on the edge of the planter as if he regretted putting it down.

"Not exactly," he added.

I kept my expression composed.

"Not exactly?"

"No."

"Care to explain what you mean by that? Exactly?"

He smiled slightly, but said nothing. It looked like we'd have to have a direct discussion after all, but not now. Not today. It was time to change the subject.

"So," I said, "the Casting."

He gave me a look that told me he'd seen through my avoidance gambit, but tipped his head, as if allowing the conversational diversion.

"What prompted that?" I asked, shivering a little under the darkening sky.

He considered the question for a moment before answering.

"Do you know how the Silver are made?"

"No," I said.

"Then I will tell you, on the condition that you allow me

to take you somewhere a little warmer before I do so."

"Not the Palace," I said quickly. The last thing I wanted was to run into Ben again.

"Very well. Downstairs?"

"The VIP bar," I replied. I needed to be somewhere cosy and quiet. With the club shut tonight, it should be perfect.

He stood from his chair and walked towards me, arms outstretched, as if he were going to carry me, and I panicked, not wanting him to touch me, not sure how I'd react. I stood quickly, so quickly that I caught the blanket under my foot and started to fall forwards. With my arms trapped, I was heading face-first for the gravel, but in a fraction of a second my cheek was resting on the soft cotton of Sol's shirt.

As he righted me, I freed my arms and put my hands on his chest, intending to push away, but he caught my wrists and held them there. The blanket pooled on the ground around my feet and a chill coursed down my spine. But then I inhaled his fresh, spicy scent and heat rushed through me.

I forgot where I was. In the open, under the now dark sky above us, it was as if I were back on the terrace in his arms.

He released one of my hands and ran a finger along the underside of my chin, tipping my face up towards his so I was looking into his bright eyes, the silver in their whites glinting darkly in the night.

"Sol…"

He leaned forwards a fraction.

He's going to kiss me, I thought.

Then he bent at the knees until he was crouching on the ground on his haunches and for a moment I thought things might be getting out of hand.

Gathering up the blanket from where it had fallen, he folded it roughly and put it under his arm. He spotted the cake box on the floor next to where I had been sitting and picked it up and, standing up once more, passed it to me.

Then he started to walk away, heading for the stairs down to the first floor.

I gawped after him, unsure what had just happened.

I was confused and, in all honesty, a little disappointed. That was it? I wouldn't have let him kiss me or anything, but I thought he was going to try at least. Then I realised how pathetic that sounded, even in my head, and hurried after him with my box of cake. I wondered if I was ever going to get to eat it, or if I'd just carry it around with me for the rest of time.

The staircase clung to the side of the building, suspended over the alley below, running from the roof down to the first-floor terrace. There was a metal handrail along the wall on its inner edge, but there was nothing between the outer edge and the three-storey drop to the tarmac. Like the rest of the roof garden, it was new. When I reached the top Sol was already halfway down, his soles scuffing lightly on the concrete as he sailed down the steps, his broad shoulders rolling gently with the movement.

I found the prospect of the precipitous descent a little more intimidating, but I stuck close to the wall and followed him slowly down to the terrace. I watched my feet carefully, making sure I didn't miss my step, so I didn't see that he was waiting for me at the bottom. Next to the wall. Right in the place where we had…

Was he teasing me? I felt like he was prodding gently at my defences to get me to give in, to talk about 'us', to give in to him.

Well, he could go swivel.

I clutched my cake and strode past him, wrenching open the door leading from the terrace to the first-floor bar. I wasn't going to play this game with him. I was going to go downstairs, make myself some tea and eat my damn cake.

At least dessert guarantees satisfaction.

I made my way down the stairs and across the floor of the main bar to the VIP bar, pushing through the doors without bothering to hold them open behind me for Sol. Yes, it was petty and rude, but it had been a shitty couple of days and I wasn't in the mood to be manipulated.

Then again, maybe it was all in my head and I was being rude for no reason.

Dammit.

The room was empty, as expected. We still kept a kettle behind the bar, just like in the old days when the club was Parker's rather than Sol's. A hollow opened in my chest as I realised that the 'old days' were just a week ago. The pace of change in those few days had been staggering. A week ago I'd stood in this bar with my friends at the end of a busy shift and everything had been right, normal. Now here I was in the same place, but everything had changed: the room completely remodelled, my friends gone, and a vampire at my side.

But I could still make myself a cup of tea.

I walked into the circular bar in the centre of the room and clicked the kettle on. The bar was shaped like a ring doughnut, the inner circle filled with fridges and optics and the outer circle edged with the bar itself, beer taps glinting on its top. The glasses hung down from a rack above the bar that mirrored the shape of the wood.

I reached up for the tea bags, but before I could grab them Sol was there beside me, lifting the box down and taking two bags out before replacing the packet. He hooked a couple of mugs down too and placed them on the bar, putting a tea bag in each.

Deprived of my busy work, I crossed my arms over my chest and leaned back against the fridges, fidgeting impatiently. Then Sol took up a position on my right, barely an inch away from me.

I immediately fell still.

He exhaled gently and settled back, watching the kettle on the bar, apparently completely relaxed. I couldn't help but be intimately aware of his every inhalation and exhalation. His presence was so imposing that it overwhelmed me, sending shivers across my skin and setting my blood alive with impatience.

I stared at the kettle, willing it to boil so I could legitimately move away without letting on that his proximity was bothering me.

The tension rose.

Every second felt like a minute.

And the damn kettle still wouldn't boil.

"Milk!" I said, jumping away from the fridges. "I have to get the milk."

Which would have been fine, except the milk was in the fridge Sol was leaning against. I gave up, grabbing my cake and walking out from behind the bar.

"You make the tea," I said irritably.

"As you wish," he replied, a trace a of smile dancing on his lips.

Maybe the awkwardness was only in my head. I felt like I was losing my mind a little. I needed some food and some sleep, then everything would be better.

Well, maybe it would seem less awful, at least.

I slid into the bench of the booth in the corner closest to the bar, my back to Sol, and popped open the box. The cake looked incredible, if a bit battered after its many adventures today. We didn't have much cutlery in the bar, so I was going to be eating with my fingers.

Sol walked over with the blanket draped over his arm and carrying two steaming mugs of tea. He sat down opposite me, gently placing the mugs on the table in front of us, and passed the blanket to me. I wrapped it gratefully around myself, still a little chilled from the roof.

"Shall I tell you about the Casting while you eat?" he asked with some amusement.

"Er, sure."

I wasn't particularly comfortable with him watching me eat, but I was determined not to show him I was anything other than perfectly at my ease, so I scooped the carrot cake up and dug in as decorously as possible, smearing cream cheese icing on my mouth and hands in the process. It was a big piece of cake.

And it was worth the wait.

Suddenly feeling much more myself, and caring a lot less about what Sol thought, whatever that might be, I licked my lips happily and nodded at him to talk while I chewed.

He intertwined his fingers, resting his elbows on the table between us.

"You will recall that, in order to stop the transformation from human to Weeper, it is possible for a human's blood to be drained to extract the Weeper infection. The human must then drink the blood of a Silver to reinvigorate him or her, which should trigger restoration."

I nodded as I took another bite of my cake. Drew had explained this to me earlier in the week when we feared that some Weeper blood had got into my bloodstream.

"However, as you know, sometimes this reversal process fails and, instead of being restored to humanity, the individual becomes Silver. That is because the procedure for turning a human Silver is very similar to restoration, save that to turn Silver the human drinks the blood of the Silver before being drained himself, rather than afterwards."

I swallowed my mouthful and licked the frosting from my lips.

"Hang on," I interrupted, wiping the corners of my mouth, "that doesn't make sense. If it's just a matter of whether the human drinks vampire blood," I shuddered involuntarily, "before or after being drained, then how can it go either way? Unless they're happening at the same time?"

"As with so many things, the process is not binary. There is a whole spectrum of experience from one extreme to the other, and there are no absolutes. Whatever process is followed, there is a significant margin for error, which we surmise is due to the fact that every human reacts a little differently to vampire blood, each absorbing it at a different rate. There is a brief window of opportunity for transformation or restoration, and that window varies."

I was totally lost.

Sol apparently noticed, because he paused in thought for a moment before continuing, as he were trying to find the best explanation.

"Imagine a set of scales. One side represents the likelihood of turning Silver, and the other represents the likelihood of being restored to humanity. Whichever side of the scales is lowest, is heaped with the greatest weight, it will be that transformation that prevails. Understood?"

"Yes," I replied.

"Good. Then we add the weights. If the human drinks the blood of the Silver before being drained, we add a weight to the Silver side, but if it is drunk afterwards, then we add a weight to the human side. But there are potential complications. So, say that a human drinks the blood of a Silver after being drained."

"So there's a weight on the human side, right?"

"Yes. But if the human has particularly fast absorption, so it takes a shorter time for the Silver blood to suffuse the body, we add a weight to the Silver side. Depending on the rate of absorption, the weight on the Silver side might be heavier than the weight on the human side, so the scales might nonetheless tip to Silver."

"But that must be something you can establish in advance, isn't it?"

I was never particularly good at biology or, in fact, science in general, but it seemed to stand to reason that if people's bodies processed... substances at different rates then there must be something controlling that, some way to test whether or not someone would process it quickly or slowly.

"In theory, yes," Sol replied, "but you will appreciate that, with so few Silver having been turned until the past few years, the research into this area has not been abundant. In addition, there appear to be other factors that affect the success or failure of the intended outcome. From the limited study we have made of the subject, those factors appear to have an even greater, often overriding, effect on the outcome when compared with the physical elements that would otherwise guide the result."

He'd lost me again. I was completely confused.

"I don't understand," I replied. "What does that mean?"

"It means that there may be something that has a greater influence than absorption rate on whether a human is restored or turned Silver; a heavier weight than all of the rest combined."

That, I understood. I nodded to Sol to continue as I put the last piece of cake in my mouth and licked my fingers.

"There is a circumstance that seems to bias the human towards turning Silver, whatever the intended outcome of the transformation and whatever ordering is used in the ritual."

"And that is?"

Sol was quiet for a moment as he took a sip of his tea.

"The Silver bond," he replied.

I stared at him.

When there had been a chance that I was infected earlier this week, Drew had tried to convince me to go through the restoration process. He wanted to guarantee that I wouldn't turn into a Weeper. Sol had stopped him, told him it was pre-emptive. Then he'd told me vaguely of the danger that I might turn Silver.

I hadn't realised how likely that eventuality would have been.

"What are you telling me, Sol?"

"Andrew's bond to you makes it more likely that, if he had tried to restore you, he would actually have turned you Silver."

"That's why…"

"Yes, Emmy. That is why I prevented him from attempting it."

"And if you'd tried to do it yourself?"

"It is not certain," he replied, "but the scant evidence we have suggests that the Silver bond will only influence the turning or restoration process when that process is administered by the Silver who holds the bond."

"You didn't think it was worth trying to restore me yourself then?" I asked, a little hurt.

He looked down at his hands.

"The risk was unclear."

I had no idea what he meant by that, but I wasn't going to ask because I suspected the answer would be something I really didn't want to hear. I gulped down my tea.

"So," I said, "what has this got to do with the Casting? Why do you think it's a good idea to offer a select number of your human subjects the chance to become one of you?"

"You think it unwise?"

I shrugged.

"A few of us have been swayed, but mostly we're split half and half. Those who liked the Silver now love you and those who disliked you now loathe you. Personally, I'm not sure that escalating things is the most sensible thing in the circumstances. Emotions were fraught enough to begin with. I think you'd do better to give us something to take our minds off the situation."

"For instance?"

"Well, the café is a start, but how about letting us humans have somewhere to drink? Somewhere else to socialise? You told me that the intention was eventually to open the club up to humans, so why not do it now? The café is hardly large enough to accommodate even a fraction of our numbers. You're offering the Casting like it's a prize, but in the short term it's just going to focus our minds on the disparity between the races. We need a distraction from that, somewhere to mingle and concentrate on our similarities rather than our differences."

"I take your point, but my main concern is not for the reactions of the humans."

"Seriously?" I asked, affronted on behalf of humankind. "You don't care if your population, your food supply, turns rebellious on you?"

"You misunderstand, Emmy. I mean that there are other wheels in motion. Let me explain."

I simmered down and drank my tea in mock compliance.

"The humans aren't the problem. The problem is the Silver."

I raised an eyebrow.

"You will have gathered that not every attempt to turn a human Silver will succeed. In fact, anecdotal evidence and laboratory research suggest that in the vast majority of cases, turning a human Silver is difficult in the absence of a Silver bond, or at least fraternal love, between the individuals concerned."

He sipped his tea again and looked into my eyes.

"Although it is rare for Silver to have children, most of us are born, not turned," he said.

"But not you?"

"No," he said quietly. "I am one of the few Silver who were born human."

I finished my tea and, resting my elbow on the table, propped my chin up on my hand.

"So what you're telling me," I said irritably, "is that, despite everything I've been told about how Silver and humans never get together, a Silver has to love a human for that human to be turned Silver? So every time a Silver has been made rather than born, it's because there was love between a Silver and a human?"

"It is a theory."

"Then it can't be all that rare after all." I was a little dejected.

"Are you irritated because you feel you've been misled, or because it would mean that you are not as unique as you might have thought?"

A nerve twitched in his cheek. He was laughing at me and trying not to show it.

Bastard.

I gave him a caustic look.

"Emilia," he said gently, reaching across the table to take my free hand, "I assure you that you are exceptional. Silver and human pairings are incredibly rare."

His fingers wrapped around the side of my hand and settled into my palm, his fingertips brushing against the delicate skin. It sent a frisson of sensation bussing through me so that I had to take a second to compose myself before I remembered what it was I wanted to ask him.

"Then how can you possibly expect the Casting to work?"

"I don't expect it to be successful," he replied, "at least not in the inaugural year."

I looked at him quizzically.

"But," he continued, "my aspiration is to achieve acceptance of the concepts of our kind silvering for humans and of your kind turning Silver. In that endeavour, my primary target is the Silver."

He withdrew his hand slowly from mine, his touch trailing along my skin as he pulled away, and wrapped it around his tea mug once more.

I was confused. If there were so few Silver and human couples, then why go to the trouble of the Casting? It seemed like a dramatic solution when the 'problem' apparently affected only a miniscule proportion of the population. Was it something to do with Drew? Or Ben?

"Why?" I asked. "Why do all this?"

"There are those who need that acceptance."

He drained his tea mug and, sliding out of the booth, took both of our mugs and put them in the glass washer behind the bar.

"Drew?" I asked. "Me?"

Walking back towards me, he picked up my empty cake box. He had a distant look in his eyes again, like a shutter had come down between us.

"Ultimately, it will foster cohesion between our two races. There will doubtless be a period of adjustment, but if we can see each other as people rather than as predator and prey, rather than rulers and slaves, then it will be to the benefit of Silver and human alike."

I felt like he was reading from a campaign speech. This was rhetoric for the recalcitrant Silver, an attempt to pour honeyed words on a bitter pill.

I didn't think it was going to work; not on the Silver and not on the humans. Humans turning Silver was one thing, but the fact that love was needed to make the transition successful... I thought of Ben. The Silver would never agree.

But Tommy had told me that he and Ben had both been born human. Did that mean a Silver had loved each of them to turn them into what they now were?

"Do they know?" I asked as Sol headed back to the bar.

"Who?"

"The Silver. Do they know about the 'other factors'? Do they know there has to be love?"

He paused in the act of throwing the cake box in the bin behind the bar.

"They know," he said.

"And Ben? What about his transformation? How can he be so militant in his condemnation of Drew if the same thing happened to the Silver who turned him?"

"Benedict was turned Silver a long time ago in difficult circumstances. Suffice it to say that he considers those who silver for humans to be weak, a liability. We know that he will take advantage of Drew's bond to you if he is permitted an opportunity to do so."

"And the rest of the Silver? They accept the Casting? They're letting you try this? Why the hell would they support that?"

"Partly because I have more power than you have grasped."

"Partly?" I asked.

"In all honesty, the majority considers that the Casting is bound to fail. They assume that I realise this and that I am simply using it as a method for placating the humans, a promise I have no intention of keeping. I have not disillusioned them."

"But you're going to go through with it?"

"If one of the applicants is viable, then yes, but it rather depends on the sponsor. Either way, the four who are selected will have to make the attempt."

I remembered what Tommy had said earlier about the sponsors, that I shouldn't volunteer Drew or Sol to act as sponsor for Alice without understanding what their role would entail. A dark suspicion grew in my stomach, uncoiling and spreading through me.

"And what will the role of the sponsors be?" I asked

hesitantly.

"I should imagine that it would be obvious to you now."

I nodded dumbly. The sponsor was there to bond to the applicant. Alice had asked me to find her a sponsor, but I didn't realise she'd effectively asked me to set her up with a vampire.

And Tommy had offered to act as my sponsor.

Ew.

"We expect that the applicants will be successful only if the required conditions are fulfilled."

"You mean if they fall in love?"

"Yes," he replied, "or something similar. Now I shall escort you back to your dormitory. It is late."

I extricated myself from the booth and joined him at the door leading into the main bar.

"Aren't you going to ask me the question?" I said.

Surely he wanted to know?

"I already know your answer," he replied. "You have no desire to be Silver."

"Then why all this?"

He smiled slightly.

"You have a lifetime in which to change your mind."

When we arrived at the entrance to the dorm he reached into his pocket, pulling his hand out again in a fist, which he opened palm-up to reveal my choker. Or a choker, at any rate.

"I suppose that you will refuse to accept this now that you know it is not unique?" he asked.

I looked at him uncertainly, searching his face with my eyes.

"You could simply ask me about them," he said. "I would rather that you refrained from allowing my Invicti to manipulate the situation for their own purposes."

I crossed my arms, shifting my weight onto my back foot.

I didn't want to ask him about the other girls. I thought that, although it had been brief, what we'd had might have meant something to him. But it was egotistical and selfish for me to want that, particularly when I didn't even know what it had meant to me. All I knew was that I didn't want to hear him confirm what I'd been told: that I was, as Ben had suggested, one of many 'donors'.

But, most of all, I didn't want to admit that I cared either way.

He smiled wryly.

"Your sin, Emmy," he said.

"What?"

A word whispered through the air and then he was gone, leaving the slip of lace draped over my arm.

"Pride."

CHAPTER VII

Friday

It was still relatively early by the time I had brushed my teeth and rolled into bed. I was used to staying up till four in the morning for my shifts behind the bar, but it was only just past midnight when I tucked myself in. I was surprised to see that most of the beds in the dorm were empty and could only imagine that everyone was out at the café, still mulling over today's announcement.

Despite it being a little before my usual bedtime, I was shattered. It had been an incredibly long day of emotional ups and downs, following hot on the heels of a difficult week. I'd nearly died yesterday at the hands of a superhuman creature who wanted me dead. I was the only thing standing between him and a kingdom, which had to be one hell of a big motivation. I supposed I had good reason to be afraid.

I recalled his manic expression from last night and the cold determination beneath his deliberately effusive performance this afternoon. He was planning something. He had to be. Earlier today he had been almost smug, playing with my fear because he was confident that I was a problem he knew how to solve.

I shuddered. Crazy though it might sound, this calculating Ben was undeniably more terrifying than the erratic Ben who had left me to die on the roof last night. Now he had a score to settle and I was certain that he would make sure he balanced things out before long.

I pulled the covers up to my chin and wrapped myself up tightly against the cool breeze from the open window by my bed.

On top of that, I had a feeling that it wouldn't be long before I had more than the Silver to worry about. I thought Sol was underestimating the threat of discontent in the human population. It could be a bigger problem than he was willing to credit. I could feel the malaise growing in the people around me, ripples of muttered dissent and confidential glances skittering through the crowds and multiplying like a virus.

There was a gentle thump on the floorboards next to me and I jumped, sitting bolt upright in bed, before realising it was just Nix coming in for the night. I sighed and lay back in bed, rolling onto my side as she meowed quietly in an inquisitive chirrup then leapt onto the mattress. She curled herself up behind my knees against the curve of my body and started to purr gently, so softly that I felt the vibration more than I heard the sound.

I started to relax and drifted off in seconds, but I slept fitfully, plagued by disturbing dreams. In the last nightmare before I woke, I was standing in front of the line of sinks in the dorm bathroom, brushing my teeth. One of my top premolars started to wobble with the motion of the brush as it swished from side to side along the line of my teeth. Within moments my molars and canines were coming loose as well. I looked down in horror as, one after the other, my teeth fell from my mouth and plinked, shining and clean, into the sink, rattling around before disappearing down the plughole. A single canine tooth was left lying between the taps.

I was grateful to be awakened by the smell of cigarette

smoke wafting in through the open window.

"Have you seen him?" a male voice said softly, faint but audible.

"Not yet," came the reply, also male. I thought the voice was familiar, but it was distorted by distance and I couldn't put a name to it. It was coming from the fire escape, or maybe the roof above the window.

"Can we trust him?" the first voice asked again.

"Do we have a choice?" the second replied.

"Why don't we just run? Leave?"

"And how do you suggest that we do so with the Weepers out there, waiting for us, biding their time for nightfall? Without a Silver escort, we'd be dinner within minutes of dusk."

I rolled over in the bed as quietly as I could, turning my face towards the open window so I could hear the words more clearly.

"Look, Johnny," the second voice continued, "I've considered the alternatives. This is the only viable option: we facilitate the transition. We become the inner circle."

It sounded like at least a couple of humans were considering accepting Sol's offer to participate in the Casting. I wracked my brain. I didn't know anyone called Johnny, not in this place. But then again, I didn't know many humans here at all.

"So, is he coming?" the first voice asked, anxiety evident in the shake of his voice.

"He'll be here."

Minutes passed in silence, the scent of cigarette smoke continuing to linger in the air.

"I don't think he's going to come."

"He said he would."

A pause.

"I don't like it," the first voice said.

A gentle, metallic thudding sounded through the night.

"Knock it off."

They must be out on the fire escape. It sounded like one

of them had been tapping his fingers on the rickety metal handrail.

"Sorry."

A few more minutes passed, then a noise like leaves blowing down the street rustled through the night.

"Holy shit!"

"Jesus, shut up," the second voice hissed at Johnny.

There was a pause.

"You came," the second voice continued.

Another pause.

"Tomorrow," a new, male voice said.

"It's too soon." That was the second voice.

"It must be tomorrow. It's time for you to make your first move."

"But we haven't got enough support yet," the second voice pleaded in a panicked tone. "We need a few more days. We're still clearing the tunnels. It's too early to tip them off. They'll find us."

"Do you have so little faith in me? I'll keep them away. You'll be safe. Trust me."

"But…"

"Do you want to be subjugated in this way? Do you enjoy being treated as an inferior race, kept alive only for your blood and your labour?"

The new voice was answered only by silence.

"Tomorrow," the new voice insisted.

"Tomorrow, then," the second voice added quietly.

A breeze gusted in through the open window, chilling the bare skin of my arms.

"That's it? He's gone?" the first voice asked tentatively.

"Looks that way."

"I don't like this. Working with one of them… it just feels wrong."

"Oh, shut up."

Muffled footsteps clanged on the fire escape and disappeared away. It sounded like the meeting was over.

I rolled away from the window and looked around the

room to see if anyone else had heard the exchange, but the moonlight illuminated only still, sleeping figures. I wondered what was going to happen tomorrow, and guessed it wouldn't be anything good. Maybe Johnny and his friend weren't so interested in turning Silver after all.

The door to the dorm opened and light spilled in from the kitchen beyond, silhouetting a figure against it. It was tall and wide-shouldered: a man's shape. I wondered whether he was one of the men from the fire escape and decided it was likely that he was. He shut the door quietly and slipped into one of the beds to the right of the room. I'd lost my night vision when the kitchen door opened, so I wasn't sure which bed he'd gone to.

Something to investigate in the morning.

CHAPTER VIII

I got up early the next morning, but not early enough. Three of the beds on the right of the dorm by the door were already empty. From the look of the clothes that were folded, or strewn, next to the beds, they were all occupied by men. That was the limit of my sleuthing powers for the day.

I had a lot of hours to kill before my shift, which wasn't due to start until later this afternoon. Alice wasn't around. I wondered whether she was back over at the café, indulging her sweet tooth.

Walking across the dorm to the deserted bathroom area, I squared up to my morning hair in the mirror and took stock. The scratches on my face were healing up well and the fake puncture marks on my neck looked passably realistic. I checked to make sure the room was still empty before stripping my nightshirt over my head and wrapping a towel under my arms.

A flash of silver in the mirror caught my eye and I clapped my hand to my chest in a panic. The mark was still there, the shape of Drew's handprint glistening with oily splendour under the surface of my skin. I rubbed at it, trying to move the shining particles from under the skin, but they were going nowhere.

I stared at my reflection in incomprehension, at the possessive brand covering my heart. It had been more than a day since he had healed me. The mark should have been gone, melted away into my flesh.

What had gone wrong?

I brushed my teeth, showered and got dressed as quickly as I could, slipping an appropriately high-necked top over a sleeveless T-shirt. Sol's choker was still where I had left it last night: stuffed into the pocket of my jeans. I couldn't bring myself to put it on, but I put the jeans on instead and left the choker where it was by way of compromise.

I needed some space, so I headed up to the roof terrace with a bowl of cereal for my breakfast. Thankfully, there was no one else up there at this time of day.

Settling into a cast iron chair that faced out over towards St Paul's Cathedral, I put my bowl on the table next to it and tried to relax. It was a beautiful morning. The sun was already burning the dew from the terrace pot plants and starlings were skittering joyfully through the sky after one another as I watched.

If I kept looking up, I could almost make myself believe that I was back on the balcony of the flat I shared with Cass before all this began. Breakfasting in the open air had become something of a ritual for the two of us and we'd become practised enough at it that we could blank out the traffic noise and fumes, and just enjoy being outside. Now there was no traffic to ignore, the tranquillity so complete that I could hear the gentle clicking of the plastic fittings expanding in the growing heat as the sun rose on the buildings around me.

I could have been the last person in the world. Maybe that would have been better.

I ate my cereal as I looked around the terrace, taking in all the changes that the Silver had made. The jasmine flowers were closed this morning, all except for the single bloom that Sol had picked last night, which lay limply on the side of the planter.

I sighed to myself.

I wasn't sure where to go from here. I was isolated in a group of humans from whom I had set myself apart, willingly or unwillingly, and I was caught in the middle of at least one Silver power struggle.

And I'd put myself on the roof terrace, alone. Again. Like an idiot.

I looked around and exhaled heavily when I saw I was, indeed alone.

Still alone.

I ran my fingers through my hair, exasperated at my continuing stupidity. Standing, I picked up my cereal bowl and turned to go back downstairs to the dorm.

"Emmy!" a shout echoed up from the street.

I put the bowl back down and walked cautiously to the edge of the roof, looking down into the street that was overlooked by the window next to my bed. Cam was standing in the road, scruffy in jeans and a T-shirt, his face lighting with a happy grin when he saw me. He motioned for me to step back from the edge of the roof, then leapt up onto the fire escape, and from there onto the roof itself.

"Show off," I huffed, crossing my arms over my chest. Cam was unperturbed and swept me up into a hug, lifting me off my feet and spinning me round. I hastily fastened my arms around his neck, worried that I would slip from his grip. Of course, he'd never let me fall. Within seconds I was laughing with delight as he spun me until I was dizzy.

"Enough, Cam!" I gasped. "You're going to make me ill!"

He put me gently on my feet and held my arm so I could walk in a straight line back to my breakfast.

"It's good to see you, Ems."

"You too," I smiled at him, genuinely pleased to see him.

When we reached the table he turned me to face him, his expression suddenly serious. It looked out of place on his boyishly cheerful face.

"What's wrong?" I asked, worried that something terrible had happened overnight. I thought back to the men talking on the fire escape last night and started to panic. "Is everyone okay? What happened?"

"No, no," he said quickly, "everyone's fine. I'm just so sorry, Emmy."

I waved my hand in a dismissive gesture.

"I know. It's okay, I've already had this from Tommy…"

"No," he cut me off, "it's not okay. I let you down. I keep letting you down. First with the capture, then that night we got drunk, and now this." He shook his head in a gesture of despair.

Cam had been the Silver who had duped me into a trap that landed me back in the hands of Drew last week. Then he'd got really drunk with me and bailed when Sol showed up, the night I was attacked by a Weeper.

"Look, Cam," I held his face and tilted it down so he was looking into my eyes. "You didn't know me when you helped with the capture. You couldn't have known I was going to get attacked by that Weeper. As for Ben, well, we all dropped the ball there. I don't blame you. None of us knew he'd worked out the Silver bond."

I kissed him on the cheek and pulled him into a hug.

"Now come and sit down," I continued. "My cornflakes are getting soggier by the second."

I sat down again and returned to eating my cereal. He took a chair opposite me and rested his elbows on the table, his gangly arms sprawling across most of its surface.

"So…" he said.

"You're going to ask me about Drew, aren't you?" I interrupted.

"No," he replied, feigning nonchalance, "no. I was going to talk about something completely different. I mean, why would I want to talk to you about Drew? Boring old Drew. Nothing to talk about there."

"Just say it."

He paused, then leaned forwards intently.

"Fine, yes, I want to talk about Drew. He loves you, he's silvered for you, and isn't that an awesome and amazing thing? And with the Casting, you can turn Silver, then you'll both be safe and you can be together. Forever. Why wouldn't you be excited right now?"

Forever.

Forever was… well, forever. And forever was really forever if you were Silver.

"I barely know him. I know you better than I know Drew. And I don't want to be Silver, you know that."

I flicked my spoon in frustration and it rattled around on the inside of the bowl, splashing milk on the table.

"But he loves you," he replied, his face clouding with incomprehension.

"So what? Is all love necessarily requited? Why should what he feels for me have anything to do with how I feel about him?"

"Is this about the Primus?"

I gritted my teeth. I was starting to feel like I was stuck in a loop.

"I can't keep having this same conversation, Cam, over and over and over. There's Sol, and there's Drew, and whatever I feel about each of them, they're not linked. It's not a contest."

He leaned back and tilted his chair back and forth on two legs.

"Are you sure about that?" he asked quietly. "It isn't for Drew. Drew's all in. But as for the Primus…," he shrugged.

This was verging worryingly closely on my own thoughts of last night. If Sol was only interested in possession, if he was intent on avarice, then his interest in me might have been entirely dependent on Drew's own. Anyway, given the tone of our discussion last night I wasn't sure that Sol still had any real interest in me at all anymore.

"I really don't want to talk about this again," I said as patiently as I could manage.

"Okay," Cam replied with a conciliatory grin, holding up his hands in a gesture of surrender. "Say no more."

We sat for a moment in companionable silence as I finished my cereal.

"I do need to talk about the Primus though," he continued.

I groaned.

"It's too early in the morning for this, Cam."

"No, look, he asked me to come over and speak to you. He's been thinking about what you were saying last night."

I cast my mind back, but there'd been a lot going on and I couldn't think what Cam might be talking about.

"About the Casting?"

"No. About humans and the Silver needing somewhere to socialise. The Primus thought it was a sensible way to starting breaking down barriers, so he wants to open up the club to humans as well as the Silver."

I looked down at the table top. It had sounded like a good idea at the time, but after the meeting I'd overheard on the balcony last night… something was up, and I didn't think a shared watering hole was going to be much more than a tiny band aid on the gaping wound between the races. In fact, I wondered if it might not just make things worse.

I needed to talk to Drew, if only to tell him about this potential security threat. In his position as head of the Solis Invicti, he might know something, or be able to do something to help.

Then again, maybe I should be encouraging this dissent rather than helping the Silver quell it. Wasn't that what I had wanted in the first place? Didn't people have a right to object to this slavery, and to live their lives on their own terms rather than as dictated by the needs of the Silver?

I just couldn't see a clear way through anymore, my moral objectivity non-existent in light of the friendships (and more) that I had built with the Silver who had taken over our world.

Screw it. I'd made my choice, and it was Drew and Sol, in whatever order I finally decided was appropriate. I was with the Silver and it was time that I accepted that.

"People aren't happy, Cam. There are things going on, people are talking… I need to talk to Drew about it."

Guilt churned in my stomach as I spoke. I was helping the Silver police human rebels. I couldn't think of any way to dress that up so it didn't make me a race traitor. That's what I was: a traitor. The thought twisted through me, insidious and unwelcome.

But siding with the humans wouldn't even keep me safe from the Weepers, let alone from Ben.

"Viv's on her way over."

I raised my eyebrows, blinking in surprise at the non-sequitur.

"She wants to talk about the, you know, plan."

"Of course," I replied quietly. "The 'you know' plan."

The plan where Viv pretended she was the girl Drew had silvered for to draw attention away from me. The plan where Drew convinced people that it was the truth. The plan where they probably had to do a lot of stuff in public to back up the lie.

That plan.

I hated that plan.

"You don't like the plan?" Cam asked nonchalantly.

"The plan is fine. Why wouldn't I like the plan?"

He grinned back at me.

"So, humans in the club?" I said, fiddling with a loose lock of hair. "You think that's a good thing?" The subject change couldn't have been more obvious, but Cam let me get away with it.

"Sure, if you're in charge."

"Come again?"

His grin expanded.

"You're in charge. That's what Sol wanted me to talk to you about. He wants you to run the club."

"What? What about Laila?"

"You've met Laila, right? You know how she feels about humans?"

Laila had been disdainful and dismissive of me when we first met, and she hadn't warmed up at all over the course of the past week. She was deep into the Silver rituals and history, so it was perhaps unsurprising that she viewed humans as a food source and little else.

To be frank, she was kind of a bitch.

"She's managing a lounge over at the Palace now," Cam continued. "Sol's keeping the Palace open to escorted humans only, and I don't think that's going to change, but you've got the club now."

"He wants me to run the club?"

Cam nodded back.

I couldn't believe it. Ever since the Silver had taken the place over I'd been feeling ousted, displaced from somewhere that had previously been a sanctuary for me, Jeff's business and home contaminated by the awful things that had happened here. Now I had a chance to take control of that, to make it mine again.

"You have to keep the VIP bar as a Silver area, human guests by invitation only, but the main bar and the first-floor bar can be all mixed. What do you think?"

I didn't know what to say. There was so much to think about.

How was I going to staff the different bars? Did I even have enough staff? Did we have entertainment we could put on for the first-floor stage? Should I limit the humans to a certain number of drinks so they didn't go crazy on the free booze? How was I going to sort out the clogging in the blood-barrel pipes?

"You look scared," Cam said, obviously expecting a different reaction.

It had to be controversial that I was being given this kind of responsibility, this kind of control over a venue that accommodated not just the humans, but also the Silver. There were three establishments up and running, and I was in charge of one of them. Me: a human. I was sure it was part of Sol's integration plans, but how could Sol expect me to exercise any kind of authority over the Silver patrons?

"It's a big deal."

"Oh, come on, Emmy. You'll love being in charge. You barely even have to do anything tonight because Laila's already done the rota for the week. Everyone knows what they're doing, so you can just take your time to get to grips with things. The office off the first-floor bar is all yours."

Jeff's office. I hadn't been in there since before I had been captured. The last time I'd seen Jeff alive he had been in that room with Sarah, keeping an eye on the monitors banked on his desk for any sign of the Silver or the Weepers in the street below.

"It's different now," Cam said, catching the look on my face.

I nodded silently, not sure whether the fact that the room had changed would make it better or worse. I was excited and terrified at the same time. I was also concerned that this new role would ally me more strongly with the Silver. I didn't want to be a target for humans looking for an easy way to get to them.

"Here," he said, reaching into the pocket of his jeans. He pulled out a keyring with two keys on it and handed it to me. "These are the keys to the office. I'll take you down there when we're done speaking to Viv."

My heart sank a little at the prospect of talking to her. I really liked her. She was vivacious and kind, and there was nothing not to like about her, except she was going to be playing decoy with Drew.

I just couldn't seem to control my jealousy.

I looked up and watched the starlings dancing through the sky once more, yearning for the balcony of my old flat. We used to get birds nesting in the gaps in the guttering. They'd swoop up and under the balcony ledge above us to the concert of their chicks' cheeping.

"I wish I could go home," I said aloud.

"Home?" Cam asked.

"I shared a flat in Archway. It was tiny, but it was home for a few months."

Cam traced my line of sight as I followed the birds across the sky.

"You miss it," he said simply.

I nodded, then closed my eyes and let the morning sun

warm my eyelids. I raised my hand to my chest, rubbing absent-mindedly at the mark through my shirt as the sun heated the skin beneath. It felt prickly and hot. I wished it would just hurry up and fade away.

"Hey guys! What's going on?"

I snapped my eyes open as I recognised the chirpy voice. Viv was bouncing up the stairs from the first-floor terrace, her lithe shape dancing along as her glorious red hair played in the breeze behind her. Her pale skin gleamed in the morning sunlight, a gentle blush tingeing her cheeks.

I groaned internally.

I was trying not to think of her as the competition, but it was difficult not to draw comparisons. None of them were in my favour. This was the woman, the Silver, who was going to be cosying up to Drew.

She clocked my grim expression as she crossed the roof towards us and frowned daintily.

"Oh crap," she said, looking at Cam. "She's not doing the Casting, is she?"

"Nope," he replied.

"Well, why the hell not?" she asked as she reached the table. The wind caught her hair and blew it round her face, carrying a familiar musky scent of leather and wood towards me.

It was the smell of Drew.

So Viv had already started laying the groundwork for the ruse. She'd probably come straight from seeing him.

I stiffened slightly in my chair. Viv caught the gesture and cast a puzzled glance in my direction.

"You smell of him," I mumbled apologetically.

"You can tell? But you're human."

"Yeah, but I've still got a nose," I replied in a scathing tone of voice. I was being unfairly hostile towards Viv, but I didn't seem to be able to calm myself down.

"I didn't realise humans could smell the mark," she thought aloud.

"The mark? What mark?"

I paused as I reluctantly processed this new information. When the Silver kissed, they could leave a scent mark behind. I didn't quite understand the parameters, but it seemed only to happen where the kisser intended to create a bond and the kissee accepted it. It was a ritualistic thing among the Silver; the equivalent of saying 'hands off, this one's mine'.

Sol had marked me twice last week, once without me knowing what it meant. I was starting to understand how that must have made Drew feel.

"I'm busting a gut here trying to play Juliet to the Secundus's Romeo," Viv continued, "and that's no barrel of laughs, I can tell you."

"Wait a second," I said, slowly getting to my feet. "He's marked you? Already?" I ran my fingers through my hair to push it back from my face then picked up my bowl, making to leave. "You didn't hang around, did you?"

Cam laughed out loud, making me jump.

"What's so bloody funny?" I demanded, whirling round to face him.

"Well if this is how you feel about him, why all the indecision? Come on, admit it, you care about him."

I had to restrain myself from kicking him.

"Yes," I replied impatiently, "I have feelings for Drew. But this isn't as simple as you seem to think it is, Cam. You don't just get to say 'happily ever after' and close the book."

I walked away across the roof and headed down the stairs to the first floor.

"Emmy, I'm sorry," Viv shouted after me.

I glanced back at her and saw that her pretty elven face was filled with desperate contrition. Cam was still sitting at the table, an unrepentant smirk on his face. I waved my hand at Viv, dismissing her anxiety.

"It's not your fault," I called back, "just give me some time."

I knew she was just trying to help. It couldn't be fun for her, having to play out this charade with the Silver who was, for all intents and purposes, her boss. That said, on paper they looked like the perfect match: the leader of the Solis Invicti and a slender warrior woman. With amazing hair, damn her.

CHAPTER IX

I sighed heavily as I reached the door leading into the first floor bar and pushed my way through it. I wasn't helping myself by playing out the Drew and Viv show in my head. I needed a distraction.

I thought I may as well go and check out the office while I was here, so I left my cereal bowl on the bar and pulled the office keys out of my pocket. The first was familiar, a key I recognised from before the Revelation, from last week.

The office was accessed through a door next to the bar, which led into a cupboard-like space that contained two more doors, one on either side. The one on the right led to the taproom and the one on the left led to the office. I fitted the key into the single lock on the office door, wondering what the second key was for; I couldn't see any new locks.

A fresh, spicy scent rushed over me as I swung the door open, and I knew what I'd see before the door was more than an inch away from the jamb.

It was the smell of Sol.

But when I opened the door I saw only an empty office. I opened the outer door and checked the dance floor behind me, but he wasn't there either. Puzzled, I walked into the room and closed both doors behind me. The office was fairly similar to the way it had always been, the monitors banked up against the inner wall showing feeds from various cameras around the club. The furniture was different, and the computer equipment was all a little slicker, but the familiar dimensions of the room enveloped me in its cosy space, an odd echo of past. It was as if someone had wound a clock forward to show me Parker's ten years into the future, rather than just a week.

I sat in one of the office seats arrayed in front of the monitors and tried to put my feet up on the desk, but the new chairs were clearly designed for good posture so were fiendishly uncomfortable in that position. The old Parker's chairs had probably started out like this, hard and unyielding, but had been thoroughly bashed into submission over years of abuse until their springs were as pliant as cotton wool.

Nostalgia pricked in my chest. This was going to take some getting used to.

The lingering scent of Sol was an odd juxtaposition to the vivid spectre of Parker's. I breathed it in and it lit up my nerve endings, burning across the sensitive handprint on my chest as if the two were uncomfortable sharing the same space.

That made a lot of sense, psychologically speaking. The itching and burning of the healing Silver mark probably had more to do with my discomfort about its meaning than it did with actual physical symptoms. No wonder it was flaring up when I thought about Sol: the other Silver, as it were.

But why was I smelling him here?

I leaned forward in my seat and scanned the monitors. They'd added more cameras: two on the roof terrace, one on the first-floor terrace and a few up in the dorm. I had a slight panic attack until I had verified that there was no camera in the dorm bathroom.

It looked like most people were still in bed. I saw Alice in the dorm and realised that she must have stayed out all night at the café. I was pretty impressed at her staying power and wondered what I had missed that had been worth the all-nighter. Then I realised that her ability to tend bar this evening was now my problem and felt a stab of anger at the fact that she was probably going to be falling asleep during her shift.

Dammit.

I didn't want to be the killjoy. For that matter, I didn't want to be the human enforcing conformity with the Silver regime. Last time I'd been looking at the monitors in this room I'd been planning ways to rebel against Sol's rule, not trying to support it. I supposed I didn't feel like there was much of a choice anymore.

There were a few people having breakfast in the dorm kitchen, but there was no one in the club itself. The humans were discouraged from wandering around out of bounds, although that didn't stop me from doing so. The street was empty apart from a couple of guards on the Palace and the new wall at the end of the road, whom I assumed were Silver.

No sign of Sol.

I watched Cam and Viv talk on the roof terrace for a few minutes. They were joking with each other, relaxing back in their chairs and laughing. Feeling like a creep for intruding on them, I looked away and scanned the other monitors.

Nothing was going on. The morning was clearly a boring time in the Silver world. I slumped forward onto the desk, putting my elbow on its surface and propping my chin in my raised hand.

What now?

There was the sound of a throat clearing behind me and I spun the swivel chair round. Sol looked down at me, the door to the office's storage cupboard clicking shut behind him. I felt my heart thumping in my chest.

He was here; I hadn't just imagined the scent.

"I take it that you have spoken to Cameron?" he asked, indicating the office keys on the desk with a nod of his head.

A lock of his blonde hair tumbled forward across his forehead as he leaned forward, trailing down towards his ice-blue eyes. My pulse raced faster and I was sure that he would be able to hear my heartbeat. My cheeks heated in embarrassment.

"Yes," I replied.

"And you are happy to replace Laila?"

I didn't really want to answer that question, because I was pretty sure the answer was 'no'. I knew that wasn't what Sol wanted to hear, and it was probably a bad idea to reject his offer.

"Why are you hiding in the cupboard?" I asked instead.

He took a step away from the cupboard door and I saw that it had been fixed with a new lock. I realised that it must be the lock into which the second key fitted.

"I was delivering your belongings to your new quarters," he replied. "You arrived a little more quickly that I had anticipated. I expected that I would have departed by the time you left the roof terrace."

He hadn't wanted to see me. I could feel my cheeks burning now, both disappointed that he was hoping to avoid me and hating the fact that I cared. Whatever had been between us was supposed to be over.

The handprint on my chest was heating under my shirt. I pushed my palm against it, trying to stop it from throbbing.

"You want me to live in this office?" I asked, trying to adopt a normal tone of voice. It would be cramped, but I could manage if I spread some blankets on the floor.

"Not quite," he replied as he pulled a key from the pocket of his chinos and fitted it into the lock on the cupboard door. As he did so, he looked over his shoulder at me.

"You and I are the only people with a key to this door."

"You want me to live in a cupboard?" I asked in disbelief.

In response, he swung the door open and stepped aside so I could look into the space beyond. The normal contents of the cupboard had gone, replaced by a set of concrete stairs climbing up and to the left. I should have put two and two together given how much building work the Silver seemed to be undertaking, but I was feeling a little floored and was finding it hard to connect the dots.

"After you," he said.

There was a single flight of stairs that led to a small landing that must have been on the same level as the dorm on the second floor of the club. However, the single door on the landing led off not to the left, into the dorm, but off to the right and into the adjoining building. They had obviously knocked through the connecting wall.

As I crested the top of the stairs, Sol reached past me and inserted the same key into the lock on the new door, then stepped back to allow me to go past him into the room beyond. My body tingled at his proximity, the mark on my chest filled with pins and needles. I rubbed at it in an attempt to dissipate the sensation.

I was expecting an office building, but it was actually a living space. In fact, it looked like a small, luxury apartment.

The long wall to my left was floor to ceiling glass with a fireplace for an open fire set in its centre. It looked incongruous in the middle of the summer, but in the winter it would be perfect for warding off the cold air from the windows. Two sets of glass double doors opened out from the room onto a wooden-decked area beyond that was littered with pot plants and small trees in large planters. Patio furniture and sun loungers sat out on the deck.

The room in which I was standing was entirely open plan. Immediately to my left and against the wall was an antique bureau and chair. Further into the room and in line with the fireplace were a sofa and a couple of arm chairs arranged around a coffee table, with a small television off to one side. In the back corner of the room to the right was a gleaming kitchen, in front of which sat a small dining table with four chairs.

I was expecting that the apartment would be a single floor, but a set of wooden stairs running along the wall to my right climbed up to the floor above.

"Wow," I said stupidly, not sure how to react.

"This will be a safe place for you," Sol said as he moved into the room and closed the door behind us. "The club is invariably guarded by my Invicti. The glass is mirrored from the outside, so you will be unseen if anyone should stumble across this place, and that is unlikely to happen. Very few people are aware of its existence. The terrace is surrounded by brick walls, so from the roof terrace next door it appears to be part of the same building." He paused for a moment. "If you remain intent on talking to my Secundus, you can do so here without fear of being overheard."

"You did this to keep me safe?" I asked, not quite able to believe what I was hearing.

Sol looked slightly taken aback.

"No, Emilia. This apartment has been here for years. I constructed the connecting staircase with the intention of offering a convenient and discreet residence for Laila. However, as you know, she has chosen instead to return to the Palace, so it is standing vacant."

Of course, I thought. Why would the Silver go to the effort of constructing something like this for a human? Why would Sol care? This last thought twisted unpleasantly in my stomach.

"You understand that this is a temporary arrangement?" he asked, furrowing his brow. "You realise that you are simply an interim manager until such time as a Silver replacement is appointed?"

I nodded dumbly.

"Yes, of course," I lied, feeling my cheeks reddening once more.

Now it made sense. The Silver would never accept a human holding any kind of responsibility here, particularly not when it came to their blood supply. I had been foolish even to entertain the thought that they might.

"But until such a replacement is found, you may stay here," he added. "Your experience of working in this club should leave you in a position to keep it going for a short period of time. You will not, of course, be expected to arrange events or manage the VIP bar, which will be delegated to an appropriate Silver in due course."

The sense of control and belonging that I had begun to

reclaim slipped away, leaving me cold. Emptiness flooded into my chest as I processed the implications of this development. I'd never be a person in this new world, I'd never be anyone. Although I would be the first to admit that one of them could take me hands down in a fight, I didn't think I was any less intelligent than them. They may have lived longer, but that didn't necessarily make them wiser.

But in their eyes, in Sol's eyes, I'd only ever be human. I'd always be less capable than the Silver. So much so that apparently Sol needed nineteen other human girls a week to make up for my inadequacies. Apparently I'd have to turn Silver before I was enough for him.

"Great," I replied as brightly as I could manage.

I spotted my rucksack on the sofa in the middle of the room and used it as an excuse to head upstairs before I embarrassed myself further by getting emotional in front of Sol. I couldn't face the thought of him seeing me as weak or, worse still, him pitying me.

There were three doors off the landing. One led into a small bedroom at the back of the apartment, one led into a neat shower room at the top of the stairs and the third opened on my left into the master bedroom. I pushed inside and closed the door behind me, dropping the rucksack onto the floor as I took in the room. It was glorious.

The wall in front of me mirrored the one in the room below. It, too, was floor to ceiling glass, a single set of double doors opening onto a wide balcony that ran the length of the wall. To my right, next to what looked like an antique chaise longue, was a door leading to an en suite bathroom with, I was delighted to see, a bath tub. To my left, behind a comfortable-looking double bed, was a large built-in cupboard. Scooping up my rucksack, I pulled open the cupboard door and swung the bag inside. I paused when I realised that the cupboard had been populated with the clothes Drew had swiped for me last week, the ones that had been left in the guest suite at the Palace. I wondered whether I had Sol to thank for that.

I sat on the edge of the bed for a moment and tried to pull

myself together. I should make the most of this amazing living space while I had it, and try my best to make a good job of running the club. That way, maybe I would be given better opportunities in the future.

Of course, the other way of looking at that scenario was that I was being placated into compliance, bribed for the price of a fancy apartment. I sighed heavily and pulled myself onto my feet.

I was expecting Sol to have left by the time I got back downstairs, and at first I thought he had. Then I saw that one of the doors onto the terrace was open. He was standing out on the deck with his back to me, the breeze catching at his crisp, white shirt. Pushing my hair back from my face and plastering on a smile, I stepped out into the morning sunshine.

"This place is amazing," I said. "Thank you for letting me use it."

He turned to face me with a faint smile on his face and I was completely disarmed.

My step faltered and I stumbled to regain my footing, blushing again with embarrassment. He lunged towards me and caught my arm, sending my heartbeat through the roof as the rich, clean smell of him enveloped me. It penetrated every inch of me, filling my head and tracing down to my fingertips. My reaction to his residual scent in the office earlier this morning was nothing compared with this. I felt light-headed with it and the strength went from my legs.

Before I knew it I was in his arms, and I felt like my temperature was soaring. The palm-print on my chest began to burn painfully, throbbing in time with my pulse.

"Emmy, your heart is racing," he said, a touch of concern in his voice.

"I'm really warm," I replied, wrapping my arms around his neck as I tried to regain my balance. My chest pressed against Sol's and in that instant a searing pain clawed into the skin where Drew's healing silver marked me.

I cried aloud and pushed away from Sol as tears sprung to my eyes, but he instinctively pulled me closer to stop me from falling, pressing my chest into his. It felt like the silver-marked skin was being held against red-hot metal.

I screamed.

"Let me go! Let me go, Sol!" I begged. "Please!"

He loosened his grip on me with an expression of incomprehension and horror. I stumbled backwards and fell onto the deck, my legs sprawled out in front of me as I curled my arms protectively over my chest.

The mark was still uncomfortably hot, but most of the pain had passed.

"It's you," I said in disbelief.

"What do you mean?"

He took a step towards me and crouched by my side. The heat in the skin under my collarbone increased to the point of pain.

"Just stay there," I pleaded as I shifted away from him.

He moved back a little, a look of concern crossing his face. He obviously thought he'd hurt me, or that he'd done something to upset me.

"What is this, Emilia?"

I stripped the high-necked top over my head so I was left in the vest top I wore underneath. The skin around the silver mark was bright red, the silver particles seeming to pulse under the surface.

His mouth twitched down for a fraction of a second, as if it displeased him to see Drew's handprint on me.

"It burns," I explained simply.

He leaned forward carefully from a distance to examine the mark, his expression carefully schooled into nonchalance.

"It has not faded," he said. "If anything, it is stronger than it was two days ago."

"I don't get it," I said. "The last mark faded in a day, and it never burned like this."

"This is different. Not only was it the second healing in a short period, but it was also more extreme. Were it not for the Silver bond, you would likely have died."

He pushed his hair back from his face, running his fingers

through it, and the movement sent a fresh wave of his spicy scent in my direction. I groaned and backed further away as tiny needles of pain stabbed at the skin on my chest.

"What?" he asked, pausing with his hand raised to the back of his head.

"Your smell," I admitted. "I can smell your scent, and it hurts."

Emotion rippled briefly across his face, but in a moment his expression returned to its usual contained composure.

"How strongly can you smell it?" he asked. It seemed like a peculiar question in the circumstances. I was going to tell him so when he interrupted me. "Can you smell my scent more strongly than usual?"

I thought about it. I had always noticed the smell of him and it had always affected me, but I did seem more sensitive to it this morning. It was odd that I had known he had been in the office just by the scent he left behind.

"Yes," I replied, "I suppose so."

"When did this first happen?"

"This morning, I think. And not just you; I could smell Drew..." I stopped myself mid-sentence, horrified that I'd nearly blabbed about Viv's fake girlfriend ruse.

"You saw Andrew?" Sol asked calmly.

"No. I saw... some of the Invicti who had just been with him," I replied. "One of them smelled of him."

Sol looked slightly suspicious, but either that suspicion was directed at my heightened sense of smell or he had decided to play along even though he knew I wasn't being entirely honest.

"And there was no pain in the mark, just heat?"

"Yes," I said. "Why? Do you know what's happening to me?"

He inhaled slowly, closing his eyes for a second, then nodded once in reply.

"Well?" I asked impatiently.

"The Silver bond," Sol said, anger flashing in his cold eyes, "is asserting its claim."

I stared at him in incomprehension.

"What does that mean?"

"Although I have heard once of this reaction occurring in bonded Silver, I was unaware that it would also affect you as a bonded human. It is a brand," he said, "created by successive healings. In the Silver I knew, it took decades to develop. In you, the process appears to have been accelerated by the severity of your injuries."

As he spoke, the Silver particles under my skin were attacking me, burning me up from the inside, and I was starting to panic. I winced.

Sol stood from his crouch on the deck and walked away towards the other side of the garden, his feet crunching into the gravelled surface until he reached the perimeter fence. Turning to face me, he indicated one of the sun loungers on the deck to my right with an economical gesture. I gathered myself up from where I was sprawled on the wood and lay back on the seat, crossing my ankles in front of me. The heat in my chest ratcheted down a notch.

"How do I get rid of it?" I asked, pressing my hand against the burning skin.

"The only way is to break the Silver bond."

"And I do that how?"

"There is no method that you will consider acceptable."

I narrowed my eyes at him.

"The simplest way is to kill Andrew," he said.

"Well, that's out then. And even if it wasn't, if Drew died, wouldn't I die too because of the Silver bond? Isn't that the point?"

"You misunderstand. Andrew is bonded to you; you are not bonded to him. He would die; you would live." I recalled my conversation with Tommy the previous day: bound in silver, sealed in gold.

My bond with Drew was just a one-way thing.

"But, as you say," he continued, "killing my Secundus is not a viable strategy."

"Isn't there another way? I'm not prepared to spend the rest of my life experiencing agonising pain every time someone touches me."

"That is not the effect of the bond, and the reaction can be mitigated to a certain extent."

"Okay, then how do I do that?"

"You don't," he said, tension subtly pinching at the edges of his mouth. "Andrew does."

"What do you mean?"

He fixed his gaze on the gravel at his feet, his body immobile as if he were lost in thought.

"Sol?" I asked.

He nodded to himself decisively then looked back over at me.

"Move into the apartment and lock the door behind you."

"Why?" I asked, sitting up on the lounger. "What's going on?"

"Emilia, I cannot help you," he said sharply.

I stared at him, surprised by his tone.

"I'm sorry that this has happened to you," he added quietly, "but my presence here will only cause you pain."

Then he disappeared over the fence in a streak of black and gold.

The moment he was out of sight, the heat in my skin dissipated, leaving me feeling confused at his abrupt exit, empty and alone. I looked after him for a moment before I realised how foolish it was for me to be alone out here.

Running into the apartment, I locked the door behind me, stopping only to scoop up my shirt from where it had pooled on the deck.

I didn't know how to process the odd interaction. Sol had been distant and distracted. He was always measured and quite formal, but this morning he had felt... off. Then, as if suddenly becoming bored of dealing with me and my pain, he was gone.

And what about the pain in the mark? He couldn't even spare me the time to tell me how Drew could help make it better. I felt lost, unsure what to do next.

I needed to go back down to the office to work out what

was happening tonight, but it was still early and I was too unsettled to want to leave the apartment. I kept myself busy for about half an hour, unpacking my rucksack properly; the small pile of clothes into the chest of drawers in the bedroom and the food into the kitchen cupboards. There was a lot of food already in there: rice, lentils, cans of tuna, jam and teas. Pretty much everything you would expect to see in a normal kitchen. There was nothing in the fridge freezer, although it had power. It smelled of disinfectant, as if it had been bleached to within an inch of its life.

I filled the kettle and made myself a cup of black tea.

The place felt like a well-loved home. None of the fittings were particularly new, so although they'd been maintained well enough there were still scratches on the granite counters in the kitchen, scuff marks on the wooden floor and sealant peeling from the inside of the shower upstairs. A large bookcase in the seating area held dog-eared books. I pulled out a crime novel and, flicking through the pages, saw an inscription in the front cover:

Robert – Happy Birthday you old bastard! Penny.

Probably both dead now. Or Weepers, I thought.

I wondered how I had worked so close by for so many months without even realising there was a flat up here. It was a safe retreat, a secret hiding place. Most importantly, unlike at the Palace or the dorm, I was actually in control here. This was my space, for the time being. Ever since the Revelation I had felt like things were messy, as if problems and dangers were spilling out from every direction. Now I felt self-contained.

I took my tea to the sofa and sat down with the book. I felt unwell: wrung out and cold, like I had a killer hangover. My fingers were tingling and my stomach thought I was on a rollercoaster. A sheen of sweat covered the skin over the mark, even though it had now cooled with the rest of my body.

I didn't want to run the club, didn't want to have to deal with that kind of responsibility. In all honesty, I didn't feel strong enough at that moment even to be on my feet. I was exhausted and just wanted to wrap myself up in a blanket and write off the day.

Sadly, I didn't have a choice about tonight. I did, however, have a choice about the next couple of hours.

I let myself fall back into the sofa cushions and drank my tea, my eyes closing gratefully against the brightness of the glass-walled room.

CHAPTER X

I dozed and read for an hour or so until I was feeling a little more relaxed and centred. By midday the weight of my anticipated obligations was starting to become oppressive, so I made myself a cup of tea and took it down to the office, making sure the door to the apartment locked securely behind me.

Settling into one of the office chairs, I pulled open the desk drawers one after the other and finally found a few files of papers. The rotas for this week and the coming week were pinned to a small board on the back of the office door and one of the files held more copies of the printed template, waiting to be filled in by hand. This was not a high-tech operation. The Apple desktop in the office wasn't even plugged in, which made me wonder whether Laila was uncomfortable with computers. After all, if she'd been around for centuries then computers had only been in use for a very small portion of her life. At this rate, they may not be in use for much longer.

Other files held records of stock levels and employees, a schematic of each of the bars and their taprooms, and operating instructions for the various taps and barrels. I looked through them as I drank my tea.

There were instructions for the blood barrels, but they were limited to the barrels themselves. They seemed to operate on standard beer pipes, which I thought was a bit short-sighted. The blood was heated and circulated in the barrels, but cooled and coagulated in the pipes until the next pint was pulled, blocking the flow. I could try to get that sorted out during my short tenure as bar manager. I guessed there was a good chance the Silver would want to invest in it, given that it affected their blood supply.

I'd have to get a bit more comfortable with that aspect of the bar as well. From the operating instructions, it looked like the blood was poured into a receptacle that was then placed inside the heated keg. When the blood barrel ran empty, the receptacle was taken out and replaced with a full one. The old receptacle was then cleaned and refilled, by hand. I wasn't sure where to get the blood to refill it, but I'd have to find out. And I'd probably have to be the one refilling it.

I also didn't know what to do with the purple tokens the Silver used to purchase their blood. They were the only currency we had now: blood and tokens. There was a locked box set into the wall of each of the bars to collect the tokens, and I found keys to the boxes in the desk drawers.

My heart sinking, I realised I needed to talk to Laila. She'd be the one with the answers I was missing.

A faint beeping noise coming through the wall from the dance floor caught my attention. The office must have been soundproofed, because when I opened the door to investigate the noise became deafeningly loud. It continued for perhaps fifteen seconds before being replaced by a computerised female voice.

"All humans please congregate at your designated meeting point. All humans please congregate at your designated meeting point."

All humans. The wording sounded incongruous in the context of the voice, which reminded me of the automated platform notifications transmitted in train stations. I wondered what was happening, an ominous feeling settling in my stomach.

Walking across the dance floor, I pushed out into the stairwell and was met by a crush of bodies walking down from the dorm upstairs. I cast around for a familiar face and spotted Oliver. Left with no viable alternative, I slipped into the stream next to him.

"What's going on?" I asked.

"Ah, the famous Emilia," he replied. "How are your monsters today?"

"This is the girl?" said a young guy, leaning forward from behind me.

"This is her," Oliver replied grimly.

"What exactly is your problem?" I asked them both, fury igniting under my skin.

Oliver was silent for a moment, his eyes fixed ahead of him as we pushed through the door to the main bar.

"You've chosen your side," he replied, quickening his pace.

I didn't know how to respond, so I pulled out of the crowd and stood to one side in the bar. When I spotted Mary, I fell into step beside her. I'd met Mary and her two teenaged children, Jane and Mia, in the dorm last week. The girls had taken a shine to Nix, so we were seeing more and more of each other. Mary had been suspicious of me at first, but she seemed to have warmed up to me a bit. I imagined she had bigger things to worry about: she was looking increasingly tired as the days went on. She'd lost her husband in the Revelation and it was taking its toll.

"How are you?" I asked her.

"Oh, hello, Emmy," she replied. "Yes, I'm fine, thank you. The girls are over at the café feeding their newfound caffeine addiction, so hopefully I'll be able to find them in the Square." She looked drawn and her face was tight with anxiety. It couldn't be easy having to worry about teenaged kids in this environment.

"Is that where we're going? Do you know what's going on?"

She looked at me strangely, her brow furrowing for a second before realisation dawned.

"Of course, you weren't here for the others. It's what they did in the safe house every time there was a broadcast, and they started doing it here for yesterday's broadcast. They must have just got the speakers set up in the club."

"Any idea what the broadcast is for?" I asked as we walked out into the sunlit street.

"It's been a week since the last 'donations'. I think it might be time for more," she said ominously.

We walked the rest of the way to the Square in silence, both of us worrying about the broadcast and Mary probably anxious to see Jane and Mia. The stage was set up at the nearest end of the Square as it had been for the previous broadcasts. Solis Invicti surrounded it, but there was no one at the podium yet.

Mary sighed in relief beside me and I followed her line of sight to see the girls trotting towards us from across the Square, smiling brightly. Mia was the elder of the two, tall and dark-haired, and I guessed she was about sixteen. Jane was much smaller, a red-head with pale skin, and looked to be only about thirteen. They were each holding a takeaway cup, and Mia had two.

"Here, Mum," she said, handing one of the cups to Mary. Mary smiled at her as she took the cup and pulled both of the girls into a loose hug. Alice joined us a few seconds later, following the girls over from the café.

There was a scream of feedback as the microphone on the stage was turned on.

"We'd better gather up," I said quietly.

The Square was packed with people, with humans. We pushed forwards until we had a clear view of the stage, and Mary stationed the girls directly in front of us, presumably so she could see them and know they were safe. Drew was on the stage with a few other Silver, and Sol stepped up behind him, walking towards the microphone.

"A week ago today, we admitted you into our safe houses

and verified your blood. Some of you completed your first donations. Since then, we have ensured that you have had access to food and drink, and have provided venues in which you may congregate to enjoy them," he said, raising his hand to indicate the café behind us. "As of today, we are also opening the club for your use, free of charge."

He paused and surveyed the audience, his eyes drawing us in. My heart began to race as he cast his gaze over my group, heat building in the mark on my chest as it did so, but he looked right through me as if I was just another human, and moved on.

"It is time for each of you to hold up your end of the bargain," he continued. "You have been divided into four groups, based on the results of your blood tests. A different one of those groups will donate each Friday. Every Friday, following those donations, we will hold a market here in the Square at which you can each collect whatever food and other necessities you need.

"Today, you will be allocated to your groups and collect a ration of basic provisions for the coming week from the stations behind you, starting with those whose meeting point is here in the Square. Those whose meeting point is in their dormitory will be escorted here later today." Again, Sol gestured towards the café. I turned to see that there was now a line of about ten tables set up in the wide space in front of the café, each one manned by a Silver and surrounded with Solis Invicti.

"The marks you receive today will last until you are next due to donate, the length of their duration determined by your group. Group one donated last week, group two will donate this week and so on.

"From this point onwards," Sol continued, "you may only collect your provisions, and have the free use of the café and the club, for as long as you comply with the bargain. If you cannot demonstrate your compliance by showing your mark, you will not be permitted our hospitality."

With that, he stepped back from the microphone and

walked off the stage, followed by a small entourage of Solis Invicti. The remaining Silver circled around the edges of the crowd and started ushering us towards the stations like dogs herding sheep. I couldn't tell whether Alice was scared or excited, but Jane and Mia started to panic.

"I thought this might happen," said Mary. "I've got to get the girls out of here."

We pushed towards the outside of the crowd until we came up against a dark-haired Silver man patrolling the edge. Each exit from the Square was blocked by a Silver guard, and more Silver were bringing people into the Square in front of us, clearly rounding them up from elsewhere in the safe zone.

"My daughters," Mary said to the dark-haired Silver, "they're too young to donate, and I donated last week."

Other people saw that Mary was trying to break out of the crowd and backed away from us, clearly afraid of the terrifying Silver guard. It was a testament to the dominance the Silver had already achieved over the humans that more people weren't trying to get out of the Square. Mary showed him her left wrist, where there was a circle in which her blood type was tattooed; it was a mark we all bore. For the first time, I saw that there was a second mark within the circle on her wrist, a smaller version of the stylised 'SI' symbol that was tattooed on our right wrists, but this time in a fainter brown colour.

The Silver nodded at Mary and waved her and the girls through and out of the Square, leaving me behind with Alice.

"What was that about?" I asked her as we watched Mary leave.

The dark-haired Silver motioned us back towards the crowd, and we joined the flow towards the stations in front of the café.

"It's a temporary tattoo thing," Alice replied. "All the people who had to give blood have them. They last for about four weeks, so they can tell if we've donated when we're supposed to."

"Have you got one?"

"No," she said, "I haven't donated yet, but I was talking to one of the guys who works in the Palace about it yesterday, and apparently all the girls over at the restaurant have them. Some of them have loads, but if they get so many they don't fit in the circle then they have to stop for a while."

Some people enjoyed the sensation of vampire bite so they volunteered themselves for table service at the Palace, and having experienced a bite for myself I could understand why. It could be exciting, but then again maybe that was just Sol.

The brand on my chest pinched, apparently reacting to the memory.

"It sounds like we're getting some kind of mark today even if we don't donate," I said.

The crowd was eerily orderly. No one was pushing. No one was shouting. Most people stood silently, holding hands or looking quietly down at the ground. After everything that had happened, it was as if the only people that were left alive were those who were willing to comply, but I knew that wasn't true. I knew Oliver was here somewhere with his friends, but they didn't seem to be making a fuss.

The queue was moving quickly, and when we approached the front I realised why. There weren't just ten stations, even though there were only ten tables. There was a whole line of Silver in front of the tables crossing the entire width of the Square, and there was a second line behind them.

I watched as a blonde woman in front of me reached one of the Silver in the front line. The dark-skinned Silver took her hand and pulled a short black tube out of his pocket. It looked like she'd seen the device before, because she didn't display any kind of concern as he pushed it against her finger. There was a click and he withdrew it, turning it sideways to read an electronic display on its side. The woman put her finger in her mouth and I realised he had tested her blood.

"Group four," he pronounced in a deep tone of voice.

As he spoke, he drew another device out of his pocket and rotated a dial on its top, then took her left hand in his, turning it over to expose the circle tattooed on the underside of her wrist. He pressed the device against a clear area of skin inside the circle and pressed the top until it clicked.

"Next."

The woman walked past him to a Silver woman in the second line, who examined her wrist then passed her a large and full plastic bag before ushering her past. The whole process took no more than five seconds.

Alice was next.

"Group two," the man said as he ushered her through without marking her. I watched as she was given a bag by a second Silver, then a third directed her to join a stream of people being escorted towards a building next to the café. She looked over her shoulder at me and mouthed a 'see you later', trying to smile through her anxiety. It looked like she was off to donate.

When my turn came, the dark-skinned Silver loomed over me as he clicked the black tube onto my finger tip. A sharp pain pricked my finger then he checked the readout. He shook the tube and pricked my finger again.

"Your blood has not been tested?" he asked me suspiciously.

"Oh, right," I muttered, as I pulled the choker out from where I had stuffed it into my pocket.

"Why are you not wearing it, if it is yours?" the Silver boomed at me.

"Er, I forgot?" I hazarded.

I could feel the weight of the queue building up behind me. I was making a scene and holding up the line. I could feel myself blushing.

The Silver whistled, and a Silver woman came trotting up from where she had been supervising the line of donors. She was heavily muscled with close-cropped blonde hair, and from the way she was dressed I guessed she was Solis Invicti. When she reached us, the Silver man turned to her.

"Her blood hasn't been tested," he said to her, "and she says the choker is hers, but she's not wearing it."

"It's fine," she replied, looking me up and down. "She's the one filling in for Laila at the club. The choker only matters if you wear it," she said to me emphatically, "which you must do at all times."

Nodding mutely, I fastened the choker around my neck.

The big Silver waved me through and the woman fell into step beside me. The Silver in the second row clocked my choker and handed me a bag, which the Silver woman took and carried for me. I felt like an entitled idiot, being escorted past the irritated glances of my fellow humans. The woman by my side seemed to sense my discomfort.

"The Primus wishes to protect you, and you must let him."

I wondered whether she was talking to me specifically, if she was saying that it was me Sol wanted to protect, or whether she was simply making a general statement that Sol wanted to protect all the humans to whom he chose to give chokers.

"I'm Tamsin," she added, extending her right hand towards me. I took it tentatively and shook it. People were staring, and I was feeling incredibly self-conscious.

"I'm Emilia," I said, stumbling over my words a little as I caught sight of Oliver and his friends over Tamsin's shoulder. They were watching us with interest as they walked slowly past us towards the club, Oliver's eyes flicking down to the choker at my throat before returning to my face. He wasn't missing anything.

"You don't have to come down here to the market, sweetheart; if you talk to the receptionists at the Palace they'll deliver whatever you need. You can call them by dialling zero from the phone in your office, and they'll sort out anything you need for the club or for yourself and send it over. The Palace restaurant will even do you some extended room service to your office if you like."

"I can't just hide myself away up there," I replied, wondering how much Tamsin knew. She obviously knew that I had some kind of relationship with Sol, but did she know about Drew? Did she know about Ben and the attack? Did she know about the new apartment, or did she just know about the office? I didn't know how far I could trust her.

"I thought I was supposed to come down to the broadcast. Did the others not come?" I asked.

"What, the other chained girls? Yes, they did, but they were wearing their chokers, so we could identify them and move them away from the crowd."

Chained girls? I was chained to Sol? That didn't sound particularly appealing.

"Chained?" I asked.

Tamsin screwed up her face a little in distaste.

"It's not a nice term, I know, but it's a legacy thing. Has the Primus not spoken to you about it? I thought he had an induction for all of you."

I dreaded to think what that might entail.

"Anyway," she continued, "it doesn't really apply these days, not when there are so few of you."

So few of us? I supposed a lot of them must have died in the Weeper attacks.

"Shit," she said as we approached the Palace, focussing on two figures sitting on the steps. "Here we go again."

It was Drew and Viv.

Kissing.

A lot.

"Revolting, isn't it?" Tamsin said, turning towards me.

Heat flared in the mark on my chest and I struggled to keep my temper in check. I stopped dead on the pavement outside the club and stared at them. My heartbeat was thumping in my ears so loudly that it blocked out the rest of the world and I felt like my head was going to explode.

Drew's head snapped up in my direction and locked eyes with me across the distance. The colour drained from his face.

"I guess it's just what happens when someone silvers," Tamsin continued in a light tone, her voice muffled through the noise rushing in my ears, "but I never thought it would happen to the Secundus."

"We're all slaves to love," I mumbled quietly.

"True enough," she replied briskly. "Well, it was good to meet you, Emilia, but I've got to go babysit some redundant leaders." She handed me my bag and started walking across the street towards the Palace. "Catch you later."

"You too," I replied, my eyes drifting back towards Drew. He was holding Viv's hand in his lap and looking anxiously in my direction. I spun on my heel and headed into the club as quickly as I could. After all, I had work to do.

I walked back up to the office and called over to the Palace reception, asking whether we could get a solution to the coagulating blood in the pipes. The receptionist said they'd send someone over tomorrow to get it sorted before the club opened. For tonight, we'd just have to manage. She also told me that I needed to hand the purple tokens to the Solis Invicti at the end of each night, so I didn't have to talk to Laila after all, which was a relief.

I still had an hour or so before I needed to open the club for the afternoon, so I took my bag upstairs to the apartment and carried it into the kitchen. It was full to the brim with fresh produce marked 'fresh from Silver Farm'. I recognised the name from before the Revelation and wondered who the comedian was who'd thought it up. There was some fresh meat, cheese, milk, butter, a loaf of bread and lots of fruit and vegetables, which I packed away into the fridge and cupboards.

There was also a small bundle of basic toiletries and medicines at the bottom of the bag. I took it upstairs to the en suite bathroom, pausing in the bedroom to stare out across the city. The view was beautiful from this height, but for me it was marred by the towering wall that separated my tiny circle of existence from the rest of London. Glinting towers winked in the distance, the uniform reflection from the glass of the tower blocks disrupted by broken windows and destruction.

I felt like I could see the future, a future in which we stood still in this spot and watched the towers of our civilisation crumble and fall around us, a world brought to its knees by the Weepers, just as we were brought to our knees by the Silver.

CHAPTER XI

I made myself a quick sandwich and took it back down to the office. I was running short on time and needed to get things in order before the club opened. I ate whilst I worked out from the rotas who was working where tonight, but Laila's plans seemed nonsensical to me so I decided I'd just ignore them and arrange the staff my own way. Who cared anyway?

I made my way quickly down to the ground floor bar. Alice was already there, along with Chris, Josh and Sam, all of whom usually worked the VIP bar. I said a quick hello and asked Alice if she was okay, worried that she might be suffering after donating blood this afternoon.

She smiled at me and showed me the new mark on the inside of her left wrist, beaming like it was a mark of achievement.

"It was fine, Emmy, just the same as normal blood donation, except they gave me a load of booster shots and vitamins and stuff afterwards. I feel awesome! It was nothing to worry about."

I was about to ask about the vitamins when Cam came in from the street with four girls in tow.

"Hey," he grinned at me as he loped across the floor towards me, "I brought you some more barmaids."

I breathed a sigh of relief. I had been wondering how we were going to accommodate the extra human drinkers with our usual skeleton staff.

"I think we'll need them," I replied.

"These are Ella, Pru, Danielle and...," he scrunched up his eyes, clearly unable to remember the last name.

"Fiona," one of the girls supplied helpfully.

"That's right," Cam said, slapping himself on the forehead, "Fiona. They've been working at the Palace, but we're a bit overstaffed. Ladies, this is Emilia."

Fiona was perhaps thirty years old, with striking blue eyes in a sharp face, and her hair was barely styled in a messy brown bob. Danielle had a similar hairstyle, but she was a little younger and softer in the face and her body was lean and wiry in a way that made her look incredibly strong. The remaining girls, Ella and Pru, were both generically young and pretty with long hair, Pru a brunette and Ella a blonde. Ella was about five foot six, and Pru was about an inch shorter.

I looked them over and saw that they had each already been issued with the tiny black outfits that passed for uniforms in this place, and realised that I had forgotten to put on my own uniform. A great start to the night.

With consternation, I also noted that Ella and Pru were wearing chokers to match my own. That made me feel a little awkward, but they displayed no reaction to my own choker. They probably thought of them as commonplace.

I pulled myself together and quickly worked out how I was going to divide everyone up. We only had about twenty minutes left.

"So," I said to them all, "I'm not sure if anyone's told you, but Laila's moved back to the Palace, so we're on our own for the time being. They've asked me to cover for the moment until there's a new bar manager in place."

Alice smiled hugely, raising her eyebrows in excitement. I guessed she thought this meant I was more likely to be able to get her a sponsor. Given all I had learnt since the broadcast, I was now even more unwilling to help. I didn't want to be her vampire matchmaker.

"Okay, have you all worked behind a bar before?"

Each of the four new girls nodded back at me.

"Great, then two of you can go on this bar with Alice," I said, indicating the main bar, "and the other two can man the upstairs bar with me. You can sort out who goes where amongst yourselves. The boys can look after the cocktail bar as usual. Cam, are you on door duty?"

We always had a few of the Solis Invicti in the bar as makeshift bouncers, and I guessed we'd need even more tonight after the introduction of humans to the mix.

"Yep, me and eleven others," he replied.

"Good. You," I said to my temporary staff, "go set up your bars. I need to get changed quickly. Chris, could you help set up the bar upstairs until I get there, please?"

He nodded and set off towards the stairs.

I took a deep breath. Tonight was going to be tough.

"Cam, have you got a moment?" I asked.

"Sure," he replied. "I'll walk you upstairs."

I smiled at him gratefully as we pushed through the doors to the stairwell. Behind us, Alice was sorting out which of the girls was working with whom. I thought I would prefer not to be with Ella and Pru, but that was irrational. I'd rejected any claim I might have had on Sol, so I had no right to be irked.

"What's up?" Cam asked, clearly seeing the emotion playing over my expression.

I shook my head, dismissing the subject from my mind. The last thing I wanted was to get into another conversation about how Sol could never feel anything for me.

"How are things over at the Palace with the defunct dignitaries?" I asked instead, as we climbed the stairs to the first floor.

"Oh, fine," Cam replied affably. "You know, petty in-fighting and posturing. Same old, same old."

"Can you spare the Invicti for tonight?"

"Sure. Most of the ex-leaders will be here in the VIP area

tonight anyway. Including Charles," he added hesitantly.

"He's still here?" I asked incredulously.

Charles was the creep who had bitten me at Ben's incitement, taking so much blood he would have killed me if he hadn't been interrupted by the Solis Invicti. I'd felt sure they would have punished him, or at least sent him packing from the safe zone.

"I'm afraid so," Cam eyed me regretfully as he pushed through the doors at the top of the stairs into the bar area. Chris was already busy emptying the glass washer, so I ushered Cam into the office, shutting the doors carefully behind us.

"Seriously?" I asked. "After he attacked me?"

"He said you asked him to," Cam replied, squirming. "You weren't wearing the choker, no one had marked you and so he technically hadn't done anything wrong. He said he'd just got a bit carried away."

"And people believed that?"

"Of course not, Ems. We know what really happened, but what could we say? We didn't have any evidence to prove him wrong, and, well, his word just means more than yours does to most of the Silver. Not me," he added quickly before looking down at his shoes. "I'm sorry."

"Fuck," I replied.

"Maybe you should stay up on the first floor tonight. He's not going to be out mixing with the humans anyway."

I nodded grimly.

"You know how crazy tonight is going to be, right? Are the Silver going to behave themselves?" I asked as I opened the door to the stairwell that led up to my new (and temporary) apartment and held it for him.

"If they don't, they'll get chucked out. The club is strictly a 'no biting' venue."

"Good," I replied, ushering him up the stairs. I'd seen the Solis Invicti at work in the club before, and I knew how brutally they enforced order. We'd be safe enough.

Cam looked back at me with worry in his big, brown eyes as I closed the door and started up the stairs behind him.

"I didn't mean to, but I heard you with the Primus earlier," he said. "Viv and I were still on the terrace."

That statement hung in the air between us as I silently unlocked the apartment door. Cam followed me inside and clicked the door shut behind us. I turned round to face him.

"Are you okay?" he asked.

Cam seemed to be the only one who ever asked me that. I wished he hadn't, because it made my emotions bubble up. I could feel my eyes filling with tears.

"Not really," I replied. "I count one lovesick vampire whose brand burns me when I get close to anyone, two psychotic vampires trying to kill me, and three dead friends. When is this going to be over?"

He made to stride towards me, but I held my hand out to stop him, warning him to keep his distance.

"You'll only set it burning again," I said with resignation as the tears overflowed my eyes and tripped down my cheeks.

"No," he said, "I don't think I will. Let me try."

I looked at him for a second then nodded. He walked towards me hesitantly and gently wrapped his arms around me, pulling me against his chest. I held dead still, my entire body tensed, and waited.

There was nothing.

No burning, no tingling, no change at all.

I exhaled with relief and wrapped my arms around Cam's back, relaxing into his arms as I wiped my tears on his chest.

"It doesn't burn, does it?" he asked.

"No," I said, pulling away from him. "Why is that? When Sol touched me it was like someone was holding a flame to my skin."

"I'm not a threat," Cam said simply.

"And he is? I can't believe that he wanted to hurt me."

"Maybe not," Cam replied, "but he's bitten you before, marked you before. Maybe without him in the picture..."

"No, Cam."

I was running late, and I wasn't prepared to go over this again. He held up his hands in a gesture of surrender.

I left him downstairs as I went to my room to put on my work outfit: a minuscule black skirt and corset, which I paired with knee-high, flat-soled, black boots. Pausing briefly to run a brush through my hair, I settled it over my shoulders and readjusted each of my fake bandages.

When I got back downstairs, Cam was talking into the radio clipped to his collar.

"Viv's going to be on your bar this evening," he said.

I shuddered involuntarily.

"What's up with you two?" he asked me.

"It's this stupid thing," I said, indicating the brand on my chest. "It's making me crazy. When I got too close to Sol…" I shook my head, the tears threatening to come once more. "I can't describe the pain. It was agony, Cam. And when I saw her and Drew with their tongues down each other's throats today I wanted to punch her."

I shook myself and wiped my eyes as I walked towards the door leading back to the club.

"Er, Emmy," Cam said, looking at my chest, "you know you can't go to work like that, right?"

I looked down at myself and saw the silver mark glinting under my irritated skin, fully exposed by the cut of the corset.

"Shit! What's wrong with me today?"

"Just go and change," he said quietly. "I'll wait. It won't matter if you're a few minutes late."

Cam gave me a concerned look and moved towards the patio doors, letting himself out onto the terrace as he spoke into his radio. I turned and ran upstairs, quickly unlacing the top and replacing it with a high-necked, short-sleeved, black T-shirt.

"I'm losing my mind, here, Cam," I yelled at him as I hurried back down the stairs. "I've got too many secrets to keep, and this isn't going to end well."

But it wasn't Cam waiting for me at the foot of the stairs. It was Drew. He was dressed more smartly than usual tonight, in chinos and a long-sleeved T-shirt rather than his usual khakis and leather. His unruly hair was nearly tidy.

I stopped dead.

"What are you doing here?" I asked.

"Cam called," he replied, his emerald-coloured eyes boring into mine as I slowly walked down the rest of the stairs towards him.

"You can't be here," I said urgently. "It's too dangerous. What about…"

"Sol told me to come. He knows I'm here, Emmy."

"What?" I replied, completely nonplussed. I was standing ten feet away from him, but it was still close enough that I could smell his familiar scent of sawdust and leather. It washed over me in a wave of heat and desire. I shuddered as I detected a dissonant note in the scent, a foreign odour. It was Viv's mark, I realised, and anger started banking high in my chest. It derailed my train of thought immediately.

"Don't you think it was going a little far to mark each other? To sit out on the steps of the Palace in front of everyone?"

He walked forwards and put his hands on my shoulders, running them down my arms.

"The whole point was that people had to see it. You know that, it's just the brand talking." He gazed into my eyes. "Sol and Cam told me. That's why I'm here. I can calm it down, make it less volatile. Okay?"

I was feeling agitated and hot, scratchy under the skin, my pulse racing, and I was acutely aware that I was late for my first day running the club.

"I have to get downstairs," I said, looking beyond him to the door.

"No, you don't. You have some time," he replied. "Cam has it under control."

I looked at his hands on my arms, taking in our proximity, and stepped backwards out of the circle of his embrace. Despite my reservations, every inch of my body was telling me to stick to him like glue, but I knew we shouldn't be this close. I looked at him mournfully.

"We can't," I said.

He matched my step to close the distance again.

"It's okay," he said. "We can touch and Viv's mark will mask it, as long as we don't kiss. Just let me help."

I paused for a moment and looked at him uncertainly, but he nodded back at me. That was all the encouragement I needed. I threw myself into his arms and buried my face in his neck, drawing in his scent.

"Woah," he said in surprise. "I think this is a reaction to the brand. We'd better sort that out."

He carried me towards the sofa, laying me on its length before settling down on the floor next to me.

"I need to touch the handprint," he said, "skin to skin, and that should help to draw the heat out. At least, we think it will," he added.

Leaning forward, I grabbed the bottom of my T-shirt and pulled it off over my head, leaving me lying on the sofa in just the tiny skirt and my bra. I watched with satisfaction as Drew's pupils dilated, a growl rumbling from the depths of his throat. It drew a rising ache from my core, racing my heart and sending a flush up to my cheeks. I wanted to kiss him so badly I felt like my chest was going to explode.

He exhaled heavily, clearly trying to get a grip on himself, and placed his hand firmly over the palm print on my chest.

My whole body suddenly felt like it was floating upwards.

There was a pulling sensation, like energy was running through me towards him. It built in my centre and ramped up, charging me with an electric current of sensation.

After only seconds I began to writhe uncontrollably, twisting on the sofa as waves of pleasure were drawn through me and out into Drew through the point where his hand met my chest. He groaned and ran his other hand behind my head, fisting it in my hair as I gripped the front of his shirt and pulled him on top of me.

His weight settled onto my hips and he pushed his leg between my own, parting my thighs and pressing against me. I pushed my spare hand into his dark, now messy locks, releasing his scent so that it wrapped around us.

Something flickered in his silvered eyes as he focussed on my neck, running his hand around it from the back of my head. Material tugged at my throat and Drew ripped the choker from it, his face twisting with anger as he threw it onto the ground.

"You're not his," he snarled. "You're mine."

His words stirred something inside me and it was as if I had stepped outside of myself, had become someone else. Despite all my better judgement, despite my illusions towards independence, in that moment there was nothing I wanted more than to be possessed by him, to be marked by him, and his aggressive declaration spun me higher, my stomach plunging in the giddiness of elation. He wanted me, wanted to own every inch of me, and I was ready to be his.

His eyes widened as if he had detected my reaction and, pulling my head backwards, he brought his face down to meet mine, caution thrown to the wind in the ecstasy of the moment.

At that second, the intensity abruptly peaked to a climax, and we both threw our heads back, me screaming and Drew yelling into the echoing space of the apartment before we both collapsed down onto the sofa, entwined and exhausted.

We were still. The whole episode had lasted less than a minute.

A few seconds passed in silence.

I opened my eyes and stared at the ceiling, trying to find space in my brain for the enormity of what had just happened.

Drew nuzzled his face into the side of my newly-bared neck, and for one terrible moment I thought he was going to bite me.

"Drew," I said sharply, putting my hands against his chest and pushing him away. He held himself above me with one hand on the back of the sofa, his eyes soft and contented.

"What the hell was that?" I asked, an unconscious tremor entering my voice. "Did you know that was going to happen? And you nearly kissed me!"

His brow wrinkled. He levered himself off the sofa and

moved to sit down in one of the armchairs set at right angles to it. He pushed his hands through his hair.

"I was expecting something pleasant," he replied unsteadily. He lifted his eyes to meet mine, running up the length of my body on the way. "I wasn't expecting that. That was…"

"A mistake," I interjected, quickly grabbing my T-shirt from behind me and pulling it over my head. I was sure this wasn't what Sol had meant when he said the apartment would be a place where Drew and I could talk in private.

"No," he said, ruefully, "it's a necessity."

"What do you mean? That wasn't me, Drew. That was just… crazy."

"That heat you were feeling, that burning sensation?"

I nodded.

"It's the only way to stop it, to soothe it. Well, there are other ways too," he said, his eyes twinkling with mischief, "but this is the best one and the only safe way in the circumstances."

I couldn't believe what I was hearing. What was this sadistic voodoo the Silver seemed to spread around? He wasn't supposed to touch me, but without his touch I'd burn up whenever I was close someone who was a 'threat' to him.

And Sol was apparently such a threat.

"Does this mean it won't burn anymore when I touch Sol?" I asked.

Drew closed his eyes in pain, as if I had slapped him.

"I don't think so," he replied, gritting the words out through his teeth. He sighed in resignation. "It will be less painful, at least. For a short time."

"Fucking Silver and your insane rites of ownership," I grumbled.

I scooped up the choker from where it lay ripped and discarded on the floor and ran it through my fingers. The lace had torn in two places, a partial tear at the side and another close to the clasp that split the material across its width. I managed to hook some of the frayed edges around the fastening at the back so the choker would hold together, but I couldn't do anything to hide the damage on the side.

It would have to do for now. I wasn't going back down into the club without it, not while Charles was there.

"So it's going to start burning again? You're telling me this… whatever it was, is something we're going to have to keep doing? Forever?" I said as I fastened the choker back around my throat.

"So that you can go back to Sol? Is that what you want? So he can use you up, drain you dry and throw you away?"

He groaned and shook his head, his dark hair falling across his cheeks.

"I didn't say that," I said quietly.

"Is it really the end of the world that it's so mind-blowingly pleasurable?" he said. "Do you feel so little for me? I'm sorry that you aren't happy with the way I feel about you, but it's not something I can help, and it's not something sordid either."

He took a deep breath, as if trying to regain his composure. Rising from his seat, he started towards me as he spoke. "I wasn't going to let you die, Emmy, so I healed you. This brand is the consequence of that. I'm sorry that we have to keep it secret, and I'm sorry that I'm not even allowed to kiss you, but I'm not going to apologise for the fact that I love you or that I enjoyed that experience. A lot."

My cheeks flushed with the recollection. He knelt down at the edge of the sofa and took my hand in his. I let him.

"I love you. The way you feel when the brand's working? That's how I've always felt about you. I don't need a mark on my skin to be filled with desire whenever I see you. Even when you're far away from me, I wish you were in my arms. Every time I see you with Sol, every time I smell his scent on you like it is today and know he's touched you, I feel like the rage and pain is going to eat me alive. This is real, Emmy, so real that I literally can't live in a world that doesn't have you in it."

He was right. It was real, terrifyingly so.

"This is meant to be. We're meant to be together, Emmy. But he'll break you. Can't you see that?"

He leaned in towards me and ran his hand along my jaw, tipping my chin down so my eyes met his from inches away.

"I'm yours," he said disarmingly, "and I always will be."

How could I argue with that?

Sol would never be mine; I would have to share with his whole harem.

And however much I might want to believe otherwise, whatever constructs of the imagination I might create to avoid reality, there was no escaping the truth: I had given up my chance with Sol days ago. I pushed him away and he slipped out of my grasp.

Now he kept his distance. The past few days, I felt like I had been crossing the line towards him, willing every gesture to mean more than it did. But he hadn't tried anything, hadn't said anything. I was no longer a priority, if I ever had been.

He'd moved on.

And for that ghost of a memory, I was going to pass up a chance with someone who loved me, someone who had kept caring for me, kept trying to make himself available to me when all I did was push him away, poisoned by Ben's lies.

It was time I gave up on Sol and started listening to what Drew had to say.

"I have to go to work," I said.

"I know. I'll make sure I'm here when you get back. We're not done yet."

With that ominous farewell, I straightened myself up and headed down to the club, leaving Drew to let himself out.

CHAPTER XII

Cam was standing in front of the bar when I walked onto the dance floor.

"Hey, we're not open yet?" I asked in confusion, touching the choker self-consciously. We were fifteen minutes behind schedule.

"No," he replied calmly. "As it happened, we were able to find someone to come over to fix those blocked pipes at the last minute. We're going to open late so they have time to fit them."

"Oh," I replied, not sure what to do with myself now.

"Downstairs is open," he continued, "so the girls are down there helping. They'll be up a bit later. We've fixed the pipes in the VIP bar and the guys are just sorting out the ones in the main bar now. They'll be up here in a jiff, I'm sure."

"And how are things going downstairs?" I asked, concerned that the sudden influx of humans might have caused some tension.

"Fine," he replied. "How are things going upstairs?" He grinned at me cheekily.

I blushed instantly.

"I don't know," I said, deciding to answer him honestly.

His brow creased, his boyish face crunched up in

perplexity.

I guessed he had probably heard the ecstatic screaming and yelling, but maybe not the rest.

"Cam, if you go eavesdropping you're going to hear things out of context."

He actually looked offended.

"I wasn't eavesdropping per se, Ems. I just, you know, heard... stuff."

"Look," I said softly, pulling him into a quick hug, "I know you want things to work out for Drew, but it's not as cut and dried as either of you seem to think it is. I'm going to talk to him, okay? And that's all I'm going to say about it. Now help me get this place set up while we wait for the guys to fix the pipes."

He nodded, apparently placated. I trotted over to the door on the other side of the dance floor and tried to work out how to raise the wall, which had been replaced with slats of metal that rolled up, lifting away to reveal the open terrace beyond.

"You know what?" he asked.

"What?" I asked, distracted.

"This job has made you even bossier."

I looked over my shoulder at him, raising my eyebrows.

"I like it," he added with a grin.

"Get the spare furniture out of the taproom," I replied, feigning a weary tone of voice with a smile. He smiled back and loped off to do as I asked.

After pressing a few buttons on a device next to the door, and finally resorting to mashing the entire keypad with my fist, I got the wall to detach from the floor. It started to whirr upwards, lifting slowly to reveal an eerie view of the dark, dead city beyond. The last time I had stood here there had been fires lighting the night sky. Now there were none. Maybe they had all been extinguished by the rain we had had overnight. Maybe there was no one left out there to light them again.

No one except the Weepers, I was reminded as a distant howl echoed through the air.

I stepped out onto the terrace with a shudder and started rearranging the outdoor tables and chairs as Cam carried the indoor furniture onto the dance floor.

"Where do you want these, Em?" he called out to me.

"All over the place," I called back to him, glad for his company. I stepped inside to give him a hand. "We don't want it raucous tonight, so we're going to make like this is a bar rather than a nightclub. If things go well, we can pump up the music later in the week."

"No DJ?" he asked.

"Nope, just set up one of the playlists at low level and let it run, same as downstairs."

"Aye aye, sir," he replied, snapping a salute.

"You're such a goof," I muttered, shaking my head at him.

"It's why you love me," he grinned.

Two Silver came upstairs a couple of minutes later, just as we were finishing setting out the tables and chairs. They went through to the taproom and sorted the pipes in lightning speed, and just like that we were ready to open the doors. My assigned barmaids came upstairs to join us and, with a crushing sense of inevitability, I saw that I had been allotted Pru and Ella, the girls wearing Sol's chokers. Of course.

I wondered if Alice had thought she was doing me a favour, that we girls would have just so much to gossip about.

I sighed.

Time to slap on my happy face and pretend there weren't twenty different things happening that were making me want to scream. I was safe with Cam, and everything was just hunky dory.

I smiled at the girls as I joined them behind the bar.

The music kicked in and the lights dimmed, the gloom seeping into the corners of the room and turning it into a place with atmosphere, instead of a sterile, featureless box.

"Ready?" I asked.

They each nodded back at me, a little nervously, I thought.

"Open them up then, Cam."

The first people through the door were three more of the

Solis Invicti, clearly assigned to this floor for the night. I was a little surprised to see that Viv wasn't among them.

"I thought Viv was going to be on this floor?" I called to Cam, a sneaking suspicion in my mind.

"Yeah," he shrugged, "but it's okay. She's downstairs in the VIP bar with… erm…," he cut himself off mid-sentence and walked away abruptly, ostensibly to greet one of the incoming Invicti. Cam wasn't great at subtlety.

I sighed to myself and assessed our incoming clientele, pushing thoughts of Drew to the back of my mind. At least I was no longer burning up with jealousy whenever anyone referred to the fake-girlfriend ruse.

Unsurprisingly, the influx was almost all human. I could imagine that the majority of the Silver wouldn't be that interested in hanging out with their food.

People instantly flooded the bar, queuing ten deep for service and rushing us off our feet. It was something of a baptism of fire for Pru and Ella. Among our customers were Oliver and a gaggle of his buddies, a few of whom quickly settled themselves at a table in the furthest corner of the room. I tried to keep an eye on them, but my new barmaids were struggling and I didn't have time to stand still.

I didn't recognise any of the other humans from the faces I picked out in the crowd. There were, however, a couple of friendly Silver faces that I recognised: Ed and Carrie, a couple of Cam's friends with whom I'd shared an evening last week, and far too much alcohol. I smiled at them happily as they reached the bar.

"Buy you a drink, Emmy?" Carrie asked, her round face creasing into a grin.

"Tipping's easy when the drinks are free," I laughed back at her. "Besides which, I'm not sure I'm ever going to drink again, even when I'm not at work."

"Same time again on Tuesday, then?" Ed said.

I shook my head with a smile.

"You two are trouble. What can I get you?"

I poured their drinks, reassured by the smooth flow as the

blood ran from the tap. People either side watched with a mixture of interest and revulsion as the viscous liquid ran into the pint glass, forming a thick meniscus on its surface. It barely bothered me anymore.

I passed the drinks over with a smile and watched them make their way out to the terrace as I served the next customer. As I handed over more and more orders I wondered about the steps leading up to the roof terrace, and how sensible it was to have such a precipitous edge when the alcohol was flowing so freely. Literally.

I hoped the Invicti were keeping an eye on it.

When the crush at the bar finally calmed down I saw that the club couldn't get much fuller. The room had a capacity of eight hundred, less with the tables set up inside, but more if you also accounted for the terraces outside and on the roof.

If this was going to carry on, we badly needed more bar staff.

Thankfully, once everyone had their first drinks there seemed to be limited appetite for a second. I supposed that people were unwilling to let themselves get incapacitated in these dangerous times, particularly on this first night, and a good proportion of the people here tonight probably came for the company rather than the alcohol. Maybe it had been made clear to them what the consequences would be if they were to show up to their assigned jobs impaired tomorrow.

After the first couple of hours, we had few enough customers that we could have a short breather once in a while. After a couple more hours, a few people started to leave and those who remained seemed to have drunk their fill for the night.

I turned my back to the room and leaned my back against the bar, facing Pru and Ella.

"You both doing okay?" I asked, concerned that Ella was looking pretty exhausted.

They both nodded back at me.

"You sure?" I said to Ella. "You look like you're flagging a bit."

"I didn't get much sleep," she replied with a smile. "I'll be fine by tomorrow."

I really, really didn't want to think about what might have been keeping her up at night.

"Okeydokey," I said brightly. "Then why don't you sort out the glass washer while I wipe down the bar? And Pru, can you please grab some more bottles out of the taproom and restock the fridges?"

I grabbed a cloth from the sink on the back wall and, as I turned around to face the bar, I caught a waft of a familiar, cool and spicy scent. The mark on my chest began to tingle, very slightly.

"Sol," I said steadily, feigning nonchalance.

"Emilia," he replied.

He was standing on the other side of bar, both hands in his pockets in a relaxed stance. Lucky him: three of his girls all in one place.

"Good evening, Primus," Ella piped up beside me.

"Good evening, Primus," Pru parroted.

I raised an eyebrow at him. Was this what his 'chained' girls were taught to do at induction?

He nodded at each of them dismissively then turned back to me. They exchanged a glance before hurrying off to their tasks.

Sol looked at me for a moment, his cold, blue eyes silently assessing my ripped choker. There was no judgement or condemnation in his expression, but shame burned through me nonetheless and prickled into my cheeks. I broke eye contact with him and fiddled with the beer taps on the bar, unable to meet his gaze.

"You have seen Andrew," he said, a statement rather than a question. The tone of his voice was gentle, with an edge of resignation to it, as if he had known all along what the outcome of that meeting would be. Perhaps he had, I thought. Perhaps he had told Drew to come to me fully aware of what would happen when he tried to soothe the brand.

"It no longer burns you?" he asked.

"No," I said quietly, stopping to clear my suddenly-dry throat, "although it tingles."

I looked up to meet his eyes. He returned my gaze placidly.

"I will give him a new choker for you," he said, then he tipped his head in farewell and walked away, out onto the terrace and into the night.

As I served a few older women I didn't recognise, I wondered about the meaning behind Sol's words. He wasn't going to give me a new choker; he was going to give it to Drew for him to give me. There must be some symbolism there.

Or maybe Sol just didn't care to see me more than necessary.

Either way, it was further confirmation that whatever we had had, it was over.

I followed the women with my eyes as they carried their drinks back across the floor to their table. They were sitting in the back, next to Oliver and his disciples, but they didn't seem to be part of his group. The congregation of the room seemed to be entirely human, but there were no signs that the individual groups were any more acquainted with each other than I was with each of them. Perhaps we were all isolated within our crowd.

I was grateful for the sense of security that came with being behind the bar, the sense of purpose inherent in having a designated role to perform. It made me feel that I was where I should be, that although everyone else in this room may feel lost, I knew where I was. More than that, this was my domain. This was my home, and now I was in charge of it. Temporarily, at least.

With that responsibility came the illusion of power and control, however tenuous that might be. Even the smallest measure of it centred me and made everything feel a little less dissociated. There was still a place for me in this world, a place where I was fortunate enough to be in a better position than most. Selfish as it was, the thought was comforting.

Ella had finished her task now and was manning the bar whilst Pru shuttled back and forth between the bar and the taproom stocking up the fridges. We had no customers to serve, so I decided to walk the floor and collect the empties.

I smiled at the customers as I did the circuit, collecting empty glasses with one hand and stacking them inside each other with my free hand until they towered over my head. I had to make two runs back to the bar to offload the empties before I reached Oliver's corner. I approached the women I had served a few minutes ago and cleared the glasses on their table, which was next to Oliver's. They were talking about their jobs: they all seemed to be cooks over at the Palace, and it sounded like they were actually getting a kick out of their work.

Behind me, Oliver and his crowd were talking in hushed tones, but still loudly enough for me to eavesdrop over the music. I moved quietly to an unoccupied table in front of theirs next, not wanting to interrupt them immediately.

Yes, I was being nosy. It's just who I am.

"He says it's got to be tonight?" a pretty, blonde-haired girl asked.

I put my stack of glasses down on the table I was clearing, making a show of wiping down the surface with the bar towel I had slung over my shoulder.

"It's time we made a move," Oliver replied. "Can't you see that?"

He sounded ragged around the edges, excited, all pretension removed from his language and tone.

"Yes, but…"

"Look, you're either with us or you're not. It's your choice."

No reply from the pretty blonde.

"We've been through this over and over," said a new voice. I risked a glance over my shoulder as I finished polishing up the surface and discovered that the voice had come from a man of about forty years old, with white hairs sprinkling his short dark hair and stubbled chin.

"All we have to go on is what they've told us," he continued, "but how can we trust them? Are there really

Weepers all over the country, all over the world, or is it just here? What if it's only here in London, or what if there are loads of us holed up safely out there, outside of the safe zone? What if someone's found a way to stop this? How would we know?"

"There are too many unanswered questions," Oliver said, taking up the thread. "Don't you think it's just a bit suspicious? The Weepers turn up, then suddenly here are the so-called Silver as well," he spat the word like a curse, "and it just so happens that the Weepers are scared of them, that the Silver are the only thing that can save us. I tell you this: wherever the Weepers came from, the vampires had something to do with it, I guarantee you that. It's too much of a coincidence otherwise."

Judging that if I stayed any longer I'd be pushing the boundaries of subtlety, I hefted the stack of glasses back onto my hip and walked them back to the bar.

"You both doing okay?" I asked Pru and Ella as I stacked the glasses into the glasswasher.

"Yeah," Pru said with a shrug. "The fridges are all full and the rush has slowed down."

She was right: the odd person was coming up to the bar every once in a while, but it looked like everyone had had their fill of the free drinks.

"Emilia," Ella said tentatively, with the nervousness of a child.

"It's Emmy," I replied with a smile I hoped was encouraging, feeling like I was a million years old. The girls must each have been in their late teens, and they acted like it.

Sol was a creep.

"You called the Primus 'Sol'," she said.

"It's his name," I said dismissively, concerned that they seemed to be treating him with such reverence.

They exchanged another glance, and I felt like I was missing something.

"What?" I asked.

"You just seem to know him really well," Pru said, with a

raised eyebrow.

Wow. This was a conversation I didn't want to have.

"Not that well," I said, and wasn't that the truth. Flashing them a tight smile, I walked back across the floor to Oliver's corner.

They were still deep in conversation as I approached, so I diverted to clear the table on the other side of theirs. It was occupied by a few beefy guys. They were leering at me a bit in my ridiculous slut skirt, but I wasn't really paying attention to them.

"Do we know how long the Weepers survive without food? Can we outlast them? I mean, if we're busting out of here, then what can we expect to find?" asked one of the men on Oliver's table.

"Isn't the point to find that out?" replied Oliver in a scathing tone. "The most important thing is to give the vampires a wake-up call, make it clear we won't be their blood bags, then get the hell out of here."

Shit. They were planning a revolution, and they were going to get themselves killed. Maybe some of the rest of us, too.

"Hey, how about another drink, sweetheart?" one of the beefy guys leered at me.

"No table service," I said absently. "Go to the bar."

I turned away from the beefcake table, picking up a small new stack of glasses, and approached Oliver. Time to interfere.

They fell silent as I collected their empties, Oliver facing me across the table with a defiant expression. I put my hand on the table between us.

"If I can hear you plotting," I whispered, "then they can too." I jerked my head towards the two Solis Invicti stationed by the doors to the stairwell and the opening to the terrace. One of them flicked his eyes our way almost imperceptibly. Almost.

"What are you doing," I continued, "bringing your sedition in here? Have you got a death wish?" I leaned forwards, getting in his face, and hissed: "take this somewhere else, you idiots."

Oliver dropped his eyes from me and I felt a little surge of triumph at his shame, before I saw his eyes hesitate in their downward journey and fix on my chest. I straightened abruptly and clasped my free hand to my chest, pulling my T-shirt up tight against the silver brand. It was looser at the neck than I had realised, and there was perhaps room for it to gape enough to show a shimmering glimpse.

Oliver seemed to have noticed something, but he looked confused rather than intrigued, so I prayed that he hadn't seen anything he would trust. Maybe he'd just dismiss it as a trick of the light. I smiled and tried to look casual, then remembered the message I had just delivered and realised that smiling was inappropriate. I quickly recomposed my expression and stared sternly at Oliver instead, as if to reinforce my point.

I'm not sure I was very convincing.

Fortunately, one of the beefy guys on the next table chose that moment to interrupt us. Unfortunately, he did so by putting his hand up my skirt.

"Come back here, sweetness," he slurred.

There was a blur of movement and then one of the Solis Invicti from the door, a towering black man with muscles bulging against the confines of his shirt sleeves, was holding the offending drunkard aloft by his wrists. The drunk's feet kicked at the air as he desperately sought for purchase, but he was a clear half foot off the ground. He had looked pretty well-built a few minutes ago, but the Silver next to him was a giant who made him look like a toy.

"You see this?" the Silver rumbled, pointing at the choker around my neck. "You know what this means?"

The drunk nodded back, the colour draining from his face.

"You touch one of his girls again, you go outside."

The tone of his voice made it very clear that he wouldn't be sending the man for a stroll down the street in the pleasant night air. He'd be walking on the outside, beyond the barricade, outside with the Weepers.

The drunk, who suddenly looked extremely sober, nodded frantically until the giant lowered him back down to the floor. He grabbed his jacket off the back of the chair and hurried across the floor and into the stairwell, his friends scrambling to keep up with him. I didn't blame them; I would have run from the hulking mass of Silver too if I had had the chance.

As it was, the big man simply nodded to me then started walking away back to his post by the door.

I was sure that those at Oliver's table would have noted the interaction with interest and, as I followed the huge Silver over to the bar, I snuck a quick glance over my shoulder to see. In fact, their table was now deserted. They must have left during the excitement.

I wondered if, after my warning, they had decided it was not in their best interests to be too close to one of the Solis Invicti at the moment. Either way, it was a relief to have them out of my hair.

"Look," I said to the Silver, "I appreciate your intervention, but if you're trying to foster cohesion then that's not the way to go about it."

"Maybe," he replied, "but we've got orders from the boss to protect you, so that's what I'm doing." And with that, he returned to his post by the door.

It was news to me that I was under official protection. Wouldn't that raise suspicion, if Drew singled me out like that? Of course, that was assuming that he was 'the boss'. It could equally have been Sol. Maybe those orders were just implied by the fact that I was wearing his dog collar.

Either way, the expression of those orders made me feel uneasy in the current environment, and I wondered whether the protection of the Silver would come back to bite me on the behind.

CHAPTER XIII

Saturday

By the time I had finished clearing the empties from the roof garden and the terrace, it was time for us to shut up shop. I was unsurprised to find that the majority of the Silver who were in the club tonight had been drinking outdoors. The temperature was rising again, making the evening breeze a welcome respite from the heat of the club. Nonetheless, the humans clearly felt more comfortable with a roof over their heads than they did exposed to the open darkness of the night.

Sol was up on the edge of the roof terrace with a few women I recognised as deposed safe house leaders. I knew better than to try and turf the Primus out of his own club, so I simply collected their glasses without a word before ushering the remaining customers downstairs with Cam's help.

We closed the upstairs bar half an hour before the downstairs bars, in order to give people time to filter out. This meant that Pru, Ella and I finished our shift a little earlier than everyone else, so after we had cleaned up we each grabbed a bottle of beer and took it out to the terrace to wait for the downstairs staff to join us. It was a bit of a celebration, a moment to bask in the relative success of the evening, and to give us a chance to relax like everyone else. Now that we were all entitled to free drinks, it only seemed fair.

I took a chair that was close to the stairs up to the roof and turned it away from the bar so it faced out towards the city. That way, I had the club at my back and could keep an eye on the ledge. Pru and Ella took chairs opposite me, looking back in to the bar.

This close to the building I was acutely aware of Sol's presence on the roof terrace above us, the quiet notes of his melodic voice intermittently carrying down on the breeze. I was reminded that this break afforded me the opportunity to get to know Pru and Ella better, so I could stop seeing them as competitors for Sol's affection and start seeing them as people.

The girls told me they had both been in halls together at University College London, both at the end of their first years. They'd been days away from leaving the city when the Revelation happened.

"We had rooms next to each other," Ella said, "up on the top floor of halls. I think we were the only ones on our floor still there; everyone else had already left for the end of term, but we had some late exams so we had to stay behind. I was cooking in the kitchen at the end of our corridor when it started."

"I was in my room," Pru interjected, "packing up my boxes for the move, and then I heard this distant screaming. I thought someone was just messing around, but then it seemed to get closer, almost as if it was rising through the floors of the dorm block. It got louder and clearer, and it just hit me in the stomach, like I knew I needed to run. But there was nowhere to go."

"I ran," Ella said, resuming the story. "It was coming up the stairwell next to the kitchen, this awful, screaming sound. It felt like there were hundreds of people, their footsteps were just thumping down on the floors and echoing around the place."

She looked haunted, her eyes focussing off into the middle distance as she remembered her fear.

"And I just ran down the corridor, thumping on the doors, trying to find someone who was still there."

"Scared the shit out of me," Pru laughed raggedly. "I thought they'd found me, but then Ella yelled my name and I realised it was her, so I let her in and we locked the door behind us. It wasn't long before they were at the door, though."

Pru looked down at her hands, shivering in the warm evening air. Ella took a swig from her beer and shook her head mournfully, and I wasn't sure whether or not they were going to tell me the rest.

"You don't have to tell me," I said.

"We've told it enough times that it's not so bad anymore," Pru said. "It's all anyone wants to hear, right? 'Where were you when the Revelation hit? How did you get out?' I suppose it's something we can all relate to."

I nodded glumly.

She was right. It would become the defining moment of our generation. Everyone had a story. None of them were pleasant, but some were unimaginably worse than others.

Pru took a deep breath.

"I had this big trunk, an old thing my grandparents had given me when I went off to university. It locked when it was closed and didn't open except with the key, and it was basically indestructible. We decided it was our best bet, so we pushed it into the bottom of the cupboard so it would look inconspicuous, hid the key, then we both climbed into it."

"It was a very tight fit," Ella said.

"It didn't take long for the Weepers to break down the door," Pru continued, "and then they were in the room for what felt like hours, pushing the trunk around like they knew we were there but couldn't work out where. Eventually they gave up."

"How long were you there?" I asked, not sure I wanted to know the answer.

"Nearly a day," she replied, quietly. "The trunk didn't open from the inside, it locked up solid, so we just had to wait for someone to come and find us. A couple of the Silver turned up calling for survivors, and we both screamed for all we were worth. They couldn't find the key by that point, the Weepers had made such a mess, but they bust us out of the trunk."

"Then they brought us here," Ella added.

They were avoiding telling me the worst of it, the terror they must have felt being confined in that space for such a long time. No food, no water, no light. I didn't blame them for wanting to keep it to themselves, and I could understand why they seemed so close after a shared experience like that.

"And the chokers?" I asked. I told myself I didn't care and was just asking to distract them from their painful memories, but in truth I just had to know.

"Same as you, I guess," Ella replied. "Same for everyone."

I wondered if that was really the case, but I'd lost my nerve and didn't want to ask her to explain. Maybe my night together with Sol on this terrace had just been the 'induction', the experience Tamsin said we had all shared.

It probably hadn't been exactly the same for Pru and Ella, but I imagined that the central theme was likely to be the same: blood and sex, Sol's favourite things.

"Can I ask about you and the Primus?" Pru said.

I shrugged. I'd had a couple of beers at this point, and having not eaten since before the club opened I was feeling pretty merry.

"You talk to him like he's just another guy," she said. "How do you get away with that? He's a god."

I had to admit that the sex had been pretty amazing.

Pru and Ella stared at me, and I realised I'd just said the thought aloud.

Oops. No more beer for me.

"You've slept with him?" Ella asked incredulously. From their reactions, I guessed that maybe Sol hadn't been as promiscuous with his choker club as I had assumed. I

148

desperately tried to backtrack, but I wasn't sure I'd be able to fix this one.

"No," I replied, forcing a laugh. "I was just kidding."

They both looked unconvinced, which was only fair given that I could feel my cheeks flushing furiously as I lied to them.

"Why do you say he's a god?" I continued, forcing the conversation to move on from my embarrassing slip-up. The girls briefly exchanged a glance then kindly allowed the diversion.

"Have you heard of Sol Invictus?" Pru asked.

"Not before last week," I admitted.

"Well, he's the son."

"The son of whom?"

"No," she tutted in frustration, "not a son, the sun. S-U-N. The sun god."

"What?" I replied stupidly.

She took a swig of her drink.

"My degree course is in Classics, or at least it was. Sol Invictus is the god of the sun in the late Roman Empire, a military cult for the Roman soldiery."

She and Ella looked at me meaningfully.

"No," I replied. Then I remembered what Tommy had told me last night: that some of Sol's people saw him as more than a king. And I remembered the fire in my veins when he touched me. No wonder he could set me alight with a glance.

"I think the title's just an honorific, but either way he's millennia old," Ella said reverentially, "and he has power. We're lucky that he's willing to protect us."

She touched her choker and ran the lace between her fingertips.

"Why is he?" I asked innocently, wondering whether she would tell me how they had earned their collars.

"He's a good man," she replied with a shrug.

Not what I was expecting to hear, and not what I wanted to hear either. I wanted to have something to crush down my feelings for him. I wanted her to tell me that he was a philandering jerk, so I knew that I was better off without him, so I knew Drew was the better choice. I wanted my decisions to be made for me and then have them validated.

But that was the easy road, choice by default, and it was no way to run a life.

The downstairs bar staff joined us then, so the conversation quickly veered off into stories from the night's shift. The VIP bar had apparently been slow tonight, with most of the vampires who had come out bemoaning the new human admittance policy. The Solis Invicti had escorted them out across the road back to the Palace, so it was just us and Sol's group still in the building.

Alice's bar had been as busy as mine, but more raucous. A couple of guys had got into a fight over the comparative prestige of their roles and had to be thrown out. The fight itself was boring and short-lived, but the interesting thing was that one of them was a farmer and one of them was a butcher, apparently over from Silver Farm on a delivery. They'd brought with them news from beyond the walls of the safe zone, but none of it was good.

Danielle's face was grim as she recounted a conversation she had had with the butcher: the roads had been cleared from the farm to the city walls so that deliveries could come in and out with relative ease, but the rest of the city was impassable and ruined. Weepers waited at the fringes of the streets in terrifying numbers, and they couldn't travel at night or without a Silver escort. Nonetheless, the farm itself seemed to be thriving and was apparently staggering in size, large enough to provide for all of us.

I found that a little disconcerting. The farm was too well established for this not to have been thoroughly planned. As if that wasn't enough to make me uneasy, the men from Silver Farm had also brought news of the warehouses, huge buildings on the land adjoining the farm stacked to the brim with stockpiled food and necessities. We had everything we needed to survive an apocalypse, many times over.

Despite my concern at this news, it seemed to perk everyone else up. They were reassured that they would continue to have access to all of their familiar creature comforts for the rest of their lives. I wondered how long that illusion would be sufficient to keep the more radical elements of the human population in check.

Everyone was visibly shattered, but the novelty of having a chance to sit down together and talk was so compelling that none of us wanted to leave. Aside from Alice, I'd never had a single conversation with any of the staff that wasn't about the job, and it was a relief finally to get to know them as individuals. It reinforced my sense of place and made me feel like I was right where I belonged.

Conversation quickly moved on to the Revelation, and a few of the group shared their stories. Chris and Fiona had each been in their respective homes when the news had hit, and had simply reported to their safe houses before being transported here. Pru and Ella repeated an abbreviated version of their story for the benefit of those who had just joined us, but when it was my turn I shook my head.

I'd just have to let them believe it was too horrible for me to want to relive it, and that wasn't far from the truth. Either way, I didn't think I should be telling anyone about how Drew had rescued me, then captured me after Ben had killed my friends, then delivered me to the Primus.

Josh stepped into the gap in conversation.

"I was out surfing in Bournemouth," he said.

"What, in the middle of the night?" Fiona scoffed.

"Night surfing's the best!"

He certainly looked the part of a surfer. His shoulder-length hair was a light brown at the roots, but it was bleached to blonde by the time it got to its tips. His skin was tanned and he was well muscled under his T-shirt.

"I was sitting on the board in the surf, waiting for a decent wave, when something grabbed onto my leg and pulled me off sideways. There was this tearing in the flesh of my leg, and I thought a shark had got hold of me, so I punched downwards into the water to try and scare it off, only it wasn't a shark."

"You're shitting me," Sam interrupted.

"It's true, I swear."

"No, it's not," Danielle joined in, "because if it was then you'd be a Weeper now, instead of what you are, which is an idiot."

Everyone laughed except Josh, whose face was still with anger.

"Here, check this out, then call me a liar," Josh said, rolling up his trousers to reveal a bite mark in the meat of his right calf. The pattern of the teeth looked human. "It was fucking traumatic. I had to paddle myself back to shore while all these hands were grasping at the board. In the end I had to leave it behind and swim."

A few people were still laughing, but I wasn't among them.

"They can survive in the water?" I asked quietly.

Josh saw that I was taking him seriously and nodded grimly.

"Then we can't stop them from spreading, and we'll never be safe. Even if we started killing them, how can we search the entire ocean?"

He shrugged as he rolled down his trouser leg again and stood up, taking his beer bottle with him.

"And you're not a carrier?" I asked. Some humans had been infected by Weepers without turning into Weepers themselves. Those people had been eliminated by the Silver to protect those of us who remained, because a single infected particle from a carrier could wipe out the entire safe zone.

"No," he said. "I'm clear. Maybe it was the salt water or something. I don't know. I'm calling it a night."

Danielle and Fiona stopped him on his way back to the bar, apologising for not having believed him, and they seemed to make up, but the interlude had taken the joy out of the party. Sam and Fiona trailed away shortly afterwards, just leaving Chris with me, Alice and the rest of the new girls on the terrace.

"Are you coming up to the dorm, Emmy?" Alice asked as she got to her feet.

"No, I actually have a room here off the bar now. You'll

look after Nix?”

“Sure. I didn’t know there was another room here.”

“It’s new,” I said plainly. “I’ll show you it tomorrow if you like.”

She smiled and said her goodbyes, turning to follow the others upstairs to the dorm. Pru and Ella’s eyes followed her as she went, then shifted abruptly up to the roof above us.

“Emilia,” came a familiar voice from behind me.

Sol was walking down the stairs from the roof terrace, his hands hanging casually in his pockets as he approached us. Ella and Pru jumped to their feet and bobbed their heads at him. Danielle and Chris exchanged an uncertain look then awkwardly followed suit.

“What’s up?” I asked as casually as I could manage, looking over my shoulder at him but remaining firmly planted in my seat. Ella and Pru glared at me. Watching their obsequiousness was making me extra petulant.

He was no god of mine.

There was a twitch of movement at the side of Sol’s mouth and I knew that he was trying not to smile. He paused halfway down the stairs and gave me a familiar look. He knew I was pushing him, but he didn’t mind. Perhaps I hadn’t completely lost him after all.

“I will collect the tokens whilst I am here,” he said to me before turning to the other four. “Thank you all for your hard work tonight. I am sure you are tired.”

They didn’t hesitate to take the hint, gathering up the empty bottles as they left the terrace.

“Night all,” I called after them.

“See you tomorrow,” Chris called back.

I stood up from my chair when they had left and started rearranging the chairs that we had dragged into a circle on the terrace. Sol finished walking down the stairs and stepped into the bar, activating the keypad to bring the wall of the club sliding back into place between us, then stepped back out onto the terrace through the door in the reinstated wall. He was carrying another bottle of beer, which he handed to me, and a glass of whisky for himself.

He leaned up against the wall, watching as I tided up the last few tables. He was doing it again: standing in exactly the place where we had been together. I wondered whether or not it was deliberate.

"It is nearly time for you to make your choice," he said quietly.

I turned to face him as I wracked my brain, trying to think what choice he was referring to.

"It is already Saturday morning. By this evening, it will be one week since you agreed to stay in the safe zone, to try to find a place here."

I had entirely forgotten about it. When Drew had captured me and brought me to Sol, he'd asked me to try to live within this new society for a week before dismissing it and striking out on my own again.

I felt like I'd been here forever and I'd just been assuming that I would stay here. I was itching to get out of the confines of the safe zone, but I couldn't imagine going beyond the barricade alone, and certainly not forever.

I guess that meant my choice was made, but it reminded me that I wasn't the only one who had entertained thoughts of rebellion.

"I think we both know I'm not going anywhere, but there are other people talking about getting out of here."

"When did you hear of this?" he asked curiously.

"There was a group of them in the top bar. They were planning something for tonight, but I don't know what."

"I will monitor the situation," he replied. "Thank you for bringing it to my attention."

"What will you do?"

"We will try to save them if it is possible to do so, but if they are intent on meeting their fate beyond the wall then it will be difficult for us to prevent that."

It was a terrifying prospect: suicide by Weeper.

"May I ask what changed your own mind?" he continued.

"It's safer here," I replied with a shrug.

"That didn't concern you a week ago."

He was right. I'd been hell bent on getting away from the Silver, even if it meant risking my life at the hands of the Weepers. Besides, the safe zone hadn't exactly been safe for me. By my reckoning, I'd nearly died four times in the last week.

"I like the club," I said, taking a swig from my beer.

He nodded to himself.

"And my Secundus," he said.

Actually, Drew was what would have driven me away from this place, despite the danger presented by the Weepers. Now, of course, that wasn't an option anyway, not with Ben still looking for a window of opportunity to catch me alone. But it had been an option until I had found out about his plans, about the Silver bond.

I had a shocking moment of clarity.

What had kept me here was Sol. I hadn't expected it, but something durable and tenacious had been at the core of what Sol called 'our association', something real in the centre of the wild tumble of emotions that he aroused in me.

I missed it.

I missed him.

And he'd sent Drew to me, to do what he had done earlier this evening.

"Did you know what would happen with him tonight?" I asked, wishing that the answer would be no, wishing that he would have balked at the thought of Drew giving me that experience. But why should he, when he'd so easily dismissed me?

He held my gaze, but said nothing. My chest constricted. It was just another thing that he had kept from me.

"Why didn't you tell me?"

"It would not have changed what had to be done," he replied steadily.

"I had the right to choose," I replied through gritted teeth.

"Sometimes, choice is not a gift. Without intervention, the brand will drive you to insanity. There was no choice to be made." He took a sip of his drink. "Nonetheless, I confess I am surprised that you are unhappy."

I rubbed the brand through the cloth of my T-shirt and sat down heavily on a chair opposite the place where Sol stood against the wall. The breeze carried a thread of his scent across the terrace to me: cut grass and incense.

"However much I care for Drew, I didn't choose it," I said.

I resented the fact that this emotionally and physically intense experience had been thrust upon me. I may have chosen in time to be that close with Drew, that intimate, but I felt like everything that happened earlier tonight had been acted out by someone who wasn't me, someone controlled by the will of the brand.

I felt like I was in hormonal meltdown.

But then again, that wasn't Sol's fault. He was right: there had been no choice.

"I apologise for my part," Sol said, "but I hope that you will not now choose to avoid repeating it."

Oh, right. It was only a short term cure.

"Will it start to hurt again soon?" I asked.

"The pain will get better each time. The… therapy should have a longer effect cumulatively."

"How soon, Sol?" I insisted.

He swilled the last mouthful of whisky around the inside of his glass.

"I am afraid I do not know."

I ran my fingers through my hair, pushing a few loose strands away from my face, and drank down the rest of my beer.

"It's only you, you know," I said quietly, looking down into my empty bottle. "It only burns with you."

There was a moment's silence.

"I can keep my distance if you would prefer."

I met his eyes. He was already so far away.

"It doesn't hurt at the moment. I don't feel it at all, actually."

I got to my feet and, setting my empty bottle on the table

next to me, took a few steps closer towards him. There was not so much as a tingle in the brand.

Sol pushed himself away from the wall and I held my palm out flat towards him.

"Stay there," I said. "You stay still, and I'll move towards you."

I was about six feet away from him, and our eyes locked as two more steps took me close enough to touch. His pupils were wide in the dark, the silver threading in the whites of his eyes setting off the ice blue of his irises. I took one more small step and his scent enveloped me, spinning my senses dizzyingly, and then his glass was smashing on the floor and his hands were on my hip and at my back to steady me. Heat radiated through my body from his touch and bloomed across the brand, but it flushed rather than burned me.

"Emilia…"

I put one hand on his shoulder and reached up with the other to push his golden hair back from his forehead, before trailing my fingers down the side of his face to brush across his cheek. My heart raced and my temperature rose, but there was still no pain.

We stared into each others eyes from inches away.

He tightened his grip on me, pulling my body up against his own, and inhaled.

Then he closed his eyes, breaking eye contact, and turned his head away from my hand.

"It's okay," I said, "it doesn't hurt."

But he kept his head turned to the side, abruptly taking his arms from around my body.

"Andrew is waiting for you, Emilia." His tone was forcibly distant and unaffected.

I had forgotten about Drew.

I felt utterly wrong-footed and jerked my hand back. For a moment I was embarrassed, feeling exposed and humiliated, but that quickly turned into anger and frustration. He hadn't wanted to stop; he'd made himself.

It was time to stop being a coward and start getting some

answers.

"What is this, Sol? Why do you keep pulling away from me?"

He was quiet for a moment, then seemed to come to a decision.

"You need Andrew."

"Isn't that up to me?" I asked incredulously.

"There is the brand to consider."

"And? It doesn't seem to be causing any problems right now."

There was another moment of silence before he spoke again. When he did so, he finally met my eyes again.

"This will never be anything more than a distraction."

So there was the truth of it, the confirmation I had been looking for: it meant nothing to him. He hadn't said it unkindly, but there was really no way to sugar coat it. I tried to feel some relief now that there was no choice to make, but instead I felt crushed, the pain squeezing in my chest. Just as everything had crystallised for me, just as I had realised that Sol was the only thing that had kept me here, he had verified what everyone had been telling me.

"Yes, of course," I said, trying not to show him that I was upset.

I was damned if I'd have him know it hurt me. I turned away from him to hide my face under the guise of collecting my beer bottle from the table, glancing out across the dark and silent city as I needlessly tidied the terrace furniture once more. The blackness sucked the light away, sucked reality away, and left me feeling exposed and isolated.

"Give me a moment and I'll get you the tokens," I said over my shoulder, not able to bring myself to turn and look at him.

"Do not trouble yourself," he said quietly. "I have the key."

A pause.

"Good night, Emilia."

I heard the door into the club click and looked round to

see that he had gone.

A warmth in the brand that I hadn't noticed was still there suddenly left me, chilling me to the bone as the breeze whipped across my bare arms and legs. I gasped with the sensation, empty and raw. I wanted to curl up into a ball and cry. Quiet tears rolled down my face and dripped off my chin onto my T-shirt.

The door behind me clicked again, and for a moment I thought that Sol had returned. I had a split second to worry that it might be Ben before the newcomer spoke.

"Emmy?"

"Viv," I said, recognising the voice as I rubbed the tears from my face.

"Hi. So, the Primus asked me to come and see you to your place."

I wondered sourly why he even cared. He probably just wanted to make sure he didn't lose his Secundus if Ben killed me.

"Can you just give me a second?" I sniffed. I wanted to try to pull myself together before facing her.

"Er, sorry, no can do. I'm not allowed to leave you alone."

I exhaled heavily.

"Well, just wait there a moment then, please."

I lifted the hem of my T-shirt and pulled it up to dry my eyes. There wasn't much I could do, and she would already have worked out that I'd been crying, but at least I could wipe away the tears.

I turned around with a forced smile, scooping my beer bottle from the table.

"Okay," I said brightly, "let's lock up."

CHAPTER XIV

When we'd secured all the doors and turned out the lights, Viv walked me back upstairs to the office. I fitted the key in the cupboard door and let myself into the stairwell beyond.

"Drew's waiting upstairs," Viv said, "so I'll leave you here."

"What? How did he get in?"

"The Primus gave him his set of keys," she said hesitantly. No wonder he had known Drew was waiting for me. It looked like Sol was relinquishing everything to Drew as far as I was concerned. He had to have handed over the keys before we spoke tonight, so pushing me away hadn't been an impulsive decision. I wasn't sure if that was a good thing or a bad thing.

I also resented the feeling that I was a hand-me-down, passed from one to the other. It made me feel like a thing, a worthless toy of which he had grown tired. I knew it was unfair of me to feel this way. He'd made no promises to me, quite the reverse in fact, but I'd unwittingly laid down stronger emotions than I was expecting.

"Of course," she continued, "he's worked out that we've been trying to mask your scent on Drew by marking each other and pretending we're a couple." Viv tossed her beautiful auburn hair over her shoulder as she spoke and I was reminded again of the many ways in which she outclassed me. I'd had about as much rejection as I could take for the day and I didn't want to think about her and Drew.

"I think he was quite impressed actually," she added. "Said it showed initiative. That's as good as approval for you two being together, right? And he's even set up the Casting and everything."

Great. So not only was Sol passing me on, he was happy about it as well. The least he could do was try to be a little jealous.

"Yeah, okay," I said distractedly. "Thanks, Viv."

She turned as if to leave, then paused and looked back at me.

"Do you want to talk about it?" she asked.

"No, thanks."

She was one of the last people who would want to hear about what had happened with Sol, particularly when she was working so hard to get me together with Drew. I appreciated that she was looking out for him, but it was difficult to have so many people cheering me on to a conclusion I wasn't sure I would want to reach on my own.

"Well, I'll leave you to it, then," she said. "Night, Emmy."

"Night, Viv."

When I let myself into the apartment the lights were on and Drew was sitting in an armchair next to the fireplace. He was still wearing the same clothes as earlier. He'd only turned on the table lamps in the room, so the lighting was pleasantly dim, but nonetheless it picked out the silver in his eyes, gliding along the tendrils that flowed into the beautiful emerald of his irises as he turned his head towards me.

"I was starting to worry," he said, getting to his feet.

"I was having a drink with the rest of the staff," I replied, slightly irritated that I apparently had to explain myself to him.

"Well, let me get you some food."

"I'm okay."

"Won't be a minute," he said with a smile.

He made as if to come towards me, but stopped himself and walked away to the kitchen instead. Things were a little awkward after this afternoon.

There was a blur of movement and in a few seconds he was placing two plates on the table at the far end of the room.

"Nothing exciting, I'm afraid. Tea?"

I nodded distractedly as I walked across the room and took a seat at the table. He'd made us both sandwiches with the food I'd picked up earlier from the market in the Square.

"Next time I'll bring you something over from the Palace."

"It's fine," I said. "Apparently I can ring them for food delivery, but I don't really like the idea. This is great, thanks," I added, finally remembering my manners.

I lifted up the top slice of bread and saw that tonight's fare was cheese and pickle with lettuce. I didn't really like pickle, but I wasn't going to tell Drew that, so I pressed the sandwich back together firmly.

"So," he said as he set the kettle to boiling, "how was work?"

I felt like I'd stepped out of myself and was living in a world where that would be a normal question. It was so incongruous that I laughed, and he smiled back at me, but there was a joy in his expression that broke my heart and made me look away. I felt pressured by the depth of emotion he held for me. I almost wished that he would hide it because it made me feel guilty for not returning it.

"Work was okay, but there were a few people in tonight who were talking about starting some trouble."

"What, humans?"

"Yeah, and I recognise a few of them from the dorm here. I think I heard them talking to a Silver out on the fire escape last night."

He brought us a cup of tea each over to the table and sat down opposite me, tucking his unruly hair away behind his ears before he reached down for his sandwich.

"I wouldn't worry about it if I were you."

"Why, what do you know?" I wondered if he already had

the situation in hand. After all, he was the leader of the Solis Invicti, so I supposed that he was in charge of national security.

It was odd to think of him holding such a powerful role. Sol was every inch the Primus, even when it was just the two of us, because it was part of who he was. His status was infused into every aspect of his being, but for Drew his position as Secundus was something that could be shrugged on and off, a costume he wore to do his job. With me, he was just plain old Drew.

I took a bite of my sandwich and swallowed it down.

Ugh. Pickle.

I took another bite and chewed it quickly, trying not to concentrate on the taste.

"You're safe," he said. "So don't worry."

"I'm not worried about me. I'm worried that you might have an uprising on your hands."

"Then that's my problem, not yours." He smiled at me and picked up his cup of tea. I knew that he was trying to be reassuring, but his desire to shield me from everything made me feel like a subordinate, and that was a feeling I didn't enjoy.

At least when I asked Sol a direct question he gave me a direct answer. Not that there was any point in comparing the two of them now, I reminded myself. It was a bad habit I needed to break.

We ate in silence for a couple of minutes.

"So," he said after he had finished the last bite of his food, "are we going to talk about what happened today?"

I really didn't want to have this conversation right now. I was exhausted, emotional from my encounter with Sol, and honestly still a little drunk.

"Do we have to?"

"I think we should."

"Then let's talk tomorrow," I said firmly. "It's late."

He looked down at the table for a moment. He'd obviously been gearing up for a big discussion, but I just couldn't cope with that until I'd had some sleep.

"It's important," he said. "We'll need to do it again tomorrow."

I sighed. Apparently we were going to have to talk this out now.

"Does it hurt at the moment?" he asked.

I shook my head as I finished chewing the last piece of my sandwich.

"And it feels okay? It's not hot or anything?"

"No," I replied, "it's fine. I feel… fine." Except for the gaping hole Sol had left in my chest.

"Everything I said earlier still stands. I love you. I know you don't feel the same way, but if you give me a chance then maybe I can make you happy."

What did I really have to lose at this point? The problem was that it felt wrong. It didn't feel like romance, it felt like compulsion. That wasn't what I wanted. I wanted to try to recapture the spark we had before today's 'therapy session', but I didn't know how to do that.

Maybe that had just been the bond as well.

"Drew…"

"Just think about it. Sleep on it, and we'll talk about it in the morning."

I was unconvinced, but I told him: "Okay."

He reached into his pocket and pulled out a familiar piece of material.

"This is for you," he said as he handed the choker to me.

"Oh, right." Sol had said he was going to give a new one to Drew.

I reached up to my neck to take off the torn scrap I had worn tonight, but before I could do so, Drew had zipped around the table and his fingers were gently removing it from my throat.

"I wish I could make one of my own to give you," he said as he leaned forwards to put the broken necklace on the table and scoop up the new one. "You deserve a special pattern that only you would wear."

His touch was soft on my skin as he delicately fastened the

new collar into place.

"Don't you have your own already?" I asked. "I thought all the important Silver did."

He trailed his fingers down towards my collar bone, but I unconsciously shied away from the contact. He froze.

Apparently I was pushing everyone away tonight.

"I thought you weren't going to push this, Drew," I whispered. "It's just too soon."

"I'm sorry," he said, walking back around the table to take his seat once more, "but it's difficult in the circumstances."

Looking for a distraction, I stood and, picking up our plates, put them in the sink in the kitchen. He cleared his throat and began to speak again in a consciously relaxed tone.

"I've never been much for the whole chained girls thing. It's mostly for the Primi and the regional leaders. I could have my own design if I wanted, but before now I never had that much interest. Much though I hate it, you're safer wearing his collar than you would ever be wearing mine."

I returned to my seat to drink my tea.

"I gather that Tommy spoke to you about the Primus's chained."

I nodded and looked down into my mug, remembering my rough calculation of the vast number Sol must have given out over the millennia.

"I met a couple of them tonight. They're working at the club."

"And?"

I shrugged.

"They seemed nice enough." Also very young and pretty, my treacherous brain reminded me.

"I don't like to think of you being lumped in with them. Hell, I just hate to think of you being considered to be his, one of the entourage." He reached out across the table tentatively and took one of my hands in his. "I wish I didn't have to lie to the world about how I feel about you."

Now I was uncomfortable again. Aside from the difficulties I had with him apparently loving me, I'd been thinking about this a lot over the past couple of days and the only way I could think of that Drew could be honest about loving me was if I turned Silver. He was going to ask me about it again, and I didn't know what to tell him.

"Viv said Sol knows about your fake relationship," I said, pulling my hand away from his as casually as possible.

"Yes, I know. Unfortunately, he's annoyingly astute, but he's the only one who knows apart from the people we've told."

"And Ben, of course," I said. Surely he would have worked it out.

Drew nodded reluctantly.

"I won't leave you unprotected, I promise. I'm staying here with you tonight."

"Well then you're sleeping in the spare room," I replied archly.

"If that's what you want."

What I wanted more than anything right now was a sleepover with a different vampire entirely. It was ironic and cruel that the desire had sharpened as soon as I discovered it wouldn't be fulfilled, as soon as the maintenance of the brand appeared to make a relationship with Drew inevitable.

But maybe Sol had done me a favour, in the long run.

How could I have Drew touch me that way every day, share that intensity of sensation with him every day, without feeling something for him? Part of me hoped that something would blossom from it, because if the brand was the only thing that was pulling me back to Drew then life was going to be pretty miserable. To have that kind of intimate experience with someone… better that it should mean something.

I knew it was going to be unpopular, but Drew and I needed to talk about the alternatives.

I took a deep breath.

"Sol said there was a way to break the bond."

His brows drew down over his eyes and his mouth twisted into a sneer.

"So that's what he wants, is it? He wants me dead now,

just so I'm out of the way?"

I was expecting Drew to be upset that I wanted to break the bond, but I hadn't expected him to be so angry.

"He doesn't want you dead, Drew," I replied, as calmly as I could manage.

"Anything that breaks this bond is going to kill me and, whatever you feel for me, it'll probably hurt you too." He stood up and ran his fingers through his hair, then stepped away from the table and rested his hands on the back of his chair, leaning over it towards me. "Seriously, how many times do I have to apologise for loving you? You may not want to admit it, but you feel something for me, Emmy. I'm not just going to stand aside and let him take you away from me. Not again. Can't you see he'll just end up hurting you?"

But Sol hadn't tried to take me away from Drew, not this time. He'd given up as soon as the chase was over. Maybe that was the problem: it was only exciting for as long as he was the one doing the chasing.

Either way, Drew was right. I was broken, and I couldn't cope with this level of confrontation from him.

"Emmy, what's wrong?"

"Nothing, it's fine," I said irritably, trying to hold back the tears.

"Look, I'm sorry, I didn't mean to shout."

"It's not you."

Drew's face instantly clouded.

"Did he hurt you? Did he do something to you?"

"No, he didn't do anything."

And wasn't that the truth. I wished Drew would just leave it alone and stop digging. If I thought about it, I was going to start crying again, and I really didn't want to do that in front of him. Not over Sol.

"Then why are you upset?"

"Can we just leave it, Drew? It's been a long day."

"No, we can't just leave it. His scent is all over you tonight. What did he do to upset you?"

I snapped.

"He didn't do anything!"

There was a heavy moment of silence as the tears spilled over and I turned away to wipe them from my face.

"Oh," he said. It was clearly not the answer he had been expecting.

"You really don't have to worry about Sol," I said bitterly.

And with that confession I'd had all I could take for the night.

I got up from the table and walked away.

"Emmy…"

I didn't look back, but carried on up the stairs to my bedroom, shutting the door behind me.

CHAPTER XV

I lay awake in bed, the tears streaming silently down my cheeks. I felt like I was falling apart. What little sense I had made of the world after the Revelation seemed to have been turned on its head. From the night I had met him, I'd wanted Drew. The only thing that had kept us apart I now knew to be a lie. I couldn't believe that I was finally here, in a safe space with him, and I was flinching at his touch. A week ago, he had been my safe space.

He protected me, he loved me, he looked after me, and I needed him to stop me from self-combusting as a result of the brand. Was I being a fool to keep him at a distance?

I'd fixated on Sol: Sol, who was a god, and I was passing up a good man while I wallowed in a misery that was of my own creation. Sol offered me only excitement, and he'd delivered in spades. Drew promised me love forever, and it had terrified me.

I listened as Drew padded up the stairs to the spare room about twenty minutes after me and closed the door behind him.

Time for me to move on, to put my feelings for Sol in a little box and lock it away, for real this time. I wiped away the tears and rolled over, tossing and turning until I finally sank into unconsciousness as the dawn began to colour the sky.

The next thing I knew, there was a knock at the bedroom door. It was fully light outside and the sun was blazing through the cracks in the curtains.

"Emmy, are you awake?"

That wasn't Drew.

I sat bolt upright in bed and gathered the duvet to my chest.

"Who's that?" I asked.

"Okay, so I know this is a bit weird, but it's Ed," he said through the door.

I hadn't seen Ed since he had come into the club with Carrie, and we hadn't really spoken properly since last week. I couldn't think of any reason why he'd be at my door.

"Ed? What the hell are you doing here?" I thought this place was supposed to be top secret, but everyone seemed to know about it. If civilian Ed could track me down, I wasn't filled with confidence that Ben wouldn't find me too.

"Er, yeah, Cam sent me over. The Secundus had to go, well, erm… all the Invicti are kind of busy. Cam was waiting for you but he had to go too, so he gave me the Secundus's key."

This didn't sound good.

"What's going on?"

"I'll, uh, wait downstairs for you."

"Ed…," I called, but I could already hear him halfway down the stairs. He wasn't going to talk to me until we were face to face.

I saw from the clock on the bedside table that it was already the afternoon. I only had a couple of hours before I needed to open the club up again.

I brushed my teeth, showered and threw on some clothes as quickly as I could, choosing a high-necked T-shirt and shorts in deference to the sunshine. They'd keep me cool, but meant I had to spend some time laboriously adjusting my fake knee bandage. I slipped my feet into a pair of Converse and, combing out my wet hair as I walked, took myself downstairs to talk to Ed.

"Okay," I said, "spill it. What's going on?"

"Everything's fine. The Secundus just wanted to make sure you weren't alone."

"Really?"

"Nothing to worry about."

He smiled at me desperately as he pushed his glasses up higher on his nose.

"I don't believe you," I said.

"Seriously, there's nothing going on. Let's just chill out and, erm… watch some TV? Yeah, let's watch a film or something. Carrie's going to come and join us in a bit anyway. Here, let me close the blinds…"

As he moved towards the wall of glass that separated us from the patio, I saw a plume of smoke rising into the air. It looked like it was pretty close by, practically next to the club. Something was very wrong.

I dropped my comb and rushed forward past Ed, unlocking the patio door and pushing outside. The air was acrid and heavy, the warm breeze of the sunny afternoon filled with smoke. In the distance I could hear voices, shouting, and the steady beat of drums.

I whirled round to face Ed.

"What the hell is going on?"

"Nothing…" he said unconvincingly. He was probably the least scary Silver I had ever met. Vampires didn't come much more cuddly.

"Ed, even if you weren't such a crappy liar, it would take a pretty amazing story to make me think that this," I said, gesturing towards the column of smoke, "is nothing. Explain. Now."

His shoulders sagged.

"There's been some… trouble. I'm supposed to keep you here."

I thought about Ben for a moment, but if something was happening I wanted to know what it was, and I didn't want to be stuck here like a prisoner.

"Not on your life. You can come with me. Let's go," I said as I gathered my wet hair up into a ponytail.

"Do I have to?"

"Come on!"

I practically ran down the stairs through the club and out into the street with Ed close on my heels. The pillar of smoke I had seen from the patio was rising from a pile of blackened debris that was smouldering in the alley next to the club, but it looked like it was in the process of burning out. The brick wall that formed the side of the club was charred above and around the scorched mass, but it didn't look like there had been any damage caused.

I turned to Ed with relief and saw with horror that this pile of burning rubbish was the least of our troubles. There were sheets of smoke rising up into the sky from the direction of the Square, which also seemed to be the source of the noise.

At that moment, there was a gunshot and a scream reverberated down the street.

"Shit!" I looked up and down the deserted road then made a decision. Nudging Ed along, I broke into a run and headed for the Square.

"Emmy, please don't!"

I ignored him and ran on until I reached the Square, but I didn't find what I was expecting to see. Instead of the crowds I had anticipated, there was no one here at all. The space was completely empty except for a few cardboard coffee cups that had spilled their contents and been trampled underfoot.

But there had definitely been some trouble here. The glass and stone walls of the office blocks and retail units that filled the Square were covered with silver paint, some from spray cans and some dripping down the walls in thick rivulets. A couple of pools of dark liquid spattering the light stone of the paving slabs looked like they could have been blood.

"Emmy!" came a shout from my right. Alice was running towards me from the direction of the café, apparently her new home from home, with Mary and her kids in tow. Three men I didn't recognise followed them out, heading quickly towards the club. The door to the café was firmly shut behind them, and I watched as one of the staff locked it up and stepped back from the glass.

Another gun shot rang through the air as the group reached me and Ed. We all instinctively ducked our heads and looked around, but the noise came from the other side of the Square.

"You should all get back to the club and get inside, where you'll be safe," Ed said.

"What's going on?" Mia asked, her voice quavering with panic.

I shrugged then turned to Mary.

"Get the girls back to the club, and take Ed with you. He'll keep you safe. Alice, you should go with them."

"No," Alice and Ed replied in unison.

"Ed, you're going. I'll be fine. Alice, if you want then you can come with, but I don't know what's going to happen."

I looked at her steadily, trying to impress the danger on her. She just nodded back.

"Emmy, please," Ed said, "I can't let you go off on your own."

"Ed," I took one of his hands in mine, "you have to see the girls back to the club safely. You can come find us after if you want. I know you can move quickly."

He relented, then rushed Mary and the girls out of the Square, clearly keen to get them deposited safely in their dorm so he could come back for me.

Alice and I ran through the Square to the other side, towards the pillared frontage of the London Stock Exchange, the concrete slab outside its door now overwritten with silver graffiti. The legend was topped with a silver handprint and read: 'What about Cara?'

We paused. I glanced around and saw that the silver handprint was painted in numerous places around the Square.

"Shit," I muttered to myself as the implications sank in.

"Who's Cara?" Alice asked.

"You're shitting me, right?" I said. She looked blankly

back at me.

"Cara Alton. You know, the girl in America. The one with the…" I stopped myself, realising in horror that I'd nearly said 'Silver brand'. That was a can of worms I didn't want to open.

"Oh, the one with the handprint, the one who was drained by a Silver?"

"Yup."

The one whose vampire lover had died with her because of the Silver bond, I thought. But, of course, Alice hadn't heard that story. That story had been for my ears only, for Ben's dying, captive audience.

"So, what?" she asked. "What does it mean? That we can't forget that the Silver are killers?"

"I suppose so," I replied noncommittally.

That was what the graffiti would mean to the humans, but to the Silver it would have an altogether more sinister meaning. It would mean: we know your secret, we know about the Silver bond and we know how to kill you.

Whatever idiot had painted the message had unwittingly issued not just a call to arms to the humans, but also an extreme threat to the Silver. I didn't doubt that it would be taken seriously, and that it would put the kibosh on Sol's cooperative future.

"Come on," I said, breaking into a run again. Alice fell into step beside me as we burst out of the other side of the Square. Thankfully, she'd opted for flats today.

The noise of shouting drew me on to the right and along a couple of side streets. The volume increased, individual shouts seeming to rise above the mass of voices, but not yet clearly enough for me to pick out words. After a few minutes we got our first glimpse of the commotion.

There were perhaps a hundred people lined up against the outer wall of the safe zone. Like all parts of the city immediately surrounding the wall, everything had been razed to the ground so there was an open space for a couple of hundred yards until the buildings abruptly rose to their original heights. There was a huge pair of wooden doors set in the wall, about ten feet high, and that was the centre of the activity. Fires were banked up against it, making the air dirty with smoke.

Fifty or so Silver stood with their backs to us in a barrier between us and the people against the wall, and between us and the Silver a crowd of around three hundred more people had gathered to watch, tucked into the doorways of buildings and, in some cases, inside the buildings themselves looking down from windows and balconies.

Ed zipped into place beside me as we came to a stop.

I could barely believe what I was seeing: it was a protest. They were chanting and shouting, demanding equal rights for humans. The noise was incredible, cracks and thuds and shouts reverberating in my eardrums. They had drums, and spray paint and… guns. Not a peaceful protest then.

Where had they got guns from? I couldn't imagine what they hoped to achieve with them, or by protesting in the first place. Hadn't they worked out that there was no choice?

I looked around the scene frantically, but I couldn't see anyone who was injured. There was no blood on the ground here. I remembered the scream I had heard from outside the club and hoped that it had been provoked by shock at the sight of the guns rather than by injury. This was England; we didn't do guns.

All the more surprising, then, that these humans had managed to get hold of them, and they weren't just air rifles or shotguns. Maybe one in five was holding either a hand gun or some sort of automatic weapon.

I scanned my eyes along the line of Silver in an attempt to pick out the people I knew, hoping to make sure they were okay. The back of my neck prickled as I identified Drew. Even though he had his back to me, there was no mistaking the muscular but relaxed set of his shoulders, the way he held his body in perfect control. The mark on my chest began to tingle and I was reminded that it was past time for my 'therapy'.

I was just admiring the view, thinking that Drew wasn't

such a bad choice after all, that he was actually precisely what I wanted and that if I could just wrap myself around him everything would be okay, when he turned round and met my eyes.

My heart rate started to soar. I needed him, right now.

His eyes flared then dismay suffused his expression as he recognised me, and his eyes shifted angrily to Ed. He turned abruptly back towards the line of protesters. In a second, Cam was standing in front of us.

"What the hell, Ed? I ask you to keep her safe and you bring her here?"

"She wouldn't stay in the club…"

"You're Silver for chrissake! You couldn't have stopped her from leaving?"

"What's going on?" I interrupted, not wanting Ed to take the flack for my insubordination.

"You need to get out of here, now," Cam said urgently.

I looked over his shoulder to the line of Silver and froze as I saw Ben, standing next to Drew in profile. He turned back towards the wall and I hoped he hadn't seen me. Maybe it was a good idea for me to be elsewhere.

"Okay, I'll take Alice back. But we're talking about this later," I said.

I took one last look in Drew's direction and, as if he had felt my gaze, he turned his head over his shoulder towards me once more. Only this time, he didn't stop spinning. His shoulder followed his head round, his body twisting at the hips, and then his knees crumpled under him. A dark pool of liquid began to spread out under his head, and only then did I register the fact that I had heard a gunshot.

I screamed.

I tried to move forwards, but Cam was standing like an immovable wall in front of me.

As I struggled, Ben spun around and caught my eye, a slow, satisfied grin breaking across his face until his white teeth twinkled in the sunshine.

"No!" I screamed again, straining against Cam's arms.

I watched as Viv scooped Drew's twisted, immobile body in her arms and carried him away from the wall at lightning speed. By the time she passed out of sight, she was just a blur in the wind. I guessed it was probably her right as his apparent mate to take care of him.

I sobbed and twisted my fists in Cam's T-shirt.

"Is he going to be okay?" I asked Cam desperately, tears streaming down my face. "Will be survive? Where has she taken him? Can I see him?"

"Ems," he said, pulling me close against him, "he'll be fine, but it'll take him a day or so to recover. Viv will be taking him to the Invicti quarters, and you can't go in there. I'm sorry."

I pressed my forehead to his chest and cried with a mixture of heartache and relief.

"Emmy?" Alice said from beside me. I'd forgotten she was there.

This was going to take some explaining.

I pushed away from Cam and, taking a deep, shuddering breath, hastily wiped the tears from my eyes. Ed took my hand and gently tugged me back the way we had come.

"We'll go back to the dorm and see you there later," I said pointedly to Cam.

"No, no, Emilia," Ben said, suddenly beside me, "I'll take you there myself."

My breath caught in my throat. Ed and Cam looked at each other, then at me in hopeless anguish. Ben insinuated himself at my side, a solicitous expression on his face, taking my hand from Ed.

"Cameron can look after this other girl," Ben said with a leer, nodding towards Alice. "Or perhaps you'd prefer that she came with us?" he asked me innocently.

I shook my head vigorously. I didn't want to drag her into this.

"Then let's just get you away from here. Quietly."

Ed and Cam just stared.

I couldn't understand why they weren't doing anything, why they were just watching as he led me away from them.

Then I realised: there was nothing they could do.

Ben was Tertius, the substitute leader of the Invicti. The street was filled with Solis Invicti and, with Drew out of action, Ben was in charge. Cam and Ed couldn't challenge that.

That was it. Without Drew's protection, without his authority, I was at Ben's mercy. It was that simple, that easy. I thought about shouting out, but even if anyone could hear me over the noise of the protestors, who would help me when I was being escorted by Ben? Besides which, one wrong step from me would mean Alice's death.

At least I wouldn't have to have that on my conscience as well as Drew's death, though I probably wouldn't have long to feel guilty about that.

My only advantage was that Ben wanted to get me somewhere out of sight before he killed me, which might give me a chance to get away. I couldn't think how, but it was the only vague plan I had.

Ben's mask of concern fell away as he wrapped his arm around me and steered me away from my friends, a rapacious glint twinkling in his eyes. He drew back his lips in a vicious smile and showed me his teeth.

"I'll look after you, little human, don't you worry about that."

"Benedict, please…" I bit out, gasping as his fingers dug into my arm.

"Oh, now, there's no need for that, not here." He waved his free hand dismissively then leaned down towards me so his eyes were looking directly into mine. "That will come later, I promise you."

"But Drew…"

"Will be out cold for at least the next twelve hours. And who knows what might happen during that time? Maybe he'll never wake up at all."

He laughed a sickly, nasal chuckle and dragged me away from the wall, back into the twisting, hidden corners of the city. Chills ran up my back and my hands started to shake as

I leadenly placed one foot in front of the other, walking towards my death. I'd promised myself that I wouldn't go willingly with Ben the next time, that I wouldn't let him carry me off without a fight, but what choice did I have?

Responding to my reluctance, he curled his fingers into my flesh until his fingernails cut into my skin.

"Not a sound," he demanded as I watched a bead of blood travel down my arm. I clenched my teeth together and forced my feet to keep moving.

"Good girl," he said, licking his lips. "Your blood smells good. Maybe this time I'll drain you myself."

There was a disturbance in the air and the brand fizzed on my chest, the skin almost sizzling with sudden heat. A cool scent surrounded me and I could have cried with relief.

"Thank you, Benedict," Sol said as he stepped in our path. "I will escort the human from here. You are needed to contain the protestors in the absence of the Secundus."

He hesitated.

"Your duty is here," Sol insisted, a threat creeping into his tone. "You have your orders."

A spasm of rage crossed Ben's expression for a second, then he extracted his fingernails from my arm and effected a neat little bow before turning on his heel to rejoin the Silver at the wall.

Sol moved towards me, his eyes flicking momentarily towards the blood on my arm, but I extended a hand to ward him off, the heat rising in the brand with every inch he closed between us. Lights flashed in my vision and my legs shook, threatening to collapse beneath me.

I had a momentary sensation of toppling backwards, then an arm circled around my waist whilst my own arm was wound around a narrow set of shoulders. When my sight returned to normal I looked to my side to see that Alice was propping me up, a determined expression on her face.

"Come on," she said. "I'm taking you back home."

"Emilia, you must come with me," Sol said.

I turned around in Alice's arms to face her, and gave her a

hug. She made a small, surprised noise. I smiled at her as I stepped away, reassuring her that I was okay to stand on my own.

"Alice comes with us," I said to Sol. "It's not safe." Ben had identified her as someone I cared about, and he'd try to use her as a bargaining chip if he could to get to me, and thus to Drew.

"Er, okay with me, I guess" Alice said.

Sol inclined his head in acquiescence.

"Very well, but we go at speed. Your key, Emilia?"

Ed passed me Drew's key and I handed it over. As Sol took it from me a painful heat sliced through the brand and I pressed my hand hard up against it, hoping to calm the heat myself. But only Drew could do that, and he wasn't going to be able to help me for hours.

Sol caught my gesture and took a step away from me.

"Cameron, Edmund?"

Cam scooped me into his arms as Ed grabbed Alice, and within seconds all five of us were standing in the large, open-plan room that was the bottom floor of my apartment, the noise of the protest echoing in my ears.

"Wow," Alice said with a smile as Ed set her on her feet. "That was a rush."

She looked around herself in astonishment.

"When you said you had a room off the bar, this wasn't quite what I was expecting."

"It's not forever. You'll stay here, right?" I said to her. "There's a spare room."

It occurred to me that Drew had slept in the bed, but that was really the least of my worries right now. I doubted that she would mind. Normal hospitality standards were probably out of the window at this stage.

"Sure," she said with a smile, clearly pleased as punch to be included. She didn't realise how much danger she was in.

I'd have to be the one to tell her.

"Cameron, back to help the Invicti," Sol said. "Edmund, gather Alice's belongings from downstairs in the dorm."

Alice quickly explained where her things were.

"Oh," she gasped, "what about Nix? We can't leave her down there."

I turned to Sol.

"Do you mind?"

He raised an eyebrow at me.

"She's our kitten," I said. "We rescued her."

"Then I do not mind at all," he said. "In my culture, cats were to be revered."

I marvelled at this tiny, material insight into his past. He and others had told me in vague terms about the man he had been, but this was the first concrete fact I had to go on. Perhaps Egyptian? But his colouring was all wrong, too blonde and fair for a pharaoh.

Cam gave me a hug then walked out of the patio doors with Ed, leaving me and Alice alone with Sol.

"I must prepare for a broadcast," he said, retrieving a mobile phone from his pocket. "Would you both please excuse me?"

"Of course," I said, slightly discombobulated by his studied politeness. It put distance between us that felt unnatural and awkward, but perhaps it was only right that our conversation should involve a little less familiarity than it had done recently.

A pain twisted in my chest as I remembered his words of last night.

I was a distraction.

"Before you do, could I just have a quick word, please?" I asked Sol. I'd made a decision: Alice had the right to know what was going on. More than that, I needed someone to talk to about, well, everything. Either way, I needed to hear from Sol that it was okay to tell her.

He paused on his journey to the dining table and nodded.

At that moment, Ed appeared on the patio with Alice's belongings, leaving them by the glass. He waved at us then immediately left again, presumably to try to track down Nix.

"Why don't you take your stuff upstairs," I said to Alice as

I helped her heft her two bags inside, locking the door safely again behind us. "The room's the one at the back. I'll be up in a minute."

"Sure," she said happily.

I turned to Sol when I heard the door to the spare room shut tight behind her, but made sure I kept a good ten feet of air between us.

"How painful is it?" he asked.

I shrugged.

"It's okay."

I didn't want to play the 'how close can I get?' game again.

"The Secundus will be fine, Emilia. There is no cause for concern."

The master of understatement.

"Seriously, Sol?"

He leaned towards me a little and held my gaze.

"We will talk about this later."

"No, I want to talk about it now. What's going on out there? I just watched Drew get shot in the head, and Ben nearly got to me. Again."

"And whose fault was that, Emilia?" he asked in a whisper, his composure cracking as anger sparkled in his cold, blue eyes.

I was taken aback by his vehemence, shocked into silence.

"Andrew can only protect you if you allow him to do so," he said. "Benedict has stepped into the role of Secundus during Andrew's recovery and I cannot change that. I may have reigned for centuries, but I do so by the grace of those who follow me. I am strong, but I am not stronger than a hundred Silver. Even I cannot defy the hierarchy they have instituted."

He ran his fingers through his hair, disturbing the golden curls that crowned him.

"There is a very good reason that I appointed Andrew my Secundus," he continued, speaking quietly and deliberately. "He is extremely competent, with a particular talent for identifying and fortifying weaknesses. Make no mistake, that is what you are to him in military terms: a weakness. He knows that to be the case, so has made every arrangement for your safety, for both of your sakes, but for some reason you are completely incapable of abiding by those arrangements."

He glanced away from me for a moment, pressing his lips together in exasperation.

"If you had done so, he would be standing here right now in my place."

I flushed with shame.

He was right: it was my fault. If I hadn't gone out to the wall, Drew wouldn't have looked away from the protestors. He would have dodged the bullet that found his head, and Ben would never have been in a position to try to lead me away. I wouldn't even have been there for him to see.

I had no argument to offer in my defence.

A tear trailed down my cheek, but Sol hadn't finished yet. I dashed it away impatiently, guilt churning in my stomach.

"Did you not consider that, with his many hundreds of years of experience, Andrew might know better than you? You rebel for rebellion's sake and take no responsibility for the repercussions, but this is not a game. You owe him, and me, some respect. Your insistence on this childish power struggle places both of your lives at risk, motivated by nothing but your blind arrogance. This is our entire society in the balance, such as it is, but you think only of yourself. And now another life is endangered because of you."

He tipped his head towards the spare room where Alice waited. I hoped shamefully that she wasn't able to hear our conversation.

I hadn't thought at all, but I supposed that was the point. I had got used to the Silver protecting me from Ben, to the extent that I had become complacent. I'd effectively delegated responsibility for my safety to them, assuming that they'd be there to cover my back in any situation, and it had made me reckless. I'd carried on regardless, wilfully putting myself in danger against Drew's explicit orders.

"I'm sorry," I said quietly, pushing more tears away from

my cheeks. "I didn't think."

He shook his head in disapproval.

"Your egotism astounds me," he said quietly, his tone dull with disappointment.

I was floored by how much it hurt when it was coming from him.

"Me too," I whispered, desperately trying to stem the flow of tears. This was no time for a pity party; I was the one in the wrong here.

I'd had no regard for Drew and no regard for Sol. I wasn't just playing with my own life. I'd deliberately ignored Ed, who had been nothing but sweet to me, and had been sent to protect me. I was behaving like a spoiled child: arrogant and self-involved in the extreme.

The most shocking thing was that I'd had no self awareness at all. We all write our own biographies in our heads, casting ourselves as the virtuous heroes at the centre of the narrative, but I couldn't believe that my perception of myself had been so removed from reality, that I had veered so far off course. In my head I'd been the victim, the poor human buffeted by the whims of the Silver, constrained into reluctant compliance by circumstance. To everyone else, I was an attention-seeking brat threatening to jump into traffic, a ticking time bomb doing everything to thwart all attempts to keep me safe.

No amount of introspection could absolve me now.

How had I become so deluded? The realisation was crushing and painfully humbling.

"I'm sorry. It was a mistake."

"Yes," he said mercilessly, but the anger was gone from his eyes.

He'd said his piece.

We didn't speak for a few seconds.

"I have to tell her something," I said hesitantly. "She's going to want to know why you're here."

I flushed with shame again as I realised that my selfish actions put Sol, the Primus, in a position where he was obliged to babysit me. He had no particular affection for me anymore, no reason to spend time with me except for Drew's sake.

I was an inconvenience as well as a liability.

"You can tell her, but you must not mention the bond, or the brand."

I nodded, wondering how I was going to tell her anything with those two glaring omissions.

"She's not safe," I said. "He saw her."

"We can protect her as well."

I didn't know what else to say. How could I convey to him how sorry I was?

"Is that all?" he asked, a dismissal if I ever heard one. It was another twist of the knife, the cool detachment that seemed to have entered into our conversation.

"Yes," I said, not sure how to express the regret and embarrassment I was feeling. "Thank you."

I reflected miserably that I couldn't remember ever having thanked him before for everything he had done for me. I wondered if I had ever thanked Drew.

Had I really been that selfish? I'd better add ingratitude to my sizeable list of transgressions.

Sol pulled his phone out of his pocket again and started dialling immediately. I wondered how he was still getting service. Maybe it was just a glorified walkie talkie.

Either way, he was clearly done with me.

CHAPTER XVI

I made a quick detour to my en suite to clean the blood from my arm and wash my face so Alice wouldn't know I'd been crying, then I knocked on the door to the spare room nervously, wondering how I was going to explain myself. I figured that honesty was the best policy.

"Alice? It's me."

"Come in," she said.

She was sitting on the bed, leafing through a book. I closed the door behind me and sat down next to her.

"So," she said, putting the book aside.

"So."

"Are you finally going to tell me what's going on?"

I exhaled heavily.

"I'm sorry, but I can't tell you everything. I'll tell you what I can."

She looked at me attentively, ready to hear my explanation. I didn't know how to start.

"The Silver you saw today, the scary one with the brown hair and the insane muscles?"

She nodded.

"That's Benedict. He's a sort of deputy leader of the Solis Invicti after Drew, and he's trying to kill me. Drew and Sol are trying to keep me safe."

Despite my best efforts to the contrary, I thought guiltily.

It was the simplest way I knew to explain it.

"The Secundus and the Primus are protecting you?" she asked incredulously.

"Yup."

"Wow."

Her reaction just affirmed my shame. I'd been so blasé about it, taken for granted the protection of the two most powerful Silver in the country. I'd expected it and treated it as if it were my due, assuming that any small discomfort attendant with it was their duty to rectify.

I was just surprised that it had taken this long for one of them to call me out.

We sat in silence for a moment, Alice doubtless mulling things over and me trying to work out what to say next.

"Ben's a dangerous Silver," I said finally, "and I'm worried that he'll come after you now he knows that we're friends. That's why I want you to stay here."

"Okay."

"I'm so sorry, Alice. I didn't mean to involve you in all this."

More silence.

"Not so great to be noticed by the Silver after all, then," she said wryly.

"No, not really. I'm sorry."

I remembered our conversation in the cinema the other day. It used to be that all Alice wanted was for them to see her. Now she had what she wanted, but it was putting her life in danger.

"Why is he trying to kill you?" she asked. "Is it something to do with the Primus?"

"I can't tell you the specifics. I can tell you this, though: Ben thinks that killing me will elevate him to Primus, or to Secundus at least. He's after the power."

She shook her head.

"This is crazy, Emmy."

"I know."

"How long had this been going on?"

"Pretty much since the Revelation. A little after."

"Is that why you weren't in the safe house?"

"No," I said quietly. "That was… something different."

"Can you tell me about that at least?"

"I'd really rather not. It was… bad."

She nodded and we fell silent again.

"Are we going to die?"

"I don't know. Maybe."

It was suddenly, horribly clear to me how reckless I had been. Drew and Sol couldn't protect me, not all the time. They couldn't look after me every second of every day. It was even more difficult with Drew injured, because he wasn't in control of the Invicti, he wasn't the one giving the orders.

Eventually, Ben would probably find his opportunity. It was incredible that he hadn't managed it already with all the help I'd been giving him.

"We've got to get through the Casting," Alice said decisively. "It's the only way."

"What?"

"The only way we'll be safe. We can't protect ourselves like this."

"It's not that simple."

"Yes it is."

I looked down into my lap. I couldn't tell her why it wasn't simple, couldn't tell her that while I might survive the process, without a Silver bond she was unlikely to pull through.

As if she'd read my mind, she said: "Are you two together?"

"What?"

I wondered if she meant me and Sol or me and Drew. She had to have been a little surprised by my extreme reaction to the shooting. In all honesty, I'd been unprepared for it myself.

"You and the Primus."

"No," I said firmly, "definitely not."

"Oh," she looked a little crestfallen. "But he's always

hanging around you, and then there's the choker and the bite marks…"

"That was just once," I interrupted.

I suppressed a shiver as I remembered the sensation of Sol's teeth breaking through my skin, the feeling of release and euphoria that came with it. I'd do it again in a heartbeat.

God, I missed him. Nothing had ever hurt me like his disappointment. I'd do anything to regain his esteem, to have him look at me with something other than disapproval.

There was a knock at the door.

"Emilia."

Sol's voice.

Speak of the devil, and he shall appear.

I wondered how long he'd been there, how much he'd heard. Part of me was thrilled at the thought that he would know how very few shits I gave about him or his rejection, but that was the part of me that lied, that crafted my deficiencies into virtues.

Most of me wished that, if only he knew that I still cared, he'd tell me he hadn't meant a word he'd said last night. Now, more than ever, I knew that was a fantasy. There was no way my ego could spin his emotions into anything other than disinterest. I could romanticise the situation all I liked, but he saw right through me, saw me more clearly than anyone. There was nothing in me that could impress him right now.

He saw my flaws laid bare, my whole personality spiralling around a central conceit that I was the most important person in the world.

I'd never felt so ashamed.

"I must leave for the broadcast," he continued, "and you must both come with me."

Alice looked at me and I nodded. I was doing what I was told from now on. We had to stick with Sol.

When I opened the door he was already back downstairs, waiting for us at the front door to the apartment.

"Are we going to the Square?" I asked as we followed him out and down the stairs, wondering whether it was really a good idea to gather everyone in that space again.

"No," he said. "The club." Apparently he'd suddenly become a master of monosyllables, which was unusual for him. He normally delighted in his use of language.

"Are we all going to fit?" I asked, thinking of the huge number of humans who normally met in the Square for broadcasts.

He looked over his shoulder, briefly meeting my eyes in a glance that felt like a rebuke. I resolved to ask no further questions.

How quickly things had fallen apart between us. Whatever intimacy we might have built had been shattered on the cliffs of my pride.

"Only those who reside at the dormitory here will be attending in person," he said.

Alice gasped as we emerged into the office.

"This is so cool. It's like a secret lair."

"Emphasis on the word 'secret', if you please," Sol interjected.

"Of course, Primus," she replied reverently, with a slight edge to her tone as if offended that he had though she'd tell anyone about it. I thought it was a good bet that she would have done if he had said nothing.

I could hear the tannoy system through the double doors to the office, doubtless calling people to the broadcast, and when we reached the dance floor I saw that a few humans had already made their way here. They stepped back as Sol walked past on his way to the stage. For many of them, this would be the closest they had ever come to him. For some, that was clearly an unpleasant experience, but nonetheless their expressions were coloured by awe.

I couldn't blame them.

I was surprised to see that Oliver was here with a few of his gang, sure that they would have been at the very centre of the protests this afternoon. He was watching closely as Alice and I followed Sol out and I had a moment of paranoia that he might be putting the pieces together before I realised that there was nothing for him to read into it. I was managing the club for Sol, and it was perfectly reasonable that he and I would have been meeting with one of the other bar staff in my office.

Sol was talking to one of the Invicti I didn't know at the side of the stage while a few men and women who looked human set up a camera and projector on and around the elevated platform. Alice spotted Chris and Sam and made a beeline towards them, but I didn't much feel like talking to anyone. I stepped back and leaned against the door to the taproom and office.

I watched as the room filled up with people to the sound of the speakers calling them to assemble. The noise of excited chatter increased as our numbers rose, but the space was still only sparsely populated. There weren't that many of us in the dorm at the club, not compared with the capacity of the room.

After a few minutes Oliver approached me, taking up a position against the wall at my side.

"Can we talk?" he asked.

"Now's not a good time," I replied, not wanting to get into a verbal sparring match with him. I'd had as much of a conversational beating as I could take today. All the fight had gone out of me. I was tired and scared, and I didn't think I'd ever felt more compliant in my life.

"Please? I need your help."

I turned my head to look him in the eye, wondering what he could possibly want from me.

"With what?"

His grey eyes widened emphatically as he nodded towards the stage, the implication being that he didn't want to talk about it in front of the Silver.

"I'm here for the broadcast," I replied, turning back to the stage.

"They'll be another ten minutes or so," he said. "They've got to set up the feeds to the other dorms. Can we just step into the office?"

"No, we can't."

There was no way I was leaving Sol's sight, not after the chewing out he'd just given me.

"The best I can do is talk behind the bar," I said. Sol would still be able to see me there, but the enclosure would give at least the illusion of privacy.

Oliver looked into my eyes for a moment, saw I was serious and relented. He shrugged.

"Okay then."

He followed me behind the bar and took up a position leaning against the fridges along the back wall. I faced him with my back to the room.

"Okay," I said wearily, "talk."

"You were trying to protect us last night in the bar," he said.

I shrugged, picking up a bar towel so I could polish some glasses while we talked. I wasn't going to tell him that I'd actually already reported the incident to the Silver. Let him dig himself further into a hole if he wanted to.

"Where did you get the mark?" he asked, his whisper doing nothing to mask the bluntness of his tone.

The colour drained from my face and my stomach turned.

"What mark?" I asked.

He gave me a frank look.

"Don't mess me around. The mark on your chest, the silver handprint. The one like the mark Cara Alton had on her stomach."

"I don't know what you're talking about," I said, grimacing internally as I felt my cheeks flush with the bare-faced lie.

"You're a crappy liar."

He wasn't wrong.

I crossed my arms over my chest again, indicating with my body language that I wasn't going to talk about it. He tipped his head back in frustration, his hands on his hips.

"It's going to kill you, you know," he said. "Just like it killed her."

He was probably right, but I doubted that he knew what he was talking about. He seemed to think that the problem was the brand itself, rather than what it represented. Then again, maybe I'd just burn up from the inside if Drew didn't recover soon.

"I thought you wanted my help," I replied archly.

"I do, but you could use mine too. We can't trust them. They'll kill us all unless we get away from here. Freedom is waiting for us outside of those walls."

I shook my head.

"The only thing waiting out there is a sea of Weepers."

"We've found another way," he whispered confidentially, "and today's distraction let us set things in motion."

"That was you, then? The riot, the guns, the graffiti?"

"Not me personally, but a small portion of those who feel the same way I do. There are a lot of us."

Anger bubbled up inside me. I wasn't going to try to avoid blame, but Oliver's compatriots had to share a fair amount of it for Drew's shooting.

"People were hurt, Oliver," I said through gritted teeth.

He shrugged.

"Not any humans."

I glared at him.

"Don't you see that things are the wrong way round?" he said. "We have something that they need: our blood. They should be working for us, paying us for it." Injustice burned in his eyes, his mouth twisting with distaste.

I laughed out loud, reflecting that he was even more delusional than I was if he thought that humans could ever control the Silver. I wondered who had been feeding the flames of his sense of entitlement.

"Why are you telling me this?" I asked.

Surely he knew I was close to the Silver, that I wouldn't hesitate to turn him in?

"I know you tried to run," he said. How he could possibly have found that out? "I know this isn't what you wanted. I can offer you freedom from the Silver, freedom from this subjugation."

"You can't hide from them," I said, shaking my head, "you

can't overpower them, and you can't make a better life than the one we have here."

"We can, when we have one of them helping us," he said, confirming my suspicions: it had been Oliver or his friends out on the fire escape a couple of nights ago.

I wondered why he was asking me about the brand when he could have asked his friendly neighbourhood Silver. Maybe that was a secret he had been unwilling to reveal, or maybe Oliver had been unsatisfied with his answer.

"Why trust him over all of the others?"

"He shares our vision."

A terrible suspicion crept over me. There was only one Silver I could think of who had an incentive to help humans rebel, for whom turmoil would be a distinct advantage.

Ben.

"This Silver," I said, wanting to confirm my theory, "short brown hair, one of the Invicti, looks like he took a bunch of steroids?"

"I can't tell you," he said, but his eyes told me I was spot on.

So that was his plan, then: get us to destroy ourselves, have the humans show the Silver that there was no hope of a peaceful future without enforced servitude. We'd do his job for him.

"He's a murderous psychopath, Oliver, and he'll get you all killed. You're being manipulated."

He bristled, pushing away from the fridges so he was leaning towards me.

"How would you know? I should have guessed that you wouldn't care about how the rest of us are living, how they're breaking us and using us up. You've made yourself comfortable in this cocoon of power," he said, gesturing towards my choker, "a possession to pander to our overlords."

It was bizarre to watch him segue into oration, the excesses of his language of disdain so much more practised than his normal mode of speaking. It made him seem like a fabrication, a politician in conversation, a straw man.

"When you remember what race you belong to," he continued in an acerbic tone, "it may be too late for you to find a place with your own people."

"I don't doubt that," I replied with equal vitriol, "because if you have anything to do with it soon there won't be any of us left. You chose to paint that symbol, the silver hand, all over the Square, without any understanding of its meaning?"

"Of course I know what it means," he said, affronted but clearly off balance. "Humans carrying that mark end up dead. It's a symbol for rebellion, proof that we aren't supposed to co-exist under the control of these vampires."

"You just don't have a clue, do you?"

He looked back at me blankly.

"You're a fucking idiot," I said, "and you're going to get us all killed."

I walked away from him in disgust, throwing the towel down onto the bar, and returned to my position by the door to the office. He shot a vicious glance at me as he returned to his friends, and I could only imagine that our conversation had gone much worse than he had planned.

Surely he knew that I would be passing on the information that he had given me?

The sooner the better as far as I was concerned. His group would doubtless accelerate their plans, whatever they were, once they realised they were being scrutinised. Their window of opportunity was closing by the minute.

He'd taken a gamble and lost. Now he'd have to live with the consequences.

I thought about interrupting Sol's preparations to tell him what I had learned, but then he stepped onto the stage. Time for the broadcast.

Everyone in the room fell silent.

"Today there was an assault on our defences at the northern perimeter of the safe zone. Many of you will have seen the smoke from the fires that were kindled at the only door in the wall, apparently in an attempt to break through them, to let the Weepers in. What makes this assault most concerning is that it originated not from outside the walls but from within, from humans living within our population and under our protection."

Photos of the protest appeared one after another on the wall behind Sol, which had been covered with a white sheet. None of the pictures were clear enough for individual faces to be made out, which was perhaps intentional.

There were some mutterings around the room. Although many people would have heard about the protests by now, the news had clearly not yet reached them all.

"The motivation of these people is not yet clear, but you will see that the intention appears to be to protest. I would remind each of you that this society is not a democracy, nor will it ever be. Your intransigent misapprehensions of entitlement have no place here and I most certainly will not suffer terrorists to live.

"Those who deliberately compromise our defences put all of our lives on the line, as well as inviting their own destruction. The endangerment of those within our care will not be tolerated. Accordingly, those responsible have been contained and incarcerated, and are watching this broadcast now from their cells. To them I say this: on this one occasion only, you will be detained for twenty-four hours then released. However, should there be any recurrence of the events we have seen today then the perpetrators will be imprisoned indefinitely or terminated. I sincerely hope that you will not make such action necessary.

"For tonight, we are imposing a curfew on all humans. Each of you will be confined to your dormitory from the end of this broadcast until midday tomorrow. All services are suspended, but you will resume your jobs as normal from tomorrow afternoon. That is all."

With that abrupt finish, he stepped down from the stage and walked towards me as the Invicti swiftly ushered the rest of the humans back up to the dorm. I appreciated the strategy. He was reminding people of the freedom they enjoyed at the moment and giving them a taste of what life would be like if they practised sedition.

It was brutally honest.

He had also avoided any mention of injuries to Silver, though there must have been more casualties than just Drew from the number of gunshots we had heard. I thought that it was important that the Silver appear to be unassailable, but those who had seen today's events knew that we could put them down, at least temporarily. That was dangerous knowledge to have floating about.

No wonder Sol was so livid.

My cheeks coloured again with the recollection.

"Find your friend," he said as he approached me, "and we shall return upstairs."

"Okay," I replied obediently, scanning the crowd for Alice and waving her over towards us when I caught sight I her. I saw with concern that she was talking to Oliver, her expression anxious. I walked towards her and she met me halfway, practically running the distance.

"You can't tell the Primus," she whispered to me urgently.

"What?" I said, looking over her shoulder to look at Oliver. He was smirking back at me.

"I'll explain later, just please don't say anything."

"I have to."

"No," she hissed with agitation, grabbing my hands, "you can't. Emmy, they've got Jane and Mia."

Shit.

I glared at Oliver as he was shepherded past me and spun on my heel, putting my arm around Alice's shoulders to guide her back to Sol.

"Okay," I whispered. "We'll talk later."

Sol eyed us suspiciously as he held open the door up to the apartment, but he didn't say anything. I expected that he'd have some questions for me later.

"You must both be hungry," he said as we reached the top of the stairs and entered the apartment. "I will call the Palace."

"Oh no, Primus," Alice piped up. "We can cook for you! Right, Emmy?"

"Er, I'm not exactly the best cook in the world," I said, not sure that poisoning Sol was going to help me get back on his good side.

"Oh, come on," she said cheerfully. "You can chop vegetables and I'll do the cooking."

She smiled at us both so brightly that I said yes, letting her drag me away to the kitchen. I thought I caught a hint of amusement in Sol's eyes, but perhaps that was just wishful thinking. He pulled out his phone again and started murmuring into it quietly as he stepped out onto the patio.

"Okay," said Alice, "now we can talk."

"Go on then. Let's hear it."

She opened the door of the fridge and started pulling out meat and vegetables, then rootled around in the cupboards for dry ingredients to see what she could make. It was odd to see her so in control.

"He said that Jane and Mia joined up, that they're with a group of them that have already escaped."

"There are people out there already?" I asked in disbelief. "How is that even possible? And I thought Ed took Mary and the girls back here when the shooting started?"

She passed me a chopping board and a knife, together with a pile of peppers, tomatoes, onions, garlic and carrots.

"I don't know, but it's what he wants us to believe. If you tell the Primus what Oliver told you then you heard what will happen: they'll be locked up or worse. How can we do that to them?"

"How can we say nothing?" I asked as I made a start trimming the vegetables. "How do you want these chopped?"

"The onions and garlic small, the rest chunky."

"And what if it's a lie?" I asked. "What if they're not complicit in this, if they're hostages, or if they're not out there at all? Anyway, they won't have heard the broadcast if they are outside, so they won't know what they're risking. How is that fair?"

"I don't think fair comes into it. Do you?"

"I guess not."

"Then how can we tell him? Would he see them safe as a favour to you? There's obviously some kind of, I don't know…," she waved some sheets of lasagne around as she tried to put her finger on the apposite word, "affection between the two of you."

"I wouldn't say that."

"Respect?"

"Er, historically not. Mutual regard, maybe."

"Well, whatever it is, do you think it's enough?"

"I don't know," I replied honestly. Before today's events I might have been hopeful, and before last night I would even have been confident. But now, I had no idea.

"I just think it's too important for us to say nothing," I said.

"But we'd be betraying them."

"Would we? Are they really safe where they are?"

She didn't have an answer for me.

I scraped the garlic and onion into a pan and Alice set it frying on the hob while she made the white sauce. We fell into contemplative silence as we worked, me chopping and she cooking. By the time our lasagne concoction went into the oven I still hadn't found a satisfactory solution. I didn't think there was one.

"We should tell him," I said to her.

She nodded reluctantly then looked at me sheepishly.

"Can you tell him?"

"Yes, but you're coming too."

CHAPTER XVII

"Outside the barricade?" Sol asked.

He was sitting at the dining table opposite me and Alice, and we were waiting for his verdict. After we'd all eaten, hoping that the food might put him in a better mood, we'd each recounted our conversations with Oliver. We'd tried to narrate them word for word, as far as we were able to remember, as he had asked us to do. He'd taken our news calmly, as if it had been anticipated.

"We don't know," I said. "He said they'd found another way, as if there was another way to get beyond the wall, to live out there. Alice?"

She shrugged.

"He said that some people had escaped and that Mia and Jane were with them and he insinuated that they'd be in trouble if we told you. I wasn't sure whether or not he meant that they'd gone willingly. And that was it. That was all he said about it."

"And you are certain that Benedict is involved?" he said to me.

"Well, Oliver didn't say so in as many words, but he seemed to recognise him from my description. And who else would help them destroy themselves in such an obviously hopeless way?"

He sat still for a moment, staring off behind us with a thoughtful expression on his face.

"So?" I asked after a minute or so had passed in this way.

He snapped out of his reverie and looked at me as if he was surprised that I was still there.

"Hmm?"

"What are you going to do?" I asked.

"I'll think on it," he replied.

"Please don't hurt them, Primus," Alice begged him. "They're just kids."

The phrase sounded odd coming from Alice, who was little more than a teenager herself. She was growing up quickly, I guessed.

He nodded solemnly at her. It appeared that, one way or another, he was prepared to make a concession for them.

"Thank you! Thank you so much," she said, practically in tears.

"You will need to look to your own protection as well," he said to her. "I regret that precautions are necessary, but you have become a target."

Reaching into his shirt pocket, he pulled out a length of lace that was a match to the choker around my own neck and handed it to her. Despite everything that had happened, despite knowing that I was the one who had put her in danger, and despite my gratitude towards Sol for protecting her, it still twisted the knife in my gut.

"Wow," she said, obviously completely enraptured as she stared into his eyes. I felt like a third wheel.

He smiled back at her, his smile, the slight smile I had come to know and... well, know.

Another twist.

I stood from the table as calmly as I could and gathered our plates, taking them into the kitchen area to start the washing up. I seemed to be doing a lot of displacement table-clearing at the moment. Unfortunately, the open floor plan meant that I couldn't help but overhear their conversation.

"This symbolises that you are under my protection, and it exempts you from blood donations. In return, if I ever ask for you then you must come to me willingly."

That was a euphemism if I'd ever heard one.

Another twist.

"Do you accept?" he asked.

"Of course! Primus, thank you so much. I just can't ever thank you enough for all you've done for me."

"You're very welcome, Alice."

I could hear the smile in his voice, the warmth, the approval.

Alice giggled happily.

"Do you want a glass of wine?" she asked him. "I'm sure I saw a bottle in the cupboard."

"That would be delightful, thank you."

I couldn't take it anymore.

I finished the washing up and turned round to face them both with my happiest smile plastered on my face.

"I'm beat," I said to them cheerfully, "so I'm going to make the most of the fact that the club is closed and get a nice early night. I'll see you in the morning."

"Okay, night Emmy," Alice replied distractedly, barely taking her eyes away from Sol's.

He didn't even bother to look round.

I tidied up the kitchen and left them to it, feeling utterly surplus to requirements. He had Alice to induct now, a new girl for his harem. As I reached the top of the stairs she finished telling a story about a night out she'd had at university, some stupid drunken prank, and he laughed. His laugh, the one I'd only ever heard once or twice, and only then when we were alone.

That was the final nail in the coffin, so to speak.

I felt as though our time together had been undermined, cheapened by the fact that Alice had more rapport with him in ten minutes than I had managed in ten days.

I closed the bedroom door behind me quietly as the tears began to stream down my face for the umpteenth time today.

I was a mess. I wished I'd had the foresight to bring a glass of wine upstairs with me. There was no way I was going to sleep without some assistance.

I riffled through the drawers of the bedside table on the off chance that I'd find some sleeping pills. No such luck, but I did find a packet of cigarettes and a load of tiny bottles of bourbon, like the type you get on airplanes. I wasn't really a whisky girl, but it would do.

I wondered whether I'd be safe out on the balcony. Ben would be busy babysitting a dorm somewhere out in the safe zone, but I didn't want to take any chances. I cautiously opened the door and, peering around from side to side, saw that it was almost completely shielded by ivy and other climbing plants, which hung down in great sheets from the roof above us. It was a wonderful, private hidey hole. As an extra advantage, when I closed the balcony door behind me I couldn't hear the laughter from downstairs.

I sighed with relief and opened the pack of cigarettes. Its previous owner had helpfully left a lighter tucked in next to the cancer sticks, and I gratefully pulled it out and lit one up. Although I'd never had a particular habit, I'd been a social smoker back in university and it reminded me of a better time, a time when I'd felt invincible.

I threw myself down into one of the cast iron chairs ornamenting the balcony and pulled my legs up to my chest. Taking a heavy drag on the cigarette, I lined the tiny bottles up on the table next to me, twelve of them, and cracked the first one open. The taste of chemicals and tar spread across my tongue as I exhaled and I suddenly remembered why I didn't smoke anymore, but I chased the taste down with the bourbon and took another drag.

I was hitting the self-destruct button, hard. I could see myself doing it, could analyse every single action and know it was stupid, but it didn't stop me from lifting the cigarette and the bottle to my mouth, turn by turn.

My mind was filled with guilt and sorrow at the events of the day. First I cursed myself for the idiocy that had sent me to the wall and the terrible selfishness that had incited it, that had ended up with Drew so hurt, then I reminded myself that Sol had rejected me, probably because of that and other character flaws, before concluding with the big finish: he was downstairs right now having a much better time with Alice than he had ever had with me, probably getting ready to take her upstairs.

Or stay downstairs, whatever.

He was the Primus, after all. He could do whatever the hell, and whomever the hell, he wanted.

How could I go back into the building with that possibly going on? Far worse than imagining it would be going back inside and hearing evidence that it was actually happening.

I'd take blind denial every time.

I wondered how Drew was, then instantly felt guilty for not having thought of him more this evening, for not asking Sol about him.

I was a terrible person.

No wonder Sol was fucking Alice.

By the time I hit the third bottle I was spiralling out, my head spinning with the heady combination of alcohol and nicotine as the tears dried on my face. I was done crying.

I moved unsteadily from the chair to a bench that sat on the other side of the balcony and stretched out on my back along its length. The cast iron seat dug into my shoulders and my hips, and it was cold outside in just my shorts and T-shirt, but I didn't really care. The bourbon bottles and cigarettes had come along with me, after all.

I could see the stars above me, twinkling through the vegetation supported on the trellised roof above me. It was utterly beautiful, and utterly heartbreaking. You shouldn't be able to see stars that bright in central London.

I downed another bottle, grimacing at the taste, and picked up one of its friends. With a further judder of guilt I realised that I was having my pity party after all, but at least there was no one here to see it.

A few bottles later I closed my eyes and put my foot down

onto the floor of the balcony, willing it to stay still.

It didn't.

Stupid disobedient floor.

I started to float upwards, starting with my shoulders, and then my head was cushioned beneath me. There was a pleasant heat in my chest, spreading out to warm my chilled limbs.

"Emmy," Sol said on a whispered sigh. "What are you doing?"

"Trying to stay out of earshot," I replied, or at least that's how the words sounded in my head. They came out in a barely decipherable slur, but Sol managed to translate.

"Of?"

"You. Alice."

"Ah."

I opened my eyes as my brain finally processed the fact that Sol was actually here, my head in his lap, his hand stroking my hair away from my face.

Here we were, just the two of us, and I didn't have a single shred of pride left in me. How could I?

It was time for the question.

"Do you have sex with all of them?" I asked bluntly.

I needed to find my peace with this, to find some peace with him, before I could move on. The more I tried to make myself forget about him, the more haunted I was by what I had lost, the fire burned out.

"You ask me this now? Are you sure you want to know my answer? Would you not prefer that I were the villain of this piece?"

"Not if it would be a lie," I replied.

His eyes shone down at me in the moonlight, looking more silver than I had ever seen them. I prepared myself for the blow, whatever the truth might be.

"As you wish," he said, looking away from me and up towards the stars. I pushed myself into a sitting position and curled up against him. I was too drunk to trust myself to sit up straight, although in all honesty the adrenaline from his presence had burned off some of the effect, but he'd given every indication that he didn't mind our proximity tonight.

May as well go for broke.

He paused for a moment.

"You are sure you wish to know?"

I nodded.

"Then the answer is no," he said softly. "I have not done so for many years now."

"And Alice?" I said, hating to ask but needing to know.

"No, Emilia."

I closed my eyes and listened to the gentle screeching of the bats reeling in the sky above us. I didn't even know that there were bats in London, but I supposed they probably got in everywhere.

"I'm not sure whether that makes it better or worse," I said finally.

"I know."

He pulled my knees onto his lap and wrapped his arms around me, pulling me closer. The affectionate gesture was a pleasant surprise after all that had passed between us in the past twenty-four hours.

"The brand does not burn?" he asked.

"Apparently not."

"Do you think that the human will tell others about it?"

"Who?" I asked. "Oliver?"

I hadn't thought about the possibility. He had no proof, and as far as I knew he only had one Silver he could tell, who was already well aware of the bond the brand betrayed.

"It's knowledge that he thinks gives him power over me," I thought aloud. "As soon as he uses that knowledge, he's spent all his bargaining chips. I don't think he's ready to do that yet. Besides, he doesn't know what it means."

"Are you certain?"

"I think so. Ben is using him as a pawn, not a confidant."

I pressed my cheek to his chest, smelling his scent through the thin cotton of his shirt.

"I must spend more time with you when you are

inebriated," he said. "You are much more…manageable."

"You didn't like it last time," I pointed out, remembering his reaction to my drinking session with Cam at the club.

"Last time you were a little less tactile. With me, at least."

"I was grumpy with you."

"And now?"

"Now I'm not," I replied simply.

Now I couldn't believe I'd ever pushed him away. What I had felt for him, what I still felt for him, had made me feel vulnerable and weak, so I'd denied that it was there. Toss in a healthy dose of confusion about my feelings for Drew and my only option had been retreat. When in doubt, I stood alone.

That was the problem, really. Self-sufficiency wasn't an option when more than my own existence hinged on my life.

I listened to his breath flowing in and out of his lungs, the movement soothing me with its regularity.

"So have you forgiven me for being a self-involved egomaniac?" I asked.

"I will if it will mean that you will stop putting yourself in harm's way."

"I'll try. I'm so sorry."

"Obstinacy is in your nature, and were circumstances different I would not ask you to temper it. It is who you are. You cannot be contained, will not comply, will not surrender."

I wondered at the fact that there was no censure in his tone, just quiet appreciation. He stroked my hair again and pressed his face to the top of my head in a kiss.

"It doesn't feel like this is over, Sol," I said quietly.

He trailed his fingers down my cheek and along my neck, pausing at my collarbone before travelling a little further down and gently tugging at the neck of my T-shirt to reveal the brand.

"It has to be."

"Because of Drew?"

"Not only him."

"It doesn't hurt."

I took his hand in mine and pressed his palm against Drew's brand. My skin sang at his touch, the heat building under the surface, but the pain never came. My heartbeat raced and his eyes locked with mine, his pupils large and dark in the shade of the flower-flecked vine curtain at our backs.

"Is this really just a distraction?" I asked.

He pressed his cheek against mine and whispered into my ear, his breath warm across my skin.

"It cannot be more."

"Why?" I asked, pressing my lips against his jawline as my hand curled around the other side of his face and came to rest at his neck.

"Emmy," he whispered, "this has to stop." But as he spoke he wrapped his hand gently into my hair and moved his head downwards, his lips tracing a line from my cheek to the crook of my neck.

"I don't believe you."

My breath caught in my throat as his teeth scraped against my skin and I imagined how it would feel for them to puncture it again. I pulled at the back of his head, pressing his mouth down on my neck as I shifted my position until I was straddling him on the bench. He pulled my ponytail down with one hand and wrapped the other tightly around my waist, drawing me close to him and making my back arch with the movement.

I shuddered at his proximity, eliciting a groan from Sol as I rubbed against him.

"No," he whispered, bringing his hands to my arms and gently pushing me away. He closed his eyes as if trying to compose himself, then raised one hand to my chin and looked into my eyes.

"We have to stop," he said.

"Why?" I asked again. "You keep saying that, but I'm not stopping until you tell me why."

"Firstly, you are inebriated."

"Yes," I said, "I know. So what?"

He raised his eyebrows at me, the half smile that I loved

playing at the corners of his mouth.

I placed my hands on either side of his face, looking into the depths of his dilated pupils.

"This is what I want, Sol. I want you."

Desire flared in his eyes, and I thought I had him for a moment, but then reason overruled him again and something like sorrow filled his expression.

"Your emotions are as changeable as the wind."

"We're living in confusing times."

"Perhaps, but our time has passed, Emmy, our window of opportunity gone. We cannot undo the brand," he said, touching his fingers to the tips of the silver mark on my chest. Little bursts of warmth flared under the skin, but the sensation wasn't unpleasant. "It will win out. It is time to move on."

"I could just stay drunk all the time," I suggested, but Sol shook his head.

"There is more to the brand than the pain. I have no idea what it might mean for you to defy it, to offer your blood, your body or your lips to another Silver. The risk is too great."

"And that's why?" I asked.

"It is the most compelling reason. Also, you smell of cigarettes."

I laughed and he treated me to another smile, which seemed to turn me melancholy almost instantly.

"I missed you," I said desperately, the words laying me bare. I didn't care.

He stroked his hand across my cheek and pulled my head towards him to press a kiss to my forehead.

"This is still goodbye," he said.

"Can goodbye wait until the morning?"

"The longer we leave it, the more difficult it will be."

"Just stay," I whispered. "Just hold me until the morning, and then you'll have your goodbye."

So he carried me inside and, gently removing my boots, laid me down on the bed beside him. Wilfully ignoring the prospect of tomorrow, I wrapped myself around his body and fell asleep peacefully in his arms. It was the best sleep I'd had all week.

CHAPTER XVIII

Sunday

I'd half expected to wake up and find that Sol had left, but it didn't hurt any less when I reached a sleepy arm across the bed to touch only the cool smoothness of the sheets. His clean yet exotic scent was still lingering in the air, but he was gone. I could feel the emptiness in the room, the void he had created by his departure.

At least I hadn't had to say goodbye.

I rubbed my eyes and tried to force them open, but they felt like they were glued together by the excesses of the previous night, so I squinted my way to the bathroom groggily. Brushing my teeth helped, but not even a boiling hot shower managed to put the warmth back in my bones.

I groaned, having to sit on the side of the bath as I brushed out my wet hair, and thought that I hadn't been this hungover since... well, Tuesday actually, but in the circumstances I decided to let myself off. I wished I hadn't had to wash my hair again today, but the lingering smell of the cigarettes made it something of a necessity.

It was still early, about eight o'clock in the morning. Last night had been eventful, but quick. I probably hadn't been out of bed yesterday for more than about eight hours in total, but it felt like a week's worth of activity had been crammed into that time.

I couldn't face proper clothes, and I didn't need to leave the apartment until the afternoon, so I found some soft cotton pyjamas and slipped them on, plaited my hair into a braid so it was out of the way and wrapped myself into a fleecy dressing gown that was hanging on the back of the bedroom door. A little more digging in the wardrobe turned up a new pair of slippers, which completed the hangover look.

I felt like a Weeper as I shuffled out of the bedroom, my eyes scrunched up against the light. I'd seen myself in the bathroom mirror, black bags under my puffy, bloodshot eyes, and thought it was a fairly apt comparison.

My nose detected something wonderful as I came down the stairs, a heavenly smell that called to my fragile, battered body.

"Mmmm?" I murmured as I turned towards the kitchen area to see Alice at the stove again.

"Morning!" she chirped at me, her blonde curls bouncing around her shoulders. She had managed to track down some pyjamas too, together with some slippers sporting fluffy rabbit ears, but despite her bright smile she looked like she was also nursing a sore head.

"You too?" I asked.

For a moment I thought she was going to continue to put a brave face on it, but then she nodded very carefully and pressed her hand against her forehead.

"Turns out that the Primus drinks very slowly. About one glass for every five of mine, in fact. And it would have been rude to give him only one glass…"

"Sounds about right."

"What about you?" she asked. "I thought you were going to bed."

"Yeah," I said, "but then I accidentally drank a shitload of bourbon."

"Accidentally?"

"That's my story, and I'm sticking to it. What's cooking?"

"I heard you get up, so I put some bacon on. I thought it might help."

"You're such a hero."

She smiled through what looked like a killer headache and I took a moment to appreciate how lucky I was to have her here with me. Here we were, in this amazing place, apparently under lockdown for the next few hours, and I finally had someone to talk to about Ben, someone human. Not that I much felt like talking right now, but I was grateful for her company nonetheless.

"So," I said, "Sol's gone. Does that mean Drew's better now?"

"Dunno," she replied. "I left the Primus on the sofa last night when I went to bed, shockingly early on in the evening I'm afraid, but he'd already left when I got down here this morning. So, I was thinking bacon sandwiches."

"Perfect."

I passed her the chopping board and she took a few slices off the loaf that had been in the bag I collected yesterday. It felt comfortable and homey, like Sunday mornings back at Cass's flat before the Revelation.

"I had no idea the Primus was such a nice guy," she said. "He's so intimidating on the broadcasts, but then he's so charming in person. And now we both have these chokers," she said as she touched the lace at her neck. "It's like we're in the same club or something."

"Mmm," I murmured noncommittally, not sure how to feel about it.

"And for all that protection, we have to do absolutely nothing."

"He said that?" I asked, intrigued. Hadn't he said something about coming to him willingly when he asked?

"Well, okay, we might occasionally have to let someone take a pint or so of blood for him, but it's not like we wouldn't have been doing that more regularly anyway without the chokers."

"What, no biting?" I was surprised. Was it really as simple as letting someone stick a needle in our arms so he could cultivate a select supply?

"Yeah, I was a bit disappointed. I'd be more than happy for him to sink his teeth into me." She paused. "Not just his teeth, actually."

"Alice!"

"Seriously, the man's delicious."

She didn't need to tell me that.

"Shame his girlfriend's such a bitch," she added.

"What?" I asked, a little taken aback. I wondered for a moment if she was talking about me.

"You know. Laila."

"Laila?" I repeated dumbly.

"He was telling me about it," she added.

He'd said nothing at all to me.

How could he not have told me? I couldn't believe it.

"Laila?"

"I know, right? Apparently she's his consort, or whatever."

A mess of emotions was running through me: jealousy, anguish and a fair dose of anger. How could he? All the time we had spent together last night, and he'd already been seeing Laila?

"But… why?" I said, more to myself than to Alice.

I was having a lot of trouble processing this. It was becoming apparent that I hadn't really considered last night to be a proper goodbye, but now he wasn't just rejecting me because of the brand, he was rejecting me because he'd found someone else.

And that just sucked.

"I guess it's like a monarchy," Alice said. "If you're a monarch then you have to get married and have kids to ensure the stability of your reign. If you're the Primus, maybe you take a consort and hold a Casting. Makes sense, right?"

"I suppose so."

I could understand that maybe the Primus had to show willing by settling down with a Silver, but of all the Silver he could have picked, he'd chosen Laila, who was an utter cow. She loathed humans, and was firmly entrenched in Ben's school of thought: humans were food, and nothing more.

But maybe that was the point. If he was trying to foster cohesion not only between Silver and humans but also amongst the Silver themselves, then it made perfect sense for him to take up with a Silver who was on the other side of the debate from his own. It didn't make their relationship real. It could just be a show, a display of unity.

I felt much better thinking about it that way than I did imagining that he'd fallen for her, hard-hearted bitch that she was, so I decided that it was undeniably an association of convenience. He couldn't feel anything for her, surely?

Alice checked on the bacon, then, as she got it out from under the grill, I grabbed a couple of plates and we each assembled a sandwich on the kitchen counter.

"So," I said as I squirted ketchup onto my bacon, slapping on my happy face again, "what shall we do for the rest of the morning?"

"I dunno, what do you want to do?"

I felt like my brain was pounding at the inside of my skull, and finding out about Laila had hollowed me out completely.

I groaned and rubbed my hands over my face.

"Honestly, I want to go back to bed and pretend the day hasn't started yet. I can't really face anything right now other than sitting on the sofa and doing nothing."

"Sounds good to me."

I took our plates over to the coffee table while Alice made us tea. I was looking through the DVD selection when a stroke of genius hit me and I followed up on it, discovering to my absolute joy that the sofa was in fact a sofa bed. It even had clean sheets and a duvet already made up on the foldaway mattress, ready for use.

"No way," Alice said as she carried our tea over.

"It's like the world knew we needed a duvet day."

I left her to choose a film while I ran upstairs to grab our pillows, and by the time I returned she had loaded an innocuous romantic comedy into the DVD player.

"We should do this every Sunday," I said as we both climbed into the bed and snuggled under the covers. I'd moved the coffee table that held our breakfast to what was now Alice's side of the bed, so she handed me my plate and mug and we settled in for the morning.

"Cheers," she said, tapping her mug against my own, and I smiled sleepily back at her. I may have been hungover and broken hearted, but I hadn't felt this safe and comfortable for weeks.

We spent the next couple of hours in a happy fog of tea and no-brain television, and eventually I began to feel normal again. Alice was actually really relaxing company, and it was amazing to be able to wrap myself in a safe cocoon of easy, human, female companionship and try to forget everything that was going on. I even succeeded to a certain extent, but I was still intermittently plagued by pangs of pain at the thought of Laila and Sol together, and by pangs of guilt and anxiety as I worried about Drew's recovery, and about Mia and Jane.

Alice and I took it in turns to make tea, and I was bringing her a fourth mug whilst she picked out a second film from the collection.

"Er, Emmy?" she said, looking down at the tea mug I was handing her as I tucked back into the sofa bed. "What happened to your bandage?"

Shit. I'd forgotten to put the dressings back on after my shower this morning.

"Oh. Well, see, the thing is…"

How did I explain this away? She inserted a DVD, climbed back into bed and then looked at me expectantly.

"It got better."

"Really?" She said sceptically. "In less than a week?"

"I heal quickly."

"Really."

She was obviously completely unconvinced.

"Maybe not entirely on my own. Look, I'm sorry, but I can't talk about it. If I could, I would, but it's just one of those things."

She reached for my hand, so I put my own mug down and let her see it.

"There isn't even a scar," she said.

"I know."

"And your knee?"

"That's better too."

Her eyebrows rose.

"So you've been faking with the bandages?"

I looked down at my hand in hers.

"I had to."

"What about the scratches on your face? The bite marks?"

"I couldn't cover them up, so I had to make them again."

She didn't speak, but I could tell she was feeling hurt that I had deceived her.

"Alice…"

She shook her head, like she couldn't understand what was going on.

This wasn't fair. She deserved to know what she was up against, and I needed to talk about it. To hell with Sol and his disclosure rules. I could trust Alice.

I took a deep breath.

"Benedict very nearly killed me on Wednesday," I said without emotion.

She went very still.

"What?"

"I was drained of most of my blood and then he left me on a rooftop outside the safe zone to die, either from the blood loss or at the hands of the Weepers."

I paused.

"Like I said, he's dangerous. He's nearly killed me three times now. The Weeper in the dorm? That was him too."

"So that's where you were on Thursday? Why didn't you say anything?"

"I shouldn't even be telling you this much."

"Are… are you okay?"

"Yes. One of the other Solis Invicti saved me." I paused, hesitating before I took the final, irreversible step towards the truth. "He healed me."

That was it. The cat was thoroughly out of the bag now.

"Healed you?"

"It's like a sort of magic they have, I suppose."

"Magic? Get serious, Emmy."

"I'm deadly serious," I replied, pulling down the neck of my T-shirt to show her the silver handprint.

She was silent for a moment, shock on her face as she digested my words. She reached out tentatively and rubbed gently at the brand, checking them to see that the shine hadn't transferred to her fingers, that it wasn't painted on.

"Cara Alton?" she asked.

I nodded.

"What does it mean?"

"It doesn't mean anything," I lied. "It's just a mark left behind by the healing. But it's very, very secret, so please don't say anything to anyone."

She was quiet for another few seconds.

"And they can all do this?" she asked.

"Only in certain, occasional circumstances. I was very lucky. Please don't tell anyone I told you that. Sol would be… unhappy."

"Of course I won't. Who healed you?"

"I really can't tell you that."

She nodded, apparently satisfied enough by the answers I'd given her.

"Okay then," she said.

So we watched a second film together as we both tried to come to terms with what we'd learned that morning. I managed to get about halfway through the film before I crashed out, the white noise of the television soothing me to sleep. I'd slept for hours last night, but apparently I still had some catching up to do.

I woke up again when the film had finished. It was already

the afternoon, so we tidied the sofa bed away and Alice went upstairs to get dressed so she could go over to the café. She was desperate to see if they'd cleared up the Square and to gather as much gossip as she could about the protest, but I was feeling so guilty about yesterday that I wasn't sure I'd ever go outside again.

After extracting several heartfelt promises from her that she wouldn't breathe a word to anyone about the apartment, Ben, my injuries, the Silver magic, Sol or anything else that she had learned over the past twenty-four hours, I gave her Drew's key to the apartment, which Sol had left on the kitchen table, asked her to bring me back some cake and waved her goodbye.

I contemplated getting out of my pyjamas, but reasoned that since I would have to change into my work clothes in a few hours I may as well not bother. I was too anxious to leave the apartment anyway.

I wondered how Drew was recovering. Would he have any scars, or would the traces of the gunshot be erased by whatever crazy healing processes the Silver employed? How long would it take? Ben had said at least twelve hours, but he'd been shot in the head. Surely that would take time to heal?

I was just contemplating what felt like the endless prospect of the few hours before work when a tapping noise at the patio door caught my attention. My heart raced with excitement and I turned around expectantly.

But it wasn't Drew; it was Ed, holding Nix in one arm and tapping on the glass of the door with his other hand. It had just started to rain again in big, fat droplets, so Ed had tucked Nix into his jacket and all I could see was her colourful face peering out from behind it.

The disappointment was utterly crushing, a hole opening in my chest, so I knew it was past time for my 'brand therapy'. Ed and Nix had become two of my favourite people.

I unlocked the door to let them both inside. "You found her!"

"Yeah, she was hiding away in one of the subways chasing mice. I finally tracked her down late yesterday, but then the curfew was in place so I thought I'd better wait until it lifted to bring her over."

Nix was nestled back in Ed's arms, happily purring and rubbing her face up against his chin.

"Looks like you've made a friend," I said.

He smiled at me happily.

"I like cats."

Fortunately, it looked like the people who used to live in the apartment had had cats of their own. Hell, for all I knew Nix might have been theirs. There were cat bowls and some food and biscuits, and even a cat flap set into one of the floor-to-ceiling windows leading onto the patio. She'd be able to come and go as she pleased here.

I filled up her bowls with food as Ed carried her over to set her on the floor in front of the tray designed to hold them.

"Better than rodents, right?" I said as I put a plate of food in front of her.

She eyed me dubiously, unconvinced, but settled down to her meal when I tickled her behind the ears.

"Can I get you a drink?" I asked Ed.

"I've got to shoot off, actually, but thanks."

"Any news about Drew?"

"None that I've heard. Sorry."

"No, I'm sorry," I said, flushing as I remembered Sol's harsh words. "I behaved like an idiot yesterday. It was my fault that it happened at all."

Guilt twisted in my stomach. It had been my fault he was shot, my fault Ben had nearly got to me, my fault…

"It's okay, Emmy. It's not like you could stop a bullet. And he'll be fine, I'm sure."

A thought occurred to me.

"Hey, Ed, you did see Mary and her girls back here safe yesterday, right?"

I thought that maybe Oliver had hijacked them on their way to the club, but I knew I was wrong when Ed looked a little affronted.

"Of course," he said. "I saw them all the way to the dorm."

"Okay, thanks."

He made as if to leave.

"Why do you ask?"

"I just… haven't seen them, that's all." I didn't want to panic him. I'd made his life difficult enough already. "Thanks for finding Nix."

He smiled.

"She's a cute kitten. Maybe I'll come visit."

"Whenever you like. Carrie, too."

I locked the door behind him and shucked out of my dressing gown, feeling too warm to wear it. I decided I needed more caffeine, so I fired up the kettle and made myself another cup of tea. At this rate, I was going to run out of milk.

There was another tapping at the patio door as I spooned the teabag into the bin and I whirled around expectantly once more.

Finally, there he was.

The wind was whipping his dark hair across his face, the rain splashing heavily against his leather jacket as it thudded down on him.

I needed him, suddenly and extremely.

I dropped the spoon on the countertop and ran across to the glass doors, pulling them open, and catapulted myself into his arms, jumping up to wrap my legs around his waist.

"You're okay," I murmured into his neck. "I'm sorry, so sorry…"

The rain soaked my thin pyjamas in seconds, plastering them to my skin as Drew pulled me to him. He stepped inside, carrying me with him, and locked the door behind us.

"It's okay, Emmy. I'm fine."

I lifted my head from his neck and ran my hands through his hair, checking for traces of the gunshot that had thrown him backwards as I watched yesterday. There was nothing.

Every mark was gone, every imperfection erased.

"I'm so sorry. I shouldn't have been there."

"It's okay," he said soothingly, his silvered emerald eyes mapping my face like it had been weeks, instead of hours, since I had seen him last. "I missed you," he said.

The words, echoing my own confession to Sol last night, jarred awkwardly in my chest. I looked away, a little ashamed of myself. Now that Drew was here, I was yearning for him, aching to kiss his lips and taste his skin.

Sol was right: the brand would win.

How had I let things get so messed up?

Drew moved his hands to my waist so I slid down until my feet touched the floor, then he curved his hand around my cheek and gently tipped my face up so I looked into his eyes.

"What's wrong?"

"It's the brand," I said.

"It's bad?"

I could barely restrain myself from rubbing up against him and moaning. I knew what was coming, knew he'd have to put his hands on me again and forge that maddening connection, and all I felt was impatient desire. I wanted him to touch me, now, and not just on the brand.

"It's bad," I whispered.

He inhaled and his eyelids flickered for a moment.

"Yup," he said unsteadily, "it's bad."

My cheeks flushed as I imagined what he would be scenting.

Stupid vampire senses.

In a split-second I was in his arms again and he was carrying me across the apartment.

"Upstairs," I said breathlessly.

He hesitated for a moment.

"You're sure?"

"No, but take me there anyway."

"Emmy…"

"Just do it, Sol."

Drew stopped dead.

The world stopped moving.

"Sol?" he said.

I felt like I was falling through a hole in the centre of the earth, my stomach plummeting so fast it made me nauseated.

"That doesn't mean anything," I said.

He set me on my feet and stepped away. I became acutely aware that I was standing in front of him in thin cotton pyjamas that were soaking wet, so completely see-through, and quickly crossed my arms over my chest.

Turning away with a noise of exasperation, he watched the rain running down the glass and pushed his hands back through his hair.

"He was here with you last night."

I nodded. I wondered whether someone had told him, or if he could smell his presence in the room. He probably worked it out; without Drew around, Sol was the only person who could really protect me from Ben.

"And?" he asked.

"And what?"

"Emmy, at some point you're going to have to make a decision. Do you want to give us a chance or do you want to let him destroy you? Because if it's the latter, I'd really like to know so I can stay the hell away from you."

"I've told you it's over."

It had to be, Sol had made that much clear last night. My feelings were irrelevant.

"And you know he's with Laila?"

Despite myself, that knife just kept on twisting.

"I know that," I gritted out between my teeth. "I've said my goodbyes."

"That doesn't mean anything if you're thinking of him every second you're with me."

"What?"

"With or without the brand, I'm not going to hang around while you reject me and pine after him," he said, his voice rising to a shout.

"You said that this… whatever this is, was enough for

you."

"Well it's not, okay? How do you expect it to be, when every other day I have to connect with the brand, to put us so close together I feel like you're under my skin?" He backed me against the wall and pressed his leg between mine to pin me there, his hands either side of my head caging me in his arms. When he spoke, his voice was deep and ragged. "This bond is getting stronger, not weaker, and every time I touch you it runs a little deeper, the hooks burrowing into my flesh."

"Drew…"

"Now you can remember my name," he rasped.

His eyes locked with mine, filled with fierce possession. He moved one of his hands from the wall behind me and curved it over my waist to pull my hips tight against his. His chest was pressed against mine, his lips inches away, and the movement rubbed his leg against my core.

I moaned.

"You won't forget it again, Emmy."

He grabbed the neck of my pyjama top with both hands and pulled it until it ripped down to my navel, revealing the brand shining under the surface of my skin.

"This is mine," he said, touching the tip of his index finger to its silver silhouette on my chest. A thread of pleasure pulled through me, pulsing to the single point of contact on the brand. I stared into his eyes as they dilated black, their intensity interrupted for a moment as the sensation took him.

"This is my brand," he continued as he pressed each of his fingertips into place on my flesh, the pressure notching up and building with each subsequent connection.

He leaned into me, his forehead pressing against mine as he looked down into my eyes. The urge to press my lips against his, to breathe him into me, was almost irresistible. But if I did so, he'd mark me with his scent and then the secret would be well and truly out.

"You are mine," he growled as he thrust his palm down onto my flesh, dragging the waves of ecstasy through me until my head tipped back against the wall, pushing my chest further into his hand. The involuntary movement bared my throat to him and before I had realised that the gesture had issued an invitation his mouth was at my neck, his free hand moving up to rip the new choker away.

Somehow I managed to gather together enough composure to stop him.

"Not the neck!" I gasped urgently, trying to push him away from me with both hands. "Drew, don't! It'll heal silver."

If he bit me, his mouth on my broken skin would trigger the healing process, leaving threads of silver tracing across the wound. There was no way I could hide a silver bite mark on my neck, not even under the choker.

He growled again in the back of his throat and pressed harder on the brand, pushing me into the wall as his skin melded into mine. Then he trailed his mouth down my body to where the torn shirt had exposed the curve of the upper side of my breast and, pushing it up from below, sank his teeth in.

I cried out as he punctured the skin, but I was in no pain. Bliss thrilled through me as he pulled blood from my veins, the suction only enhancing the tugging sensation of the brand until it built to a peak that was almost painful in its intensity. Then it broke.

His teeth pulled out and he pressed his head against my shoulder, yelling as we flipped over the edge.

"Emmy," he whispered.

My legs were no longer able to carry my weight and we slid down the wall together until we were curled up on the floor as he licked at the bite. When the wound was closed he laid his head on my chest and wrapped his arms around me, his dark hair spreading in a messy shadow around his head.

"Emmy?"

I didn't know how to feel. The brand had done its magic, leaving me unsure how things had got this far. Again.

"Please don't push me away this time," he said, lifting his head to look into my eyes.

I shuffled backwards and out of his arms, sitting up with

my back against the wall, and pulled my shirt together across my chest. I felt hollowed out and raw, like I'd been violated by my own treacherous emotions, by the brand.

But I'd been expecting it this time.

"Please, Emmy," he said. "Don't shut me out. We have to talk about this."

This time, there was no shock, no outrage at the effect of the brand. This time, I wanted him to gather me up in his arms and hold me. I wanted to taste his lips, to run my fingers through his hair and hold his face to mine.

I didn't trust it at all.

"It makes me feel things that aren't real," I whispered, looking down at my hands.

"No, it's real."

The illusion of safety was back, the feeling that I was home when I was in his arms, the absolute certainty in my bones that he would shield me from the world.

"It's too much for it to be real," I said.

"But it is."

I met his eyes, the irises suffused with the silver that marked the bond. Our bond.

CHAPTER XIX

"I want to talk about the Casting," he said.

"I thought you might."

If he was trying to start off with an easy subject then he'd picked the wrong one. But then, nothing we had to talk about was easy.

I wrapped my dressing gown over my torn pyjamas and settled down on the sofa with my tea. Drew took a seat next to me, leaving a careful distance between us. I wasn't going to be the one to close the gap, not when I was still so unsure about what had passed between us through the brand.

I'd agreed not to run away this time, to stick around and talk it out. We'd had precious little time together since I'd learned the truth about Jeff and Sarah's deaths, so I felt I owed it to him.

Also, much though I hated to admit it, I was reluctant to let him to leave.

"Viv told me you don't want to do it."

"You know I don't want to be Silver."

"You don't want to live forever?"

"Not particularly. Not in this world."

Not as a monster that would have to drink human blood to survive, that would be part of this dominant regime. Oliver was an idiot, but a rebellious part of me was with him in spirit.

"Do you think anything could change your mind?" he asked quietly.

I looked at him appraisingly as I sipped my tea.

"I'm mortal, and you don't want to die," I said, the truth of the statement self-evident.

"Don't get me wrong; I wouldn't want to carry on living without you, but I'm worried that if you don't turn Silver we won't even have a human lifetime together."

I shook my head in disbelief. He was talking about the big, forever love.

"You want something I'm not sure I can give you. Bond or not, you can't manufacture emotion. It's either there or it's not."

"It's there, Emmy. You know it's there."

I pushed a few loose strands of hair away from my face and leaned towards him. If I needed to be brutal to get my point across then that's what I'd have to do.

"There's something there," I said, "but it's not love."

"Not yet."

"Maybe not ever. And how will that make you feel? If nothing changes and, after a few years, I move on?"

"I'll be miserable for a few hundred years."

I looked at him meaningfully.

"Would you rather I died?" he asked incredulously.

"No!"

"Then why are you agonising over this? I'll die when you do, until the bond fades. Give me a couple of centuries to get over it. And in the meantime, for a little while at least, give us a chance."

Here comes the painful part of the conversation, I thought.

"What does that entail?" I asked.

His face clouded over, determination setting his jaw. He knew what I was asking.

"It means you and me being the only people in this relationship."

"You might not like it, but I can't change how I feel, Drew, or who I think about."

"Maybe not, but can you try?" he asked desperately. "It's not like Sol will be thinking about you anymore, Emmy. You do know that?"

I shrugged.

"Maybe not," I said.

"Definitely not. The Silver bond gives you something of a one-track mind."

"What?"

He furrowed his brow.

"I thought you said you knew? Sol's silvered for Laila."

That's why his eyes had been so bright last night. What had he said? Something about Drew not being the only reason we had to stop seeing each other?

But he'd never said, never even mentioned her.

I didn't think it was possible for it to hurt any more than it already did, but that knife just kept on turning. The floor fell out of my stomach and I was in freefall again.

"He's silvered?" I whispered, unable to meet Drew's eye.

"There's a lot of it going around," he said. "Something about us all being together in such close quarters. He's the fifth this week, by my count."

So last night really had been goodbye. That was it. He was gone. There was no going back from this.

I tried to push it down, push it away. I could take out the pain and brood over it later, but not now.

He was in love with a vampire bitch, and sooner or later her poison would start infecting him. We were insects under her feet and before long Sol would see us the same way, would see me the same way. I had a feeling that life was about to get inexorably more unpleasant for humans in the near future.

"Do you believe me now when I say it's over?" I asked.

We sat in silence for a few moments.

"And us?" he asked. "Will you give us a chance?"

It felt like it was too soon, and before I even thought about it my head started shaking of its own accord.

"Will you give it a week?" he asked. "The Casting's more than a week away."

It was always a week with Drew. A week to decide whether or not I could tolerate life as a human ruled by the Silver, a week to decide whether or not I could love him, a week to decide whether or not I'd make him die with me.

That was a power I didn't want to wield.

"And the risks?" I asked, remembering my conversation with Sol. "What if I die when you try to turn me?"

"It won't happen," he said, putting my tea on the coffee table and taking my hands in his. "You see the silver in my eyes." He put his hand to the brand, and even through the dressing gown I felt the tendrils of desire rush to meet the touch of his fingers. "You're marked by my brand. There's no danger here, Emmy."

"I don't want to become something I'm not," I whispered.

"You won't. You'll still be the woman I love. Turning Silver won't change that, but it might save both of our lives."

He took his hand from my chest and ran his fingers through the loose hairs at the back of my neck, his touch gentle and coaxing. My mind flashed back to last night, Sol's hand wrapped tightly into my ponytail as he pulled my head back to bare my neck, demanding and in control. He inveigled me with his words but his actions were imbued with confidence and devoid of hesitation.

Drew persuaded me with his touch.

The flash of comparison was unwelcome and sobering. I pulled away from Drew and sat back into the sofa, picking up my tea to stand as a barrier between us.

"What happens if it doesn't work?" I asked. "Would I die instantly?"

"It's irrelevant. It'll work, I promise you."

"I haven't agreed to it yet."

He sighed and mirrored my pose on the sofa.

"You wouldn't feel any pain," he said in a hollow tone of voice. "It would be over in a second. For both of us."

I nodded to myself, thinking it over.

"I wouldn't even be suggesting this if I thought it posed the slightest risk to you."

I believed him. Every part of me was irrationally convinced that he would always act in my best interests and that he would always protect me. It was an insidiously dangerous conviction and I mistrusted it on instinct. It had to be an effect of the bond, of the brand.

But that didn't mean it wasn't true.

"How would it feel? How would I change?"

"I'm not sure. I was born this way."

"Tommy told me."

He nodded.

"I've heard stories from those who have been turned Silver, including Tommy," he said, "and I've watched it happen."

"Does it hurt?"

"Yes," he said quietly. "The Silver blood burns through your body, healing and replacing. It makes you quicker, stronger, more sensitive. That takes some getting used to. For a while, everything will seem like it's too much, but you'll learn to filter things out. When the whites of your eyes silver, it's over."

"How long does it take?"

"It depends."

"On?"

"How strong you are. How strong the bond is. A lot of different things."

"How long would it take for me?"

"I can't tell you that, Emmy. That's part of what the Casting is designed to figure out. There will be tests."

"What kind of tests?"

He smiled a vulpine grin.

"For someone who doesn't want to turn Silver you're asking a lot of questions about the Casting."

I tutted in irritation.

"Are you trying to convince me here, or what?"

He smiled again, thinking he'd already won this one.

"I don't know what the tests will be. Would you like to find out?"

"I'll think about it," I said.

The grin was still there.

"That's not a 'yes'," I added.

"I know."

I drank my tea quietly for a few seconds while he watched, following the movement with his eyes.

"I'd rather you weren't here," he said.

I was confused.

"What do you mean?"

"I'd rather that you were at my apartment. I could keep you safe there, and you'd be hidden from prying eyes."

"You can't lock me away, Drew."

"It would probably be safer for both of us if I could."

There was no way I was going to let that happen, but I didn't think he was serious in any case.

"I really am sorry about your head," I said.

"You're not very good at doing what you're told."

As Sol had made crystal clear to me yesterday. Even the recollection of his disappointment tightened my chest. But what did it matter what he thought, when he'd silvered for that human-hating witch?

"I'll work on it," I said.

"It would help my stress levels. You have a habit of getting yourself into trouble, and you're too much of a target to be wandering around the city unprotected. The choker will help, but nothing will stop Ben if he catches you on your own."

"I know."

He shook his head in despair.

"I keep losing you, Emmy. First you leave the broadcast when you're supposed to be going into the safe house, then when I track you down you go racing into Sol's arms, and now that we finally have a chance to work things out you're taking every opportunity to put yourself in Ben's way. Or Sol's."

"I know, Drew." I thought I couldn't feel any worse about it than I already did, but I was wrong. I'd never considered what it must have been like for Drew, what he must have gone through over the past ten days since we'd first met.

"I'm not sure you do. You never stand still, never do what I think you're going to do. It's like trying to protect a moth from a flame." He inhaled and closed his eyes for a second, then fixed me with his gaze.

"When I got to the safe house on that day, the day after the Revelation, and you weren't there… I knew you had run. I searched and searched for you, round the whole city, and when we found you, you were so convinced that I was a monster, that I was a murderer, but you couldn't see that in Sol. How could you put the two of us side by side and think that Sol was more moral, that he was a better person than me?"

"What are you saying?" I asked, sensing that he was hinting at something greater.

He leaned back in his seat.

"God, Emmy, if you only knew. But you weren't going to listen to me, so I had to watch. I had to watch him paw at you, watch him mark you, smell his scent all over you and see the scars of his teeth in your throat. Worst of all, I had to watch you wanting him, watch you welcome in the darkness he brings."

"What darkness?"

"He's Sol Invictus, the unconquered sun."

"So it's true then? He's a god?"

"That depends on your perspective. There's a reason he earned that name, Emmy, and it's not just because of the colour of his hair. During the day the sun shines, but what happens at night?"

"It goes away?" I hazarded.

"It's overcome by darkness. You can only break the horizon in the morning if you're pulled beneath it at dusk. Every day he leaves the darkness behind him, but if he's dragged you down into it with him then that's where you'll stay, waiting for him to come back to the night. He'll always rise again, but one day you'd stay behind, alone in the dark."

I remembered the black anonymity of my encounter with Sol on the terrace, and again last night on the balcony, the comforting warmth as the night wrapped around us, permissive and intoxicating.

Then the morning after, the shock of self-conscious realisation, the stark vulnerability of exposure when the dark blanket was pulled away. That was then, but this morning there was nothing but an aching desire for his return.

"You can call him a god," he continued, "but some call him other names. I wasn't lying when I said he'd break you."

"Nor was I when I said it was over, Drew."

I didn't want to keep dredging this up, to keep rehearsing events that had already happened. There was no going back from here, and I knew it.

His eyes flicked to my throat.

"You're still wearing his collar."

"And you know why."

"I don't have to like it. You know that I've officially committed treason by biting you?"

"Well, I'm already wearing high-necked T-shirts to cover the brand so no one's going to see the mark, and I'm not going to tell anyone. Are you?"

He smiled at me. That was a no, then.

"Would my teeth grow?" I asked.

"What?"

"You know, would I get vampire fangs if I turned Silver?"

He chuckled in the back of his throat.

"No, our teeth are just like yours, just a bit sharper."

He opened his mouth to show me. They looked pretty normal.

"They don't look that sharp."

"They are, and don't forget that we have the extra speed and strength to pierce through the skin cleanly, so the wounds are neat."

The mark on my breast had healed under his mouth, the skin knitting together with threads of silver lining the breaks. It would last a day or so, the silver gradually dispersing into the skin until it was gone entirely. Unlike the brand, which was apparently here to stay.

I finished my tea and put my cup down on the table, my eyes lingering on my hand, on the unmarked spot where I had cut myself on a bottle last week, the wound that had healed when Drew had branded me.

"You know when you healed me, on the rooftop outside the barricades?"

I assumed that was what had happened, but all I could remember before I had passed out was Sol calling for someone to get Drew. He'd known I was nearly dead.

Drew's face twisted with anguish, shying away as if I'd slapped him.

"I remember."

"Why didn't it leave any silver in the wounds? They just healed up, like they were never there."

"I don't know. It's a different process, I guess. I wasn't healing individual wounds, I was trying to get your whole body to heal itself in one go, like I was sending an electric current through you."

"And you knew how to do that?"

"Not really," he said, his expression thoughtful. "I wasn't really thinking at all. It was just instinct. I did what felt right, and it worked. Thank god."

He leaned forward and wrapped his arms around me, scooping me up until I was sitting across his lap, my head resting against his shoulder. I didn't stop him, the warmth of his arms around me soothing and strong.

"I could feel you dying," he whispered. "First in the club with Charles, then on that roof. I knew you were slipping away. It was like your heart was stuttering in my chest."

"Can you feel the bond like that?" I asked, curious about how much he might experience with me.

"Only in certain circumstances."

"When I'm in pain?"

"If you stub your toe, then no, but if your life is actually leaving your body then the bond gets stretched thin and I feel like it's going to blink out and take me with it. It came like a rush on the night of the Revelation. As soon as I saw you it flowed through me, sinking its claws into my skin, tingling across my eyeballs and into my soul."

He made it sound like an assault, like an invasion, like a disease. It wasn't something he had welcomed or wanted, it was just something that had happened. Something he was stuck with.

There was no romance in it.

"Now there's the brand," he continued, "and the bond has changed. When I'm touching you, the brand is like a feedback loop, enhancing and intensifying every second of the experience, designed to make me sensitive to your pleasure. And now I can always feel it, whether or not it's me causing it."

Oh god.

"So, last night…"

"If I hadn't been immobilised by the healing process, I would have been over here like a shot." His arms tightened around my body, then he shifted me over back onto my side of the sofa and leaned away. "Every time he touches you I feel it, vibrating under my skin, phantom reactions that have nothing to do with me."

Did he really want me to apologise for how I felt about Sol?

"I don't know what you expect me to say."

"Nothing. He's the Primus, and he takes what he wants. I just hope that's not you anymore."

There was a clattering noise behind us and I jumped to my feet, suddenly remembering that Alice had a key.

"Hey Emmy," she said absently as she walked in, "still in your PJs? So I got you lemon drizz…"

She froze on the spot as she registered Drew's presence.

"Er, sorry. I, uh, didn't mean to interrupt."

"You're not interrupting," I said. "I was about to get changed for work. Alice, this is Drew."

"I know," she whispered, still standing in the doorway.

I rolled my eyes and turned back towards Drew to see his eyes fixed on Alice's throat, where the dark lace contrasted against her pale skin.

"Ben saw her," I explained to him. "Sol's trying to keep her safe, so she's got the choker. And she's sort of moved in here."

He raised his eyebrow at me and I realised that Alice staying here with me might have put a crimp in his plans for tonight, and every night after that. It would be difficult for us to get close to each other with Alice chaperoning.

"If things are too cramped then I can find space for you elsewhere," Drew said to me.

But I wasn't about to let him lock me away in his apartment.

"Thanks, but there's plenty of room. Alice and I are very happy being roomies."

I smiled at him, wilfully misunderstanding the intention behind his offer as Alice snapped out of her stupor.

"Can I get you a drink, Secundus?" she asked.

"Thanks, but no."

"Well, I'm going to go and get changed," I said. "Alice is here, and we're both perfectly safe, as you can see, so you don't need to hang around."

"Actually, Alice, on second thought I'd really love a coffee if you have some," he said, smirking at me.

"Of course!"

Alice beamed at him then bustled off to the kitchen.

I glared at Drew and took myself upstairs to switch clothes and put my fake bandages on. By the time I got back downstairs Drew was sitting on the sofa with his coffee, whilst Alice pushed things around in the fridge. She heard my footsteps on the stairs and shouted up to me.

"I'm making cheese and ham toasties for lunch. You want some?"

"Sure," I replied. It didn't seem like it had been that long since breakfast, but given how late our shifts finished we probably wouldn't have a chance to eat again until tomorrow.

"Alice has been telling me about your friends the rebels," Drew said.

"My friends?" I asked.

"Mia and Jane," Alice said from the kitchen area.

"Has anyone seen them?" I asked.

"No," Drew said.

"No one's seen Mary either," Alice added.

"Shit. They've got them, haven't they?"

"Or they've decided to join them," Drew said.

"No," Alice said. "Mary wouldn't do that to her kids. They were pretty safe here, all things considered. They didn't have to donate, they had jobs at the Palace, they were far away from the Weepers. She wouldn't put them in danger."

"Did you find out anything else at the café?" I asked her.

"Just that there are more of them than we thought. I didn't expect so many people to be lining up to support them, but I guess a lot of people haven't got anything left to lose."

"What are you going to do?" I asked Drew. As Secundus, security was his job.

"We're dealing with it."

"How?"

"We have a plan."

"And you can't tell us?" He met my gaze. "Of course not. Well, Sol promised that Mia and Jane would be safe, okay?"

"Okay," he said solemnly as he took a sip of his coffee.

"Oh, hey, Alice?" I said, remembering Ed's visit of earlier today.

"Yeah?" she said as she plated up the toasted sandwiches and put two on the coffee table: one for me and one for Drew.

"Ed found Nix. Last I saw her she was asleep on your bed."

"I can't believe it!" she said, and ran upstairs to her room to see the little tortoiseshell kitten.

"We're leaving in five minutes," I yelled after her.

"Yeah, okay."

I sighed and dropped down onto the sofa next to Drew, pulling a plate into my lap.

"You don't have to babysit me every moment of the day, you know."

"What if I want to?" he asked.

"Then everyone will work out the bond and then we're both screwed."

I bit into my toastie and watched him as he did the same. It was so strange to watch him do something as normal as eating. It was so easy to forget that he was Silver, to think that he was just like one of us. But that's what it was now: us and them. I had to choose.

"Alice wants to turn Silver," I said between mouthfuls.

"Sensible girl, but bad circumstances."

"Tommy said he'd sponsor her if I let you sponsor me."

Drew paused with the sandwich halfway to his mouth.

"Did he now?"

"Yes."

"Has he met her?"

"I don't know. Can you find out if he's genuine?"

He put his sandwich back onto his plate and fixed me with his gaze.

"Are you telling me you're willing to go ahead with the Casting?" he asked.

"No. I'm still thinking about it."

"But you're considering it?"

I hesitated. I was scared of turning Silver, scared of what it might make me become, but I didn't want to die this week either. The way things were going, I thought it was unlikely that I'd last long as a human, and that meant the end of Drew too. There was Alice to consider as well, who was only in danger because I'd put her there.

It was time for me to get serious and stop being selfish.

"Yes."

CHAPTER XX

I was on the top bar again tonight with Pru and Ella. It seemed to work out well the night before last and I didn't want to go shifting people around before they'd really got the hang of things.

Drew had left just before Alice and I headed downstairs, but said he'd be back later that night. He didn't even try to explain that one away to Alice. She'd asked me about it as we headed down the stairs to the club, jumping to the inevitable conclusion that we were involved.

I'd had to lie to her.

I didn't feel good about it. She was the closest human friend I had in this place and I was keeping so much from her, but this was no time for honesty. There was too much at stake and, much though I was fond of Alice, she had a big mouth. I could only hope that she'd manage to keep the secrets she already knew.

Pru looked like she was struggling tonight. The bar was busier than it had ever been, people crushing up against the wood at the beginning of the night until the Invicti had to settle them down. It took no more than their appearance for things to become a lot more orderly.

I'd set out the tables inside again, trying to keep the

atmosphere relaxed, but although the bar was busy most people seemed to be heading out of the room to the roof and the terrace. The rain had stopped a few hours ago, so I'd cranked up the terrace wall and let the sunset in, the colours in the sky suffusing the light with a pinkish hue.

Red sky at night. It was going to be a beautiful day tomorrow.

The problem was that everyone drinking outside made every errand to clear tables about ten times more difficult because we had to go out and climb up to the top of the building to collect the glasses. That left just two people on the bar for much longer than would otherwise be the case, so we were feeling distinctly short handed.

Pru set out the latest load of dirty glasses on the bar and I shuttled them to the glass washer.

"It's insane out there," she said. "People keep trying to give me drink orders, and they're so... handsy." She shuddered. "The Invicti have thrown out about fifty people already."

"Wow," I said, "you must have been getting some serious action."

"They're not just chucking people out for that." She pushed a few strands of her long, brown hair out of her eyes. "They're all getting drunk."

"On the roof?" Ella asked as she pulled a pint of lager.

"Sounds dangerous," I said.

"Yeah, well, they're pretty rowdy," Pru continued as she swung round the bar to help me stack the washer. "They're saying some dangerous things. I think things might be about to blow up."

I nodded grimly.

"I'm getting that feeling. Can you two manage here while I take the next glass run?"

"Sure," Ella said.

Pru smiled, obviously relieved that she didn't have to go back outside.

Things were a little quieter now, everyone having already

loaded up on alcohol, and it seemed like behind the bar was the safest place to be. I didn't want to keep sending Pru and Ella out into the scrum, even if they were wearing Sol's choker.

I could see Tommy on the corner of the terrace, and I knew he'd keep an eye on me. I'd be safe. I made a beeline for him, collecting a few glasses on my way. He was standing on his own in watchful mode, keeping an eye on the tables in his view.

"How's it going?" I asked him as I drew near.

"This was a bad idea, Emmy."

"What?"

"This humans drinking thing. They're going to get themselves in trouble. This isn't the political climate for Dutch courage."

He might have been right, but Sol could hardly take it back now.

"What's done is done," I said.

"A lot of Silver are upset, and too many idiot humans are making threats they can't even hope to back up with action. This is going to end badly."

"Everyone keeps saying that."

"Well, it's true," he said. "The sooner you're Silver the better."

I turned to scoop up the glasses on the tables around us, not sure I wanted to have this conversation. I was still mulling things over.

"I've spoken to Drew," he said.

"Already?"

"He stopped by. I know the girl."

"And?"

"And she won't get through the first round, but if you want me to sponsor her then I will, as long as you'll keep to the deal."

"What's the first round?"

"I don't know."

I looked at him dubiously as I stacked the glasses on my

hip.

"Look," he said quietly, "they're not going to let these kids get through the first round, whatever it is, unless they have some kind of connection with their sponsor. A connection is a prerequisite. If they get to the end of the selection process then they have to take it all the way, do or die. She's not going to get that far."

"Would I?" I asked, the whole thing suddenly seeming very real.

"I hope so," he whispered, turning away from me as a group of guys took a seat at a table next to us, "for your and Drew's sakes."

I'd not even decided to put myself in the running, and already I was feeling intimidated at the prospect of the challenges I'd have to overcome to have even a chance of turning Silver. My nervousness was only exacerbated by Tommy's lack of confidence.

I walked back into the building and put the glasses on the bar then headed up to clear the roof terrace. On the furthest corner, half hidden behind a planter filled with small trees, I found exactly what I was expecting: Oliver and a bunch of his friends sitting secretively around a table. So they'd come up here to hide, to make sure they weren't overheard.

I was glad they'd actually listened to my warning of the other night, but disconcerted to note how many other huddles of humans seemed to be here for the same reason. No Silver on the roof tonight.

Oliver saw me the moment I crested the top of the stairs. I'd been hoping to eavesdrop for a while, but it didn't look like that was going to happen so I decided to take the direct approach.

"Oliver," I said as I made my way across the roof towards his group, collecting glasses as I went.

"Emmy." He dipped his head in an incongruously respectful gesture, and I was instantly on the alert.

"What's going on?"

He exchanged glances with the group of people sitting

around him, a couple of teenagers and four men and women in their twenties or thirties, then stood up and crossed the roof towards me.

"Can we talk?" he asked.

"What, again? I thought you'd said all you had to say yesterday. You know, when you threatened two of my friends? Two of my very young friends?"

He took the stack of glasses from my hands and set it down on a nearby table, ushering me quickly towards a quieter area of the roof.

"Look, I had to say something. You were going to tell the Silver about us."

"I did," I said frankly, not willing to let him be under any illusions as to whose side I was on. "You threatened Jane and Mia, and I made sure that they won't be hurt. I can't speak for the rest of you."

He just looked at me.

Then everything was clear, clicking into place in my mind. I couldn't believe I'd been so stupid.

"You knew I was going to tell them." Dammit, he'd played me.

"Yes."

"And Jane and Mia?"

"They're safe, I promise you."

"Then what was the point of that whole ruse?"

His grey eyes flicked briefly away before settling back on my face.

"It wasn't a ruse. I haven't told you anything that wasn't the truth. You chose how to act on that information."

"Why?" I asked, unable to fathom why he'd want me to tell the Silver about Jane and Mia if the information was true. Did he want them to hesitate, to think twice before killing them all?

"You know why I can't tell you that," he said.

He was right not to trust me. I'd tell Drew in the blink of an eye.

"I wanted to offer you one last chance," he continued.

"One last chance to join us, to help us change the world."

His bright eyes were intense, staring into mine, the breeze picking at strands of his hair and blowing them away from his face.

"The world's already changed and there's no way you can change it back."

"No, but we can make it better." He hesitated for a moment then reached out and took my hand in his. "I know this isn't the life you wanted to lead. I know you're trapped as much as we are, maybe even more so. That mark on your chest, it's a symbol people can get behind."

"You don't even know what it is," I said, trying to pull my hand away, but he caught it in both of his own and squeezed.

"Yes I do," he said. "I know all about it. It's a violation, an imposition. The Silver call it a brand."

A shiver ran down my spine. Ben had been speaking out of school again.

"I know how to break it, Emmy."

"So do I," trying again to pull my hand away, "but I don't want anyone to die. I don't want a war, Oliver. They'd wipe us out. Surely you can see that?"

"I know another way."

I stopped struggling. He knew a way to get rid of the brand without killing Drew? I wanted to ask whether it would break the bond as well, but I didn't want to tell him about that unless he already knew.

So I said nothing.

"Don't you want to be free?" he asked. "This brand, it's got you caged and contained. You're a slave to it, and I know you're not the type to submit. It's got to be scratching under your skin, that chain around you, controlling not just your actions but your emotions as well. Do you even remember what it's like to have nothing in your head, nothing in your heart, but you?"

I was quiet for a moment, trying to piece together how much of my feelings in the past few days had been real and how much had been down to the brand. The truth was that I didn't even know anymore which emotions were real and which were fabricated.

"How?" I asked.

"I can't tell you unless you're with us."

It would mean betraying Drew and Sol, betraying all my Silver friends. Other than Alice, Mary and the girls, they were all I had. They meant more to me than anyone else still alive in this world.

"I'm trying to help you," Oliver said, leaning forward to catch my eye. "And I have answers. We can save you from this."

"I'm not sure I want to be saved."

"And is that how you feel, or how this brand is making you feel? How do you know?"

I couldn't answer that question, because I didn't know. But what I did know was that even before the brand I had given up fighting. Whatever Oliver said, this was a fight the humans would never win.

"You'll still end up killing us all. The brand is irrelevant."

He tipped his head back in exasperation and exhaled.

"Just think about it," he said as he let go of my hand and stood up from his seat. "If you want to be alone in your head then I can help. We'll talk again tomorrow. And I'll make you a deal: don't tell them about my offer and I won't tell anyone about the brand."

I stood and gathered the glasses back to my hip. I was uncomfortable about it, but it seemed to be more in my favour than his and the last thing I wanted to do was talk to Drew about how I might get rid of the brand.

"Deal."

We shook on it and Oliver walked away to join his friends. They smiled as he reached them, flicking glances my way, clearly thinking that our handshake evidenced some kind of victory. I was almost certain that they wouldn't be smiling tomorrow after we'd spoken again.

I collected a few more glasses then turned to carry them back down to the bar. Tommy was on the other side of the roof, watching my progress back towards him. I wondered how long he'd been watching, whether he'd been listening, but he said nothing as I passed him on my way to the stairs.

The bar was still fairly busy when I brought the glasses down, but the pace slackened off over the course of the next few hours as our human customers took themselves back to their dorms, either mindful of early starts tomorrow or having been encouraged to leave by the Invicti for having enjoyed themselves a little too much.

Pru and Ella were both falling into a gentle rhythm at the taps and they seemed to be starting to enjoy themselves. It made me wonder whether the club could be a family again, if we could get back some of what I had lost in the Revelation. I was actually looking forward to having a drink with the rest of the staff tonight.

The prospect of a life without the brand was starting to look increasingly more appealing.

It was late, about an hour before closing, when I was overwhelmed by the scent of cool spice as I replaced one of the optic bottles. Even if I hadn't recognised the scent I would have known who had arrived from Ella and Pru's rote greetings.

"Good evening, Primus."

"Good evening, Primus."

I turned around to say my line, starting to feel like this was becoming a routine.

"Hey, Sol."

The corner of his mouth twitched into his nearly-smile and it instantly took the edge off my cockiness. I didn't need this. We'd said our goodbyes, sort of, so what the hell was he doing here?

"Emilia," he said softly, breathing my name like a caress.

I could have believed that there was desire in his voice, but his eyes glinted in the dull lighting of the room, the silver threading through his ice-blue irises betraying his bond to Laila.

Never one to leave an open wound unprodded, I decided

to get right to the point, but I couldn't find the right words to express the mess of emotions I was feeling.

"You didn't tell me," I said.

"No."

No explanation. No apology. Just: no.

He rested one arm on the bar and leaned into it, surveying the room around him with quiet detachment, assessing but not quite engaged.

"Why didn't you tell me? And Laila?" I asked incredulously. "Really?"

Pru and Ella set themselves busily about various tasks behind the bar, acting like they weren't listening in, but I could feel their attention in the deliberate care of their movements. They were trying not to make too much noise so they could still hear our conversation.

"Is it so hard to believe?" he asked.

"She's vicious, Sol."

He leaned towards me, pausing to make sure he had my attention before he spoke.

"So am I."

"No, you're not. You don't hate us like she does. You're not a monster."

"I am inhuman, Emilia." The silver seemed to run like mercury through the threads of his irises, as if to emphasise his point. "That will never change."

"I don't believe you."

"But you know it to be true. You see it in me. You know in your heart that I have held human life in my hands and drained it dry without remorse, that I am not a moral creature."

A chill crept over the surface of my skin, standing the hairs on end.

"Why are you here?" I asked, hoping that he had just come in for a whisky.

"I would like a drink, Emilia, if you would be so kind."

I breathed a silent sigh of relief.

"Scotch with an ice cube?" I asked, naming his regular

order.

"Not that kind of drink," he replied.

This surprised me. I knew that Sol only ever drank blood in private, considering it vulgar to do so in company. Well, certain kinds of company at least. Apparently that had changed now Laila was on the scene.

"And what does your girlfriend think of you drinking blood in public?"

"Emilia, I am Primus, and she is my consort, not my queen."

"And? What's the difference?"

"A consort removes distractions that prevent a sovereign from ruling effectively."

Distractions. Distractions like our relationship, whatever it was. The use of the word incited a flash of anger in my veins.

"Oh?" I asked, impatient for him to get to the point.

He turned towards me and caught my gaze in his, the silver lending a sharpness to the blue that was already so cold.

"A queen rules her king," he continued quietly, "but I am no king and I will have no queen."

So that was the problem: Laila had power over him because of the bond.

I wasn't really surprised that he was struggling. It couldn't be easy for a man like Sol to be ruled by emotion, to have his control taken away from him. He was wishing the bond away.

I felt for him.

"So," I said, gentling my tone, "do you want it in a bottle or warm from the tap?"

"Neither."

I looked at him in confusion for a moment until comprehension dawned, unwelcome excitement following close on its heels, but I was unsettled by something in his tone. I had never seen Sol like this before, determination setting his jaw as if he had something to prove to himself, and I worried that he might be here to test the worth of my life to him.

"You're not a monster, Sol," I whispered, "and you don't

have to do this."

"You wear my choker," he said quietly, leaning across the bar towards me. "It is time for me to collect my dues."

The blood rushed in my veins as if rising to the invitation.

"Your dues?" I whispered dumbly.

Behind me, Ella and Pru were utterly still, giving up all pretence that they were otherwise occupied.

"I have come for what is mine," he said. "Will you deny me?"

He pushed off the bar and walked to its end, extending his hand to me.

"Sol…" I said hesitantly, my feet moving me towards him despite myself until I was standing in front of him. He took my hand in his, sending a wave of heat through me.

Every set of eyes in the room was watching us now, following the exchange. He was pushing me, daring me to shame him publicly by refusing him my blood.

It was his by rights, after all.

"I am Primus and you wear my sign," he said, reaching out to run his fingers along the lace at my neck. "So I ask again: will you deny me?"

I lifted my chin and met his gaze unflinchingly. What choice did I have?

"Just take it," I said to him under my breath, my voice breaking with sorrow at this sudden brutality.

His pupils dilated as I watched, erasing in their path the hateful silver that coloured his irises, and he pulled me towards the door that led to the office and the taproom. I stepped through as he held the door open for me and as soon as it shut behind us he pinned me up against the wall in the unlit, confined space, holding my arms above my head by the wrists. His mouth was at my neck, his free hand at my hip and in a dizzying rush his scent spiralled around me, the exotic smell curling between my lips.

"Sol, what are you doing?" I asked breathlessly. "This isn't you."

"I will have what I require from you."

"And if I say I don't want to give it?"

He trailed his teeth down my neck and my heart started to race, blood thrumming through me in a rush of heat.

"That would be a lie," he whispered into my ear.

He was right. He was lighting up my senses, explosions igniting behind my eyelids and under the surface of my skin with every contact. I never wanted it to stop.

"Last night was supposed to be the end of this."

He pulled back to look into my eyes, almost invisible in the darkness of the space between the doors.

"This is about blood, not sex."

"Is there any difference to you?"

"Sometimes."

"Tonight?"

He brushed his cheek along mine until his lips rested against my ear again.

"Tonight you issued an invitation you cannot rescind," he whispered.

"You'd rather that I'd said no? In front of everyone?"

He moved his hand from my hip to my face, pushing his fingers back into my hair.

"I could have taken what is mine regardless," he whispered. "But you would not have refused me."

He was right. I knew with a certainty that scared me that I would never turn him away.

"But what about the brand?" I asked, the heat rising gently with his proximity.

"You were with Andrew earlier today. It will suffice."

"But the brand and the bond," I said helplessly as he kissed his way down my throat. "I belong to Drew."

"No, he belongs to you. You," he said, pulling back to spread his hand along the choker, "you belong to me."

"Then you belong to Laila," I whispered back.

"Have a care." He applied a gentle but steady pressure to my neck, to the point that it slightly restricted my breathing. "I am the Primus. I belong to no one."

"You don't scare me, Sol," I whispered. "You only take

what's freely given, remember?"

It was part of the excitement for him: the thrill of conquest, the surrender of his prey.

"And you offered your blood to me freely," he said, the intensity of his clear voice almost menacing in the dark.

I swallowed awkwardly against his hand at my throat.

"I did."

He released my hands from above my head and started to unwind my unnecessary bandage from the wrist of my healed right hand, lifting the bared skin to his mouth in the small space between our faces. He leaned against me, keeping me trapped against the wall, and looked up into my eyes.

A second later his teeth were digging into my flesh, pulling an exquisite ache through every inch of my body as tendrils of flame skittered through my bones. His tongue lapped against the delicate skin at the base of my hand, inciting connections I didn't want to dwell on.

If I did, I'd probably self-combust.

I moaned and rolled my head back against the wall, but he pulled my gaze back towards him, back towards his teeth in my wrist, as if he wanted me to watch it, wanted me to be fully conscious of what he was doing, of what I'd asked him to do.

My eyelids flickered as a bolt of sensation ran straight to my centre, urging me into oblivion, and I needed more. I pressed my free hand against his chest and he let me push him up against the door behind him with a thud, the door leading back out into the club. My fingers were fisting in his hair, pulling his mouth from my wrist, because if I couldn't take his taste into my mouth, if I couldn't kiss him, I thought I might melt away entirely.

It was impossible not to draw comparisons between him and Drew, but Sol was incomparable.

He caught my face in his hands, licking a drop of blood from the corner of his mouth.

"Emilia, stop. In this state, I cannot help but mark you." His lips were a fraction of an inch away from mine, and I remembered a vow I had made to myself last week. I had promised myself that I wouldn't kiss him again until it meant to me what it meant to the Silver: that I was his and he was mine.

But he didn't belong to me, and much though Sol might think the choker gave him ownership of me I suspected that the brand would trump it, in Drew's eyes at least.

I pulled my face away from his. He was not mine.

"We cannot hide in the dark together forever," he whispered.

"No," I agreed, disappointment tempering the thudding desire running through me.

He tucked a few stray strands of hair behind my ear and ran his hand over my cheek, his eyes following the movement in the minimal light as if he were memorising its contours.

"Why are you here?" I asked. "Why all this? Why the blood?"

"I wanted to see you," he said. "I needed to taste you, one more time."

The simplicity of the statement disarmed me, and I wished with all my heart that he'd never come here tonight.

"Your taste…," he paused with his hand on my cheek, searching for the words, "like honeyed wine on my tongue, the headiest mixture of sweetness and sin." His tone was almost reverent, so full of emotion that I felt like we were standing on the precipice, waiting to pitch forward into the uncharted darkness beyond.

He was not mine.

I stepped backwards, unable to bear the temptation to cross that line.

"So this is our goodbye?" I asked, my voice breaking on the words.

There was a noise to my right and the door leading into the office crashed open, pushing me even further into Sol's arms.

Drew was silhouetted in the doorway, his fists clenching at his sides as the light from the office spilled into the small space between the doors. Embarrassment heated my cheeks as I realised he would have lived through that experience with me through the bond.

This wasn't going to be pretty.

"Get away from her," Drew said, practically growling the words.

"I was simply taking my entitlement," Sol replied, stroking his fingers possessively down my bare arm. "Or do you wish to challenge my exclusive right to Emilia's blood?"

The light shimmered across the surface of Sol's eyes as he drew himself up to his full height, and I realised in a rush that he knew what had happened earlier today. He knew that Drew had bitten me, had tasted my blood, and he wanted Drew to know it.

This whole interlude had just been a power play.

He wasn't here to see me at all.

It didn't mean a thing.

Betrayal crashed through me. I didn't think Sol was capable of such cruelty, such cold-blooded manipulation. Not where I was concerned, at least. But wasn't detachment his watchword? Hadn't he always manipulated circumstances, twisting words to make horror seem palatable?

I hoped that this change in him was just Laila's influence, her inhumanity bringing out the darkness, but that was naïve in the extreme. The man was a god of Silver.

"I need to get back to work," I said, pointless guilt and regret filling me up as I pushed away from Sol. It's not like I could have said no to him, even if I had wanted to.

"Emmy," Drew growled, but I interrupted him.

"We'll talk later, okay? See you upstairs?"

He nodded once, but his face remained set in a mask of pure vitriol. I turned to leave, wanting to give him some time to cool off, but Sol was still blocking the doorway back into the club.

"Get out of the way," I said to him brusquely as I rewound the bandage around my wrist.

He stepped to one side and held the door open for me.

"I was wrong," I said, biting out the words, "you *are* a

monster."

CHAPTER XXI

Monday

There were more eyes following me than normal for the rest of my shift, searching my skin for signs of the Primus's teeth. Pru and Ella had obviously picked up on my mood when I returned to the bar, so there was no chit chat until we were joined by the staff from downstairs after closing. Even then, no one seemed to feel much like talking and we called it a night after one drink.

I was in a dangerous frame of mind, anger clawing tension into my neck and shoulders. I knew that Drew would be waiting for me to return to the apartment and I was dreading it, both wanting to postpone it and impatient to get it over with. Between Drew, Sol and Oliver, the week was turning into a string of confrontations that were gradually eroding my mental defences to tissue paper.

On top of it all, I felt like I'd lost Sol three times over: once to his goodbye, once to Laila and once to the monster he now was, perhaps had always been.

Viv was helping me lock up the club's front door, the scent of Drew's mark on her scratching further against my nerves, when a couple of Silver streaked along the street in a blur, heading towards the Square.

"What's going on?" I asked.

Viv put hands over her ears, blocking out the ambient sound so she could hear her earpiece, and fell still. The moonlight admitted by the front door shone off her loose hair, falling in waving tumbles past her shoulders.

I wished she wasn't so beautiful.

"More trouble," she said quietly.

"Protestors?"

"No. Worse."

I looked at her expectantly, waiting for her to fill me in.

"Not humans," she said, "Silver."

She frowned, her perfect forehead wrinkling perfectly above her perfect eyebrows.

"There's a body," she continued.

"Oh, god."

The words crushed something in my soul: that little piece of me that had dared to wish that one day I might feel safe again.

"Silver?" I asked, almost hopefully.

"No."

"Who? How?"

"Shot to the head."

"Who, Viv?"

She held her hand out to silence me, her face frozen in concentration as she listened to whatever was being communicated across the receiver. The seconds ticked away, each one feeling like it was a minute, as I waited for her to say a name I knew. My legs were feeling jerky and I was yearning to run off in the same direction as the Silver, to see for myself, but I'd made a promise to Sol, for all that was worth.

For Drew's sake, I stayed put.

"Don't know," Viv said eventually. "Male."

I breathed a sigh of relief. Not Mary or either of her girls, at least.

"They think it was a Silver who did it?" I asked.

"Yes, there's a scent mark."

I knew of two scent marks that the Silver could leave. One was a mark of possession, the mark given with a kiss, that left behind the distinctive scent of the individual Silver. The second was a mark of anger and violence, a scent that designated a target, a weakness, and left no trace of the identity of its maker. I was guessing that this scent mark was the latter.

"Where's the body?"

"He's propped up against that stone tablet sign in the Square, the one with the graffiti."

The phrase flitted through my mind: What about Cara?

Well, here was the Silver's answer to that question.

First Drew was shot, and now this. It was retaliation and escalation, and a salutary reminder of our fragility. The Silver would heal, but the human would stay dead. If Oliver and his friends wanted a war, apparently they were going to get one.

There was a shout from the dorm window above us, a man's cry, heartrending with the depth of despair it conveyed. I stepped out of the door to see what was happening, but Viv pulled me back inside quickly.

"Graham!" the voice continued. "Graham!," closer now as the voice approached the window above, which must have been open from the volume of the shout.

Viv met my eyes.

"I think we know who," she said grimly.

A thudding ring above heralded the impending arrival of the shouting man, clambering down the fire escape towards the ground. His footsteps faltered as he approached the door of the club, stopping and starting as if he were tracking signs on the ground. Viv stepped in front of me, barring me from the doorway, as the man approached.

He started to walk past the door then, seeing that it was open, turned towards us. It was Oliver.

His eyes flicked towards me before coming to rest on Viv's face, his expression hardening and turning sour as he glared at her.

"Where is he?" he demanded of Viv.

"Graham?" she asked.

"Yes, Graham," he snapped impatiently. "He's not in his bed and there's… blood." It was as if the fight had suddenly gone out of him, his voice trailing off into haunted resignation.

Viv said nothing.

I watched Oliver's eyes search her face desperately for a few moments, then he turned away as his face creased up, collapsing into grief. He pressed his fist to his lips, tilting his head back to the sky, and took a few moments to get himself under control.

"He's dead, isn't he? Fucking bastards got him, didn't they?"

"Who's Graham?" I asked quietly from behind Viv.

"My brother," he whispered. "My little brother."

A tear ran down his cheek and his lip trembled, his agony so palpable that it was painful to watch.

"I'm sorry," I said.

He sniffed and turned back to us.

"Where?"

"I'll take you," Viv said before activating the microphone at her collar and speaking into it. "Leaving for the Square, boss. Need assist on lockup."

A second later I was overwhelmed by the smell of sawdust and leather. Drew was at my back, his hands on my arms as he gently pulled me away from the door and back into the club.

"Come on," he said. "You can't help here."

I cast one last glance back at Oliver, who was now crouched on the ground with his face in his hands, before Drew locked the door on his distress.

I felt empty and impotent, scoured raw by the depth of Oliver's emotion but unable to provide any comfort when I didn't know his brother, couldn't even bring his face to mind, and felt nothing at his death other than a rising dread at what it might portend.

For me, the death was a harbinger. For Oliver, it would

be a motive.

If he hadn't already wanted to rebel, vengeance would have pushed him to it. He was in a state of devastation now, but soon enough that would turn to a burning flame of anger that he'd wield as a sword against the Silver.

I hoped for the sake of his compatriots, for the sake of us all, that he had something else to live for.

Drew took my hand in his, leading me back up to the first floor to bring down the wall and lock it up tight.

We didn't speak, but he touched my arm, took my hand, rubbed my back, and generally made as much casual contact with me as he could until we were back in the apartment. I was grateful for the silence and, despite the conversation I knew was coming, I was comforted by his proximity.

I wondered if Oliver was right, if it was just the brand making me feel like he was a balm to my soul.

"Did you know him?" he asked as we walked through the door and into the apartment.

"No," I said.

I looked upstairs and saw that Alice's bedroom door was shut, so she must already have gone to bed. I wondered if she had known Graham and dreaded the prospect of breakfast chitchat tomorrow.

A human had shot a Silver, and now a Silver had killed a human. How did we recover from this?

I dropped down onto the sofa and sighed heavily, letting my head fall back so it rested along the top of the seat cushions. Drew walked into the kitchen and put the kettle on to boil, then came and sat next to me. He reached out and took my right hand, slowly unwrapping the bandage from my wrist.

So that's how he was going to broach the subject.

He ran his thumb over the bared wound and I shivered with the intimate sensation, but there was no discomfort. Surprised, I straightened in my seat and looked at the place where Sol's teeth had broken my skin.

The surface was smooth and healthy, silver particles

joining the neat bite marks together like glue.

"It's the brand," Drew said. "I think it must keep the healing silver circulating in your bloodstream."

"So I'm, what, invincible now?"

"I don't know. Please don't try to find out."

"I won't," I said. "Not on purpose, at least."

He looked down at the bite, tracing it with his fingertips, then looked up at me with pain in his eyes.

"Tell me again that it's over, Emmy," he said bitterly.

"It is."

"What you feel when you're with him…"

"Look, it's not going to happen again."

He looked at me sceptically.

"He's entitled to ask you for more blood. You've got his bloody collar on."

"I'm entitled to refuse."

"No," he said, "you're not. He's right: it's the whole point of the choker."

I remembered the stunt Sol had pulled earlier in the evening and my blood began to boil all over again. But chasing hot on the heels of that memory was a ghost of the effect of his bite, of the soaring joy of his touch.

I resented the power he had over me. Perhaps this was how he felt about his bond to Laila, I thought.

Then the anger rose in my chest again.

"What do you want me to say? That he's a bastard? That I hate him? That I wish to god that I never had to see him again? Because that's true, but it can't change how he makes me feel. I can't control that for your sake or my own."

"You don't hate him. You may wish that you did, but you don't."

He was right. I didn't hate Sol, not the Sol I knew. But he'd changed. Something benign that had always been there had twisted inside him, making him sharper, crueller, a distant tyrant for the Silver extremists.

"I'm trying," I said.

"I know."

His voice was heavy with sorrow, but he didn't push me any further. When the kettle boiled he made us each a cup of tea and brought them to the coffee table.

My mind kept pulling me back to what might be happening outside, to Oliver, to his brother.

"What happened tonight?" I asked.

"With what?"

"The murder. It was Silver?"

He handed me my tea and took a sip of his own.

"It looks that way," he said.

"And?"

"And what?"

"What happened?" I asked impatiently. "Who did it? Why did they do it? Is there some kind of rift happening in the Silver?"

"Why would you ask that?"

"Oh, come on. The body's found under the 'What about Cara?' graffiti, the victim is Oliver's brother of all people, and the poor boy's been shot in the head, just like you were. That sounds like a deliberate statement to me. So what's going on?"

"We're investigating."

"But you have a theory. Was it Ben?" I asked, frustration starting to unravel within me.

"Like I said, we're investigating."

"And that's it? That's all you're going to tell me?"

"There's nothing else to tell."

"Bollocks."

"Emmy…"

"No, Drew, you listen to me. I get that you're trying to protect me, and I appreciate it, but don't you think that I should know what's happening? With everything that's going on with Ben, with him scheming right in the middle of this nascent revolution, aren't you putting me in danger if you keep me in the dark?"

"I'll keep you safe. I promise you that."

I exhaled heavily, a claustrophobic impotence settling into my skin, twitching in my limbs and making me feel like my emotions were too big to be contained within it.

"They're offering me answers," I said.

"Who are?" he asked, instantly on the alert.

"Some of the rebels."

"You know you can't trust them."

"But I can trust you?" I said.

Pain suffused his expression.

"I love you, Emmy. I'd never do anything to hurt you."

"But you won't tell me anything, either. You won't let me in, Drew, won't let me understand what's going on. Can't you understand how terrifying that is? I don't know where the danger is, so I don't know how to avoid it. You're setting me up for a fall."

He was silent for a moment.

"No," he said, "I'm keeping you safe. It would be easier to do that if you'd agree to come to my apartment."

"We've been over this."

"It's more secure than here," he insisted.

"More secure than Sol's secret safe house? I don't think so."

"Sol doesn't know where my place is," he said. "So yes, it's safer."

I snorted disdainfully.

"Depends who you're trying to protect me from, I guess."

"Yes," Drew acknowledged quietly. "I suppose so."

"He'll lose interest soon anyway," I said, more to myself than to Drew. "He has Laila now.""

"And she's loving every second of it, obviously."

"I bet," I said, envy coiling in my stomach.

A light bulb went off in my brain.

There it was: the seventh deadly sin.

Envy.

"Oh, god," I muttered under my breath.

"What?" Drew asked.

I stood and picked up my tea then made my way to the stairs.

"I'm going to turn in," I said distractedly. "Night."

"Emmy, what's wrong?"

"Nothing. I'm fine. It's just, you know, long day. Tired."
I forced a smile.

"Really," I continued. "I've just got a headache, is all. I just need to sleep."

He examined me suspiciously for a moment then nodded, apparently satisfied, and stood up. I waited patiently, crushing down the panic in my heart, as he walked over and dropped a kiss onto my forehead.

"I'll check on you later," he said, making it obvious that he was worried I would try and sneak out. I wasn't sure where he thought I could go.

I smiled at him again and walked with deliberate slowness up to my room, closing the door softly behind me, then put my tea on the bedside table and fell face-down onto the bed. I buried my face into my pillow as a cry of despair rose in my chest and burst from my mouth, ripping through me like it was pulling part of my soul along with it.

Envy, I thought.

Sol envied Drew, and that was his sin. That was what he had been trying to tell me.

And now he had bonded to Laila, and there was nothing I could do.

It was too late.

CHAPTER XXII

Ben's hand was round my throat, pressing me down into the soft bedding and keeping me there. He was strong, his musculature defined and honed, and there was no way I was going to be able to move him until he wanted me to. His brown eyes bored into mine with a look of such intensity I thought it might break me, and then it did, pleasure cresting as he pushed inside me, his free hand grasping my hip in a grip that was needful and frantic.

"We can hide here forever, Emmy," he said as darkness fell around us, plunging the room into indistinct gloom. "You'll never leave."

I reached up and put my hands on his back, pulling him down towards me until his naked chest lay against my own, and I knew he was right.

"I love you," I whispered.

He smiled kindly and squeezed my throat. The night crowded in from my peripheral vision, pulling the curtains across my eyes until I saw nothing and felt nothing but heat, want and peace.

I could stay in his arms until the end of time.

The sound of fabric rustling against fabric intruded into my cocoon, the pleasure dissipating as it grew louder. I moaned a protest.

"Sorry," a voice whispered. "I didn't mean to wake you."

My eyes flew open.

I was in the master bedroom of the apartment, lying on my back and looking at the ceiling.

Horror and revulsion crashed through me. I'd dreamt I'd been having sex with Ben. And I enjoyed it. What was wrong with me?

I blinked a few times to try to scrub the dream from my mind. I wished I'd had another nightmare instead, anything other than the gift of that disturbing imagery to carry around with me.

I turned my head to my right and there was Drew, stretched out on the chaise longue opposite the bed, his boots lined up neatly at its foot. He looked awkward, too big for the delicate piece of furniture, his shoulders too wide to be accommodated by it.

"What time is it?" I asked, my voice croaky with sleep.

"Still early. You've only been asleep about four hours."

"What are you doing here, Drew?"

He sat up and swung his feet to the floor, pushing his hair away from his face to tuck it behind his ears.

"I just... I'm sorry, but it's difficult for me not to be with you. It sort of hurts."

"The brand?" I asked.

"No. The bond, I think."

"So you've been, what? Watching me sleep?"

"A little."

"That's kind of creepy," I said.

"I know. Are you okay?"

I nodded vaguely, wondering if he was picking up on my distress from the dream.

"How's the brand?" he asked. "Do you need me to, you know..."

He raised his eyebrow at me and wiggled his fingers. It was such a comical gesture that I had to laugh.

"No, thanks," I said, rolling onto my side to face him.

"Not with Alice next door."

"Later, then," he said, and I knew what he was asking. We both knew that I'd probably be alright for another couple of days. He was asking for intimacy.

I said nothing in reply and after a few moments he stretched himself out on the chaise longue again, fidgeting in a vain attempt to find a comfortable position.

I made a decision. I needed the comfort of his presence, needed his warmth next to my skin to chase away the lingering spectre of Ben's face in my mind.

"There's plenty of room in this bed, Drew," I said.

He stopped dead.

"Are you sure?"

"Yes," I said. "But I'm going back to sleep. No funny business."

"Of course." The enthusiasm had gone out of him a little, but it was replaced by a strange nervousness evident in his stance as he got to his feet and walked towards the bed.

I shifted backwards so I was on one side of it and lifted up the duvet so he could slide in.

"I'll lie on top of the covers," he said.

"Don't be ridiculous."

He hesitated a moment before indicating his fly buttons.

"Do you mind if I…?"

"Sure," I said, turning around to face the other way.

Watching him take his trousers off was a step too far for me. What with the brand and everything, it would probably send me over the edge. The intimacy we'd shared wasn't skin on skin, flesh to flesh. It was all channelled through the brand. Sanitised.

Things were suddenly getting a little more real. I was glad that at least I was wearing pyjamas.

The bed depressed next to me with his weight and my body tipped back towards him, rolling me into his arms. The bed was a double, but it wasn't that big. His hands settled hesitantly on my stomach and, when I didn't resist, pulled me firmly against his body, curling his legs into the back of mine.

His face found the crook of my neck and nuzzled in, his stubbled cheeks rubbing up against the sensitive skin.

I sighed, letting out a breath I hadn't realised I'd been holding, then breathed in the scent of him. It was earthy, familiar and comforting, the smell of forests and sunshine. It centred me, settling my mind and my body until I felt aligned and unified.

"I love you," he whispered.

I put my hand over his where it rested around my middle and squeezed it lightly. His fingers intertwined with mine and he held on tight, tucking himself around me until I couldn't feel more secure and I drifted off to sleep.

When I woke we were in exactly the same position, but I knew from the colour of the light peeking through the curtains and from the feeling of restfulness in my limbs that the day had long since started. I also knew exactly where I was, here in Drew's arms, and I was happy about it.

I wondered how much of that the brand had to answer for and how much was real.

"Morning," I murmured.

"You're awake," he whispered back, pressing a kiss onto my shoulder.

"Yup. What time is it?"

"I'd say about midday."

I groaned and rolled onto my back in his arms, turning my face towards him. I had a few hours still before work, but I could do with spending some time in the office beforehand doing the rota for next week and checking stock.

"Don't you have things to do?" I asked, and then the events of yesterday came rushing back into my mind. "Haven't you got to go and deal with the investigation?"

"I've made some calls while you've been sleeping, but it's all in hand."

"Oh." I wondered about kicking up a fuss again about his unwillingness to give me any information whatsoever, but then I remembered Sol's admonishment of the other day. Drew probably did know best, even if it did irk me to be out of the loop.

At least, that was the reason I told myself, but really I was just extremely warm and comfortable and didn't want to ruin the moment.

Drew and I were having a moment.

The thought sank in.

Was this real?

Looking into my eyes, he stroked his hand down the side of my face and down my neck until it rested on my shoulder. With the curtains in the room drawn, his eyes were dark and deep, the silver tendrils glinting on the surface. His hair was falling across his face, messier than usual, and I pushed it back with my fingers. When I made to withdraw my hand, he caught my wrist and held my hand against his face as he pressed a kiss into my palm.

The temperature in the room shot up a few degrees.

"Drew…"

"I know, not with Alice in the apartment."

"No."

It was as good an excuse as any. There was an awkward silence as Drew adjusted his expectations.

"I need to talk to her about the Casting," I continued.

There was a pregnant pause.

"You mean…" he said.

"I think it's the only way to keep us safe. Tommy said he'd sponsor her."

A smile of joy crossed Drew's face and he pulled me closer, his arms tight around me, our legs entwined. My face was pressed into his neck, his warmth and his scent enveloping me.

"Thank you," he said, his relief heartfelt. "I promise it'll all be fine. I'll keep you safe."

"And Alice?"

"We'll keep her safe too."

He pulled away from me, his hand resting on my face as he grinned at me.

"Forever, Emmy," he said. "We'll be together forever."

My heart fisted in my chest, anxiety clutching it into a tight ball. Forever was a long time.

"I'm not making any promises," I said.

"I know. But you're giving it a chance, and that's enough."

For now, I thought. But how long would that be enough for him?

"So what happens now?" I asked, wriggling back on the bed so there was more space between us.

It was time to talk business.

"Now I sign you up, and Tommy signs Alice up."

"You have to tell people? Now? Isn't that a bit dangerous? I mean, if you put my name on that list with you as sponsor then won't people find out, you know, about the bond?"

"The list won't be public knowledge until the Casting itself. It's sealed before then, revealed only to the Silver administering the Casting."

"Who?"

"Alyssa."

"Who's she?"

"Her territory was South London. I know you've met her because she mentioned you the other night. She's on our side, fiercely loyal to Sol."

I wasn't sure whether that meant she was on our side or not. Sol's side didn't feel the same as my and Drew's side. Not anymore.

"One of the former leaders?"

"Yes," he said. "She talks about Wimbledon a lot."

"Oh, yeah. I did meet her."

I'd liked her as well. She gave the impression that she was ancient, kind and cheekily shameless in the way that some people became as they got older. She had been without pretension or artifice, and I'd taken to her immediately.

"But once your name's on that list you're in the Casting," he said. "No backing out."

I nodded. This was a commitment I had to follow through on, and so did Alice.

"What will happen at the Casting?"

"It's sort of archaic. Castings have been around for centuries, since Silver started to spread and gather in any kind of number. There are rituals that some people expect us to follow. Certain bits have been modernised, but some of it will seem strange."

"How common are these Castings? Before now, I mean." The way everyone had been talking about them I figured they were pretty rare.

"Not common at all. In the past they've usually only been for one or two humans at a time at the request of a Silver." He paused. "Things are changing. There are more silverings, so I can only imagine there'll be more successful Castings too."

"Not everyone will be happy about that," I observed.

"No."

The sound of Alice's door opening carried through the bedroom door to us, followed by her footsteps taking her to the bathroom. When I heard the bathroom door shut I pushed away from Drew and swung myself out of bed.

"Come on," I said to him. "Get yourself back downstairs while Alice is in the bathroom."

"You don't need to hide me from her if you trust her."

"Sol said no talking about the brand or the bond."

"Because you always do what Sol says," Drew muttered sarcastically as he climbed out of bed and pulled his trousers back on. I tried not to concentrate on the view.

"In this instance, yes, I do. Sort of."

Maybe not at all, actually, when I came to think about it.

Shit. It had seemed so reasonable at the time.

"As it happens," I continued, "she's seen the brand and she worked out the healing thing. But she doesn't know it happened because of the bond, and she doesn't know it was you who did it. So go on. I'm going to have a shower then I'll see you downstairs."

CHAPTER XXIII

The sun was streaming through the windows when I came down the stairs; a beautiful day as promised. Drew was already explaining the Casting to Alice as she sat at the table eating her cereal, so I just let him get on with it while I made myself some tea and toast for breakfast.

"I get it," she said. "I understand the risks, and I want to do it. When can I meet Tommy?"

"I'll call him," he said, pushing away from the table as he took a phone out of his pocket. He stepped out onto the terrace, closing the door behind him as he dialled.

Alice shot out of her chair and came to wrap her arms around me.

"Thank you so much, Emmy. I can't tell you how much this means to me."

"It's the least I could do after I essentially stuck a vampire target on your back. You know I'm probably not doing you a favour, right? If you die in the Casting I'll never forgive myself."

"I'm not going to die," she said.

"Well, see what you think of Tommy. And tell me honestly before you sign up for sure. Okay? You've got till Wednesday anyway."

"But I know now that I want to do it."

"I know, but please, Alice. Humour me. Just talk to me before you commit."

"Okay, I promise."

"Thank you."

Her face lit up again as if she'd just remembered she now had a sponsor, and she jumped up and down excitedly.

"Don't tell anyone!" I said, worried that her enthusiasm would overspill and make her say something we'd all regret.

"Don't worry, I won't," she said. "I hope he's hot." That was Alice: superficial to the core.

"Oh, he's hot," I said.

Weren't they all? Even Ben, I thought as the chilling memory skittered across my mind.

Drew came back inside and, to Alice's delight, told her that Tommy would meet her downstairs. She gathered up her things and, with a last primp in the mirror, went off for her date with a vampire. I tried to enjoy her happiness, but anxiety was eating me up.

She'd heard about Graham, but it didn't seem as portentous to her as it did to me. I felt like we were on the threshold of the downward spiral to oblivion.

I sat myself down at the table to eat my breakfast and Drew reclaimed his seat opposite me.

"What are you doing for the next couple of hours?" he asked. "I've got to get back to the Palace, but with everything that's happened I don't really want to leave you alone."

"I'm going to sort some stuff out downstairs," I said. "Stock check, rotas and all that jazz."

"Could you use some help?"

"I guess," I replied, thinking that I might need to move crates and barrels from one taproom to another.

Then he was back on the phone, calling for my own personal Silver bodyguard. Cam was with us within the minute, waving manically through the one-way glass as he hopped over the wall to the patio.

"Emmy!" he said cheerfully as Drew unlocked the patio

doors and let him inside. He loped over to me, gathered me into a hug and squeezed me tight. "I missed you. I didn't see you yesterday."

I laughed, his casual intimacy warming my heart. It was so easy to love and feel loved when there was no sexual attraction to get in its way.

"I missed you too," I said as I kissed him on the cheek.

"Easy there, tiger," Drew said in a warning tone.

"Scared by a little competition, boss?" Cam asked, his eyes lighting up with mischief as he scooped me up into his arms and spun me round.

"You're a menace," Drew muttered back, his attempt at nonchalance somewhat marred by the look of yearning and regret in his eyes as he watched me and Cam together. "I've got to go," he said to me, "but I'll see you after you close up, okay?"

"Sure," I said brightly as Cam set me back on my feet.

He moved towards me as if he were going to hug me goodbye, but then paused mid-step and turned away, clearly thinking better of it.

"Drew, wait" I said, walking after him to wrap my arms around his neck. He held me, his face pressed into my neck, and squeezed me tight. After a few seconds he pulled back and looked into my eyes.

"Bye, Emmy," he said.

I pressed a kiss to his cheek before leaning in for a final embrace.

"See you later."

He smiled back at me as he stepped away and out into the midday sun, leaving me wondering where we went from here.

"Nice to see you two getting on so well," Cam said.

"Yeah," I replied vaguely.

"Still not sure?" he asked.

I just shook my head, not wanting to open that particular can of worms.

"Come on," I said. "I need to find some crates for you to carry."

"At your service," he said with a salute, and just like that the fun was back in the room.

It took us a couple of hours to get the stock moved around the various bars and taprooms, and to get the rota drawn up. I called over to the Palace to let them know what we were running low on, and they promised to send more supplies round tomorrow. They also promised to send someone over to refill the blood barrels, which were finally starting to run a bit low. We'd had so few Silver customers over the past few days that we hadn't needed to change the tanks until now.

We had a quick bite to eat upstairs, and then it was time for me to get back behind the bar. I saw Alice only briefly before we opened for the night, but she promised to fill me in later. From the look on her face, I thought she was probably smitten with Tommy. Since he elected to replace the Invictus who was due to work on Alice's bar for the evening, I wondered whether he might feel the same way. I couldn't blame him; the girl was gorgeous.

Cam stayed in the top bar for the night, close by me at all times. He was jovial, joking around with me in the quieter moments, but when we were busy I noticed his eyes scanning the room, his face threatening and hard. Something had given the Invicti a scare, and I was willing to bet it was the discovery of Graham's body.

The humans weren't much more comfortable, subdued and mournful, and they cleared out early. No one was particularly interested in socialising this evening. The Silver, however, were back in force, pretty much back to their numbers from last week.

I felt like we were being squeezed out.

Oliver and his friends weren't out tonight, which was hardly surprising in the circumstances, but one of the women I recognised from his entourage was. She walked directly towards me at the bar in a way that made me think I was the reason she had come here.

That worried me.

"Emilia?" she asked as I passed a few drinks over the bar

to a customer.

"Yup," I said. "What can I get you?"

"Nothing. I'm here with a message from Oliver."

"I was sorry to hear about his brother."

She nodded, acknowledging the pleasantry, but she didn't seem convinced that my concern was genuine, dismissing it quickly.

"Are you with us?" she asked.

"Who's us?"

"You know who. Let's be clear on this: I'm only here for Oliver's sake, because he asked me to give you a chance. So are you coming with us, or are you siding with the demons?"

"Demons?"

"You think they're anything else?"

A few heads turned towards us and I wished she would lower her voice. There were too many Silver around us, too many chances to be overheard by the wrong person.

"I'm not siding with anyone."

"Then that's all I need to know."

I wanted to ask how Oliver was, wanted some reassurance that he was going to be okay, to erase the image of his desolating grief that was hauntingly fresh in my mind, but I didn't get a chance. She turned on her heel before I could say another word and marched herself out of the room and back downstairs.

So that was that.

As the night dragged on we were serving more blood and less alcohol, the purple counters filling up the lockbox set into the wall at the back of the bar. By the time we got near to closing, there were no humans left in the place. It was like Sol had never invited them in, the room eerie with the inhuman stillness of the Silver. It was something I only noticed when I saw them crowded together, but the oddness of their immobility, moving only to speak or to lift a glass to their lips, was so unnatural it was almost like being surrounded by mannequins.

I'd forgotten in the past few days how truly terrifying they were en masse, in a darkened room.

My hand lifted to my neck and I stroked the choker surrounding it, reassuring myself that I was safe. There was Cam on the other side of the room, watching me, and I had Sol's collar covering my throat.

I was safe.

But the end of the night couldn't come soon enough.

Finally, the lights came up, the music came down, and the Silver emptied out and back to the Palace and, I assumed, to their own apartments in some cases, wherever they were. Drew couldn't be the only one to have his own place. For all I knew there might be Silver living outside of the wall; it's not like the Weepers bothered them.

The world outside the barricades belonged to monsters now.

By unspoken consensus, there were no drinks tonight for the staff. None of us wanted to hang around this late at night, not after what had happened to Graham. They had us scared, which had probably been the plan all along: put the humans in their place.

But I worried about the visit from Oliver's emissary earlier in the night. It sounded like they were getting ready to make a move, incited to action rather than fear by the death of one of their number.

These were dangerous times.

I locked up the downstairs bar with Cam's help, waving off Alice and Tommy who were apparently going over to the Palace for some food. They seemed to be hitting it off after all.

After a quick check of the VIP bar, we went back upstairs and got the tables in. I was thumping the keypad by the terrace in the top bar, trying vainly to beat it into submission, when the air rippled, carrying with it a coolly familiar scent. An arm reached around me and pressed a series of buttons in a blur until the mechanism whirred into action, the wall settling perfectly into place and locking itself tight.

"What are you doing here?" I asked, the blood under the

skin of the brand heating with his proximity.

"This is my club," Sol said monosyllabically as I turned to face him. His voice was toneless and he looked out of sorts, his hair oddly dishevelled and his perfect complexion marred by bruising under his eyes. He looked exhausted.

I could guess why.

"Well, then, knock yourself out, but leave me alone."

I left him standing by the door to the terrace and helped Cam put away the last of the tables. At this rate, tomorrow night we'd be back to full-on dance floor mode for the Silver. I couldn't see the humans flocking back here any time soon.

Sol walked behind the bar and poured himself a glass of whisky, then leaned against the wall and watched.

"Thanks, Cam," I said, ignoring Sol. "Are you coming upstairs?"

"No," he said, flicking nervous glances in Sol's direction. "Drew's waiting, so I'll see you to the door then leave you there, but I'll be back before work tomorrow."

"No need," Sol interrupted. "You are dismissed, Cameron. I will see Emilia to her quarters safely."

"No, you won't," I said.

"Emmy…" Cam said, a look of intense discomfort on his face.

Rage rose within me.

"Oh, don't you do this to me again, Cam. Don't you dare bail on me. Not just because he says so."

Cam wrapped his arms around me and lifted me until my toes left the ground. He whispered in my ear: "I'm sorry, Ems, but it's just the way it is. He's my Primus."

"He's a dick."

"Whatever he is, I trust him and I obey him. I'll see you tomorrow."

He nodded to Sol in a curt manner that made it look like a salute, then turned and let himself out into the night through the terrace door. I looked after him in disbelief.

He'd left me here with Sol.

His scent was working its way under my skin, the blood in

my veins ripping across the brand. The worst thing was that, after all he'd done, I still wanted him. It sharpened the edges of my mood, making me feel volatile and out of control.

"Emilia."

"Why are you here?" I asked, rounding on him in desperate irritation. "Why are you always where I am? How many goodbyes do you want from me before you'll actually leave? And last night…"

I looked away from him, closing my eyes against the pain of the memory. I'd come to think of sharing my blood as something intimate, something precious, and his cold calculation had turned it into nothing more than a chess move.

I opened my eyes and stared him down.

"You're moving me around like a pawn, pushing at Drew, for no other reason than that you can."

"I apologise for my words to Andrew last night," he said quietly. "I was not myself. I am finding the bond… difficult."

This wasn't news to me. I sighed and walked past him to the area behind the bar, grabbing myself a bottle of beer and cracking it open.

"You're with Laila now," I said, taking a generous swig.

"Yes."

It hadn't been a question, but the stark confirmation was something I needed to hear.

"And I…" I hesitated, accepting the thought in my head before I could say it out loud. "I'm with Drew."

He took a couple of steps towards me, pulling up a stool on the other side of the bar, and sat with his hands resting in front of him.

"I see," he said, swilling his whisky in his glass. "Then all has worked out for the best."

"Yes." The hollowness in my voice was audible even to me, belying my answer.

"But you are unhappy."

I took another slug from my bottle and put it down between us, turning it gently on its base as I fought with my emotions.

"I don't want to see you," I said, slowly and deliberately. "I don't want to hear your voice, and I don't want to smell your scent on the air or on my skin. I want to erase you so I can move on, but you're everywhere. I keep saying goodbye, but you're still here."

"I will keep my distance," he said,

I shook my head hopelessly. Yes, his presence was making things more difficult, but even when he wasn't here he was still with me. He was in my head, under my skin, and I couldn't scrub him out. How many times had I tried to seal him away into the past? But every time I closed that door and locked it tight, somehow it got opened again.

"I want to hate you," I whispered.

The unspoken truth lingered in the air between us as I met his eyes.

"The brand, and Andrew's bond, will win out," he said quietly.

"I hope so, because right now I feel like I'm being torn in two."

He looked into my eyes, the silver filaments threading into his irises like cracks through ice, then knocked back the rest of his drink and put the glass down on the bar with an air of finality.

He took my hand and kissed the skin above the knuckles, his touch sending a shot of fire across the brand, then pressed it to his cheek for a moment before releasing it.

"Goodbye, Emilia."

I took a breath, steeling myself.

"Goodbye."

And he was gone, the terrace door clicking shut behind him as the bolt slid home.

CHAPTER XXIV

Tuesday

Drew was waiting out on the patio when I got upstairs, lying on one of the recliners and watching the stars.

"Hi," I said.

"Hi yourself. How's the brand?"

I shrugged.

"Okay," I said.

He raised an eyebrow at me.

"Not great," I admitted.

He sat up and swivelled towards me, putting his feet down on the deck.

"Well, Alice is out."

He was about as subtle as a sledgehammer.

"I know. Is there any food left in the fridge?" I asked, walking back into the apartment and into the kitchen area. He followed me.

"You saw Sol," he said.

I kept on walking. There was nothing in the fridge but milk and some vegetables, so I made myself a bowl of cereal.

"Yes," I said as I sat down at the table. "I saw him. Did

you hear?"

"No. I can smell him on you."

"He barely touched me, and I told him to leave me alone. Happy?"

He said nothing, taking the chair opposite me and watching as I spooned the cereal into my mouth. After a night on my feet, I was ravenous. What I really wanted was chips, late-night takeaway like we'd sometimes ordered in to the club after work, back when it was Parker's. I was missing the familiar things tonight. I craved comfort.

"Did you find out anything about Graham's murder?" I asked after a few minutes of silence.

"We're dealing with it. Don't worry about it."

I rolled my eyes and scraped the bowl clean, then got to my feet and rinsed it and my spoon in the sink, leaving them to drain on the side.

"How can I not be worried?" I asked as I turned back towards him. "Can't you see what's happening? Look around you: everything is falling to pieces. We're on the verge of outright rebellion and you're telling me not to worry?"

"Yes. Things will take a while to settle down, but it'll happen. It's inevitable that there'll be some resistance."

"Resistance? Drew, we're in a state of complete instability. Everything's out of control. Not only are humans protesting, shooting at the Silver, but the Silver are killing humans. This isn't a readjustment period, this is constant escalation. Where is it going to end? How much blood do you expect to be spilled before this is over?"

"Trust me, Emmy. I've seen this time and time again. It will all blow over."

I shook my head.

"I wish I had your faith. There's so much you won't tell me, so many unanswered questions. You're asking me to take a lot on trust, and I know more than most, am closer to the Silver than most. Can't you understand how they feel, how we feel? We're completely impotent, powerless to protect ourselves, and without the information that would tell us whether or not we're in danger in the first place."

"You don't need to protect yourself. That's my job."

Frustration crawled under my skin.

"Now you're just being facile. I'm not a child."

"No," he said, "but you do need my protection. Please just let me keep you safe."

Sol's words of the other day came back to me again, drawing me up short: Andrew can only protect you if you allow him to do so.

I got my temper under control, with some difficulty, and sighed, relenting reluctantly.

"One day you're going to tell me everything," I said.

"When you're Silver, I'll be able to."

I crossed my arms and leaned back against the kitchen counter. Apparently that was a foregone conclusion, now: that the Casting would be a success. I wished I hadn't had to agree to it. It was no choice, really.

It would change my life irrevocably in so many ways: speed, strength, eternal life. Blood.

"What's it like," I asked, "when you drink blood? How does it feel?"

"It's invigorating," he said. "It buzzes through me, like… like I can't even describe. It's incredible."

He stood from his seat and walked up to me, taking my hands in his.

"I can share all these experiences with you, Emmy. I'll be there every step of the way. You know that?"

I nodded mutely. He moved one of his hands up to my face and used it to brush my hair back. His touch sent an involuntarily shiver across my skin, raising goose bumps in its path, and I knew I was in trouble.

Stupid brand.

"I can make you happy," he said, his breath whispering over my cheek. I felt my heartbeat quicken, my pulse thudding in the heat of the brand, and tried to resist its pull. But as I pushed against it, a warm wash of desire spread through me, erasing in its wake every logical reason I had to step away from him.

It was taking my mind away, but almost every conscious part of me didn't give a damn.

"Let me make it better," he said.

Helpless to do otherwise, I gave myself over to the irresistible.

"Do it," I said.

He wrapped his arms around my waist and lifted me up until I was sitting on the edge of the countertop, my legs wrapped around him. Taking hold of the bottom of my T-shirt, he pulled it off over my head, dropping it carelessly onto the floor.

"God, I missed you," he said, stroking his hands over my shoulders and down my arms.

He raised his right hand to hover over the silver palm print on my chest and I braced myself breathlessly, knowing what was coming and yearning for it.

But when his fingertips touched the brand the sensation was more extreme than it had ever been, so intense that I ached painfully with the force of it, crying out in discomfort until the first few seconds of contact took away the edge and all that was left was the pleasure of his touch, the rhythmic tugging of the brand's magic.

I tightened my legs around him and gasped, drawing him closer as my fists clenched in a death grip over the edge of the countertop.

"Shit," Drew gritted out through his teeth, sweat beading on his forehead. "God, Emmy."

And then his eyes locked onto mine and I couldn't look away. His free hand reached up to curl around the back of my neck, and he was drawing my face down, drawing my lips towards his own, and I was doing absolutely nothing to prevent him.

The world exploded and, as the ecstasy from the brand reached its apex, we kissed.

The moment his lips touched mine it was as if my entire body clicked into place, as if suddenly everything was right.

Here I was, where I was supposed to be, and Drew was kissing me, just like he should be. The balance was restored, the taste of his breath settling every part of me into perfection as his lips met the demanding beat of my heart.

This time when he cried out in release the noise was muffled by our kiss, the exclamation reverberating through my body as the urgency left my limbs and normality reasserted itself.

Whatever passed for normality these days, anyway.

He'd finally kissed me, and it had been perfect; the most perfect kiss in the world.

But for some reason, the fact sent a note of alarm sounding through the post-orgasmic haze. There was something wrong with this picture.

Something was wrong.

Really wrong.

Consciousness returned and I pulled away abruptly.

The heat left my body in a shiver and suddenly I was chilled to the bone.

"We just kissed," I said numbly, touching my fingers to my lips in dismay.

"Yes, we did," Drew replied smugly, his voice liquid with relaxation as he leaned his body against mine.

"That's not a good thing! Did you mark me?"

He hesitated a moment then stood up straight, a look of horror passing over his face as he met my eyes. His nostrils twitched, as if he were scenting the air, checking for the mark.

"Yes," he said, the blood draining from his cheeks.

Every Silver I bumped into over the next twenty-four hours would know that Drew had kissed me, know that he had marked me as his own. Even with the fake-girlfriend charade, I thought chances were good that at least some of them would suspect the truth, suspect the bond.

Shit.

I couldn't believe that either of us could have been so stupid, but then we weren't ourselves, taken over by the allure of the bond. It made us each into something we were not.

"Well? What the hell do we do now?" I asked, my voice rising.

A brief look of panic passed over his face before he got it under control and started making a plan.

"We do nothing," he said after a moment.

"What?"

"We do nothing. We stay right here for the next twenty-four hours until it's faded. You take the night off. It's usually your night off on Tuesday's anyway, isn't it?"

"Yeah, but…"

"It's fine," he interrupted. "I'll stay here with you, and no one will ever find out about it. It's fine."

"I'm managing the place now," I said. "I don't think I get nights off."

"Well, you're having one. Alice can manage without you, right?"

"I don't know…"

"Emmy, come on. How much can she really screw it up? It's only a bar. It's not exactly rocket science."

I went dead still for a moment.

I was willing to admit that managing a bar wasn't the most intellectually demanding job in the world, but it was what I did. More than that, I loved this place. Parker's had been everything to me for the few months before the Revelation, and his off-hand dismissal of it burned like acid in my stomach. I could cope with him belittling my job, but to have him belittle something I cared about just irritated me.

On top of the emotional exposure left behind in the wake of the touch of the brand, I was primed and ready to blow my top. The slightest thing would have done it, and his words were enough. The irrational core of me was willing to turn this into the row of the century.

I knew it was unfair, but I was so furious that I didn't care about the right or wrong of it.

He seemed to realise he'd made an error of judgement, regret crossing his face as I glared at him.

"Only a bar? Only a bar?"

"Emmy..."

"This place is all I have left! Do you not understand that?"

"I didn't mean..."

"Yes, you did. You meant every word."

He stepped away in the face of my rage and I slid down from the countertop and moved away from him, the indignant gesture only slightly spoiled by the fact that my skirt ended up bunched up around my waist. I readjusted it with as much dignity as I could muster and, scooping up my top from the floor, pulled it over my head.

"Seriously," I continued as I paced around the kitchen, trying to get back into my stride, "what's the point of this? You don't respect my job or my abilities, you won't trust me enough to tell me the truth of what's going on around me..."

I paused, struggling to find the right words, exasperation making me inarticulate.

"Emmy..."

"No, let me finish," I snapped.

I took a deep breath and tried to think through what was at the root of my anger, why I was flying off the handle at him over nothing. I tried again, more calmly this time.

"Love is sharing your life with someone, sharing yourself with someone. You don't hold things back from the people you love. Real relationships, adult relationships, aren't based on dishonesty, or on magic. So how is this love? Why do you love me?"

"The bond..."

"Not good enough," I interrupted. "There has to be a reason."

"It's chemistry," Drew said helplessly, "just like human attraction. That's how the bond works."

"That might be how human attraction works, but it's not how human love works. You love someone because they make you laugh, or because they make you a better person, or because their smile is so beautiful it makes your heart sing, and for fifty other reasons. Not because of chemistry."

He looked at me as if he thought I was crazy, but I'd

started this and I was damn well going to finish it. This was the source, this was the problem. I wasn't going to let things progress any further without some reassurance that there was something to this other than the bond, that he wanted me for some reason other than that the bond told him he had to.

The magic of fate wasn't enough for me, not when I was so unsure of him.

"So why do you love me?" I asked again.

He opened his mouth, then closed it.

"Nothing?" I asked, with quiet resignation. "You can't think of even one thing?"

He shrugged, exasperation making his movements jerky and awkward.

I was surprised to find that his response hurt, that the confirmation crushed a little flame inside me. His feelings for me were so dissociated from reality, from the tangible, that there was absolutely nothing for him to hang them on. They had nothing to do with me or who I was.

"It's not how the bond works," he said.

"Who cares how the bond works? It isn't real."

"It's so real it could kill me, Emmy," he replied, deadly serious.

"And what about me?" I asked. "This brand is changing me, giving me feelings I don't feel, and without the bond you probably wouldn't even have looked at me twice. This is a scenario that's being engineered around us, a relationship we're being coerced into. Doesn't that bother you?"

"No." His voice was soft, empty with hopelessness. "I just love you, and I want to be with you every moment of every day. I don't care why I feel the way I do, I just know that I want you, and that's not going to change. The 'why' doesn't matter to me."

"And if the bond somehow gets broken, but you still live?"

I was thinking about Oliver's offer, about the possibility he offered of an escape from the cage of emotions elicited by the bond and the brand.

"That's not going to happen," he said.

Maybe not, I thought. But maybe.

I sighed and picked up my keys from the bowl on the counter where I'd left them.

"I'm going to go down to the office and write out some instructions for Alice," I said.

"I'll come with you."

The last thing I wanted was his company. The only reason I was willing to do anything other than sleep at this hour of the morning was to get out of his immediate proximity for a moment, to give myself some time to think.

"No," I said. "I'll be fine, and I won't be long. Just… just give me some time, okay?"

"I can't…"

"Look, the building's all locked up, the office door is locked up, and there's no one in here but us and my fellow humans in the dormitory. So just give me the time I need."

"How long?" he asked.

I thought for a moment. What I really wanted was another plan, a way to get me out of the apartment while the mark wore off, but I was conscious of Sol's warning not to put myself in harm's way.

Dammit. I was going to have to speak to him.

Or maybe not…

"Give me an hour," I said. "I won't leave the building, okay?"

"Okay. I'll be waiting."

And with that I was free, bolting out of the apartment door and down the stairs to the office. First order of business: a willing accomplice.

I picked up the phone and dialled the Palace.

"Good morning, Solomon's Palace," a female voice answered on the second ring.

I nearly laughed. The name made it sound like a casino.

"Oh, hello. Erm, could I speak to Cameron, please?"

I realised I had no other way of identifying him. Did the Silver even have surnames?

"He's one of the Solis Invicti?" I hazarded.

"May I ask who's calling please?"

"It's Emilia, from the club."

She put me on hold without another word, and for a moment I thought she had cut me off. After about a minute I started to worry that she wasn't going to put me through to him, but then a reassuringly familiar voice came on the line.

"Hey Ems, what can I do for you at this ungodly hour of the morning?"

"Oh, hey Cam," I said, smiling to myself at the sound of his voice. "I hope I didn't wake you?"

"Nope, I was just coming to the end of my shift."

"Okay, good," I said, relieved.

There was a moment of silence on the line.

"So?" he asked after a moment, amusement rather than irritation colouring his tone.

"Oh, right, so, yeah." I was suddenly nervous at making this confession. "Um, I have a favour to ask."

"Okay."

"Er, is this line secure?"

He laughed at me.

"Why, who are you, James Bond?"

"Seriously," I persisted. "Is it okay to talk openly?"

"Yeah, sure, just give me a sec."

I heard the noise of a door closing in the background and gathered that he had probably just shut himself into a quiet room.

"Okay," he said, "go ahead."

I paused for a moment, not sure how to break the news, then decided to go straight in.

"Drew marked me," I said.

Cam sighed.

"It was bound to happen sooner or later. You guys are, like, electric."

I rolled my eyes at the phone.

"Not helpful," I said. "We had a bit of a falling out, and I don't want to hang out here alone with him for a whole day."

"Ems, the apartment is pretty much the only safe place for

you with his mark on you. Actually, you're probably not even safe there. You'd be safer with the Weepers if any of the Silver caught wind of the mark."

"See, that's the thing. In fact…" I hesitated, knowing this was going to be difficult to swing. "I want to go outside the walls, back to my old flat, to see things for myself, to see if there's any sign of my flatmate."

I hated to admit it, but Oliver's words had raised some doubts in my mind. I had to see the outside world in the flesh, not just in the distance from the top of the club. For all I knew, we were living inside a dome, a real-life Truman Show.

"I need an escort," I added.

"You want me to come with you?"

"Would you?"

There was a pause.

"It's actually not an awful plan," he said. "No one would think to look for you outside the safe zone."

He avoided saying what we both knew he meant: Ben would never look for me out there, not after he left me to die on that rooftop, not now that he'd instilled such a terrifying fear of the Weepers in me.

I immediately started to have second thoughts myself.

But I needed to see it. I needed to see the city. I had to know that it was real, and that it wasn't all a fairytale the Silver had concocted to keep us compliant. I was almost certain it was the truth.

Almost.

More than that, I needed to see the flat, to see if there was any trace of Cass having got out of there safely.

"Would you run it past Sol?" I asked tentatively.

"You want his approval?"

"I'm not asking for Drew's. I don't want him to come and find me. Sol can make sure he doesn't."

"You want me to go behind Drew's back? Ems, look, I love you and all, but he's the boss."

"Please, Cam," I begged. "I just need some time."

"And you can't ask Sol yourself?"

"No," I replied simply. There was no way I was going to speak to him ever again if I could possibly avoid it.

"Okay. I'll call you back," he said, and hung up.

I replaced the phone in its cradle and typed up a list of instructions for Alice while I waited for Cam's call. As it happened, there wasn't much to list out. I told her to get one of the guys from the VIP bar to help on the top bar, told her which barrels were running low and how to get hold of the Palace in case the blood barrels malfunctioned again, and after that I ran out of things to say. She knew about opening and closing times, knew about how to work all of the gear in the taproom. It wasn't like I was doing anything complicated while I was filling in here.

Drew was right: a monkey could do my job.

Cam called back just as I was printing out the brief sheet of instructions.

"Hey," I answered nervously.

"Hey, Em."

"So?"

"He said yes, I can take you. The three of us will be the only ones who know about it. He won't tell the boss where we are."

Relief rushed through me, followed very shortly by a healthy dose of trepidation and anxiety.

"Okay."

"Don't go back to the apartment, don't pack anything, just crack a bottle of beer for me and I'll see you in the top bar in ten minutes. I'll bring everything we need."

"Thanks, Cam," I said with feeling. "Really, thanks."

"Anything for you, Ems. See you in a few."

I breathed a huge sigh of relief and, pinning the instructions on the back of the office door next to the rota, walked outside to wait for Cam.

Despite the soft soles of my boots, my footsteps echoed around the empty room until I stepped behind the bar, the enclosed space muffling my tread. Ten minutes seemed like an eternity to wait for Cam. I was impatient to get out of here now. I knew that I'd locked everything up tight downstairs, but nonetheless I kept expecting one of the Silver to walk in from the stairwell, to see me, to scent the mark. Then all hell would break loose.

I sighed and grabbed a couple of beers out of one of the fridges, cracking them open with a hiss. I set one on the bar for Cam when he arrived, then came back around front and hopped up onto a bar stool, facing out towards the terrace wall. If things were different I would have stepped outside and felt the air on my skin until the tense knot in my stomach unwound itself, but that would have been dangerous even before Drew marked me. Now it would have been practically suicidal.

I lifted the bottle to my lips, inhaling the flavour of hops and alcohol, but I was interrupted before I could take the first sip. The room was plunged into darkness and for a tiny moment I thought the lights had gone out, but then a piece of fabric was pulled down over my head, crushing my nose with its force, another piece was shoved into my mouth so roughly that it tore the skin at the corner of my mouth, and strong arms were around my body in an immovable cage, pinning my own arms to my sides.

The beer bottle fell to the ground beside me, detonating in a deafening crash of glass.

The material over my head smelt stale and mouldy, as if it had held muddy old potatoes, but the fabric in my mouth was acrid and bitter, almost smoky. I tried to scream against it, but the only noise I could make was a strangled moan, the noise so dampened that I doubted I would have been heard beyond this room, even by the Silver. But maybe Drew would have heard the bottle break.

"Shut up," a male voice growled.

I started to wriggle in his grip, kicking out to try to get free, but it was useless. I felt my boot connect with the bar stool, sending it toppling over, but there was no clatter, no crack of the wood hitting the floor. It must have been caught, but not by the man who was holding me.

There was more than one of them.

One of my arms was slightly released, but only enough to allow the man to twist it up behind my back so far that I thought my shoulder was going to dislocate. I moaned as pain shot through the limb.

"Listen up, vampire whore," he hissed. "Far as I'm concerned, you've picked your side, and you're as good as dead anyway. If I have to break every bone in your body, you won't see me shedding no tears. So shut the fuck up and walk."

I walked. It didn't seem like I had any other choice.

He steered me effortlessly by my twisted arm, navigating my course by forcing me to move to one side or the other to relieve the pain in my shoulder. I was disoriented until I heard the creak of doors in front of me, quickly followed by a breeze on my skin and an echoing quality to the sound around us. We were in the club's main stairwell.

"Up," the man said.

To the dormitory.

I stretched out my foot tentatively until I felt the edge of the first step, then started to climb the stairs. I thought frantically, trying to work out what was going on.

The people who had attacked me were human, no doubt about that. Firstly, they were taking me to the dormitory. Secondly, no one had mentioned Drew's mark. Thirdly, and probably more obviously, they'd called me a vampire whore, which wasn't something the Silver would ever say. Or, at least, I thought not.

I didn't know where they were going with this, but I didn't think anything good started with being gagged, blindfolded and called a whore. My tastes didn't really run that way.

It must have been the rebels, I thought, but the guy who was speaking didn't sound like Oliver. He'd said it, though: I'd chosen my side. Now, apparently, I was facing the consequences of that decision.

Fear prickled across my skin, sweat tingling on my hands and neck in the still air of the stairwell. I couldn't scream, couldn't fight. I was going nowhere.

I was pushed roughly into the door at the top of the stairs, used as a tool to open it wide. It cracked across my cheekbone and into my hip, sending agonising bursts of pain radiating out across my body. This man was brutal, and I wasn't going to get any mercy from him.

We walked through the kitchen and I knew when we'd entered the dormitory because the breeze from the open window above what used to be my bed hit my bare thighs, chilling me to the bone. But it was too quiet, the normally omnipresent murmurs and snorts of sleeping people oddly absent. Where was everyone? I'd assumed that they were taking me to see Oliver or the other rebels, that they were going to try to beat information out of me about the Silver. Oliver had probably realised that I'd been holding back, and I thought he'd want to know what I knew.

But the room felt practically empty, as if the dormitory was unoccupied.

There was a clanking, metallic sound by the window as I was marched in that direction.

"Is it true?" a male voice by the window asked.

There was a movement from the man holding me, the motion sending a further jet of pain through my shoulder. He'd clearly made some sort of gesture, but I couldn't guess what it might have been.

There were a few footsteps towards me and then hands at the neck of my shirt, tearing the thin fabric open.

"See?" said the voice again, now right in front of me.

"Damn. He was right," the man at my back replied.

"It's going to make a fucking big statement, I'll tell you that much," came the response.

"Should never have taken that bribe, little girl," another voice said from the direction of the window, female this time, as fingers stroked over the choker around my neck. The fingers were replaced by heavy metal that was draped around my throat in a loop.

Chains, I thought.

"Too late now," the man said, and I belatedly realised from the finality of his tone that they were going to kill me. Dear god, they were going to kill me.

Humans were going to kill me.

Not Ben, not any of the Silver, but humans.

It was time to start thinking about best options to avoid dying, rather than avoiding injury. But before I could make a move I was pushed forward quickly, my arms released as the man behind me grabbed the back of my legs and lifted me up.

Over the sill of the window, I realised, and out. Out into space, with a chain around my neck. I kicked out with my legs as quickly as I could and managed to make the man stumble enough to give me some time to get my hands between the chain and my neck, but he had me fast now and was walking me ever forward.

Hands reached up and at the last moment the bag was removed from my eyes, the gag pulled from my mouth, and I had just enough time to push the chain over my head before I sailed through the window towards the tarmac below, a scream ripping from my throat as I tumbled.

Then there was a wrenching yank, an excruciating jolt through my right shoulder, and my body slammed back against the wall of the building. I looked up to see that my hand was caught in the chain that had been intended as a noose, the bones crushed as it constricted over my knuckles. I hung there screaming for a moment until my fingers slipped through the loop of metal and out, depositing me painfully onto the pavement below in a heap of agony.

Tears streamed from my eyes as I cradled the hand to my chest. The decoy bandage was still wound around it and had probably saved me from surface injuries, but I guessed that the chain had broken a few bones. At least it hadn't ended up around my neck. I was also grateful that it had slowed my descent to the ground, although I was still going to have a colossal bruise on my backside.

But I wasn't out of danger yet.

I looked back up to the window, expecting to see the faces

of my attackers looking down at me, but there were no faces peering out from the dorm. Instead, there were more chains. With the oddness of the steep perspective, it took me a moment to realise what I was looking at.

When I did I froze, nausea pressing urgently at the back of my throat.

I hadn't been the first.

There were two figures halfway up the wall, hanging from the dorm window by the chains around their necks, staring sightlessly across the road towards the Palace. Their faces were grotesquely distorted and discoloured, barely recognisable, but each wore a choker around her neck and each wore the skimpy uniform of the girls who worked in the club.

In the darkness of the night the light from the moon and from the Palace windows reflected faintly off highlights on the bodies: the glint of a silver bracelet, the shine of patent leather, the glow of exposed skin. Their feet swung gently in the breeze above my head, twisting from side to side as their otherwise inert bodies moved against the wall, the chains ringing softly with the motion.

One of them was wearing Alice's boots.

CHAPTER XXV

"Almost poetic, isn't it? The chained girls hanged in chains."

I looked up, a horrible sense of inevitability creeping under my skin, into Ben's face.

"Two hanged whores and Emmy makes three," he continued. "I heard the screaming and obviously volunteered to come to the rescue."

I started edging away from him painfully, my battered limbs awkward and ungainly.

"Oh, don't you worry," he said with a grin that showed more of his teeth than I wanted to see. "There's no time for us now, not with the other Invicti on their way. It's an experience I want to savour. Trust me."

The grin again.

I turned back towards the Palace and saw the door opening, but as I did so Ben hunkered down beside me, leaning in close in an apparently solicitous gesture that made my skin crawl. I cowered away, protecting my injured hand, but he took it from me, sending spears of agony through it, and unwrapped the bandage around it to reveal the bite at my wrist.

"I smell his mark on you," he whispered.

Suddenly the prospect of the approaching Silver was a

mixed blessing, and I had no idea where to turn.

"Does he enjoy hearing you scream, or do you enjoy the feeling of his teeth in your flesh? Maybe both?"

But the bite mark on my wrist wasn't Drew's. It was Sol's. I subconsciously fingered the choker at my neck with my free hand, but he caught the gesture.

"Or do you think of the Primus when he bites into you?" He laughed and leaned in closer, his eyes drilling into mine. "You're not so unlike me after all. Drew will die for your sake, but all you care about is the power. Well, none of it's yours," he hissed. "That choker around your neck? You wear it like it's a badge of honour, a mark of prestige, but once upon a time those chains were real and you knew you were slaves."

I looked back at him, trapped in an awful realisation.

"You told them to do this," I whispered. "This was your idea, this retaliation."

It fitted perfectly. I would have died tonight, Drew would have died, and the rebels would have been seen to have made a direct attack on Sol's regime through his chained girls, in Ben's twisted poetry. I may not have died, but this was still a strike against the Primus.

"Yes, well, if you want something doing right around here, apparently you have to do it yourself."

"You want a war."

"Peace is boring," he replied with a darkly mischievous smile that made him look like he'd lost all his marbles.

He thought this was peace? That this was boring, this bleak and brutal future we were carving out for ourselves?

There was a rush of air and I looked up in a panic to see Cam at my side. He didn't stop to talk; he just scooped me up in his arms and carried me away at such speed that when he stopped I was promptly and violently sick, again. That probably also had something to do with the pain all over my body, and the shock of terror and grief. At least I managed to push away from Cam first and find a convenient flowerbed.

I was aware of noise around me, but I was too preoccupied to pay much attention to what was going on. When the retching finally passed, I stood up straight to find myself standing on the terrace of my apartment. The pain in my hand was extremely distracting.

"Shit," I said, tears starting to flow down my face. "What the fuck took you so long?"

I hit Cam hard with my uninjured hand, then collapsed against him, sobbing uncontrollably as he wrapped his arms around me.

"I'm so sorry, Ems," he said. "Ben was running the shift and he took the call. I didn't know it was you; I thought you were safe."

"Alice," I whispered.

"I know," he said. "But Em, we've got to go, particularly after this. I'm not confident that it's secure here anymore. We need to get you healed, then I'm taking you somewhere safe. Remember?"

I nodded against his chest, unable to speak through the pain and sorrow. We had to go. It wasn't safe here.

Then his words penetrated the fog around my brain.

"Healed?" I croaked.

"Yes," said a voice from behind me.

I turned around awkwardly to find myself looking at Drew. Obviously, he was still here. He would have seen us come in.

He raised his hand towards the brand and I leaned back, uncomfortable with him touching it after everything that had happened tonight, before I left the apartment and after.

"It'll be different, I think," he said. "I'm sorry, but we don't have time to argue about it."

With that, he put his palm over the brand. Fire burned through me, but this wasn't pleasant. It felt like I was roasting from the inside out. I opened my mouth to scream and Drew covered my mouth with his hand, deadening the noise before it could attract attention. The bones in my hand cracked together, my knee and my cheekbone felt like they were exploding with pain, and then there was nothing.

"Go," Drew said as he stepped away. "But you," he continued, turning to Cam, "will tell me everything when you get back."

Cam nodded and, shucking onto his shoulder a pack I hadn't realised he'd been carrying, scooped me up into his arms again, carrying me away in a flash of movement. When he stopped we were outside the wall, standing in the dark on the barricade beyond it, our surroundings lit only by the light of the moon.

He set me on my feet and adjusted his pack on his back.

"Why have we stopped here?" I whispered, worried that we might be heard by Silver on the other side of the wall. Or by Weepers on this side, for that matter. We were now thoroughly out of bounds.

"We'll have to walk at normal speed," he whispered back. "It gives the Weepers time to notice me, to move out of our way. Also, I've used a lot of energy this evening already and I'm not going to be able to get any blood till tomorrow. I need to save my strength, just in case."

I didn't want to ask what he was expecting to need it for.

"Okay," I said. "Then let's go."

I turned out to the city to get my bearings and had to stifle a scream. Arrayed in front of me, filling the street, was a crowd of thousands upon thousands of Weepers, their eyes following my every movement. There were so many of them that I couldn't see an end to their numbers, crammed into alleyways, spilling out of broken shop fronts and lining the windows and roofs of the surrounding buildings.

The Silver were eerily still en masse, but the Weepers couldn't have been more different. They were a wave of constant individual motions that somehow gave the impression that they were moving in concert, silently oscillating to the beat of a song only they could hear. In the dim light, the features of each Weeper were obscured, distinctions between bodies unclear and ill-defined, but the appearance of the cohesive whole was startlingly imposing.

How could I ever have doubted that the Weepers had inundated us?

The reason that the Silver had built the wall was now

blindingly obvious. They couldn't have expected us to build a future, to move on and trust them to keep us safe, with the Weepers looming so darkly and numerously into our sanctum. For some of us, the faces would hold more horror than for others. They wanted us to forget.

I shuddered, wondering what familiar faces I might be able to see in the crowd if the light were stronger.

I backed up against Cam, terrified and feeling extremely exposed on the peak of the barricade. His hands rested on my shoulders.

"We walk," he whispered, "and they'll move. I promise."

He steered me gently forward, my knees locking against the movement as every cell in my body screamed for me to run in the opposite direction. Progress was extremely slow because I had to check my footing on the unstable rubble of the barricade before moving, and as soon as I had planted a step my eyes snapped irresistibly back up to the Weepers to check that they weren't any closer.

It was like a tortuously painful game of Grandmother's Footsteps. But there were no wolves here, just people who had once been children, parents, grandparents, lovers.

I couldn't take my eyes away from them, congregating here in their multitudes beyond the walls.

"Why are they here?" I whispered as we inched our way down the slope, towards the road and the crowd occupying it.

"They're always here, looking for you. They know there are humans inside the wall, but they know we're there too, so they're waiting."

"For how long?"

"Forever, maybe. Until we find a way to kill them or control them safely."

"Or a cure?" I asked. Sol had told me they were researching a cure for the Weeper plague, trying to find a way to eliminate the threat that the virus they carried presented to the remaining human population.

"Or that."

As we approached the tarmac at the base of the barricade,

the Weepers started to back away, keeping a distance of about ten feet between us. Their eyes glinted in the moonlight as they followed our progress, individual faces now visible but unidentifiable under the grime over their skin and the bloody tears smeared across their cheeks. The faces were different, but the expressions were all the same: blank and inanimate.

Despite that, I felt scrutinised and harried, prey being tracked by a hunter. By thousands of hunters, in fact.

"They're staying pretty close," I whispered.

"There are a lot of them, and only one of me, but don't worry, they won't come any closer. I've got you covered. Which way?"

I looked around nervously until I saw buildings I recognised. We were on the right side of the city at least.

"This way," I whispered, nodding with my head straight down the road in front of us, "about twenty minutes' walk."

I thanked god it wasn't any further.

"Then let's go."

With Cam pushing me forward, I walked slowly towards the mass of Weepers in front of us. They split down the middle as we approached, as if the length of the road was unzipping, to leave a clear area around us for about ten feet in each direction. Initially I thought the crowd would part all the way along, but as soon as we were about fifteen feet in to the congregation the bodies closed across the road behind us, barring the way back to the wall until we were completely encircled.

"Cam," I whispered urgently as I glanced behind us.

"It's okay, they'll keep this distance. Now let's pick up the pace."

I increased my walking speed very gradually, fear churning in my stomach and my heartbeat thumping in my throat, until I was comfortable that the Weepers were, indeed, moving back to match my pace, anticipating our course. It didn't fill me with a great deal of confidence that they were capable of making those calculations, and of such foresight.

I didn't doubt that they were even more dangerous than

they looked.

I was blinkered and isolated by the mass of bodies around us, distracted by my fear, and unsure of exactly where we were. It didn't help that the buildings out here seemed to have suffered even more damage than those I had seen before the wall went up. A lot of them were missing their frontages entirely, the walls pulled from the faces of the buildings so that it was possible to look right inside them, to see their furniture and fittings precariously placed on their outside ledges, as if they were giant dolls houses.

There was rubble and rubbish in the street, but nothing so big that we had to climb it. The road here was wide enough that when we came across abandoned cars, of which there were several, we simply walked around them, the chorus circle widening and skewing to accommodate the diversion, a macabre hokey cokey.

We carried on in silence for ten minutes or more, the Weepers around us similarly quiet. I'd heard their calls in the night, keening and howling to each other across the city, calling and responding like the world's biggest wolf pack, but right now they apparently had nothing to say.

"Why are they so quiet?" I asked.

"Mostly they call when they find something. Someone. But I'm here, so there's no reason for them to call."

"Why don't they attack you? There are so many of them."

I regretted asking the question almost as soon as it was out of my mouth.

"They never have," he replied softly, "and they never will. It's instinctive. Stop worrying, Ems, and just walk."

Five more minutes of tense walking brought us into narrower roads and alleys with buildings overhanging from above, so that in places we were walking directly underneath Weepers who were looking down from second, third and fourth floor balconies and roofs, silhouetted against the moonlight. My anxiety levels peaked as the road constricted further, claustrophobia overwhelming me as I imagined hundreds of Weepers dropping down on our heads.

My lungs crushed in my chest, my breath coming quicker and quicker as I was consumed with panic, sweat breaking out on my forehead and upper lip.

"I can't do it," I gasped.

"Yes, you can," Cam replied, confident and forceful in a way that was unlike him.

"I can't."

"We're nearly there," he said.

But I froze. I couldn't take another step.

He turned me round to face him and lifted me up, wrapping my legs around his middle and my arms around his neck so that I clung to his front like a monkey, balancing out the pack at his back.

"Close your eyes and breathe," he said.

I did as I was told.

He walked on as if the extra weight was nothing, his arms holding me securely against him, covering my back so I didn't feel exposed. I tried to slow my heartbeat, to slow my breathing, but my brain still knew what was going on around me even if my eyes couldn't see it.

"I used to live around here, you know," he said.

"Mmm?" I replied, still trying to concentrate on getting myself under control.

"Yeah, me and Ed had a place out this way a few centuries ago. It was very different back then, but we had a pub that we bought and ran, pretending we were brothers at the time if I remember correctly. Now, I know what you're thinking. You look at me, and you look at Ed, and you think we couldn't look less like we're related to each other, right? Well, you'd be right, but Ed has that older brother thing going on, and I'm so obviously boyish and charming that no one seemed to mind much."

I realised that he was trying to distract me, but I was grateful for it. It seemed to be working, so I just let myself zone out to the sound of his voice.

"Plus," he continued, "back in those days there were a lot of kids who were illegitimate, you know, back when the word was 'bastards'. Babies delivered by the milkman, that sort of thing. It wasn't something polite people asked about, because you really didn't want to know the answer, and you were probably going to get in trouble for the question. Plus, Ed might not look like much, but he was pretty imposing once upon a time, and he was also a bit reclusive then, which added to that impression.

"So, anyway, we're running this pub and we think what we really need is a nice, comely wench around the place to bring in the customers, because that's what it's all about really: booze and chat and gambling and barmaids. We go through a few of them, and we pay them well and look after them, give them a room, make sure no one gets too friendly with them unless the girls ask them to, but they just don't seem to want to stay. After a while, we're getting a bit suspicious about this, thinking maybe there's something wrong, maybe there are stories we're not hearing that are putting them off, but we can't get to the bottom of it. Months go by, and these girls just keep leaving, sometimes packing up in the middle of the night.

"Now, back then, things were a little less organised. Just before the Revelation, the Silver were pretty well set up for living incognito. There were blood banks and a whole raft of willing vampire devotees, so we had easy access to guilt-free blood. But years ago we didn't have any of that, and things were much more fragmented, the Silver more suspicious and not as willing to risk humans finding out what we are. So we had to improvise, but the ethical options were sort of limited.

"I'm sorry to say that most Silver used to bite the weakest, the people who were least likely to remember and least likely to be believed even if they did: the insane, the old, the young and the poor, women more than men. Lots of humans were killed that way. It wasn't much better, but we used to take blood from those of our patrons who passed out from too much drink. But we didn't bite them, we used a needle to take blood from their veins and siphon it into bottles, kind of like blood donations today in fact. You see Ed's actually insanely clever, really good at science, and he's something of a master physician."

I thought of Ed with his beard and glasses. I could picture him in a lab coat or in a physician's coat.

"He worked out the best way for us to do it, how much blood to take, where from, how to keep it, all that jazz. He looked after us, and he used to spend a lot up time in his makeshift lab trying things out while I ran the place."

Cam described the pub to me, its rooms and the food and drink it offered, together with a few stories about its most regular and distinctive customers. He also described his and Ed's rooms within it, and how Ed had converted a cupboard in one of them into a cool box that kept the blood chilled, using a process that Cam didn't quite understand.

He sounded almost nostalgic, like he missed that period of history, or perhaps missed his time alone with Ed. I wondered how close they really were now, if Carrie was the reason for that tinge of regret in his voice.

"So anyway, these barmaids are all leaving the pub and we can't work out why. Then this new girl starts and we hear a scream in the middle of the night at the end of her first day. I go running downstairs to her room, which was on the first floor below ours, and barrel inside to find her staring up at the ceiling, at a dark stain that had let a few red drops fall down, right onto her pillow as she slept. Poor girl was scared half to death.

"Turns out that there was a tiny leak in one of the water pipes that led into the cooling cupboard, and it was letting the odd drip through, and gradually those drips built up until they fell into the room below, pulling grime and rust with them until they looked like nothing as much as blood. Ironic really.

"She stayed with us, that girl, once we explained about the water pipes and showed her the empty cool box. But then the Great Plague came and took her with it, along with a load of other people, piling the bodies in the street. It wasn't so different from this, really. Seems like there was a lot of plague around then.

"Okay," he said, "we're through. Open your eyes, Ems."

He put me down and I looked over his shoulder to see a wall of Weepers with their backs to us, blocking the way we had come. I thought he had meant that we were through the narrow streets, but we were actually through the Weepers completely. They were a blockade, a mass encircling the city, waiting for the Silver to leave, for their chance to come in, but they weren't interested in me and Cam. I was small fry.

"They're stacked this deep all the way around the walls?" I asked as I looked back at the crowd of swaying sentinels.

"In most places," he replied. "Deeper in some. They've been gradually following the trucks and deliveries in."

"There must be thousands of them."

"Millions."

The nebulous protection the Silver offered was suddenly starting to look pretty flimsy. With that many Weepers crowding at our gates, how long would it be before they decided that the threat of the Silver wasn't a sufficient deterrent to stop them from piling over the walls?

The Silver couldn't kill billions of Weepers before they got to the rest of the humans, particularly when the humans were actively trying to get away from the Silver.

"So there are no humans out here anymore?" I asked, wondering about Cass, about Mary and her girls. And then I remembered: they'd be devastated about Alice.

Cam shrugged.

"Who knows? We searched everywhere before we locked down the safe zone, but I suppose it's possible we missed some people. We do hear the Weepers call every now and then. Which way from here?"

I gave myself a mental shake. I just had to get to the flat, then I could think about what had happened tonight.

"It's just round the corner," I said. "That tower block behind the next street."

There was a bus skewed onto its side blocking the road in front of us, cars stacked up against it in what looked to have been an awful accident. It had brought part of the buildings either side of it down into the narrow street, and they didn't look very stable. We were going to have to go over the top of the pile up.

Cam gave me a leg up onto the bonnet of the closest car, then hopped up after me and helped guide me up and over the wreckage in the dark until we were standing on the side of the bus.

"Are a lot of the roads like this?" I asked. How were the Silver keeping everything operational if they couldn't get anywhere?

"Most of them, yeah. We cleared the ones we use, the ones between the safe zones, but we haven't bothered with the others. There's no need right now. The more energy we use shifting stuff that doesn't need to be moved, the more blood we need, and we're trying to be careful about that. We're under rationing."

This was news to me, but then I thought about the tokens at the club. They weren't about prestige, or about power; they were about how much blood you had earned, just like our food supplies were earned by our labour and our blood.

"Is it very different?" I asked as we picked our way across the carcass of the bus and down the other side.

"What?"

"Life after the Revelation. Are things better for you, now the Silver are in charge?"

"No," he said. "Why would you think that? Everything's harder, and everyone's all crammed together like sardines, and the Silver really don't do well in confined spaces together. Too many sharks, not enough goldfish. And rationing sucks.

"Also, a lot of us enjoyed the anonymity we had when we were pretending to be human. I miss it, but others don't mind the spotlight so much. Unfortunately, they tend to be the wrong people, the egomaniacs, the Silver who would be king."

"Like Sol?" I asked.

"No," he said, looking at me as if I were being ridiculous. "The Primus isn't like that. Not at all."

He jumped back down to the tarmac and held his hand up

to me. I took it and hopped down after him. The rest of the way looked relatively clear, the rubble on the road low and sporadic, so we could weave through it and the various cars abandoned in the street without much difficulty.

There were more gutted buildings out here, their contents clawed out and pulled into the road, banking up against the towers at either side of the street. I started to worry that Cass's flat might not even be there anymore, that it might have been turned inside out by the degradations of the Weepers, and my feet started to move faster.

I turned the corner onto our road, Cam hot on my heels, and caught my toe on a brick that was lying on the pavement, sending me sprawling to my hands and knees.

"Shit!"

"Ems, are you okay?"

It hadn't done much damage, just bruising my knees and slightly skinning my unbandaged palm, but it hurt like hell and had me screwing up my face for a few seconds until the pain passed. When it had done so, I checked out the graze and realised it had barely broken the skin, just a couple of tiny spheres of blood pushing through the surface.

"I'm fine," I said, getting to my feet. "It's fine."

I unwound the bandage a little from my right wrist and used its inner edge to blot gently at the graze. It needed a wash, really, but it didn't look like anything was stuck in it, for once. As I tied the bandage back together the healed skin of my right wrist caught my eye, and then I looked back to my grazed palm in perplexity.

"Why isn't it healing?" I asked Cam.

"Why would it?"

"I thought it was something about the brand, that it kept the healing thing going. That's what Drew said. Surely it should have healed this, should have healed me earlier without Drew needing to do anything?"

"I dunno, "Cam said. "Maybe it needs recharging or something, or maybe it only works for a certain amount of time." He shrugged. "It's all new to me."

That would have to be a question to file away and think about later.

"It's just in here," I said, pointing to the left side of the road. The block was set back from the pavement behind a bike rack and a few scraggly shrubs and trees. I was overwhelmingly relieved to see that it was still intact. It wasn't a pretty building, but it had been cheap and relatively safe. It had been a sort of home for a while.

The front door of the building was locked up tight, and I hadn't thought to bring my keys with me, if I even still had them. I was reluctant to break the door to get in, firstly for my own safety once we were in there, but secondly because an optimistic excitement had started to build up in my chest that, if the building was still locked, it might be possible that people were still alive inside. Fortunately, Cam's past lives had apparently required him to pick a lock or two, so he managed to jimmy it open without damaging the mechanism. I stood and watched while he worked, impatient to get inside, to get to the flat, my mind painting hopeful pictures of Cass, still there having been holed up since the Revelation.

My enthusiasm was short-lived. When Cam pushed on the door, it opened only about a foot before jamming on something stuck behind it. He pushed harder and there was a crack, wood splintering behind the door under the force of the pressure. He passed me a torch from a side pocket of his pack.

"Keep the beam pointed down," he cautioned.

I clicked on the switch and a dull, yellow light illuminated the building's entrance hall. Someone had barricaded the door with a bookcase, but it hadn't done much good; the Weepers had come in through the service entrance, which gaped open on the other side of the building, bloody trails leading through it to the alley beyond.

"Oh god," I whispered.

There were a couple of lifts in the middle of the room, but I imagined they probably weren't operational anymore. The stairs led up to our right and they were strewn with clothing, papers and wrapped food, a suitcase split open on the landing above that had clearly spilled its contents and been left behind. Maybe Cass had got out, I thought.

I took a steadying breath and started to move up the stairs, Cam close by my side.

"It's on the tenth floor," I said.

I was anticipating further scenes of carnage with each flight we scaled, but the concrete stairwell and corridors beyond were empty until we reached the seventh floor. There had clearly been some fighting here, as evidenced by a broken baseball bat and a few holes punched into a nearby door, but there was no blood on the floor. A few other doors were hanging open, as if the building had been deserted in a hurry.

We carried on up to the eighth floor, and there the torchlight found the blood that had been missing from the seventh, smeared in handprints along the wall and sitting in pools on the floor of the corridor. I took one glance and broke into a run, racing up the staircase to the tenth floor without even bothering to look in at the ninth, the light bouncing with my steps. Cam said nothing, right by my side as we hurried upwards.

The tenth floor was empty, the doors all shut. Everything was normal. It was as if none of this had ever happened, as if I had walked home that Thursday night as usual and was about to open the door and find Cass on the sofa waiting for me.

"This one's ours," I said as we reached the fifth door on the right.

Cam picked the lock quickly and silently, then pushed the door open in front of me.

I swung the torchlight carefully into the doorway and looked around the room that had been our sitting room, kitchen and dining room. Everything seemed to be in its place, nothing disrupted. I walked into Cass's bedroom, hoping desperately that I would find her curled up comfortably asleep, but the bed didn't look as if it had been slept in. I opened her cupboards and shone the torch under her bed, but her clothes and suitcase were still where they always were.

If she had got out, she hadn't taken anything with her. I walked back into the main room and walked into the kitchen area. Cam had closed and locked the front door behind him and, setting his pack down on the floor next to the sofa, he took a seat. I opened the fridge and was hit by the foul smell of rotting food. The electricity hadn't been on out here for about ten days and the weather had been roasting hot, so it was hardly surprising.

Holding my breath as I tried to ignore the smell, I scanned the shelves of the fridge for the thing I was hoping not to see, for Cass's favourite dinner that she had been intending to eat the moment she got back from work that Thursday.

But it was still there. Her clothes were here, she hadn't slept in her bed, hadn't eaten her dinner and the flat was otherwise untouched, just as it had been when I left for work that day.

"She never made it back here," I said aloud.

I felt crushed, my last faint, glimmer of hope dashed in the face of the evidence. Whatever I had wanted to find here, whatever closure I thought coming here might bring, it suddenly seemed like I had been an idiot ever to think this trip might end differently. I slammed the fridge door shut and turned back to face Cam.

"I was just hoping, after Alice…"

"I'm sorry, Ems."

His tone was sympathetic, but not surprised. He'd always known this was a fool's errand, but he held me tight as the tears came again.

CHAPTER XXVI

"So this was your place?" he asked me.

I nodded dumbly as I sat down next to him on the sofa. The past tense couldn't have been more appropriate. The flat felt empty and lifeless now, all the rose-tinted memories of the joy and security it had given me wiped away in the face of reality.

My eyes filled with tears again as the vision of Alice's horrible death rose grotesquely in my mind. I'd nearly died the same way, and it had been terrifying. I couldn't pretend that it would have been otherwise for her. I had finally had a friend, a human ally to whom I could talk about the Silver, and now she was gone. I was flattened by the grief, the pathos of such a senseless death, but I was also burning with fury at the way it had happened, the calculated way that her life had been taken.

And it was all my fault, again. Guilt pulled at me, tearing with sharp and vicious teeth. If I had done what I was told, had stayed at the club instead of running off to the wall on the day of the protest, then she would never have been a target for Ben, would never have been wearing the choker that was the reason for her death. She was killed just to send a message to the Silver and to Sol. She had been nothing more than a tool to them, and it was all so pointless.

"Is your world always so cruel?" I asked, pushing the tears from my cheeks.

"Isn't yours? Silver didn't kill Alice, Ems."

"I know that." I paused. "How do you know?"

"There was no scent mark on the body. If a Silver had been the one to do it then there would have been."

Then Ben really hadn't touched her. It wasn't much by way of consolation, but it was something.

"Who was the other?"

"The other girl?" Cam asked me.

I nodded.

"Ella."

I put my face in my hands. Ella, who had survived the Weepers after a day locked in a trunk, who had survived the Revelation and the Silver, only to die at the hands of the humans she lived with. Cam was right: the human world was just as brutal as the world of the Silver.

I was sure it had been the rebels. I could understand how they had got to Ella; after all, she shared a dorm with them, but how had they managed to take Alice?

"Wasn't Alice with Tommy?" I asked.

"Yes."

"Well?" I asked. "Why the hell didn't he bring her back to the apartment?"

"He did," Cam said quietly. "But he left her in the top bar instead of taking her to the patio doors. They must have grabbed her there. I don't think he's ever going to forgive himself for that decision, so don't go hard on him. He really liked her, Ems."

Against all expectations, I had really liked her too. When I first met her I found her immature and irritating, but she seemed to have come into herself in the past week and we'd become a lot closer. I hadn't understood why she wanted to be Silver so badly, but I supposed she'd always felt like she wasn't enough. She was always trying to be better, trying to be everyone's friend, but that desire was borne out of a sense of powerlessness. She was pretty as anything, but she wanted to be strong too, was desperate to be tougher than she was. It was so difficult not to like her when she wore her insecurities so openly on her sleeve.

I remembered her looking out for me at the wall when I almost passed out after Drew was shot. She'd stared down Sol and Cam, daring them to tell her that she wasn't going to be the one to take me back to the club. She was stronger than she'd thought.

Yes, she'd said what she thought without thinking, and she couldn't keep a secret to save her life, but at the heart of it she was a comforting and predictable presence in a sea of the unfamiliar. I was going to miss her like hell.

A howl cut through the quiet of the night and was answered by hundreds of others, an animal ululation that sent shivers down my spine. It sounded like it was just outside. I quickly switched my torch off, worried that the Weepers might have seen the light through the heavy curtains.

"Are we safe here?" I asked, panic creeping into my tone.

"You're completely safe, but if they're following the light then until they get close they won't realise I'm with you. They might come to investigate, so maybe it's better if we keep the torch off for now."

I handed it back to him and he stowed it in the pack. Without the light it was pretty much pitch black, but he seemed to be able to see well enough.

Now that I was sitting still, the shock, tiredness and exertion were starting to catch up with me. A chill ran through me and I realised how cold I was, how little I was wearing. The deserted flat was far from the cosy nest I had expected it to be.

There was no going back, no returning to this life that had been taken from us.

"Come on," Cam said. "We need to get you into some warmer clothes, then you can get some sleep. Where's your room?"

"It's the door on the other side of the flat from Cass's.

The bathroom is the door in the middle, but I don't suppose there'll be any running water."

"It doesn't matter," Cam said, "I brought enough." There were a couple of heavy thumps, and I guessed that he had patted the pack.

"Take my hand," he continued, "and I'll lead you to your room. We can probably risk using the torch enough to let you find something else to wear."

His hand slid into my own and he used it to guide my steps, shutting the bedroom door behind us once we were inside. Thankfully, my clothes were all kept in a very small walk-in wardrobe, so once Cam had made sure the curtains were tightly closed we both walked inside it and shut the door behind us before turning on the torch.

"Just as I left it," I said.

I started sorting through the clothes on the shelves and rail, pulling out some new underwear, a pair of jeans, a clean top and a warm jumper. I contemplated pyjamas, but I wanted to be ready to run if I had to.

"I need to get changed," I said, "so you need to get back out of this cupboard."

"Oh," he said with a cheeky grin, "are you sure you don't need some help?"

I punched him in the chest.

"Don't flirt, Cam. It's weird."

"Yeah, it is, isn't it? I'll be right outside."

I took off the grubby old bandages and stripped out of my mangled uniform. I seemed to go through two or three a week at the moment. Once I had dressed in the new clothes I slipped my feet into some trainers and flicked the torch back off, stepping out into the bedroom.

"Cam?"

"Right here," he said from the direction of the bed. "I found some extra blankets under the bed so I've put them on top of your duvet. You should be snug."

"Thanks, but I'm not sure I can sleep yet. Can you put these in your bag?" I held out the uniform and my boots, and he put them away for me. At least, I assumed that he had from the noise of rustling material.

"Well," he said, taking my hand, "get tucked in and we'll see."

"You won't leave me?" I asked, surprised that I felt so vulnerable in such a familiar and cherished place, here in the dark.

"Ems, I'm right here," he said, settling me under the covers then snuggling in next to me. "I'm going nowhere and you're safe. Also, I brought snacks."

"Really?" I hadn't realised how starving I was until he'd said the words.

"Here," he said, handing me a clingfilmed package.

"What's this?"

"That's a sandwich," he said, "salami and salad, and this is a cup of tea." He pressed a cup into my hand. I inhaled the wonderful, comforting steam and sighed, a broken and jerky sound pulled through the depth of my being after the horrors of the night.

"You brought a flask? You are my absolute hero."

"No, I'm not. I keep letting you down, Ems. If I'd been there earlier…"

"No. I keep letting myself down. It's not your fault. Now talk to me while I eat."

He dropped the subject for the moment, but I knew he felt as much guilt as I did, and Tommy did, for Alice's death.

"Okay, let me ask you a question. You and the boss kissed, so why are you still trying to get away from him?"

"Ask me a different question."

If he had been trying to distract me then it had been a good question to pick.

"Is it…"

I interrupted him.

"If you ask me if it's Sol then I'm going to run out into the street and let the Weepers have me. I'm not having this conversation again."

"That's just your knee-jerk reaction, Ems. Have you

actually thought about it? If you have feelings for the Primus, then maybe that's getting in the way."

"I've thought about it, but it's not like I have a finite amount of emotion that's being shared. The two aren't connected like that. It just doesn't work like that."

"So you love the Primus?"

Another question I didn't want to answer.

"Look, I'm not going to tell him or the boss," he said. "You can talk to me, and only me."

I took a sip of my tea. In the confidentiality of the darkness it actually helped to have Cam there, someone to talk this through with, someone with respect for Sol and Drew. I decided it couldn't hurt to say it out loud.

"There wasn't time for love," I said, "but there was… something."

"You humans have some funny ideas about love, you know that? You're always trying to limit love, to catch love, to pin it down and keep it, as if that were in its nature. Love isn't something you can box up, and it's not a switch that flips on. It builds. It's fluid, like all emotions, growing and ebbing to its object like the tide to the moon. You can't confine or define it."

"But he's out of the picture, Cam. It's all academic now that he's silvered for Laila."

"Even when you're Silver, love isn't always forever. When it is, it isn't always as strong."

"But you're rooting for Drew. You're not exactly unbiased here."

"I love my king and I love my leader, but if all other things were equal then I do think that the boss has a worthier claim. The bond is a burden. Can you imagine how much it hurts to be reminded every time you look in a mirror that the love of your life doesn't love you back? That's what the silver in his eyes means to him: you don't love him."

There was an awful sadness to his words and I wondered who had left him pining. Cam had always been so carefree, so cheerful, that I'd never really put him in the same camp as the rest of the Silver. He didn't give the impression that he'd lived for centuries because he was still full of the same joie de vivre as a seven-year-old with a toy airplane.

But I was meeting a different Cam today. He was more thoughtful, his words coloured by loss. I felt with certainty that he understood my grief over Alice and my heartache over Drew and Sol, not because he was particularly empathetic but because he'd lived it himself and had stood in my shoes an age ago.

I wanted to ask to hear about it, but I felt like we'd had enough of sad stories today.

"More than that," he continued, "much as I respect him, I worry that the Primus would never tolerate a partner when he can have a concubine instead."

I thought back to his words of the other night: I am no king and I will have no queen.

"So you're going to tell me all about Drew's virtues?"

"I'll tell you whatever you ask me," he said. "I'm your friend, Ems, not your matchmaker."

"You're awesome," I replied, leaning back against him for warmth as I unwrapped my sandwich.

"I was actually pretty surprised when you and the Primus… you know," he said.

"Really?"

"Well, yeah. I know him better than most, I think."

"You do?"

"Yeah, but that's a whole other story. Either way, it's not really… I mean, he just isn't like that anymore."

"Everyone else seems to think it's perfectly in character," I said.

"Well, people don't see him clearly. They see the suit, not who's wearing it. You ever see him without the suit?"

I flushed as my imagination conjured up all sorts of visuals. I was glad that I could hide my reaction in the darkness.

"No."

"He's not like the rest of us, Ems."

I knew what he meant.

"I've heard he's a god."

"He's something like it. To me, he's a warrior king."

"Tell me about it," I said, handing my tea to him so I could unwrap my sandwich.

"Another slice of history then," he said. "How much do you know about the Roman Empire?"

"Assume I know nothing," I replied through a mouthful of bread.

"Well, you've probably heard of a few of the early emperors, and you probably know they were into expansion. At the Empire's height, they had a whole load of provinces, stretching from Babylon to northern Africa to France, and across the channel to England, and all of that land was hard-won by the Empire's soldiery. But those soldiers weren't just Romans; they were Illyrians and Armenians and Greeks. Most of the emperors had an approach that I think the Primus sort of admires: it was all about assimilation. They came into these backwater regions that had been subjugated by war, looked around at their gods and consciously decided that the local deity was just another manifestation of Jupiter, or Juno, or Mars, or whatever god best suited the bill. Then they brought trade, and wine, and bathhouses, and everything they considered to be civilised, and made their captives into Romans. It got to the point where some of the regions actively wanted to be Romanised.

"But not all of them.

"The Germanic tribes refused to be subdued. They fought back against the Romans time and time again, battling over the Rhine for hundreds of years. I'll tell you the story I heard from someone who was there when it happened. As far as I know, he was the only person other than Sol who was there that day and who was still alive, but he died in America in the Revelation, so I guess Sol is the only one who knows the truth now. Nevertheless, the legend is pervasive. It's something the Silver tell their children, something they tell their newly-turned, but they all tell it wrong."

He shifted position slightly so he could reach behind

himself to put my tea down on the windowsill, then settled down into the story.

"My friend was a legionary, fighting the tribes in the front line. He wasn't yet twenty and he'd just been recruited from the eastern provinces. For the Roman legionaries, some of whom had been raised in far warmer lands, the reality of warfare in the cold, dark, wet forests of Germany was hard and unyielding. The way that Roman legions fought, arrayed in tight lines behind the protection of large shields, was difficult to adapt to battles amongst the towering trees against an enemy who knew the terrain extremely well and was much more comfortable with the sort of guerrilla warfare that the situation required. They were losing, badly. Their men were dying or injured in horrifying numbers, their blood soaking into the rich leaf litter carpeting the forest and running red in its streams.

"To say the least, it was demoralising. And when people are demoralised, I've found that's often when they look for outside help. That's why cults had always been popular in the Roman army, and when I say 'cult' I don't mean the word like it's understood today. I mean a niche religion, a following that's specific to the people, the time and the place. It's safe to say that the Roman troops in Germany were on the look out for that kind of personalised saviour.

"So, my friend the legionary, he had a god back home, a god of the sun. He's in this dank, vegetal mire and all he can think about is how much he misses the sunshine on his skin, how much he misses the warmth and how he wishes that he were anywhere other than under the cold shade of the soaring pines surrounding them, watching friends and strangers die. Those of his friends who are still alive, they aren't exactly happy either, so they pray.

"They gather together one evening, a pathetically small group, a little way away from the rest of the camp but still close enough to be in earshot, and they pray to their sun god to give them strength, to bring them courage and to find them a way to overcome the warrior tribes they faced. Back home, they'd normally have offered some kind of sacrifice to the god to seal their prayer, to bring them favour, but stuck out in their encampment they had nothing to offer, no meat to burn, just bare rations. So they improvise, each of them making a small cut on their arm and letting the blood flow to the ground, a libation to speed their requests to the ears of their deity.

"Maybe the god was listening, maybe not, but what they got was not what they were expecting. Just as the last man in the group is running his blade along his skin, a hollow sound comes out of the woods, like someone is knocking on the trunk of a dead tree, and it scares them half to death. They scramble up to their feet, thinking it's the enemy, but then a voice calls out softly to them from the darkness in their own language.

"Now, despite the size of the Roman Empire, the world was pretty small back then. It only went as far north as Germany in the west, and Scandinavia was uncharted land for the Romans, so blonde hair was fairly rare in their society, particularly amongst those who spoke the language of the eastern edges of the Empire. When our Primus strolled forward out of the shade of the tree canopy towards the soldiers, clothed in nothing but a pair of loose trousers, can you imagine how he must have looked to them? His eyes such a clear blue with their silver markings reflecting the little light that there was, his voice clear and his accent perfect, and, above all, his hair crowning him in a blaze of gold that resembled nothing so much as a burning halo of light.

"No wonder they thought he was a god. They might even be right. There's no denying that there's something supernatural about the light, and the darkness, he seems to carry in him, even for a Silver. Maybe that's what happens when you're that old, when you've lived so long. Or maybe that's just Solomon."

I reached out to take the tea from Cam, crumpling the empty clingfilm in my hand as I did so and dropping it to the floor by the bed.

"Do you believe that?" I asked.

"I don't know what to believe about him, really, but I wouldn't bow to anyone else. All I know is that only a complete idiot would stand against him and expect to come out on top. Don't let the fact that he has us as his guard fool you into thinking that he needs us for his own protection, because he's fifty times stronger than any one of us, even Drew. We're his enforcers, not his bodyguard. Until Laila came along, I wasn't sure it was even possible for him to die."

"Because of the bond? You think someone will try to kill Laila?"

"There are a lot of stupid people out there who might think it's a great opportunity. They'll find it hard, though; she's damn strong herself and she's under even heavier protection than you are."

I sighed. It was a hell of a situation for them to be in, with Sol and Drew both silvered at the same time, but at least Laila wasn't the same weakness to Sol that I was to Drew. I wondered again about Oliver's offer to break the bond. It would probably be for the best in the long run, if it was genuine, but I was hardly going to trust him now. Not after Alice.

"So what happened?" I asked, trying to distract myself. "What about the soldiers?"

"Oh, right. So, the Primus steps out of the darkness like some kind of terrible beacon, and he offers the soldiers a trade. He says that, in return for their blood, he'll save their lives by fighting at the head of their army to help them to defeat the tribes."

"That sounds like a familiar bargain."

"In very different circumstances, though. I'm not sure what had happened to him, but apparently he was on the verge of collapse that day, so it must have been weeks since he had last fed. He doesn't like to take blood by force."

I knew that all too well; he liked to persuade and seduce it willingly, to win it from your veins.

"Now," Cam continued, "for the soldiers, this is completely in keeping with what they expect from their gods.

The eastern manifestations of their deities in particular were pretty demanding in terms of sacrifices, and being asked to feed a god your blood to win a war was nothing compared with being required to murder your babies on his altar to bring back the rain. So they fall on their knees, agreeing with only a moderate amount of trepidation, and by the time the Primus has fed from the wounds of each of them he looks to the soldiers like he's almost glowing with strength and fire. As they return to their tents to sleep it off, they couldn't be more convinced that he is both their god and their salvation.

"When the next day dawns, the troops are lined up as far as possible amongst the trees and sent forward in their diminished numbers to meet their enemy, in a last desperate attempt not only to bring the tribes under Roman rule, but also to clear a path home for the soldiers who otherwise have no hope of ever escaping the forests. Those forests had claimed legion after legion over the previous centuries, and the soldiers had even come across heaped piles of their bones in their march, their standards driven into the mud, the material tattered and defiled, beneath hundreds of skulls arranged like trophies in the arms of the trees. The spectre that the forest might also become their graveyard was hanging heavily in the soldiers' minds that day.

"Then there's shouting and whooping in the trees ahead of them, so they know the battle's drawing nearer and nearer, and my friend looks for his saviour to come, but there's no sign of him. Arrows fly through the air from both sides and men fall all around them, but still Solomon doesn't come. Finally, as sword clashes against sword and shield there's a detonation in the centre of the melee, like something has thudded down into the earth with massive force, and before the leaves can settle Solomon is tearing through the barbarian ranks, his golden crown glinting and flashing as he speeds from kill to kill, ripping through hundreds of men in the space of seconds.

"He pauses in a circle of felled bodies, his golden hair shining through a coating of crimson, and throws his head back in an inhuman roar. His face is smeared with blood, and it's streaming down his bare throat and torso, and his arms are red past the elbow with the gore that drops to the ground from the tips of his fingers. He's a vision of death, a demon to the tribesmen but a terrible god to the Romans, the god they had asked for. And he'd delivered on his promise, just as they had.

"The Roman soldiers gape and step back out of the ambit of the whirlwind as their god continues in his carnage, and in less than a minute they stand arrayed in front of a pile of dead barbarians, but there's no sign of the Primus. A few seconds pass in silence, each soldier too shocked to move, and then the birds start singing again, a noise the soldiers hadn't realised was missing until they heard it once more.

"Those soldiers made it home and the legend of Sol Invictus grew with the telling. There were stories of him turning up at other battlefields, of leading the charge against the enemy, and eventually he became integrated into the Roman state religion."

"So what happened?" I asked. "Sol's still here, so why isn't his religion?"

"Christianity happened. The emperors converted. The Primus was still there in the background for a while, but he's never stayed in the same place for that long. Eternal life is difficult if you can't reinvent yourself, move on from your past and escape your mistakes. People remember though, the Silver remember, so he still carries the name. But that's not all he is to us and that wasn't the first time he'd led an army into battle. He's known by so many names and titles, followed by each of us in a different guise, but all of those personae have one thing in common: power.

"And that's part of the problem, Ems. He doesn't settle, he doesn't share, and he knows that you're interested in him. I wouldn't be surprised if the bond is the only thing that's kept you and the boss safe. When I heard he'd silvered for Laila, I was almost as relieved as Drew. He's painfully powerful, physically and mentally, and he's merciless when he needs to be. I don't know why you don't see that side of him, but to gain the kind of respect and fear he engenders in people he's had to be hard, cruel and razor sharp."

"That's not all there is in him," I said.

"No, but it's a large part. It's not something that he wants, not anymore, but it's something he has to be. People don't want emotion and fragility from their military leaders. They want terrible creatures built of granite and cold as ice, vicious in their pursuit of the enemy and uncompromising in their justice. They want a nightmare to unleash."

"Is that who he is to you?" I asked.

"To me he's what he was when I first met him: a warrior king, dripping in blood. It might not sound like a good thing, but I've been in his army for centuries and I wouldn't follow anyone else. There's a reason people worshipped him."

"And what about your friend, the legionary?"

"He never saw Solomon again during his military service. He took a blow to the shoulder in close combat a couple of years later and had to be discharged. A few months afterwards he had just stabled his horse at an inn on his journey home and was on his way back inside when a familiar voice called to him, asking if he wanted his strength back. As far as I know, he's the only Silver the Primus ever turned."

"And it worked?" I asked. "I thought it didn't work without the bond?"

"Oh no, it can, and I guess they had a connection of sorts. My friend had given his blood when the Primus needed it most, and had worshipped and revered him as his god. Isn't that love as good as any bond?"

There was another call from out in the city, further away this time, and I wondered what new quarry the Weepers had found. Some of the answering howls were very close, as if they were inside the building itself. Perhaps we had had a close reprieve after all.

"They'll move on now," Cam said, "particularly as it'll be dawn soon. Then they'll be mostly inside, and we should be able to move around a bit more freely. Why don't you try and get some sleep?"

I handed him back the empty thermos lid that had served as my cup and there was a gentle clunk as he put it down.

"You'll stay here?" I asked.

"Going nowhere, Ems. I promise."

We lay back on the bed together and he wrapped his arms around me, pillowing my head on his chest. I was crashing hard, and it couldn't have been more than a few minutes before I was dropping off, visions of Sol bathed in blood chasing me into sleep.

CHAPTER XXVII

"What time is it?" I asked as I woke later that day. There was dull light coming in through edges of the curtains.

"Pretty late. Mid-afternoon, I think."

"You don't have a watch?"

"You're lying on it," he said.

"Oops."

I sat up so he could have his arm back and he checked the dial on his wrist.

"Just past three," he said. "We've got nearly twelve hours to burn before the mark fades and we can go back."

"I'm not sure I want to."

"No choice I'm afraid."

"I know," I said. He couldn't stay out here with me forever, and if he left I'd be Weeper bait. "I just want to pretend none of it happened for a while."

"Well, come on then. Let's make that happen."

He opened the curtains and let the dreary afternoon into the room. It was chucking it down with rain again and, as we watched, lightning started to streak across the sky. It was going to be another of those heavy summer storms.

"The light's dull enough that the Weepers are probably still out on the streets in this weather," he said. "Better that we stay here anyway. It's safer for us to stay put, so the Primus knows where we are at least."

Now that I could see in the faint light of the storm I looked around the room to see if there was anything I'd want to take with me when we went back to the walled city, but it seemed like it would be a futile gesture. There was nothing here that I could reclaim.

Then I remembered my parents' rings. I kept them in my jewellery box, their wedding rings and my mum's engagement ring. I pulled out a strong silver chain from the box and slid the rings onto it then, in a fit of anxiety, threaded three similar chains through the rings as well and fastened each of them around my neck. It looked a little weird, but at least if one of the chains broke I'd have three backups.

Cam watched me quietly, but he didn't ask.

"Hungry?" he said.

"Sure. You?"

"Yeah, I could eat." He picked up his pack and we walked into the main room of the flat and opened the curtains in there too.

"What's on the menu then?" I asked. "I suppose the thermos of tea will be cold by now."

"Yeah, sorry. And all I have is more sandwiches, water and some chocolate. You want jam or cheese?"

I opted for cheese and we sat down on the sofa, wondering how we were going to spend the rest of the day and night. I didn't want to talk about Alice, or about Ben, about Sol and Drew, or about the imminent Casting.

We needed a distraction.

As Cam sorted through his pack, most of which was taken up with bottles of water, I looked around the room trying to think of something to kill the time. My gaze fell on the small stack of board games that we kept on top of the bookcase.

Perfect.

We had a few rounds of Uno then switched to Monopoly and couldn't seem to stop playing. Much to my amusement, Cam was a hilariously poor loser. Every time I bought a property he wanted, and every time he landed on one of my hotels, he'd get really huffy about it and try to pretend he wasn't. It was really endearing, like playing with a competitive six-year-old.

"I hate this game," he declared after he got sent to jail for the third time in a row. He threw his fake banknotes down on the floor and stomped off into the kitchen to put our sandwich plates in the sink. Not that it mattered; it wasn't like I was going to wash them up without running water. We weren't going to be coming back here any time soon anyway.

"Aw, Cam, don't be a sore loser."

"I'm sure you're cheating somehow."

"I'm cheating? I saw you slip that Get out of Jail Free card into your sleeve."

"Yeah, well, this game sucks."

He hated it so much that we played three more rounds.

We lost the light shortly afterwards, so we drew the curtains again and curled up on the sofa to wait for the mark to fade enough for us to go home. The club was home now, I realised, not this empty shell of a flat.

"Are you ready to talk now? If I ask you a question, will you answer it honestly?" he said.

This sounded ominous, but I guess I owed him that much.

"Okay."

"Why are you running from Drew?"

In the dark and empty flat, the answer was easy to come by. It was time to say it aloud.

"I can't be what he needs me to be. I don't love him. I can't love him."

"Why?"

"Everything I feel for him now is an illusion of the brand. Whatever was there to start with, whatever we might have had, it's just got all twisted up in this mental manipulation. I resent it now, every time it happens. I feel violated afterwards, like someone else has taken control of my body and done things with it that I never wanted. If I don't get away from it, I think I might start to hate him."

He was quiet for a moment, apparently considering what I'd said.

"And the Primus?"

"Has moved on. Nothing more to say there, Cam."

"Then what about the Casting? Why did you agree to it?" he asked.

"You wanted me to!"

"I know, but still."

"Look, my vulnerability puts him in danger, which puts the stability of the Silver hierarchy in danger."

"You mean it puts Solomon in danger?"

"That's not what I said. But yes. And I did it for Alice." A tear slipped out and ran down my cheek. "It wasn't her fault she got mixed up in this, and she so wanted to be like you. She idolised the Silver. She must have thought all of her prayers had been answered by Tommy, and then this happens."

"It's always been dangerous for humans to hang around with the Silver. It always will be, I'm afraid. It's not your fault, Ems."

"Yeah, it is, but that's my guilt and I'll deal with it."

We sat together in silence for a few minutes before either of us spoke again. There was a howl outside in the street and we moved to the window to see what was happening. The moonlight caught the movement of Weepers piling into the building over the road from us, a never-ending stream of dirty, ragged bodies in the pursuit of something.

"Do you think there's someone in there?" I asked.

"Could just be a fox or something."

"But what if it's a person? Shouldn't we do something? Can't we go over and help?"

He sighed and sat back down on the sofa, the moonlight picking up the edge of his silhouette.

"There's nothing we can do. Firstly, I'm not leaving you alone. Secondly, even if we went together I'm not taking you in there among Weepers who are in a feeding frenzy. Thirdly, we've tried helping people in this situation before, but we're always too late. When we first got the barricade up, we used to send a couple of the Invicti out when we heard a call, but every single time the Weeper to sound the call had already killed or bitten the victim before alerting its pack. The idea, we think, is to let the other Weepers know that other prey might be nearby that they can catch, rather than to invite them to come and share."

I shuddered.

"Sandwich?" he offered cheerfully, clearly not in the least bit bothered by the thought of the Weepers eating people. Well, who was he to judge? He drank our blood.

"Er, no thanks."

He tucked into one himself with apparent relish, but the thought of it made me feel queasy.

"How long till we leave?" I asked.

"About another four hours, I reckon."

"Do we have to be back tonight?"

"Not if you don't want to, but we'll have to go back tomorrow morning. Do you want to sleep here?"

I thought of the alternative, of inching back through the city surrounded by millions of Weepers for every step of the way, then coming home in the dark to the apartment I had shared with my dead friend, into the arms of a man I didn't love, but who loved me so fiercely that he wanted to keep me even though I didn't want to be kept.

"Definitely," I said.

"Okay. What do you want to do until then?"

"Will you answer a question of mine?"

"Okay, fair's fair."

"Why does Ben hate humans so much when he started out as one? Why is he so against Silver and humans bonding?"

Cam leaned back next to me, taking a swig from a bottle of water and handing it to me. I drank it gratefully.

"Well," he said, "that's actually not a story I know in detail, so I can only tell you what I've heard. Apparently, Benedict was some kind of Germanic prince a few centuries back, and a noblewoman came visiting his court from the borderlands of a nearby kingdom, bringing her daughter with her. The woman had just lost her husband in some feud between the two monarchs, and her home had been burned, her lands salted so that she had nowhere to go and no way to pay the taxes her new king was demanding.

"I don't know what happened to the woman, but the king took a shine to her daughter and decided to keep her at court. I think in all likelihood the mother probably sold her to the king in return for a new domain of her own, because that's the sort of horrible shit that happened back then. But anyway, this daughter of hers was beautiful, in her late teens, with flowing brown hair and all the attributes you'd look for in a young wife. The moment Benedict saw her, so the story goes, he fell in love with her.

"But her own feelings didn't run quite so deep. She was only a few years younger than him in appearance, but she was actually a Silver a good fifty years older than he was, and she wanted the power and money his family held. Of course he didn't know any of that because she was hiding the silver of her eyes, and he didn't know the Silver even existed."

"Is that something all of the Silver can do?" I asked, remembering when Cam himself had practised that deception on me the first time we'd met.

"Most of us, but not until we're a few decades old. It takes time to learn how to maintain it, but this girl had had time enough. What we can't do is show one part of the silver and not the whole lot, so while Drew could hide the silver in his irises and in the whites of his eyes, he couldn't do one without doing the other. When you've silvered, everyone knows about it; there's no way to conceal those telltale marks.

"So anyway, she'd already been promised to the king, but she decided she'd rather shack up with young Ben than spend her years as queen tied to an aging alcoholic who had just been widowed for the third time in circumstances that made it look like none of his wives' deaths were accidental. Can't blame her, really. She'd decided to seduce Benedict and encourage him to kill his father and take the throne, which is exactly what she did. Ben hated his father because he, like the rest of the court, suspected that he had killed Ben's mother, so he was more than happy to oblige.

"But something went wrong in the attack, and Benedict ended up with a stomach wound. The girl's plan only worked for so long as he was alive, so she turned him Silver to save him. He was on cloud nine, thinking he had eternity to spend with the girl he loved and he told her all of his plans for their future, their children, and their life together.

"She laughed at him. She'd been sleeping with half the court and she thought he was a stupid child, pretty but dumb, and she told him so."

"So?" I asked.

"So he killed her."

"But... how?"

"There are ways and means, and she was still young and inexperienced."

"But if he loved her, hadn't he silvered? Wouldn't he have killed himself?"

"There's all kinds of love, Ems, and it's not always the kind worth silvering for."

"I thought the two went together?"

"You're trying to put love in a box again. People love in lots of different ways. I love you, but I'm not silvering for you."

"But if you're in love, isn't that the point of it?"

"There are always degrees. It isn't simple, and the whole silvering thing just makes it more complicated. At the end of the day, love is just a word and people use it in different ways."

I couldn't argue with that. How did you standardise language to describe emotion when experience of that emotion isn't universal?

We chatted for another hour or so, mostly about the club. I told Cam some of the stories from before the Revelation, some of the parties we'd had for birthdays and special events, some of the horrible customers. There wasn't much to celebrate anymore.

Maybe that's what we were missing. We had the venue, but we had no reason to enjoy it.

CHAPTER XXVIII

I had an mp3 player in my bedroom that still held some of its charge, so when we ran out of enthusiasm for conversation and the night started to chill the air, we got back into the bed and shared the headphones, one earpiece each. By the time the music stopped, the battery run down, I was half asleep.

Then there was something knocking against the door of the flat.

I froze, my fingers twisting into Cam's T-shirt.

"What's that?" I hissed.

Cam said nothing, so I shook him a little, realising guiltily that he had sat up all of last night so this would have been the first sleep he'd had for two days.

"Wuh?" he said blearily.

"There's something at the door," I whispered.

He slid out of the bed stealthily and crept across to the bedroom door. I hurried after him, glad that I'd opted to keep my clothes and trainers on.

There was another knock, and it seemed rhythmic and intelligent, not the mindless thumping I would expect of the Weepers.

"Cameron?" said a voice from the corridor outside.

Oh, shit. I knew who it was.

He rushed to the front door and opened it wide to his warrior king, stepping aside to let him enter.

"Primus," he said formally.

Sol looked from one of us to the other as he entered the room.

"You are both well?" he asked.

"Yes, Primus," Cam replied.

"The mark has faded, but you have not returned to the safe zone."

"The Weepers were on the hunt in the street, so it seemed a better idea to return in the morning," he said.

I said nothing. I was looking at Sol, tracing his features in the moonlight as I tried to pick out the bloodied god, the vengeful demon that Cam had described to me last night. His hair did seem to glow a little in the darkness, his eyes were the same piercing blue in the diminished light as they were in the middle of the day, and there was a hardness there.

Cam was right: I'd been looking at the suit, not the man, not the lean strength of his body. I hadn't paid enough attention to the poise with which he held himself or the power that emanated from him. I'd heard his eloquent words but not understood the force that supported them.

I hadn't seen him roaring fury to the sky, but I'd seen him roar in triumph and could imagine how it could hold fear in it. I could well believe that this man could take down an army.

"I was concerned for your safety," he said, but he was looking at Cam, not me. "You will be missed, and you need to drink. I will escort you both back now."

Cam nodded at him once, and I knew it had been an order rather than an offer.

"Is there anything you want to take from here, Ems?"

I pressed my hand against my chest where my parents' rings hung on the chain beneath my jumper.

"I've got everything I need," I said.

Sol's face darkened a little in the light of the moon, a shadow passing over his face that made it look almost as if the blue in his eyes had dimmed.

Cam zipped up his pack and slipped his arms into the shoulder straps, then held out his arms towards me.

"Come on then, let's get out of here."

"You'll be alright?" I asked, thinking about what he had said about how much energy it took for him to travel at speed.

"Sure, I don't need to save my strength anymore and I'll have some blood as soon as I get back to the Palace. It'll be fine."

"I could carry her if you would prefer," Sol interjected.

Was I not standing right here? He hadn't said one word to me since he'd walked in the door.

"The brand won't tolerate it," I said simply as I put my arms around Cam's neck and jumped up, with his help, to wrap my legs around his waist.

"Ready?" he asked me.

"Ready."

I pressed my face into his neck and closed my eyes, and after a few seconds of frantic motion I opened them again to find that we were standing back in the garden of my temporary apartment. I was relieved to see that Sol hadn't followed us here.

"Best hop off quick, Ems, because you're starting to look sort of delicious."

I slid down to the ground and punched him on the arm.

"You're such a dick," I said.

He grinned at me happily and knocked on the patio door, which was opened a second later by Drew.

"Here she is," he said to Drew, "safe and sound."

Drew rushed out and pulled me into his arms, squeezing me tight against his chest.

"God, I'm so glad you're okay."

Cam caught my eye over Drew's shoulder and gave me a sympathetic look as I gently disengaged. After our candid discussion of last night, he knew how conflicted I felt about it. I couldn't have felt more awkward than I did at that moment.

"Where the hell have you been?"

"Outside the walls," I said, "back at my old place. We thought it would be safer than staying here."

"Safer? Safer than here with me?" he asked incredulously.

"Drew, please don't. I just… I couldn't stay here. Did Cam tell you what happened?"

"Yes, and we're investigating."

"So you don't know who killed Alice and Ella?" I asked.

"We're looking into it."

"So you do know, and you won't tell me."

"Like I said, we're looking into it."

I lost my temper.

"No, I've had enough of this. You need to tell me what's going on here, right now."

"So," said Cam awkwardly from behind me, "I'm going to head off now." He dropped his pack to the ground and handed me my boots and uniform. "Here you go, Ems. It's been a ball. See you later."

He grabbed me into a quick hug then picked up his pack and zipped off, apparently so desperate to be out of here that he was willing to use the very last of his strength to leave as quickly as possible. I couldn't blame him.

"Can we at least argue inside?" Drew said, holding the patio door open for me. I couldn't think of a reasonable objection, so I walked into the apartment and sat on the sofa as he locked the door behind us.

"What did you do with them?" I asked.

He sat down next to me and met my eyes. He looked tired and ragged, like he'd not slept since I'd left. Maybe that was true.

"Please tell me you didn't put them outside the wall," I continued.

"No, we didn't. We buried them in the cathedral, along with Graham."

At least they would be out of the hands of the Weepers, then.

"So tell me what happened," I said.

He took a breath and leaned forwards, his elbows resting

on his knees.

"From what we can gather, Ella was jumped about half an hour after she finished her shift and Alice a little after that. Then they went after you. They were all human. How many did you hear?"

I thought back to the events of the previous night.

"At least three, probably four. I heard two male voices and one female, and the way they were talking about him, Oliver wasn't with them."

"That makes sense. Graham's death made Oliver angry, but it gave him a wake-up call. We've been told that he's stepped away from the rebellion, the fight gone out of him. He might be willing to help us bring an end to this."

"And what about the Silver? We know Ben's involved. And what about Graham? Who killed him?"

"Ben didn't; I've had someone watching him the whole time." Not just for my safety anymore, I realised, but for Laila's as well.

"So who did?"

"We don't know."

"Then find out."

He nodded at me solemnly.

"And what about Mary and her kids?" I asked.

"No news. I'm sorry."

I ran my hands over my hair, pushing the dirty strands away from my face. I must have looked a state. I hadn't washed today and I was starting to feel pretty filthy after all that had happened in the past two days.

"I need a bath," I said, "and then I'm going to bed."

I stood up and was on my way to the stairs when a thought occurred to me.

"What happened today? Was the club closed?"

With me away and Alice… Well, there had been no one to run the place.

"No," he replied. "They opened."

There was something he wasn't telling me.

"What is it?" I asked.

"Emmy…," he paused. "Ed's in charge now. There are a few more staff they've brought over from the Palace too, but you're back on the bar."

Oh. At least it was Ed and not a human-hating bitch like Laila, and Ed knew what he was doing if Cam's story about their pub was anything to go on.

"Also," he continued, "Sol made another broadcast: no humans in the club anymore, not until things settle down."

"Is that his retaliation?" I asked. The humans had attacked humans under his protection, and there had to be a steeper penalty on the way.

"He'll exact his price when the time comes," he replied. "Don't worry about that."

"And this place?" I asked, indicating the apartment around us.

"Sol knows you can't go back in the dorm at the moment, but yes, we need to move you out of here soon, and Ed needs to move in here tomorrow or it'll look suspicious. I've spoken to him, and he's happy for you to stay as long as you want, but you won't need to be here after the Casting anyway."

So I had a week. That was some reassurance at least. I started heading up the stairs.

"Emmy," he said.

I turned to face him and, standing up from his seat, he walked over to me.

"I know this isn't really the time, but I get that the bond is hard for you to understand, and that it's weird, but please don't give up on us. I'm trying, I really am, and I know it might not mean much to you, but I love you. And I do have my reasons, I'm just not any good at romance. I'm a fighter, not a lover."

"Well, we certainly fight a lot."

I had been trying to lighten the mood with a joke, but the moment it was out of my mouth I realised it had been a stupid thing to say.

"You're the only one fighting this," he said.

"I know."

"And the Casting? Please don't tell me you've changed your mind."

"I haven't," I replied. Alice might be beyond my help, but I was more certain than ever that the only way Drew and I would have even half a chance of surviving was by turning me Silver.

"Thank god for that. I've signed you up," he said. "We can't back out now."

"You've signed up as my sponsor?" I asked.

"Yes. Will you still have me?"

He knew I didn't have a choice, so he wasn't asking me if I'd still let him be my sponsor. He was asking if I'd still give our relationship a chance. He looked so forlorn, so desperate, that it made me feel angry and guilty all at once.

I wondered if reality and the brand were crashing together to create that ambivalence, but the brand won out, just like Sol had said it would. As Drew came closer, comfort flowed over me like a balm and soothed the rough edges off my mood, pushing away all the negative feelings that were burning brightly in me.

I didn't have the mental strength to fight it, so I just gave in.

The brand would always win.

CHAPTER XXIX

Wednesday

I'd bathed alone and dressed in my pyjamas in the bathroom, but I'd eventually given in to the urge to keep Drew close, pulling him into bed with me just before I fell asleep.

When I woke the next day I was cradled close to him, both of his arms wrapped around my middle so I was locked in to his chest. He was holding on so tightly that I couldn't move.

"Drew?"

He mumbled into my neck, burying his face in my hair then, as he started to stir, he released his arms a little and pressed a kiss to the side of my throat.

Then I realised why I'd woken up: something was ringing.

"Drew, is that your phone?"

He lifted his head and rolled away, sitting up on the side of the bed.

"Hello?" he said. "Oh, shit." A pause. "Yes, please. See you in a couple of minutes."

I swung my legs free of the covers and got out of bed.

"That was Viv," he said. "She's reminded me that it's been a while since I... saw her, and that if I've spent the night with

355

you then there's nothing to mask the scent."

"Oh," I said. "Of course."

He was going to have to mark her, and vice versa. It felt like a lot to ask of me at the moment, when things were already so emotionally precarious between us.

"This won't be forever, Emmy. As soon as you're Silver, we can drop the charade."

"I know," I said.

"Look, I need to get back to the Palace. Ed's coming with Viv so he can bring his bags over and go through the papers in the office with you."

"Oh, right. Shall I move my stuff over to the little room?"

I didn't want to hog the master bedroom when I was only staying here by Ed's charity, but I wasn't sure I could cope with sleeping in Alice's bed.

"I don't think he'd ask you to do that."

"Well," I said, "I'll ask him then."

I wrapped a dressing gown around myself and by the time I got downstairs Viv and Ed had already arrived. Drew let them in through the patio doors and I crossed my arms over my chest, well aware that I'd only just got out of bed and had hair like a haystack, whereas Viv was her usual radiant self.

I wished it didn't still bother me so much, but I supposed it was just the power of the bond.

"Hey guys," I said.

Viv said a quick hello, then Drew kissed me on the cheek and the two of them hurried off to do what they had to do, thankfully out of sight. I locked the door behind them and turned to Ed.

"Have you got keys?" I asked.

"Yup," he said, patting his pocket. "Right here."

"Good." I didn't want to think about where they had come from. The only other set I knew about had been Alice's.

"Thank you so much for letting me stay," I continued. "I was just about to move all my stuff out of the master bedroom for you."

"Oh, god, no," he said. "Please don't. I'll have Ali…," he

stopped himself mid-sentence, her name on his lips. "I mean, the other room," he finished.

"It's okay," I said. "You can say it."

He had been trying to brazen through and avoid mentioning her, avoid acknowledging what had happened, but he gave up, his whole posture collapsing in sympathy.

"I'm so sorry about what happened, Emmy. I heard you were hurt. Are you okay?"

"I'm doing alright, thanks. It's very kind of you to let me hang around for a while. I'll try to stay out of your way."

"Oh, don't worry about that, but I imagine that Carrie and Cam will probably be in and out a fair bit, I hope you don't mind."

"Of course not. Doesn't Carrie want to move in here with you?"

He smiled at me ruefully.

"I'm trying to convince her, but she's a bit old-fashioned that way."

"Tell her I'll chaperone."

He laughed, and it made me feel pretty comfortable about this living arrangement. I couldn't imagine that Drew was thrilled that I was going to be living with another man, but since he was off kissing another woman he wasn't really in a position to throw any stones.

I went back upstairs and got changed while Ed moved his things into his new room, and by the time I was back downstairs eating my breakfast he had everything squared away.

"You didn't bring much with you," I observed.

He shrugged.

"I'm used to travelling light."

The Silver probably had to leave a lot behind through the course of their lives, I thought. Always moving from place to place, trying to find the next home.

"Cam told me about the pub you two used to have together."

"Oh, did he? And I suppose he told you that it was my

fault we kept losing all our barmaids."

"Yeah, he did mention something about a leaking pipe."

"He loves his stories."

The smile he gave me was so affectionate, so full of love, that I realised maybe Cam wasn't the only one who missed those days.

I cleared away my cereal bowl and put on my best happy face.

"Right, shall I show you where everything is downstairs, then?"

We spent a couple of hours in the office first. I showed Ed where everything was on the computer then took him through the drawings of the pump rooms, explaining how the different pumps and gas worked together so he knew how to change them, then I took him into the taproom of the top bar to show him how it all worked in the flesh. I talked him through our opening and closing processes and tried to show him how to work the lifting wall out to the first floor terrace, but of course it wouldn't do what it was told so I just ended up thumping the keypad until it made a mournful beeping sound and capitulated.

Finally, I took him through each of the bars and showed him how everything was stacked and stocked, and explained what we did with the purple tokens that the Silver used to purchase their blood.

By the time we were done he looked more confused than when we had started, so I decided I'd probably done my job. We were both starving, so we went back upstairs to grab some lunch, but when I opened the fridge there was nothing there.

Great.

"We could go to the café," Ed suggested.

I shuddered. The place just reminded me of Alice, and I couldn't face it.

"I know," he continued, catching my reluctance, "let's order in from the Palace."

A couple of minutes later the phone on the bureau rang to announce our order and Ed walked down to the front door of the club to collect our food: burgers and chips. They were pretty good, and it was nice to have some hot food after two days living on sandwiches and cereal, but I was starting to crave vegetables.

By the time my shift rolled around I already felt like I'd done a full day's work showing Ed the ropes, but I could tell that he was secretly excited about it being his first night and I didn't want to ruin that for him, however I felt about it. I was surprised that I wasn't actually that upset about having the control of the club taken from me.

I wasn't part of it anymore. I was just a human serving vampires again. Us and them, masters and slaves.

Sometimes lovers.

It was an odd world, this new civilisation.

I was working the top bar as usual tonight, with Ed and Chris. I wasn't surprised to hear that Pru had asked to be assigned to a different work detail. The Silver didn't have a reputation for letting the humans pick and choose their jobs, but I suppose there were extenuating circumstances, and as one of the chained girls she probably had more say than most.

I was sad to see her go, but it was clear that the chained weren't safe in the club. I reminded myself that I was amongst their number, and that I'd have to keep alert this evening, regardless of the recently reinstated 'no humans' rule.

The club was raucous, the volume up on the music, the chairs and tables outside where they belonged so the dance floor was cleared to serve its purpose. We served a lot of blood and not much else.

Ed was having the time of his life, chatting away to all of his friends, and I saw what a good choice he was for this job. He clearly took it seriously, but he wasn't so uptight that he was going to be a killjoy for his customers. He'd be better in the role than I would ever have managed as a human.

That grated on me a little. I didn't miss the responsibility, but the knowledge of my comparative inadequacy scraped away at the edges of my self-respect.

It was past midnight when there was a commotion by the

door to the bar, the Solis Invicti barring the way to refuse someone admittance. I finished serving a pint of blood to a petite Hispanic Silver then craned over to see if I could make out what was happening. The incident was attracting a lot of attention now, and it had the feel of a powder keg about to explode.

Tamsin hurried over to the bar from the door, speaking into the microphone at her collar, and waved me over towards her.

"What's going on?" I asked. "Is something wrong?"

"There's a guy at the door claiming he has to see you. We've told him no humans can come in, but he's insisting it's important. I rang it in, and the Secundus says to talk to him. He said his name is Oliver."

Shit.

"What's Drew expecting me to do here? Does he really think Oliver will talk to me, give up the rebels?"

Tamsin shrugged.

"Maybe. Either way, I'll have eyes on you the whole time. Just go with it."

I stared back at her. She was expecting me to be clandestine now? I was probably the least subtle person in the world.

This wasn't going to work.

I hurried along the bar and told Ed what was happening. He told me to be careful and not to worry about coming back on shift afterwards; it was pretty quiet now anyway.

As soon as I got into the stairwell that led up to the dormitory, Oliver grabbed my hand and started walking up the stairs.

"Woah," I said, not keen to go racing back to the spot where I'd nearly died in the company of an associate of the rebels who'd nearly killed me. "Why do you think I'd go anywhere with you?"

"Emmy, I don't have time…"

"Well, I've got tons of time. Your friends tried to kill me, and they did kill Alice and Ella. For no reason at all, except they were wearing the chokers. And," I dropped my voice to a whisper, "you told them about the brand, you bastard."

"I'm so sorry, I can't tell you how sorry I am about Alice, but that had nothing to do with me. Don't you think I've seen enough death now? After Graham, I'm not sure this is a war I can fight anymore. If we were killing the vampires I'd be all for it, but we're not, we're killing our own. It's madness. I'm trying to stop it, to save lives, don't you see? Please, Emmy. You have to come with me."

"What's going on, Oliver? Whose lives are you trying to save?"

"They've got Mary, Mia and Jane, and I know where they are."

"Wait a minute. You're the one who took them."

"No," he said with frustration, "Jane and Mia came to us. But then they heard about Alice and wanted to leave, but the guys, they stopped them."

"Who?"

"I'll give you names. I'll give you everything. I'll tell you how to break the brand. I'll tell you everything I know. Just come with me, please."

I was stumped, unable to tell whether this was a ruse or not. Why did he suddenly care so much about Mary and the girls? Why was he so desperate to get me to follow him? It felt like a set up and I was highly suspicious. If I hadn't known that Tamsin was following me, I probably would have said no.

But I thought about the girls and gave in, running up the stairs after him and into the dorm.

"There's something going on tonight," he said, "I know there is, but they won't tell me what they're planning."

Instead of leading us into the dorm in which he slept, in which I had slept, he took us into the second room that lay to the left of our own dorm. It was the same size, running parallel to the other, but it was crammed with bunk beds and intended for families with young children. At the far end, where our dorm had the window, this room had a door that led out onto the fire escape, and that's where we were heading.

The door opened as we neared it and two women walked in, followed by three men, obviously on the way back from their shifts at the Palace. I vaguely recognised them from the dorm.

"Guys," Oliver said frantically to them, "have you seen Dave or Carolyn?"

The newcomers looked at each other then shook their heads.

"What's wrong?" one of them asked him.

"I don't know," he replied, his voice thick with frustration and tension. "But something's going on."

They stood aside and I followed Oliver through the door and outside.

"Shit," he said. "This is bad."

We clattered down the metal staircase, racing towards the street below.

"Where are they?" I asked.

"Underneath us. There's a huge network of tunnels under the ground here: sewers, service tunnels, the London Underground. After a few days of searching, we found one that let out into a disused train tunnel that goes right under the wall and out into the city. It's still sealed up on the outside, with doors that are locked and barricaded from this side, so the Silver didn't bother to block it at the boundary line."

"So that's how you got out?" I asked.

"Yes."

We hit the pavement in the alley running alongside the club and Oliver flattened himself against the wall, creeping along its length away from the Palace, towards the street at the back of the club. When he got to the end of the alley he paused.

"Why do you think something's going to happen tonight?" I asked him as he scanned the road in front of us.

"Because we got some information this evening that made a lot of people angry."

He ran across the road and along to the alleyway that was furthest right from where we had started, close up against the perimeter wall. I followed him as quickly and quietly as I could.

As we plunged into the deeper darkness cast across the alley by the walls towering at either side of it, I thought about how close we were to the barricades. The Weepers would be massing outside, keeping their silent vigil on the city as they waited for their opening. I shuddered at the thought, grateful when Oliver stopped at a door set into the wall to our left and pushed it open so we could slip inside.

He took a torch out of his pocket as I pulled the door shut behind us, clicking it on so that by its light I could see that we were standing at the top of a narrow concrete staircase leading down into the darkness below.

"It's not far," he said, "but I think we'd better hurry."

I really didn't want to follow him down into the dark, but I was reassured by the knowledge that Tamsin would be close behind us. There was only one route she could take from here so she couldn't miss it, and maybe she would even be calling in reinforcements by now to track our path.

The staircase was a couple of flights deep and ended abruptly at another door. Oliver paused at the bottom, listening for movement, then carefully opened it. It looked sturdy, sealed with metal along its edges and secured with several strong locks, but they'd clearly managed to get round them somehow.

There was a long corridor beyond with bare brick lining its sides and poured concrete on the floor. It was slightly damp in here, as if the ceiling wasn't properly water-proofed, and the only sound was an occasional drip splashing from it onto the floor below. Maybe there was a broken water main above our heads, I thought, or maybe it was just the result of the rain.

"Our Silver contact came to see a few of the group earlier tonight," he whispered as we hurried quietly along the passage.

"Your Silver contact?" I asked.

"Yes."

"You mean Benedict."

He said nothing for a few breaths.

"Yes," he said. "Benedict. He told us where the Weepers came from."

"Oh?"

"He said Weepers are what you get when Silver try to make more Silver and fail."

It felt like my heart had stopped. The Silver had made the Weepers?

"Everyone went nuts over it," he continued, "particularly with the Casting coming up."

"I've told you before not to believe what he says," I said uncertainly.

"But doesn't it sound plausible?" he asked. "The Silver are exposed in America, so they decide they need to make a move to come into the open. As part of that, they try to make an army, to swell their numbers so they can take over. But it goes wrong."

"Do you really believe that?"

"It has the ring of truth to it, and it explains a lot. Why did the Weepers suddenly turn up at the same time as the Silver? Because one was the direct result of the other. Why are the Weepers scared of the Silver? Because they're effectively their masters, their creators, and they can control them."

It also explained why trying to restore a human from a Weeper bite might turn them Silver; the two processes were inextricably linked, two ends of the same continuum. By the same logic, trying to turn someone Silver might make them a Weeper. In retrospect, I'd been an idiot not to put it together before now.

"Shit," I said. "I'm signed up for the Casting."

Oliver whirled round to face me, his expression contorted in horror.

"Why the hell would you agree to that?"

I couldn't think of a single reason anymore. I'd done it for Alice, but she was dead. I'd done it for Drew, but he'd lied to me about the risks. I'd done it for myself, to try to avoid dying at Ben's hands, but I'd rather be dead than Weeper.

Shit.

"There's no backing out now," I said, "so let's just get on with this. Where are we going?"

He gave me a level look then faced front once more. We were running now, our feet splashing gently into the puddles on the ground as the torch traced a manic pattern on the walls around us.

"This service tunnel leads under the club, then we can get through a hatchway into the old tube tunnel. They're stockpiling down there, out beyond the wall. I reckon the girls are probably being kept somewhere between the club and the stash, but there are a load of rooms and other tunnels leading off so we've got a lot of searching to do."

"We'd better hurry up then," I said, quickening the pace so we were running full pelt down the narrow passage.

After a minute or so Oliver slowed abruptly to a halt, holding his arm out in front of me to stop my own steps.

"What's wrong?" I whispered.

He switched the torch off and pulled me flat against the wall.

"There's a light at the end. You see the glow?"

I blinked a few times while my eyes readjusted to the darkness, and then I saw it. It was brighter on one side than on the other, as if it were creeping around a corner from our left, from the direction of the wall.

"Where are we?"

"That's the corner beneath the club. There's a flight of stairs that goes right up into the building next door, but it's sealed up tight from the outside. That's where they're getting all the supplies from; the vampires are using it as a warehouse. Let's take a look."

We edged along the wall until Oliver could peek around the corner, then he stepped out and around it.

"There's no one here."

I followed him out and took in the scene. There were a couple of big spot lights on the floor of the tunnel, wires running off into the darkness, and they were trained at a single spot on the ceiling. There were more wires.

"Oh, shit," I said. "Is that what I think it is?"

The ceiling of the tunnel was honeycombed with holes, more wires hanging down from each and trailing away along the corridor ahead.

"They're going to blow the club. Holy fuck. Emmy, we've got to get out of here."

"Not without Mary and the girls," I said.

"Are you crazy? You don't know when they're going to set this thing off. We'll be buried alive down here."

"No. You go back if you want, but I'm finding them."

I couldn't lose anyone else. It just didn't bear thinking about.

He stared me down for a few seconds, then started past the lights and around the corner.

"Fine," he said, "you win, but we do this quick."

"Thank you," I said with feeling. "I won't forget this."

We didn't need the torch anymore because, although the light was very dull, there were lanterns set up intermittently along the way. The route must have been pretty well travelled, and I wondered whether they still had some work to do on their charges before they were ready to press the button.

Either way, it made us more cautious, anticipating that we might bump into the rebels every time we turned a corner.

The corridor angled steadily upwards and there were doors and corridors leading off every hundred feet or so. We checked them each, but found no sign of the girls, returning to the main tunnel after each search. Eventually we reached a place where there was a hole in the corridor wall where it looked as if the brick had been smashed through, and there was a solid metal door fifty feet or so beyond, just visible through the rift in the tunnel wall.

"This is the last lantern," Oliver said as he peered into the darkness. "That's the hatch that leads into the tube tunnel and the stash."

As he spoke, the door began to open. He grabbed my

hand and pulled me back into the main tunnel and off to the right, into the section beyond the hole in the wall that we hadn't yet explored. We ran softly and lightly until we were out of the lantern's circle of light, then he pushed me up against the wall and held me there, the weight of his body pressing up against mine.

We both turned our heads toward the light, mine tucked under the rough stubble of his chin, and watched.

Two figures stepped out through the crack in the wall, first silhouetted and then detailed by the glow of the lantern. They were a man and a woman, each carrying a spool of wire, some wire cutters and what looked like blocks of plastic explosives.

"…last run, right?" the man asked.

"Yeah, well, maybe. That's what they said last time, but they seem to keep coming up with new places for us to stick it," the woman replied.

"Between this and the stuff at the wall, if we put any more in there we're going to take down the whole block."

"Don't be such a drama queen. Anyway, what do you care? We'll be long gone by then."

They walked on in silence in the direction of the club until they were out of sight, and out of earshot.

"Shit," I whispered, pressing my forehead against Oliver's shoulder. "We've got to find the girls then get upstairs and warn the others."

Oliver said nothing, but he squeezed my shoulders encouragingly then took my hand, leading me back towards the hole in the tunnel wall.

There was a harsh noise behind us, like something thudding against metal, and he quickly pulled me back against the tunnel wall before we were touched by the light of the lantern.

We were silent for a few seconds, then we heard the noise again: a dull, hollow thunk.

"What's that?" he whispered.

"It sounds like something hitting one of the tunnel doors. Is there a door up ahead?"

"Probably."

"It could be the girls. Come on, we've got to see."

"We'll have to use the torch. Let's be quick about this."

About a hundred feet ahead of us we found the door. It was in a metal frame and barred from the outside with a length of pipe that had been inserted through the loop of the door handle then jammed into a hole in the brickwork alcove that it was set into.

As we watched, there was another thump against the door.

"Hello?" I asked quietly.

There was a pause.

"Hello?" came the reply, a young, female voice.

"Jane? Is that you? It's Emmy."

"Yes!" a frantic voice replied. "Please let us out!"

Oliver yanked the pipe free from the door and I wrenched open the door. The torchlight illuminated a small room with a lot of machinery and piping in it, out of which Mia and Jane spilled gratefully into my arms.

I looked around, but I couldn't see Mary.

"Where's your mum?" I asked, not really wanting to hear the answer.

"We don't know," Jane said. "We didn't even know she was down here until they shut us in, but we've heard them walking past this door to go further along in that direction." She pointed off into the unexplored section of the tunnel beyond.

"We need to get you out of here," Oliver interjected, "and then we'll keep looking."

"We can help," Mia said.

"No," he replied. "It'll go quicker if it's only the two of us."

I appreciated his decision not to tell them about the imminent explosion. It would just make things worse.

The only problem now was how to get them out of here, but an easy solution presented itself as we walked back towards the place where the crack in the wall led to the tube tunnel. We were moving with the torch switched off, cautiously approaching the circle of light cast by the lantern, when the man and woman we had seen earlier returned back along the corridor.

They were now empty-handed, which couldn't be a good thing.

We froze where we were in the darkness, not wanting to draw attention to ourselves, and waited for them to go past.

"After you," the woman said to the man as they approached the hole in the wall.

"You first," he replied, picking up the lantern from the ground.

"No, I'm not letting you go after me, and you know why. Firstly, you can't stop staring at my arse, and secondly, you never lock the door properly after we come through. If you fuck it up this time then we're all going to be roasted, so excuse me if I don't want to trust my fate to your fat fingers."

"Fucking bitch," the man mumbled to himself as he stepped through.

"Better bitch than dead," she said as she followed after him.

After a few seconds we heard a heavily crash and a series of duller thumps and we were left in the dark. Oliver clicked on the torch and we started running down the passage, back towards the corner under the club.

"We'll take you halfway," I said, "till there are no wrong turns for you to take, and then we'll come back for your mum."

I picked up one of the lanterns from the floor as we passed, thinking Jane and Mia could use it to light their way out, and we raced on. When we reached the corner where the charges were packed heavily above us, Oliver carefully directed the torchlight downwards so the girls wouldn't see the sword of Damocles hanging over our heads.

Shortly afterwards I switched on the lantern, which was battery-powered, and handed it over to Mia.

"Just run straight along here and up the staircase at the end. Turn right when you come out of the door at the top and then just keep running straight and you'll see the Palace. Tell them we're down here and tell them to evacuate the club right now."

Fear flooded into their expressions, but what else could I say? They had to warn them.

"What's going on?" Jane asked.

"Just go, as fast as you can," Oliver said. "Run."

They did.

We watched for a second to make sure they were out of earshot, then turned round and raced back in the other direction. I cringed as we passed under the explosives for the third time, but tried to push it out of my mind. We had to find Mary.

"They've got a load of doors behind that hatch," said Oliver, "and they've locked them from the inside. We're not going to be able to get in."

"No, but we can search the rest of the corridor where we found the girls."

He said nothing for a moment.

"This is suicide, Emmy."

I didn't reply. He was right, but I had my finger on the self-destruct button again and I just didn't seem to care. How could you balance up the lives? Was the life of Mary, mother of two children, worth less than the lives of Oliver, me and Drew, a Silver? I was endangering more lives than I was hoping to save, but wasn't that justified?

I wanted there to be a right answer, but there wasn't.

Logic couldn't help me here.

"You can always turn back," I said.

"No."

A clicking noise from behind us caught my attention, and suddenly Oliver was pulling me to one side, into an alcove and behind one of the metal doors lining the passage.

There was a heavy thud that pressed painfully against my eardrums and then the world hung for a second in silence before it crashed down around us, hurling me forward in a rush that ended with a sickening crack.

My head and ears thumped with the ringing noise of the blast, and the lights behind my eyelids were strobing and blinding. As my vision started to clear, I could see the stars blinking peacefully in the sky above me and it took a moment for me to realise what had happened, to remember where I was.

We must have been very close to the surface, because an access hatch above us had been blown up and apart, exposing us to the open air beyond. From what I could see of the rest of the tunnel from my prone position, it looked as if it had collapsed in on itself entirely, filled with rubble from its own ceiling, from the street above us.

There was a foul burning smell in the air, a mixture of nitre and sulphur that scored a painful path along the back of my throat as I inhaled. The torchlight in what remained of the room was dim and it seemed to be getting darker by the moment.

There was the sound of screaming from not very far away, mingled with something far more sinister: a howling call that echoed down into the ground where I lay. I remembered that the rebels had been talking about bringing down the wall. They were going to let the Weepers in to the city, to end their silent vigil. And I couldn't move.

I tried to reach my hand out to my right, but my shoulder was pinned at an awkward angle and I couldn't shift whatever was holding it in place. I blearily made out a figure to my left, half-buried beneath lumps of masonry and twisted pieces of metal and concrete. It was Oliver, lying on his side with a dark circle of liquid spreading from beneath his shoulder.

He wasn't moving.

Where the hell was Tamsin, and why hadn't she come to help?

Where were the rest of the Invicti?

I tried again to wriggle free, but the movement sent such a spasm of agony through me that I nearly blacked out. Not only was my shoulder pinned, but I couldn't feel my legs.

Once I'd felt the pain in the rest of my body for the first

time it just wouldn't go away. The surface of my skin stung as if I were burned and raw, my bones ached and my muscles screamed, torn and cut in ways I didn't want to imagine. It came on and on in never-ending waves, taking me under, drawing me down with it.

I was dying, I realised.

The cold night air flowed down from above us and crept into my bones, numbing my skin a little, chasing the blood away from the surface. My heartbeat was slow and irregular, and I wondered how much blood I had lost. Too much, probably, though I didn't know from where.

I tried to force my eyes to stay open, but they fluttered closed, sealing me off from the horror around me into my own personal pain, but soon even that started ebbing away.

As the cold embraced me I felt a warmth building in the brand on my chest, banking up until it felt like it was going to break, and I realised it probably was. Drew was going to die tonight, too.

But it wasn't him I called to mind in those final moments. At the last, my heart overrode my brain, and it was the scent of cold spice that followed me down into unconsciousness.

CHAPTER XXX

It can't have been much later that I came to, because the Weepers were still howling in the distance rather than right on top of us. I blinked my eyes open and tried to move.

There was no pain.

I sat up and looked myself over in confusion. There were holes in my clothes, the front of my T-shirt barely holding together, but I seemed to be absolutely fine. As I moved, a shower of various shrapnel skittered off my legs and poured into my lap from my shirt. I was reminded of the stitches that had sat so neatly in my palm after my hand was healed, expelled from the skin.

I looked down at my chest where the top half of my T-shirt was shredded and hanging loose from the neck. The brand was gone, no trace of silver left on the skin.

I didn't understand how, but it must have healed me.

There was a moan from my left and I turned around to see that Oliver was moving, trying to dig himself out from under the rubble.

"Hey," I whispered, "are you okay?"

"My shoulder," he said.

I helped him move some of the larger blocks of concrete from where they pinned his legs in place, but they had done no real damage and he was able to get to his feet. However, the worst of his injuries, a huge gash into his shoulder, was badly in need of some attention. There was a bent shard of metal sticking out from it, but I didn't want to remove it because he'd already lost a lot of blood. We needed to get out of here quickly and get him some help.

"How badly does it hurt?" I asked.

"I can bear it. You're okay?"

"Yes," I replied guiltily, conscious that I'd had some intervention on that score.

He looked me up and down suspiciously.

"There isn't a mark on you."

"I think we'd better talk about that later," I said. Now was not the time. "We need to get somewhere safe, if you can walk. The Weepers are coming."

"I can walk."

I looked around and tried to assess the best route out of here, but it was difficult to see in the dark. The torch had finally sputtered its last light, and I would have been reluctant to use it anyway as it would only draw the attention of the Weepers. For the same reason, I didn't want to call out. We might be heard by the Invicti before the Weepers got to us, but would it be the right Invicti? If Ben turned up then we'd be worse off than we were now.

There was a landslide of rubble rising out of the room in which we stood, pouring in from where the tunnel had collapsed. There was also a metal ladder rising from one side of the room towards what had probably originally been a manhole cover before the blast had blown it open. The scramble would be steep and treacherous, but I couldn't help Oliver up the ladder and he'd only have the use of one arm to climb. I opted for the scramble.

"Up this way," I whispered as I slung his arm over my shoulder and wrapped my arm around his back.

It was slow going and we missed our footing a few times in the dark, but we made it safely to the top. When we had done so I was horrified at the scene that presented itself. It took me a while to work out where we were because of the destruction around us, but I realised that we were right down by the wall at the end of the street on which the club and the Palace sat, a good few hundred feet away.

Or, at least, the street on which they usually sat. Both buildings had been utterly destroyed, razed to the ground by the blast, replaced by towering mounds of stone and metal sitting in clouds of dust and smoke, illuminated by the moonlight.

"Shit," I said.

There were Silver zipping around crazily between the two buildings, digging the masonry away from their remains as they tunnelled down to search for survivors.

There was a howl from close to our right and I saw that the Weepers were making their way over in our direction. It looked like the wall had been brought down on the next street over from here, the one that ran parallel to this one behind the club.

What used to be the club.

"We've got to run," I said to Oliver as I started to move towards the fallen buildings, hauling him alongside me.

I could feel his steps faltering as he tried to make his body do what he told it to, but he was obviously weak from the blood loss and from the pain.

"Come on," I said. "We're getting you some help."

We were moving faster than the Weepers for the moment, and they didn't seem to have spotted us yet, but I wasn't sure how long that would last. I decided to go for broke.

"Help!" I shouted towards the Silver. "Please help us!"

There was a howl behind us and I wondered whether this gamble was going to pay off. I put on some extra speed, dragging Oliver with me, and shouted for all I was worth.

"Help us, please!"

One of the Silver stopped, standing still in the dust as it swirled around in the moonlight, disturbed by the frantic movement of the others.

"Emmy?" a voice called.

"Yes! Help us!"

The figure walked out of the smoke and the light touched his face.

"Drew, the Weepers!"

He rushed forward in a blur until he was standing right in front of me and I turned to see that they were no longer following us, turning back towards the wall in search of easier prey.

"He's hurt," I said. "He needs help."

He looked at me suspiciously, like he couldn't believe his eyes, then he reached out a hand and touched it to my cheek.

"I thought you were dead," he said.

"Well, I'm not, but Oliver will be if he doesn't get some medical attention soon. Where can I take him?"

"To the Square. We're taking all the humans there and there's an infirmary set up."

He put his fingers to his lips and whistled, and in a moment Viv was right by his side.

"Emmy," she said, "thank god you're okay."

"I'm fine," I said, feeling like a broken record, "but he's not."

Drew carefully took Oliver from me and lifted him into his arms, while Viv turned round so her back was to me.

"Hop on," she said.

I was slightly weirded out by receiving a piggyback from Viv, but I jumped up anyway and a second later we were outside one of the buildings in the Square, opposite the café. The place was busy, and I realised how many people must have been displaced by the blast. The Silver might now be the only ones who patronised the club and the Palace, but a lot of humans worked and lived in those buildings.

"How many have died?" I asked them as we walked into the building, Viv going on ahead to hold the door for Drew and his burden.

"We don't know yet," he said. "We're still digging people out."

"Did you get the people who did this? Did you find

Mary?"

"We found them," said Viv. "Those girls you saved, they came straight to us and told us where to find the rebels. They're all in custody, only about fifty of them in the end."

The others must have been scared off when they realised how serious things were getting, I thought.

We walked down a corridor lined with doors then out into an open plan area where a large number of beds and some medical equipment had been set up.

"And Mary?" I persisted.

"We haven't found her yet," Drew said.

"Oh, god." Jane and Mia must be beside themselves.

Drew led us towards an empty bed and carefully laid Oliver out along its length. He'd lost consciousness at some point in the journey over here and his eyes were closed, his breathing rapid.

"We need some help over here," Drew said to a nearby Silver man dressed in an incongruous purple suit.

"You got it," he replied. "You staying, miss?" he said to me. "There's a makeshift waiting room through that door if you want to hang around."

I followed the line of his finger towards a door at the other end of the room and nodded numbly.

"Will he be okay?" I asked the Silver.

"We'll give him a transfusion and wrap him up, and he should be fine."

I breathed a sigh of relief and, taking Oliver's hand, leaned down towards his ear.

"I'll be just next door," I whispered, "and I'll be back as soon as they let me."

I wasn't sure if he could hear me, but I owed him one, so I was going nowhere. He hadn't had to take me into his confidence, but he'd done it anyway, then he'd stuck by me on a suicide mission that had landed him in this state. He'd probably saved both our lives, brand notwithstanding, by pulling us into that side room at the last minute, and I was incredibly grateful for that.

He hadn't turned out to be such a bad guy after all, just misguided and naïve.

Drew led me away from the bed as Viv said her goodbyes and went back to the club to help with the search operation.

"Don't you need to go too?" I asked him.

"We need to talk."

That sounded awfully ominous.

The waiting room was empty when we stepped inside, so it was just the two of us in a small room with four chairs and a table at its centre.

"What happened out there?" he asked as soon as the door closed behind me.

"Well, you saw it. Everything blew up."

"That's not what I mean. The brand's gone," he said, indicating the unmarked skin on my chest, "and I felt the bond... snap. I thought you were dead and I couldn't work out why I hadn't died too."

"You felt it snap?"

I took a step closer to him and looked into his eyes. Rich green irises, dark and clear, looked back at me. There was no trace of silver in them.

"It's gone," I said. "The bond's broken."

"I know."

His voice was bleak with loss, ringing with a pain I couldn't understand. His posture was one of defeat and resignation, of utter exhaustion.

"How did it happen?" he asked. "I didn't think it was even possible."

I shrugged and fell down into one of the chairs.

"I don't know. I thought I'd died, but then I woke up again and I was healed, everything in perfect working order. I assumed the brand had healed me, that it had sort of... burned itself out putting me right again."

He took a seat opposite me.

"Maybe it did."

"You're upset?" I asked.

"Yes." His voice broke a little on the single syllable.

"Isn't this a good thing, though? The bond breaking, I mean."

"No, Emmy, it's not. It's… gone. It's just empty, where before there was something. I'm empty. There's nothing inside me anymore."

"You mean you don't love me anymore," I asked, thinking that it wouldn't be the worst thing in the world.

"I don't know. I just feel… grief."

"It'll pass," I said.

"Perhaps. And what about the Casting, Emmy?"

Oh, shit. The Casting.

"There's no way to pull out?" I asked hopelessly.

"No, not now. It's too late."

We sat together in silence for a few minutes.

"So I'm going to turn into a Weeper, then," I said in a dull tone.

That gave him pause.

"How did you find out?" he asked.

"Ben told Oliver. It's true then?"

"It's true."

"And you didn't think it was something you should tell me before you asked me to make the decision?"

He shifted in his seat a little.

"It was irrelevant because of the bond. Everything would have been fine…"

"But now it won't be, Drew. Now I'm committed to something that hasn't got the slightest hope of working, for no reason. I don't want to be Silver and you don't need me to be Silver, not now you're free from the bond."

"I'll never be free from it," he said darkly. "What it was, what we had, that depth of emotion…"

"It wasn't real, and it wasn't reciprocated, so what does it matter?"

"It was real to me, and I know there were times when you felt it too, the pull of it bringing us together, how right it was."

"But it wasn't right. You don't love me, Drew, not really."

"Don't tell me how I feel," he growled.

After that, there was nothing for us to say to each other. I didn't like to see him upset, but I was pretty angry that he hadn't told me the truth about the Weepers, and I was having a hard time feeling sorry that he didn't seem to be enamoured of me anymore.

I wondered if this meant Ben would leave me the hell alone.

We sat in silence as we waited for the doctor to return, each of us locked away with our own thoughts and emotions. I was worrying for Oliver, scared that Mary might not have made it out, uncertain about the future in the wake of this disaster.

After perhaps half an hour a human girl came to fetch us.

"Your friend is still out cold, but we've finished patching him up," she said. "We've moved him to a separate room, and you can come and sit with him it you like."

I thanked her and followed her into a room leading off from the side of the open plan area, leaving Drew behind in the waiting room. I wondered if Cam would be the only real friend I had left among the Silver now.

Silver politics had put me in enough danger that I didn't think I'd miss it.

But Sol…

I couldn't think about him, or about the last time I'd seen him. He'd been so distant, so cold, as if we'd said goodbye, and that was the end of it.

I wished I could switch off my emotions in the same way.

CHAPTER XXXI

Thursday

I sat up with Oliver through the night, trying to process my thoughts. It wasn't like I had anywhere else to go now anyway; the apartment had come down with the club in the blast. I hoped Nix had got out.

The room was small and felt awkwardly cramped with the bed in the middle of it, a couple of office chairs and a desk set close up against one wall. I guessed that this building had once been office space, that the open plan room had been the main working area and the private rooms the offices for the higher echelons of whatever organisation had once inhabited it.

I pulled one of the chairs up to the side of the bed and took hold of Oliver's hand so I'd know the moment he woke up. He was topless, a bandage wrapped securely around his shoulder, the muscles of his torso highlighted by the grime that covered him. The medical staff had clearly tried to clean some of the blood and dirt off, but they hadn't had much luck. I imagined I wouldn't look much better.

I must have dropped off eventually, because the next thing

I knew I was face down on the side of the bed, my head pillowed in my hands, and someone was calling my name.

"Emmy."

I looked up blearily and saw that Oliver was awake, looking like he'd been run over by a bus.

"Jeez," I said to him, "you look like shit."

"Yeah, well, have you seen your hair?"

I patted it tentatively then pulled it out of its hairband, ran my fingers through it to tease out the knots as best I could, and put it back in a ponytail.

"Better?" I asked sarcastically.

"Sure, whatever. It actually looked okay."

"You're such a dick."

"I know," he smiled at me: a long, slow, sleepy smile that had a level of intimacy in it that I wasn't expecting from him. I supposed that sharing a near-death experience was a pretty good bonding exercise.

"How are you feeling?" I asked.

"I'm okay, I suppose. Did the girls get out okay?"

"Yeah," I said, "so I'm told, and they captured your friends."

His face clouded over with anger, his bright eyes flashing.

"They're not my friends. I just wanted to get out of here. I never wanted to hurt people, much less kill them."

"But you were a part of this. I don't want to sound childish or anything, but you started it."

Sorrow suffused his expression, the anger dissipating as he pulled it in, turning it on himself. He blamed himself for his brother's death, I thought, and everything that followed.

"I'm sorry. It was a mistake. I was so determined to reclaim our freedom that I let myself believe the lies I was hearing. I just..." he paused, running his fingers through his hair, "I didn't want to give up and lie down. I wanted something better."

We had that in common, I thought.

How could I judge him harshly for doing only what I had done myself last week? If I hadn't been so stubborn, if I had seen sense, then Danny, Jeff and Sarah might still be alive right now, but I hadn't wanted to be subjugated.

His full lips pressed together into a line, his forehead furrowing as he visibly tried to contain his grief, and I leaned forward and took his hand in mine once more.

I was in no position to throw stones, and I sympathised with him entirely. Watching his pain returned the echoes of my own, and we sat together in silence for a few moments before I spoke again.

"I don't think there's any other way now," I said in resignation. "This is it. We need them, just as much as they need us. We have to stick together."

He shook his head in despair.

"I just thought we could find another way. I was wrong."

"Well," I said, "you were right about the Silver, the secrets they were keeping."

"About the Weepers?"

"Yes."

"And you were right about Benedict. Hooray for us. Now we're both in the shit, but at least we were right about the sort of shit we're in."

I smiled at him.

"What do you think they'll do with the prisoners? Or with us?" I asked.

"You know them better than I do," he said as he slowly sat up in his bed, the sheet falling away from him. I was relieved to see that he was still wearing his jeans. "I assume you'll be fine, what with your fancy neckwear." He pointed at my choker.

"Maybe," I said.

"That Silver at the door of the club, I explained things to her. Wasn't she supposed to be with you, keeping an eye on you? What the hell happened to her?"

"I don't know," I said quietly. "I hope she didn't get caught in the explosion."

"I wouldn't lose any sleep over it," he said.

There was a knock at the door and we both turned towards

it, then caught each others' eye.

"Come in," Oliver called.

It was Cam.

I was out of my chair in a second and in his arms.

"Shit, Emmy," he said, holding me so tightly I thought I might pop. "I thought you were dead. Where the hell were you? What were you doing down there? You just disappeared."

"Didn't Tamsin tell you?" I asked as I pulled away, a horrible suspicion creeping up on me.

"Tell me what?"

Confusion was all over his face. He knew nothing about it.

Damn it, I'd been screwed over again.

"Does Tamsin happen to be bestest friends with Benedict by any chance?" I asked.

"No," he replied, "but she is very close to Laila, and Laila and Benedict are bosom buddies."

I punched his chest in frustration.

"Christ, why don't you guys tell me these things? She told me to go with Oliver, said she'd have my back." I reflected for a moment, recalling her words. "She told me Drew wanted me to go with him. I thought you knew." I kicked myself for letting her fool me. "That bitch. Fuck."

"Hey, man," Cam said to Oliver.

"Hey," he replied.

"Oh," I said, remembering my manners, "Cam, this is Oliver, reformed rebel. Oliver, this is Cam, probably the only friend I have among the Silver at the moment."

"You and Drew aren't friends anymore?" Cam asked.

"The bond broke," I said simply.

"It what?"

"Broke."

"How?" he asked.

I shrugged and sat down in my chair again. Cam took the one next to me.

"Shit," he said.

"Yup."

"I've got more bad news, I'm afraid," he said.

I looked at him expectantly, wondering if this was when he'd tell me that Mary was dead. But it was something entirely different.

"The Primus wants to see you both."

"Why?" Oliver asked, sitting up straighter in the bed.

"I don't know. I just got sent to bring both of you."

This really didn't sound good.

"From what you've told me, I think it might be a tribunal," he continued. "If Tamsin's spun some lie about what happened last night, it's going to be your word against hers and, in the circumstances, she's going to win."

"We're screwed, then," I said.

"You've got to watch your step here, Ems. However familiar you two might have been in the past, you keep your eyes on the ground and call him 'Primus', and don't speak unless he asks you a direct question. That goes for you, too," he said to Oliver. "Let's go."

"Now?" I asked.

"Now."

Oliver struggled slowly out of the bed, his shoulder making movement awkward, and got to his feet unsteadily. He was swaying, one of his legs apparently giving him some trouble.

"Any chance of a shirt?" he asked.

Cam looked around the room and shrugged.

"Doesn't look like it. Sorry."

Oliver gave me a quick once over, doubtless noting I was still wearing my shredded work uniform that was barely holding together.

"Oh well," he said, "at least we're a matching pair."

I smiled sardonically and went to his side, slinging his good arm over my shoulder. Cam watched us with interest in his eyes, following the movement as I put my arm around Oliver's torso, his fingers curling into my bare shoulder so he could support his steps without leaning too hard on his injured leg.

"What hurts?" I asked, looking up at him.

"I think I've just pulled a muscle. It's nothing serious."

He smiled at me again, his bright eyes softening in a way that was too tender, too vulnerable for the situation. Whatever was going on between us here, it wasn't something I wanted Cam to watch.

I cleared my throat.

"Come on then," I said to Cam. "Lead the way."

He went in front of us, guiding us out of the building and into the Square. Oliver limped slowly at my side, each step pressing his body close to mine in a way that felt comfortable and affectionate. The weirdest thing was that I didn't mind. I was even enjoying the closeness of him and, from the way that he was leaning into my body, I thought he might be too. Then again, it could be just my imagination.

I wondered if my reaction was something to do with the freedom from the bond, from the brand. It was as if a sudden awareness had been breathed into me.

We followed Cam across the Square and into one of the buildings next to the café. It looked like they had moved their whole base of operations over here in the wake of the explosion.

"We've got to go up some stairs," Cam said as we entered the building.

It had a large, marble entrance hall and had clearly been some kind of corporate building, maybe a head office. There were a couple of Invicti posted at the door, but otherwise the place was deserted.

"How many flights?" Oliver asked.

"Three. I can carry you if you'd like."

"No thanks," he replied without hesitation. He was clearly a man with some pride, or maybe he just didn't want to be touched by a Silver unless it was absolutely necessary.

"Suit yourself. I'll go on ahead and let them know you're on your way."

Cam ran up the stairs and left us down at their foot to negotiate them on our own.

"You're a stubborn man," I said as Oliver limped onto the

first step.

"I know," he said, and he smiled that slow smile at me again.

I blushed.

"Stop that," I said, setting my jaw and fixing my eyes on the stairs in front of us.

We climbed the stairs in silence, Oliver apparently chastened by my tone. When he spoke again, his voice was quiet and sincere.

"I can't ever apologise to you enough. I regret it like hell, and not just for Graham's sake. I was trying to make things better, to protect the people I loved, and instead I made things worse."

I started to think about all the regrets that were stacking up in my own mind. Alice, Ella, Mary, the Casting, Danny, Jeff and Sarah. I could have prevented all of it if I'd acted differently. How could I be critical of Oliver when my own mistakes had been as great, if not greater? He'd rebelled, like me, and that rebellion had cost him his remaining family. Like it had cost me mine.

We paused at the foot of the next flight of stairs and he turned to face me, his hands grasping my shoulders.

"We're in this together now," he said, almost as if he'd read my mind.

I looked up into his bright, grey eyes as he stared at me intently. There was something there, some connection there, some common ground, and it had nothing to do with bonds or blood or magic.

He understood me.

He was human, and he was flawed.

Just like me.

"Ahem."

I turned round to see Cam standing at the top of the next flight of stairs, not looking particularly happy.

"Ems, please," he said, taking in the scene, "the Primus will know. This really isn't a good day to piss him off."

"For god's sake, Cam, there's nothing going on," I replied

irritably, stepping away from Oliver. "And even if there was, it's not like Sol would give a shit. He couldn't care less. Or are you still worried about Drew? Because he doesn't give a shit about me now either."

"At the very least, you're still wearing that," he said, pointing at the choker, "and that's a problem."

"It doesn't mean he owns her," Oliver said.

"Yeah, it kind of does. Just come on, please."

I took Oliver's arm over my shoulder again.

"We'll talk later," he whispered to me.

If there was a later.

When we got up to the third floor Cam opened a set of double doors and ushered us inside a large conference room. Sol was sitting at the head of a large table, Drew at his right hand and Laila at his left.

How symbolic.

None of them looked happy to see us.

I remembered Cam's instructions and fixed my eyes on the ground.

"Oliver, Emilia," Sol said. "We have heard evidence from this tribunal that you collaborated with the rebels, leaving your assigned work details to join them in the tunnels beneath the Palace and the club, colluding in the destruction of those buildings. What do you say in your defence?"

I wanted to rage against Tamsin, to ask Sol why he'd believe I'd do something so awful, but it would be completely pointless. This felt like nothing so much as a show trial, a formality. Besides which, I had form for rebellion, as Sol well knew, and so did Oliver.

I had no idea what to say, but in the end that didn't matter.

"Primus," Oliver said, "it is true that we each left our work duties to go down into the rebel tunnels, but we only did so to save the lives of two girls I had learned were being held hostage there. We succeeded in that task, and went back to find their mother, but were caught in the explosion."

"I would find that story plausible if you had taken steps to notify us of your intentions, of the imminent danger, but we are reliably informed that you took no such action."

That was fairly transparent code for: we're not going to believe a word you say to the contrary.

We were totally screwed.

I couldn't believe that I was standing here in front of this man, this Silver, who had held me in his arms as if I were the only woman in the world, and hearing these words from his mouth. This was the ruler, the king, the godlike creature Cam described on the battlefields of the provinces. There was no mercy here.

"I should order their deaths if I were you," Laila interjected.

"But you are not," Sol replied, cutting her dead.

Trouble in paradise, apparently.

I suppressed a smile. Smirking wasn't going to help us here.

"I will pronounce my sentence at the gate, along with the others. I regret that events have brought us to this end, but action is necessary to protect the majority." His voice took on a softer, more confidential tone, and my surprise brought my eyes up to meet his.

"We all suffer for our sin," he said.

CHAPTER XXXII

I was still wondering at the meaning behind Sol's words when he and his tribunal stood from their seats and filed out of the room, Sol in the lead. Cam ushered Oliver and me behind them, followed by a couple of the Invicti, but there was no time for dallying on the stairs this time, so Cam carried Oliver down with me at his side. As soon as he hit the ground floor, Oliver hurried back to me, his arm circling my shoulders gratefully, as if he were relaxing back into my presence.

"Do you think they're going to kill us?" he asked me quietly as we walked back out into the Square.

"I don't know," I said.

I wasn't sure whether Sol had been trying to tell me that there was still something between us. Even if that had been the message, there had been a healthy dose of necessary evil in his words, and I didn't think that any feelings that might remain were going to affect his actions.

Did he know that Drew was no longer bonded to me? If so, I might be in serious danger here. He had no reason to keep me alive anymore.

A few steps outside the building we were joined by a large group of Solis Invicti who were escorting a crowd of people in the same direction: the rebels. I saw faces I knew amongst them, people I'd served in the bar and people I'd laughed with in the dorm. How could they do something so awful, these ordinary men and women?

Some of them saw Oliver and started jeering at him, but a few quick knocks from the Invicti rendered them silent once more.

We walked through the Square and out the other side, following the Silver through the streets. I realised that Sol was taking this back to where it started, back to the gates in the wall where the protestors had shot Drew.

"I think they might," I whispered to Oliver.

"Might what?"

"Kill us."

He looked at the faces of the Invicti behind us.

"Yeah."

As we walked, we were joined by humans from every building we passed on the way. They were parading us through the streets, gathering their audience for the main event. I'd had no idea that Sol had such a flair for the theatrical.

The tribunal remained out in front, the three of them walking side by side at the head of the line. Drew had given me no indication that he'd even noticed I was there, and I was starting to think that I really might be dead to him now.

They were followed by the mass of rebels, their assigned Invicti circling around them, and then Oliver and I were bringing up the rear with Cam and the other two Invicti behind us.

The spectators were following, but there was a definite divide maintained between them and us. They were distancing themselves from us, we who had attracted the censure of their masters. They were abandoning us to our fates, escorting us to our deaths.

"It's been fun, Emmy," Oliver whispered, leaning down to my cheek and pressing his lips to it softly. "I'm sorry we didn't have more time to get to know one another properly."

"Don't give up yet," I said optimistically, trying to lighten the mood, but the effect was slightly spoiled by the catch in my voice as I spoke. I felt like I was going to cry and I tried desperately to push down the tears.

I guessed it didn't really matter; if I didn't die today then I'd be turned into a Weeper in a week's time at the Casting. Maybe this was better after all.

When we finally reached the gates in the wall there were thousands of people gathered behind us, crammed into every space, desperate for a view. Sol walked up onto a platform that had been set next to the gates, his Secundus and his consort taking up their positions. There was a microphone at the front of the stage and Sol stepped up to it.

Absolute hush descended around us, the anticipation sharp and vicious, people gathering to watch the show.

Humanity disgusted me sometimes.

"Last night," he said, "a group of humans placed incendiary devices in various locations around the city: at the western wall, at the club and at the Palace. The intention, as we understand it from the perpetrators, was to kill as many Silver as possible. Two young Silver have, in fact, died in the explosion."

A lacklustre cheer rose from the rebels crowded in front of us, but the people weren't behind them. You could feel the condemnation radiating from them, tangible and hateful. They knew what was coming. They had heard the news.

"However, that alleged 'victory' has come at a cost of at least two hundred and thirty-six human lives, with still more unaccounted for."

The crowd erupted, angry and despairing. Amongst them were doubtless people who had lost their parents, their friends or their lovers in the rebels' idiotic attempt to assert control.

They were nothing but Ben's puppets. If they'd had an ounce of sense between them, they would have wondered if it was really such a good idea to bring the wall down, to invite the Weepers into the city where we lived. Or maybe they liked the idea of being the only few left alive, of being the only ones clever enough to find another way out.

Either way, they weren't the heroes they were hoping to be.

"We have repaired the wall, repaired the tunnels and sealed the safe zone so the Weepers will not be a threat to those who remain here. We have also moved our base of operations to the Square. It remains only to pass judgement on the perpetrators."

Oliver pulled me close against his side and I rested my head against his shoulder, my heart thudding in my chest.

"You forty-seven individuals were instrumental in the events of last night's tragedy," Sol continued. "You have made it clear that you have no desire to live here in these walls, to comply with the bargain we have offered you."

The Invicti led the group of rebels forward and opened the gates in front of them. The buildings immediately outside were close on either side of the road, the Weepers clearly visible crowding in the shaded alleys, bloodied tears streaming from their eyes in the dull light of the overcast day.

"Oh, god," I whispered.

I knew what he was going to do. My fingers clenched, closing tightly around Oliver's side, and he pulled me against his chest, but I couldn't look away.

The rain began to fall on us, dimming the light still further, and the Weepers crowded forward out of their dark corners.

"Those who wish to live outside our society," Sol continued in a commanding tone of voice, "will see that wish fulfilled."

The rebels looked at each other incredulously, then realised that their sentence had been passed, that they were being exiled, but this was a very different escape from the one they had hoped for. They weren't sealed off, underground, living a parasitic existence from the safe zone. This was a true representation of life without the Silver, without their resources and without the ambit of protection that they offered from the Weepers.

The Solis Invicti lined up behind the rebels, marching them forward and through the gate, out into the street beyond.

At first, the Weepers retreated, moving back in the presence of the Silver, and I could almost see the rebels relax.

But then they were gone, racing away from the street and through the gate, leaving the rebels on their own.

There was a moment of stillness, utter silence from the crowd and from the scene in front of us.

Then the Weepers ran out into the light, so starved that they were oblivious to their burning eyes as they rushed to the feast.   The rebels were obscured in seconds, a wave of Weepers muffling their screams in the press of their bodies, suffocating and tearing with each new inundation.

In the space of ten seconds they had pulled the rebels apart and disbanded, returning to their alleys with their trophies, leaving only a smear of gore on the surface of the street.

Someone in the crowd behind us retched. I couldn't blame them.

But then it was our turn.

We were shepherded forward, Oliver's limp more pronounced now after the exertion it had taken to get him to this place. My heart was thundering in my chest, my palm slick with sweat on his side.

The Invicti stepped back, leaving us standing in front of the open gate on our own, at least twenty feet of clear air between us and any of the Silver.

The Weepers turned in our direction, starting to take an interest, but not willing to come within the safe zone.

I didn't want to walk out into the city, out into the arms of the Weepers who were waiting beyond the gate. But I didn't want to join them, either, and that seemed to be the fate that would await me after the Casting.

"Oliver and Emilia," Sol said from his podium above us. "You have broken the bargain by leaving your duties and have placed lives in danger by your failure to report rebel activities promptly to the Solis Invicti."

I swallowed, my throat dry.

The sun glinted through the clouds, catching his hair in its light, and he was radiant. But I could look beyond the suit, now. I could see the blood on his hands and in his hair, the power rippling through every tendon and muscle on his body. I could see the emptiness in his icy eyes as he sent fifty men and women to their deaths at the hands of creatures that were created as slaves by the hubris of his kind.

What is a god, other than a being that has power over life and death? A Silver who turns others Silver, who gives eternal life, and who passes death sentences on others is nothing more or less than a god.

It wasn't a laudable claim. That kind of horror was something to which no moral person would aspire.

Yes, Solomon was a god, carved of ice and fire, and Laila was his muse.

He stepped down from his podium, down from the stage, and came to stand in front of us with his back to the gate. The Weepers backed away slightly. He looked from me to Oliver, to our arms around each other, and then his eyes rested on mine.

I decided to be candid. After all, there was no one near to hear me and, even if there had been, I might not get another chance.

"So is this it, Sol?" I whispered. "Do you really want to kill me, and Oliver, because of a lie?"

"Inaction is not an option," he replied.

"But this?"

"You will survive this," he said, his eyes drilling into mine as if the words were a command rather than a platitude, "and perhaps we will meet again one day."

His gaze dropped to my neck.

"You have my protection no longer," he said loudly, his voice reverberating around the congregation as he reached out to pluck the choker from me. "You are exiled indefinitely to Silver Farm to serve punishment duty."

Before I could process the sentence, an open pick-up truck that was parked by the gates and had gone unnoticed until now spluttered into life and pulled into the gateway in front of us. One of the Silver from behind us stepped forward and flipped down the rear wall of the truck bed, handing us each up onto its bare metal floor before slamming it shut behind us.

There were a few metal loops set into the floor, presumably for securing goods in transit, but they were serving a different purpose today. The second Silver stepped forwards with two pairs of handcuffs in his hands, but Cam took them from him and shooed him away. I was relieved that he apparently had the power to do so.

He leaned in close to me as he fastened the cuffs first to two loops in the floor, then onto my and Oliver's wrists.

"You won't be alone out there, Ems," he said. "I promise. I'll find a way to come and visit. I'll talk to Drew too."

I smiled at him, putting on my bravest face.

"It's kind of you, Cam, but don't worry. It's over, the bond's gone, and maybe it's for the best anyway."

He looked at me in despair.

"I can't believe this is happening. I'm so sorry."

"Don't be. For you, my lifetime's just a blink of an eye."

"Don't talk like that," he said, trying to pretend that he wasn't welling up. "It won't be forever. I'll see you again."

But I knew he was lying from the tear that slipped down his cheek.

"Have a drink on me tonight," I said cheerfully.

He forced a laugh, but it sounded hollow and mournful.

"Be seeing you," he said.

"Sure," I said, grinning through the tears.

He stepped away and Oliver took my hand in his, squeezing it tightly as I stared after Cam, the best friend I had in the world now. Rain started to fall on us once more, more heavily this time, and water splashed into the open truck bed in big, fat drops.

Then the truck moved forward with a jerk of acceleration, taking us through the gates and out into the world beyond the wall, away from the world of the Silver and into the world of the Weepers.

If you enjoyed *The Price of Silver*, why not read *Bound in Silver*? It's the third book in the *Solis Invicti* series, and it carries on right where *The Price of Silver* left off.

***

Join my Readers' Club and receive a FREE short story

www.josiejaffrey.com/subscribe

***

Please leave a review!

If you enjoyed *The Price of Silver*, I'd be so grateful if you would please review it. Book reviews can make a huge difference to the success of a novel, particularly those of self-published authors like me. If you have time to leave a review, even if it's just a sentence or two, then I'd really appreciate it.

***

Explore the rest of the Silverse…

This book is just one small part of the Silverse, a whole world of vampires that's waiting for you to explore. There are more novels, short stories, serialised story episodes, and even audio drama podcasts. They're all interrelated, although each series stands alone.

Find out more on my website at www.josiejaffrey.com

Acknowledgements

First and foremost, the author wishes to thank her wonderful husband for everything he did to make this book possible, not least by allowing her to lose entire weekends to the thrall of the story and by providing her with the 5,789 cups of tea, 567 glasses of Malbec and 267 pieces of chocolate shortbread that saw her through the many long nights of writing after work.

Huge thanks are also due to Zoë and Vicky for once again destruction-testing the first draft, and to the author's family, both this side of the pond and the other, for their unexpected and enthusiastic support of the first book in the series.

Special thanks to the author's parents for editing the text. [Yup, that's right, my parents are reading this sexy vampire novel I wrote. They read the first one too. Hi, mum and dad!]

Finally, many thanks to everyone who has read this book. I'd love to hear from you. You can contact me through my website at www.josiejaffrey.com.

A NOTE ON SOL INVICTUS
(AND SOME LATIN)

Whilst there was a god of the Roman Empire called Sol Invictus, I'm afraid that I have taken several liberties with the worship, location and origins of his cult for the purposes of this story.

In fact, Sol Invictus is believed by better scholars than me to have originated from the Syrian sun god and to have been introduced to the Roman Empire in the early third century AD by the emperor Elagabalus (although debate abounds on this subject). His cult was later popularised by the emperor Aurelian, who claimed kinship with the god and brought his worship into the Roman mainstream.

I find this self-aggrandisement that is so common in the propaganda of the Roman emperors (which was by no means limited to Aurelian) to be fascinatingly hubristic. This group of human individuals variously declared themselves to be gods, sons of gods and otherwise related to or associated with gods, all the while refusing to adopt the title of 'king' because Rome would not tolerate a monarch. I couldn't resist gently playing with that concept, and I hope any historians reading this will forgive me the licence I have taken.

Sol Invictus appears in imperial imagery alongside the emperors, and particularly on coinage, as late as the period during which the Empire was under the control of Constantine, who may be considered to be the first Christian emperor. The god is denoted in that imagery by the radiate crown described by Cameron in this book, the same crown that tops the Silver Primus's symbol that is tattooed on Emilia's (and the other London safe house humans') wrist.

Whilst we're on the subject, the title of 'Primus' is a reference to 'primus inter pares', a Roman title meaning 'first among equals'. Originally used in the Roman Senate, the title was deployed in an apparently self-deprecating way by Roman emperors to imply that they considered themselves to be equal to their fellow humans (provided that they were male, rich and free). I think it's a wonderfully obfuscatory phrase, and it is for this reason that I have given the Silver not only a Primus, but also a Secundus, a Tertius and so on.

The Romans loved to call a spade an implement by which earth is moved (that's a Tacitus joke, for you Latin fans).

CONTENT WARNINGS

Viral apocalypse: humanity has been mostly wiped out by a virus that turns them into zombie-like creatures. No zombies seen are people the characters used to know.

General warning for violence.

General warning for blood/gore, including blood drinking, description of injuries, zombie-like creatures, dead bodies.

Humans are considered servants/slaves. Issues of power disparity/class divide discussed briefly.

No racism, no homophobia, no ableism, no animal cruelty, no misogyny.

Some steamy content but no sex on page.

Some swearing (up to and including 'fuck').

Blood drinking as sexual/pleasurable behaviour.

Heroine is briefly groped.

Brief scene of self-harm (for practical rather than emotional reasons).

www.ingramcontent.com/pod-product-compliance
Lightning Source LLC
Chambersburg PA
CBHW011924190726
48285CB00011BA/2780